the nightmare

the nightmare

lars kepler

translated from the swedish by laura a. wideburg

McClelland & Stewart

Library and Archives Canada Cataloguing in Publication

Kepler, Lars
     The nightmare / Lars Kepler ; translated from
the Swedish by Laura A. Wideburg.

Translation of: Paganinikontraktet.
ISBN 978-0-7710-9578-8

     I. Wideburg, Laura A. II. Title.

PT9877.21.E65P3313 2012   839.73'8   C2012-903515-7

Grateful acknowledgment is made for permission to reprint excerpts from the following previously published material: "Starman," "Life on Mars," and "Ziggy Stardust," written by David Bowie, reprinted by permission of Hal Leonard Corporation and Tintoretto Music, administered by RZO Music, Inc.; Pablo Neruda, "Soneto XLV," *Cien sonetos de amor,* © Fundación Pablo Neruda, 2012.

Printed and bound in the United States of America

McClelland & Stewart,
a division of Random House of Canada Limited
One Toronto Street
Toronto, Ontario
M5C 2V6
www.mcclelland.com

1   2   3   4   5   16   15   14   13   12

The word "music" comes from the "art of the muses" and reflects the Greek myth of the Nine Muses. All nine were daughters of the powerful god Zeus and the titan Mnemosyne, goddess of memory. Euterpe, the muse of music, is often portrayed holding a double flute to her lips. Her name means "Giver of Joy."

The gift of musicality does not have a generally agreed-upon definition. There are people who lack the ability to hear differing frequencies in music while, on the other hand, there are people born with an exact memory for music and perfect pitch so they can reproduce a specific tone without any external reference.

Throughout the ages, a number of exceptional musical geniuses have emerged, some of whom have achieved lasting fame—Wolfgang Amadeus Mozart, who began to tour the courts of Europe at the age of six; Ludwig van Beethoven, who wrote many of his masterpieces after becoming totally deaf.

The legendary Niccolò Paganini was born in 1782 in the Italian city of Genoa. He was a self-taught violinist and composer. To this day, very few violinists have been able to perform Paganini's swift, complicated works. Until his death, Paganini was plagued by rumors that to gain his musical virtuosity he'd signed a contract with the Devil.

the nightmare

In the light of the long June night, on becalmed waters, a large pleasure craft is discovered adrift on Jungfrufjärden Bay in the southern Stockholm archipelago. The water, a sleepy blue-gray in color, moves as softly as the fog. The old man rowing in his wooden skiff calls out a few times, even though he's starting to suspect no one is going to answer. He's been watching the yacht from shore for almost an hour as it's been drifting backward, pushed by the lazy current away from land.

The man guides his boat until it bumps against the larger craft. Pulling in his oars and tying up to the swimming platform, he climbs the metal ladder and over the railing. There's nothing to see on the after-deck except for a pink recliner. The old man stands still and listens. Hearing nothing, he opens the glass door and steps down into the salon. A gray light shines through the large windows over the varnished teak brightwork and a deep blue cloth canvas settee. He continues down the steep stairs, which are paneled in more shining wood. Past a dark galley, past a bathroom, into the large cabin. Tiny windows near the ceiling offer barely enough light to reveal an arrow-shaped double berth. Near the headboard a young woman in a jean jacket sits slumped at the edge of the bed. Her thighs are spread; one hand rests on a pink pillow. She looks right into the old man's eyes with a puzzled, frightened expression.

The old man needs a moment to realize the woman is dead.

Fastened to her long black hair is a clasp shaped in the form of a white dove: the dove of peace.

As the old man moves toward her and touches her cheek, her head falls forward and a thin stream of water dribbles from her lips and on down to her chin.

1

A cold shiver runs down Penelope Fernandez's spine. Her heart beats faster and she darts a look over her shoulder. Perhaps she feels a sense of foreboding of what's to come as her day progresses.

In spite of the television studio's heat, Penelope's face feels chilled. Maybe the sensation is left over from her time in makeup when the cold powder puff was pressed to her skin and the peace-dove hair clip was taken out so they could rub in the mousse that would make her hair fall in serpentine locks.

Penelope Fernandez is the spokesperson for the Swedish Peace and Reconciliation Society. Silently, she is being ushered into the newsroom and to her spotlighted seat across from Pontus Salman, CEO of the armaments manufacturer Silencia Defense AB. The news anchor Stefanie von Sydow is narrating a report on all the layoffs resulting from the purchase of the Bofors Corporation by British BAE Systems Limited. Then she turns to Penelope.

"Penelope Fernandez, in several public debates you have been critical of the management of Swedish arms exports. In fact, you recently compared it to the French Angola-gate scandal. There, highly placed politicians and businessmen were prosecuted for bribery and weapons smuggling and given long prison sentences. But here in Sweden? We really haven't seen this, have we?"

"Well, you can interpret this in two ways," replies Penelope. "Either our politicians behave differently or our justice system works differently."

"You know very well," begins Pontus Salman, "that we have a long tradition of—"

"According to Swedish law," Penelope says, "all manufacture and export of armaments are illegal."

"You're wrong, of course," says Salman.

"Paragraphs 3 and 6 of the Military Equipment Act," Penelope points out with precision.

"We at Silencia Defense have already gotten a positive preliminary decision." Salman smiles.

"Otherwise this would be a case of major weapons crimes and—"

"But, we *do* have permission."

"Don't forget the rationale for armaments—"

"Just a moment, Penelope." Stefanie von Sydow stops her and nods to Pontus Salman, who's lifted his hand to signal that he wasn't finished.

"All business transactions are reviewed in advance," he explains. "Either directly by the government or by the National Inspectorate of Strategic Products, if you know what that is."

"France has similar regulations," says Penelope. "And yet military equipment worth eight million Swedish crowns landed in Angola despite the UN weapons embargo and in spite of a completely binding prohibition—"

"We're not talking about France, we're talking about Sweden."

"I know that people want to keep their jobs, but I still would like to hear how you can explain the export of enormous amounts of ammunition to Kenya? It's a country that—"

"You have no proof," he says. "Nothing. Not one shred. Or do you?"

"Unfortunately, I cannot—"

"You have no concrete evidence?" asks Stefanie von Sydow.

"No, but I—".

"Then I think I'm owed an apology," says Pontus Salman.

Penelope stares him in the eyes, her anger and frustration boiling up, but she tamps it down, stays silent. Pontus Salman smiles smugly and begins to talk about Silencia Defense's factory in Trollhättan. Two hundred new jobs were created when they were given permission to start production, he says. He speaks slowly and in elaborate detail, deftly truncating the time left for his opponent.

As Penelope listens, she forces aside her anger by focusing on other matters. Soon, very soon, she and Björn will board his boat. They'll make up the arrow-shaped bed in the forecabin and fill the refrigerator and tiny freezer with treats. She conjures up the frosted schnapps glasses, and the platter of marinated herring, mustard herring, soused herring, fresh potatoes, boiled eggs, and hardtack. After they anchor at a tiny island in the archipelago, they'll set the table on the afterdeck and sit there eating in the evening sun for hours.

Penelope Fernandez walks out of the Swedish Television building and heads toward Valhallavägen. She wasted two hours waiting for a slot in another morning program before the producer finally told her she'd been bumped by a segment on quick tips for a summer tummy. Far away, on the fields of Gärdet, she can make out the colorful tents of Circus Maximus and the little forms of two elephants, probably very large. One raises his trunk high in the air.

Penelope is only twenty-four years old. She has curly black hair cut to her shoulders, and a tiny crucifix, a confirmation present, glitters from a silver chain around her neck. Her skin is the soft golden color of virgin olive oil or honey, as a boy in high school said during a project where the students were supposed to describe one another. Her eyes are large and serious. More than once, she's heard herself described as looking like Sophia Loren.

Penelope pulls out her cell phone to let Björn know she's on her way. She'll be taking the subway from Karlaplan station.

"Penny? Is something wrong?" Björn sounds rushed.

"No, why do you ask?"

"Everything's set. I left a message on your machine. You're all that's missing."

"No need to stress, then, right?"

As Penelope takes the steep escalator down to the subway platform, her heart begins to beat uneasily. She closes her eyes. The escalator sinks downward, seeming to shrink as the air becomes cooler and cooler.

Penelope Fernandez comes from La Libertad, one of the largest provinces in El Salvador. She was born in a jail cell, her mother attended by fifteen female prisoners doing their best as midwives. There was a civil war going on, and Claudia Fernandez, a doctor and activist, had landed in the regime's infamous prison for encouraging the indigenous population to form unions.

Penelope opens her eyes as she reaches the platform. Her claustrophobic feeling has passed. She thinks about Björn waiting for her at the motorboat club on Långholmen. She loves skinny-dipping from his boat, diving straight into the water, seeing nothing but sea and sky.

She steps onto the subway, which rumbles on, gently swaying, until it breaks out into the open as it reaches the station at Gamla Stan and sunlight streams in through the windows.

Like her mother, Penelope is an activist and her passionate opposition to war and violence led her to get her master's in political science at Uppsala University with a specialty in peace and conflict resolution. She's worked for the French aid organization Action Contre la Faim in Darfur, southern Sudan, with Jane Oduya, and her article for *Dagens Nyheter*, on the women of the refugee camp and their struggles to regain normalcy after every attack, brought broad recognition. Two years ago, she followed Frida Blom as the spokesperson for the Swedish Peace and Reconciliation Society.

Leaving the subway at the Hornstull station, Penelope feels uneasy again, extremely uneasy, without knowing why. She runs down the hill to Söder Mälarstrand, then walks quickly over the bridge to Långholmen and follows the road to the small harbor. The dust she kicks up from the gravel creates a haze in the still air.

Björn's boat is in the shade directly underneath Väster Bridge. The movement of the water dapples the gray girders with a network of light.

Penelope spots Björn on the afterdeck. He's got on his cowboy hat, and he stands stock-still, shoulders bent, with his arms wrapped closely about him. Sticking two fingers in her mouth, she lets loose a whistle, startling him, and he turns toward her with a face naked with fear. And it's still there in his eyes when she climbs down the stairs to the dock. "What's wrong?" she asks.

"Nothing," he answers, as he straightens his hat and tries to smile.

As they hug, she notices his hands are ice-cold and the back of his shirt is damp.

"You're covered in sweat."

Björn avoids her eyes. "It's been stressful getting ready to go."

"Bring my bag?"

He nods and gestures toward the cabin. The boat rocks gently under her feet and the air smells of lacquered wood and sun-warmed plastic.

"Hello? Anybody home?" she asks, tapping his head.

His clear blue eyes are childlike and his straw-colored hair sticks out in tight dreadlocks from under the hat. "I'm here," he says. But he looks away.

"What are you thinking about? Where's your mind gone to?"

"Just that we're finally heading off together," he answers as he wraps his arms around her waist. "And that we'll be having sex out in nature."

He buries his lips in her hair.

"So that's what you're dreaming of," she whispers.

"Yes."

She laughs at his honesty.

"Most people . . . women, I mean, think that sex outdoors is a bit overrated," she says. "Lying on the ground among ants and stones and—"

"No. No. It's just like swimming naked," he insists.

"You'll have to convince me," she teases.

"I'll do that, all right."

"How?" She's laughing as the phone rings in her cloth bag.

Björn stiffens when he hears the signal. Penelope glances at the display.

"It's Viola," she says reassuringly before answering. "*Hola*, Sis."

A car horn blares over the line as her sister yells in its direction. "*Fucking idiot.*"

"Viola, what's going on?"

"It's over. I've dumped Sergei."

"Not again!" Penelope says.

"Yes, again," says Viola, noticeably depressed.

"Sorry," Penelope says. "I can tell you're upset."

"Well, I'll be all right I guess. But . . . Mamma said you were going out on the boat and I thought . . . maybe I could come, too, if you don't mind . . ."

A moment of silence.

"Sure, you can come, too," Penelope says, although she hears her own lack of enthusiasm. "Björn and I need some time to ourselves, but . . ."

2

Penelope stands at the helm. An airy blue sarong is wrapped around her hips and there's a peace sign on the right breast of her white bikini top. Spring sunlight pours through the windshield as she carefully rounds Kungshamn lighthouse and maneuvers the large motorboat into the narrow sound.

Her younger sister, Viola, gets up from the pink recliner on the afterdeck. For the past hour, she's been lying back in Björn's cowboy hat and enormous sunglasses, languidly smoking a joint.

Five times she tries to pick up a matchbox from the floor with her toes. Penelope can't help smiling. Viola walks into the cockpit and offers to take the wheel for a while. "Otherwise, I'll go downstairs and make myself a margarita," she says, as she continues down the stairs.

Björn is lying on the foredeck, a paperback copy of Ovid's *Metamorphoses* put to use as his pillow. Penelope notices that the railing near his feet is rusting. The boat was a present from his father for his twentieth birthday, but Björn hasn't had the money to keep it up. It was the only gift his father ever gave him, except one time when his father paid for a trip. When Björn's father turned fifty, he invited Björn and Penelope to one of his finest properties, a five-star hotel called Kamaya Resort on the east coast of Kenya. Penelope endured the resort for two days before she took off to join Action Contre la Faim at the refugee camp in Kubbum, Darfur.

Penelope reduces speed from eight to five knots as they reach the bridge at Skuru Sound. They've just glided into the shadows when Penelope notices the black rubber boat. Pressed against the concrete foundation, it's the same kind the military uses for their coastal rangers: an RIB with a fiberglass hull and extremely powerful engines. Penelope has almost passed beneath the bridge when she notices a man hunched in the darkness, his back turned. She doesn't know why her pulse starts to race at the sight of him; something about his neck and the black clothes he wears bothers her. She feels he's watching her even though he sits turned away.

Back into sunshine, she starts to shiver; goose bumps cover her arms. She guns the boat to fifteen knots. The two inboard engines drone powerfully, and the wake streams white behind them as the boat takes off over the smooth surface of the water.

Penelope's phone rings. It's her mother. For a moment Penelope fantasizes that she's calling to tell Penelope how wonderful she'd been on TV earlier, but she snaps back to reality.

"Hi, Mamma."

"Ay, ay."

"What's wrong?"

"My back. I'll have to go to the chiropractor," Claudia says, loudly filling a glass with tap water. "I just wanted to learn if you've talked to your sister."

"She's on the boat with us," Penelope replies, listening to her mother gulp the water down.

"She's with you . . . how nice. I thought it would be good for her to get out."

"I'm sure it is," Penelope says quietly.

"What do you have to eat?"

"Pickled herring and potatoes, eggs—"

"Viola doesn't like herring. What else do you have?"

"I've made a few meatballs," Penelope says patiently.

"Enough for everyone?"

Penelope falls silent as she looks out over the water. "I can always skip them myself," she says, collecting herself.

"Only if there aren't enough," her mother says. "That's all I'm trying to say."

"I understand."

"Am I supposed to be feeling sorry for you now?" her mother demands with irritation.

"It's just that . . . Viola is not a child—"

"I remember all the years I made you meatballs for Christmas and Midsummer and—"

"Maybe I shouldn't have eaten them."

"All right then," her mother says sharply. "If that's the way you want it."

"I'm just trying to say—"

"You don't have to come for Midsummer," Claudia snaps.

"Oh, Mamma, why do you have to—"

Her mother has hung up. Penelope shakes with frustration.

The stairs from the galley creak and a moment later Viola appears, a margarita in hand. "Was that Mamma?"

"Yes, it was."

"Worried I wouldn't get enough to eat?" Viola can't hide a smile.

"Believe me, we have food on board," Penelope says.

"Mamma doesn't believe I can take care of myself."

"She worries about you."

"She never worries about you," Viola points out.

"I can take care of myself."

Viola takes a sip of her drink and looks out through the windshield.

"I saw you on TV," she says.

"This morning? When I met Pontus Salman?"

"No, it was . . . last week," Viola replies. "You were talking to that arrogant man with the aristocratic name—"

"Palmcrona," Penelope says.

"Palmcrona, right."

"You can't believe how angry he made me! I could feel my face turning beet red, and the tears strated coming and I couldn't stop them. I felt like jumping up and reciting Bob Dylan's 'Masters of War' to his face, or like running out and slamming the studio door behind me."

Viola's only half listening. She watches Penelope stretch as she opens the roof window. "I didn't realize you've started to shave your armpits," she says.

"Well, these days I've been in the media so much that—"

"Vanity, pure vanity!" Viola says with a laugh.

"I didn't want people to dismiss me as a dogmatist just because I have some pit hair."

"What about your bikini line, then?"

"Well, that's not going so well . . ."

Penelope pulls aside her sarong and Viola laughs out loud.

"Björn likes it," Penelope says with a little smile.

"He can't talk, not with those dreads of his."

"I imagine you shave everywhere you have to," Penelope says sharply. "Just to please your married men and your big-muscled idiots and—"

"I know I have bad taste in men."

"You have good taste in most other areas."

"I've never amounted to much, though."

"If you'd just finished school, gotten good grades . . ."

Viola shrugs. "I actually got my equivalency."

The boat plows gently through the water, green now, reflecting the surrounding hillsides. Seagulls follow overhead.

"So, how did it go?"

"I thought the exam was easy," Viola says, licking salt from the edge of her glass.

"So it went well?"

Viola nods and puts her glass down.

"How well?" Penelope nudges her sister in her side.

"One hundred percent." Viola looks down modestly.

Penelope laughs with happiness and hugs her sister hard.

"Do you realize what this means? Now you can be anything you want! You can go to whichever university you want and study anything you like! You can pick anything at all! Business, medicine, journalism!"

The sisters laugh and their cheeks flush. Penelope hugs her sister so hard that the cowboy hat falls off. She smoothes Viola's hair and pats it into place just as she used to do when they were small. She removes the clip with the peace dove from her hair and slides it into her sister's, smiling contentedly.

a boat adrift in jungfrufjärden bay

With roaring engines, Penelope steers toward the bay. The bow arches up; white, frothy water parts behind the stern.

"You've lost your mind, girl!" Viola yells as she pulls the hair clip loose, just as she used to do when she was little and her mother *almost* had her hair done.

Björn wakes up when they stop at Goose Island for an ice cream. Viola insists on a round of miniature golf, too, so it's late in the afternoon when they set out again.

On their port side, the bay spreads out like a grand stone floor. It is breathtaking. The plan is to anchor at Kastskär, a long, uninhabited island with a narrow waist. On the southern side, there is a lush cove where they'll anchor the boat and swim, grill, and spend the night.

Viola yawns. "I'm going below to take a nap."

"Go ahead." Penelope smiles.

Viola walks down the companionway as Penelope stares ahead. She reduces the speed and keeps her eye on the depth sounder as they glide in toward Kastskär. The water is shoaling quickly from forty meters to five.

Björn enters the cockpit and kisses Penelope's neck.

"Would you like me to start dinner?" he asks.

"Viola needs to sleep for an hour or so."

"You sound just like your mother right now," he says softly. "Has she called you yet?"

Penelope nods.

"Did you have a fight?"

Tears spring to her eyes and she brushes them from her cheeks with a smile.

"Mamma told me I wasn't welcome at her Midsummer celebration."

Björn hugs her.

"Ignore her."

"I do."

Slowly and gently, Penelope maneuvers the boat into the innermost part of the cove. The engines rumble softly. The boat is so close to land now that she can smell the island's damp vegetation. They anchor, let it drag, and go in toward the shore. Björn jumps onto the steep, rocky ground holding the line, which he ties around a tree trunk.

The ground is covered in moss. He stands and looks at Penelope. A few birds in the treetops lift off as the anchor winch clatters.

Penelope pulls on her jogging shorts and her white sneakers, jumps on land, and takes Björn's hand.

"Want to check out the island?"

"Isn't there something you want to convince me about?" she asks hesitatingly.

"The advantages of our Swedish general-access rights," he says.

She smiles and nods as he pushes her hair off her face and lets his finger run over her high cheekbone and her thick black eyebrows.

"How can you be so beautiful?"

He kisses her lightly on the mouth and begins to lead her inland, until they reach a small meadow surrounded by tight clumps of high wild grasses. Butterflies and small bumblebees flit over the wildflowers. It's hot in the sun and the water shimmers between the trees on the north side. Björn and Penelope stand still, hesitate, study each other with shy smiles, then turn serious.

"What if someone comes?" she asks.

"We're the only ones on this island."

"Are you sure?"

"How many islands exist in Stockholm's archipelago? Thirty thousand? Probably more," he says.

Penelope slips out of her bikini top, kicks off her shoes, and pulls off her shorts and bikini bottom at the same time so that she's standing completely naked in the grass. Her initial feeling of embarrassment gives way to pure joy. There's something remarkably arousing about the cool sea air against her skin and the warmth that simultaneously arises from the earth.

Björn looks at her and mumbles that he's not sexist, but he does want to just look at her for another second. She's tall; her arms are muscular yet still have a soft roundness to them. Her narrow waist and sinewy thighs make her look like a playful ancient goddess.

Björn's hands shake as he pulls off his T-shirt and his flower-patterned swimming trunks. He's younger than she is. His body is still boyish, almost hairless.

"Now I want to look at you," she says.

He blushes and walks over to her with a smile.

"So I can't look at you?"

He shakes his head and hides his face in her neck and hair.

They begin to kiss standing still. They hold each other tightly. Penelope is so happy she has to force a huge grin from her face so that she can keep kissing. She feels Björn's warm tongue in her mouth, his erection, his heart beating faster and faster. They find a spot between the tufts of grass and stretch out. With his tongue he searches for her breasts and their brown nipples. He kisses her stomach, he opens her thighs. As he looks at her, it strikes him that their bodies have begun to glow in the evening sun, as if illuminated. Everything now is gentle. She's wet and swollen as he licks her slowly and softly until she has to move his head away. She whispers to him, pulls him to her, steers him with her hand until he slides inside her. He's breathing heavily into her ear and she stares straight up at the rosy sky.

Afterward, she stands up, naked in the warm grass, and arches toward the sky. She takes a few steps and peers between the trees.

"What is it?" Björn asks, his voice thick.

She looks back at him, sitting naked on the ground and smiling up at her.

"You've burned your shoulders."

"Happens every year."

He gently touches the pink spots.

"Let's go back—I'm hungry," she says.

"Let me swim for a bit."

She pulls her bikini bottom and shorts back on, puts on her sneakers, then stands with her bikini top in her hand. She allows her gaze to wander over his hairless chest, his strong arms, the tattoo on his shoulder, his careless sunburn . . . and his light, playful look.

"Next time, *you're* on the bottom," she says.

"Next time," he repeats cheerfully. "You're stuck on me—I knew it!"

She laughs and waves at him dismissively. She hears him whistle to himself as she walks through the forest toward the tiny, steep beach where they've anchored.

She stops for a moment to put on her bikini top before she continues down to the boat.

On board, Penelope wonders whether Viola is still sleeping in the aft cabin. She thinks she should start a pot of fresh potatoes and some crowns of dill and then wash up and change for the evening. Strangely, the deck near the stern is totally damp as if from a rain shower. Viola must have swabbed the deck for some reason. The boat feels different somehow. Penelope can't say what it is, but all at once she has goose bumps. The birds suddenly stop singing and everything is silent. Penelope is now aware of every one of her movements. She walks down the stairs. The door is open to the guest cabin and the lamp is lit, but Viola is not there. Penelope notices her hand shakes as she knocks on the door to the tiny toilet. She peers inside and returns to the deck. Looking ashore, she can see Björn walking down to the water. She waves to him, but he's not looking her way.

Penelope opens the glass doors to the salon.

"Viola?" she calls softly.

She goes down to the galley, takes out a pot, puts it on the element, and returns to the search. She peers into the large bathroom, then the main cabin where she sleeps with Björn. Looking around in the dark cabin, at first she thinks that she sees herself in a mirror.

Viola is sitting on the edge of the bed, her hand resting on the pink pillow from the Salvation Army.

"What are you doing in here?"

As Penelope hears her own voice, she's also realizing that nothing is as it should be. Viola's face is cloudy white and wet; her hair hangs down in damp streams.

Penelope takes Viola's face in her hands. She moans softly, then screams right into her sister's face, "Viola? What's wrong? *Viola!*"

But she already understands what's out of place and what's wrong. Her sister is not breathing, her sister's skin is not giving off warmth. There is nothing left of Viola. The light of life has been snuffed out.

The narrow room tightens around Penelope. Her voice is a stranger's. She wails and stumbles backward, knocking her shoulder hard on the doorpost as she turns to run up the stairs.

Up on the aft deck, she gulps down air as if she's suffocating. She glances about, ice-cold terror filling her bones. One hundred meters away on the beach, she spots a man in black. Somehow Penelope understands how things fit together. She knows this is the man who was underneath the bridge in the military inflatable. This was the man who had his back turned when she passed by. And she knows this is the man who killed Viola—and is not finished.

From the beach, the man waves to Björn, who's now swimming twenty meters from shore. He's yelling something to Björn. Penelope rushes to the steering console and rummages in the tool drawer. She finds a Mora knife and races back to the stern.

She sees Björn's slow swimming strokes and the water rings around him. He's looking at the man in confusion. The man is waving, motioning for him to come over. Björn smiles an uncertain smile and begins to swim toward land.

"Björn!" Penelope screams as loud as she can. "Swim to sea!"

The man on the beach turns toward her and begins to run toward the boat. Penelope cuts off the rope, slips on the wet stern deck, leaps back up, and runs to the steering console and starts the motor. Without looking around, she raises the anchor and engages the gear in reverse at the same time.

Björn must have heard her, because he turns away from land and starts to swim toward the boat instead. As Penelope steers in his direction, the man in black changes course and starts running toward the other side of the island. Intuitively, she knows that's where he's pulled his inflatable ashore, at the northern inlet.

And she knows without a doubt that there is no possible way for them to speed away from it.

Motor rumbling, she steers toward Björn, and as she gets closer, she slows and stretches a boat hook toward him. The water is so cold, and he looks exhausted and so frightened. His head keeps bobbing under the surface. She jabs the boat hook his way and accidentally strikes his forehead. He starts to bleed.

"Hold on to it!" Penelope cries out.

The black inflatable is rounding the island. She can clearly hear the roar of its motor. Björn grimaces in pain, but after several attempts, he finally manages to wrap his elbow around the boat hook, and Penelope hauls him as quickly as she can to the swimming platform. He reaches the edge and holds on. She lets go of the boat hook and it drops into the water and drifts away.

"Viola is dead!" she screams, and hears the panic and despair in her own voice.

As soon as Björn grabs the ladder tight she runs back to the steering console and hits the gas.

He climbs over the railing and she hears him yell that she should steer straight across to the island of Ornö and its spit.

She can hear the rubber boat draw closer. She turns in a tight curve and the boat thuds heavily underneath the hull.

Penelope can't speak, she can only whimper. "That man killed Viola!"

"Watch out for the rocks!" Björn warns through chattering teeth.

The inflatable has rounded Stora Kastskär and is now picking up speed on the smooth open water.

Blood runs down Björn's face.

They are swiftly reaching the large island. Björn turns to see that the rubber boat is now only three hundred meters behind.

"Head for the dock!"

She hits reverse, and shuts off the motor as the prow of the boat slams the dock with a crunching sound. The waves of their wake race toward the rocky shore and roll back, making the boat tip to the side. Its ladder breaks to pieces. Water sloshes over the railing. Penelope and Björn jump off and race across the dock toward land as the rubber boat roars closer. Behind them they can hear the hull knock against the dock in the swells. Penelope slips and steadies herself with her hand, then clambers up the steep rocks that edge the forest. The motor of the rubber boat falls silent and Penelope knows their head start is insignificant. She rushes into the trees with Björn. They head deeper into the woods as her thoughts whirl in panic and her eyes dart back and forth for a place where they can hide.

4

Paragraph 21 of the police law states that a police officer may enter any building, house, room, or other place if there is reason to believe that a person has died, is unconscious, or is otherwise unable to call for help.

The reason Criminal Assistant John Bengtsson has received the assignment to examine the top-floor apartment in the building at Grevgatan 2 on this Saturday in June is that Carl Palmcrona, the general director of the National Inspectorate of Strategic Products, has not appeared at work and has missed an important meeting with the foreign minister.

This is certainly not the first time that John Bengtsson has had to enter buildings to search for deceased or injured persons. He remembers silent, fearful parents waiting in the stairway while he enters rooms to find young men barely alive after heroin overdoses, or worse, murder scenes: women in their living rooms, battered to death by spouses as the TV drowns out the sound.

Bengtsson carries his breaking-and-entering tools and his picklock through the entry door and takes the elevator to the top floor. He rings the bell and waits. He examines the lock on the outer door. After a while, he hears shuffling. It sounds as if it is coming from the stairwell one floor below. It sounds as if someone is sneaking away.

Bengtsson listens for a moment, then tries the door handle. The door swings open silently.

"Anyone home?" he calls out.

Nothing. He drags his bag over the threshold, wipes his feet on the doormat, closes the door behind him, and steps into a large hallway.

Gentle music can be heard from one of the rooms so he continues in that direction, knocks at the door, and enters. It's a large drawing room, sparsely furnished—three Carl Malmsten sofas, a low glass coffee table, and a tiny painting of a ship in a storm on the wall. An ice-blue sheen comes from a music system with a modern flat, transparent design. Meandering, melancholy music comes from the speakers.

Across the room is a set of double doors. Bengtsson swings them open to reveal a salon with tall Art Nouveau windows. The late-spring light is broken by the multiple small panes at the top.

A well-dressed man swings in the middle of the white room.

John Bengtsson stands quietly in the doorway and stares at the dead man for an eternity before he notices the laundry line fastened to the ceiling-lamp hook.

The body seems poised at the moment of a jump into the air. His ankles are stretched and his toes point to the ground. He's hanged—but there's something that does not fit. Something is not as it should be.

Bengtsson cannot step through the double doors; he must keep the crime scene intact. His heart pounds and he feels the heavy rhythm of his pulse. He finds he cannot look away from the swaying man in the empty room.

The whisper of a name begins to echo in Bengtsson's brain: *Joona. I have to talk to Joona Linna immediately.*

There is no furniture in this room. Just the hanged man, who, in all probability, is none other than Carl Palmcrona, the general director of ISP.

The rope is fastened to the center of the lamp hook emerging from the rosette in the center of the ceiling.

There's nothing for him to climb on, Bengtsson thinks.

The ceiling height must be at least three and a half meters.

Bengtsson calms himself, collects his thoughts, and registers everything he sees. The hanged man's face is as blanched as damp sugar and

John Bengtsson can see only a few blood spots in the wide-open eyes. The man is wearing a thin overcoat, a light gray business suit, and black leather-soled oxfords. A black briefcase and a cell phone lie on the parquet floor a short distance from the pool of urine that has collected directly underneath the body.

The hanged man suddenly shakes.

Bengtsson takes a sharp breath.

A heavy thud from the ceiling above. The sounds of a hammer in the attic. Someone walks across the attic floor. Another thud and Palmcrona's body shakes again. The sound of a power drill. Silence. Someone calling for more cable: "Cable reel."

Bengtsson notices how his pulse begins to slow as he turns to walk away from the salon. He sees the outer door is open and he stops, sure he'd closed it. He knows he could be wrong. He leaves the apartment, but before he reports to his department, he picks up his cell phone and calls Joona Linna at the National Criminal Investigation Department.

"Shouldn't we wait for Joona Linna?" asks Tommy Kofoed.

"Well . . ." drawls Carlos.

"That man does just what he pleases," Pollock says quietly.

"Hey, come on now," Tommy Kofoed says defensively. "Give the man his due. The Tumba murders last year? He had them all figured out and I still don't know how he did it."

"Against all fucking logic," Elton says with a smile.

"I'd say I'm fairly well versed in forensics," Tommy Kofoed continues, "but Joona walked in, took a look at the blood spatters . . . He knew right away when each murder had occurred . . . Amazing . . ."

"It's true, it's true. He could see the whole picture," Pollock says. "The degree of violence, the level of force, the stress level, how the footprints found in the apartment lagged more, which showed more exhaustion than those in the locker room."

"Fucking awesome," Tommy Kofoed mutters.

Carlos clears his throat, returns to his informal agenda.

"The Coast Guard called this morning," he tells them. "An old fisherman found a dead woman."

"In his nets?"

"No, he saw a large motorboat drifting with the current near Dalarö. He rowed out, boarded the vessel, and found her sitting on her berth in the fore."

"That doesn't sound like something for us," Petter Näslund says, and smiles.

"Was she murdered?" asks Pollock.

"Probably a suicide," answers Petter quickly.

"There's no need to make snap judgments," Carlos says as he helps himself to a slice of sugar cake. "But I wanted to bring it up."

"Anything else?"

"We had a request from the police in West Götaland," Carlos says. "The form is on the table."

"I won't be able to take it on," Pollock says.

"I know how busy you are," Carlos says, slowly sweeping crumbs from the table. "Let's skip to the other end of the agenda: recruiting someone for the NHS."

Benny Rubin looks around with a sharp glance and explains that the leadership is aware of the heavy workload, and they therefore, as a first step, have allocated funds for expanding the Commission by one full-time position.

"What does everyone think?" Carlos asks.

"Shouldn't Joona Linna be here?" asks Tommy Kofoed. He leans forward and takes one of the wrapped sandwiches.

"I'm not sure he'll make it," Carlos says.

"What about a bite before we get into this?" says Elton, reaching for the tray.

Tommy Kofoed methodically unwraps the plastic from his salmon sandwich, peels back the bread, plucks off a sprig of dill, squeezes lemon juice over the salmon, and reassembles his sandwich.

Suddenly the door to the meeting room swings open and Joona Linna steps in. His short-cut blond hair stands straight up.

"*Syö tilli, pojat,*" he says in Finnish.

"That's right!" Nathan Pollock laughs. "Eat your dill, boys!"

Nathan and Joona grin at each other. Tommy Kofoed's cheeks turn red and he shakes his head with a smile.

"*Tilli.*" Nathan Pollock repeats the Finnish word and laughs out loud as Joona walks past Tommy and sticks the dill back onto his sandwich.

"Let's get back to the meeting," says Petter.

Joona shakes hands with Nathan, then takes an empty chair, slinging his black jacket over the back as he sits down.

"Please pardon my being late," he says.

"Let me welcome you as a guest of this meeting," says Carlos. "We were just bringing up recruiting. I believe I'll hand the floor over to Nathan."

"All right, and I want everyone to know that I'm not alone in this," Nathan Pollock begins. "Rather . . . we're all in agreement. Joona, we're hoping that you'll come on board with us."

The room falls silent. Niklas Dent and Erik Eriksson nod. Petter Näslund is a dark silhouette in the backlight.

"We'd really like to have you," Tommy Kofoed ventures.

"I appreciate the offer," Joona answers as he runs his hand over his hair. "You're hardworking guys, and you've proved your mettle. I respect your work . . ."

Everyone around the table smiles.

"But as for me . . . I just can't be tied down to your strict methodology. To any strict method of investigation," he explains.

"We know, we understand," Kofoed says quickly. "The way we work is a little rigid, but it's shown . . ."

Kofoed falls silent.

"We just wanted to ask," says Nathan Pollock.

"It's just not the way I work," Joona explains.

To a man, they look down at the table; someone nods. Joona's cell phone rings and he excuses himself to answer it. He stands up from the table and leaves the room. A minute later he returns and slides his jacket off the chair.

"Sorry. I would like to stay, but—"

"Something serious?" asks Carlos.

"That was John Bengtsson from Routine Patrol," Joona says. "He's just found Carl Palmcrona."

"Found?" asks Carlos.

"Hanged," Joona answers. His eyes gleam like gray glass.

"Who is Palmcrona?" asks Nathan Pollock. "I can't place the name."

"He's the general director for ISP," Tommy Kofoed says quickly. "He makes the final decisions on Swedish arms exports."

"Isn't everything at ISP classified?" asks Carlos.

"True," Kofoed answers.

"So let the guys at Säpo take it."

"I've just promised Bengtsson I'd come in person," Joona answers. "There's something not quite right about the scene."

"What?" Carlos asks.

"He said . . . well, I really have to see it myself."

"Sounds interesting," Tommy Kofoed says. "Can I come?"

"If you want," Joona answers.

"I'll come, too, then," Pollock says swiftly.

Carlos tries to remind them about the meeting in progress but sees it is pointless as the three men get up and walk out into the cool hallway.

how death came

Twenty minutes later, Detective Inspector Joona Linna parks his black Volvo on Strandvägen and gets out to wait for his colleagues from the National Criminal Investigation Department. They pull up moments later in a silver-gray Lincoln Town Car and together they walk around the corner and enter the building at Grevgatan 2.

While they ride the ancient, rattling elevator to the top, Tommy Kofoed asks what information Joona's already been given.

"The National Inspectorate of Strategic Products had put out a bulletin that Palmcrona was missing," Joona says. "He has no family and none of his colleagues knew him socially, but when he didn't show up for work, the police were asked to investigate. John Bengtsson went to Palmcrona's apartment and found him hanging. But he's not sure it's a suicide."

Nathan Pollock's weather-beaten face frowns in concentration.

"Why does he suspect something's wrong?"

The elevator stops and Joona slides the gate open. Bengtsson is waiting at the door of the apartment.

"This is Tommy Kofoed and Nathan Pollock from the CID," Joona says.

They shake hands quietly.

"So the door was unlocked when I arrived," John tells them. "I heard music and found Palmcrona hanging in one of the large rooms. Over the years, I've cut down a number of people, but this time . . . I mean . . . perhaps it is suicide, but given Palmcrona's position in society, I thought I'd better check it all out."

"You did the right thing to call," Joona agrees.

"Checked out the body?" Tommy asks in his sullen fashion.

"I didn't even enter the room," John replies.

"Good," Kofoed mumbles, and he begins to lay protective mats on the floor.

Minutes later, Joona and Nathan Pollock are able to walk into the hallway. John Bengtsson is waiting for them next to a blue sofa. He points toward the double doors that are ajar and reveal a well-lit room. Joona continues walking across the protective mats and pushes the doors wide open.

Warm sunshine pours into the room through high windows. Carl Palmcrona is hanging in the center of the spacious room. Flies creep over his white face and into his eye sockets and open mouth to lay their small, yellowish eggs. They buzz around the pool of urine as well as the sleek black briefcase on the floor. The narrow laundry line has cut into Palmcrona's throat, forming a deep red furrow. Blood has flowed out and down his shirtfront.

"Executed," Tommy Kofoed declares as he pulls on protective gloves.

Every trace of sullenness has vanished, and he smiles as he goes down on his knees to begin photographing the hanging body.

"We'll probably find injuries to the cervical vertebra," Pollock says pointing.

Joona glances up at the ceiling and back to the floor.

"Obviously it's a statement," Kofoed says triumphantly and keeps the flashing camera focused on the corpse. "I mean, the killer didn't bother to hide the body but wants to say something instead."

"That's exactly what I was thinking," Bengtsson exclaims just as eagerly. "The room is empty and there are no chairs or ladders to climb on."

"So the question is, what does the killer want to say?" Tommy Kofoed says as he lowers the camera to peer at the body. "Hanging is connected to treason and betrayal. Think of Judas Iscariot who—"

"Just a second," Joona says mildly.

They see him point at the floor.

"What is it?" asks Pollock.

"We're looking at a suicide," Joona replies.

"What a typical suicide!" Tommy Kofoed laughs. "He flaps his wings and flies—"

"The briefcase," Joona says. "If he set it upright, he'd reach the noose."

"But he couldn't have reached the ceiling," Pollock points out.

"He could have fastened the noose beforehand."

"I think you're wrong."

Joona shrugs and says, "Keep in mind the music and the knots . . ."

"Let's take a look at the briefcase," Pollock says.

"Let me just secure the area first," says Kofoed.

They watch Kofoed, his bent, short body, as he creeps forward and rolls out over the floor a sheet of black plastic film with a bottom layer of thin gelatin. Then he carefully presses on the film with a rubber roller.

"Can you get me a couple of bio-packs and a large container?" he requests as he points to his collection bag.

"Wellpapp?" asks Pollock.

"Yes, thanks," Tommy says as he catches the packs that Pollock throws in a high arch to him.

He secures any biological traces on the floor and then waves Pollock into the room.

"You'll find the marks of his shoes on the outer edge of the briefcase," Joona says. "It has fallen over backward and the body has swung diagonally."

Pollock says nothing, just walks over to the leather briefcase and gets on his knees beside it. His silver ponytail falls forward as he leans down to put the briefcase on its edge. Obvious light gray marks are clearly visible on the black leather.

"So it's so, then," Joona remarks quietly.

"Fucking awesome," Tommy Kofoed says, and his whole tired face smiles up at Joona.

"Suicide," Pollock mutters.

"Technically speaking, yes," Joona says.

They stand looking at the body for a while.

"What do we really have here?" asks Kofoed. He's still smiling. "Someone high up, with a job deciding who can export military equipment, who decides now to take his own life."

"Not our department," sighs Pollock.

Tommy Kofoed rolls off his gloves and gestures at the hanging man. "Joona? What's the deal with the knots and the music?" he asks.

"It's a double sheet bend," Joona says and points to the knots around the lamp hook. "I connect it to Palmcrona's long naval career."

"And the music?"

Joona stops and looks at him meditatively.

"What do you think?" he asks.

"Well, I know it's a sonata for violin. Early nineteenth century or—"

He is interrupted by the doorbell. The four of them glance at one another. Joona starts to walk back to the hallway and the rest follow but stop before they can be seen from the landing.

At the front door, Joona considers a quick view through the peephole but decides against it. He can feel air stream through the keyhole as he presses down the door handle. The heavy door swings open. The landing is dark. Joona's hand goes for his pistol as he checks behind the open door. A tall woman is caught in a faint gap of light by the handrail. She has huge hands. She's probably about sixty-five years old. She's completely still. Her gray hair is cut in a short, girlish pageboy style, and there's a large, skin-colored bandage on her chin. She looks Joona right in the eye without a hint of a smile.

"So have you cut him down yet?" she asks.

helpful people

Joona had thought he'd have time to make the National Criminal Investigation Department meeting at one o'clock.

But he'd wanted to have lunch with Disa first. They were to meet at Rosendal's Garden on Djurgården. Joona arrived early and had to wait for a while in the sunshine. He idly watched the mist hovering over the small vineyard. Then he saw Disa coming, her cloth purse slung over her shoulder. Her narrow, intelligent face was closely sprinkled with late-spring freckles and her hair flowed free over her shoulders, loosed from its customary tight braids. She'd prettied up in a dress patterned in small flowers; on her feet were sandals with wedge heels.

Carefully they hugged each other.

"Hi," Joona said. "You look great."

"You, too," said Disa.

Together they went to the buffet to choose their food and then sat down at an outdoor table. Joona noticed that her nails wore a new coat of polish. Usually they were short and ragged, embedded with the dirt Disa picked up in her work as an archaeologist. Joona's gaze wandered away from her hands and out over the orchard.

"Queen Kristina received a leopard as a present from the Count of Kurland. She kept it here at Djurgården."

"I didn't know that," Joona said absentmindedly.

"I read in the palace accounts that the Royal Treasury paid forty daler in silver coins, the cost of a serving girl's funeral. She was ripped apart by that leopard."

Disa leaned back in her chair and picked up her glass.

"Stop talking so much, Joona Linna," she said.

"Sorry," Joona said. "I just . . ."

He fell silent again, suddenly exhausted.

"What's up?" She was suddenly concerned.

"Please, just tell me more about the leopard."

"You look so sad."

"I was thinking about my mother . . . It's been one year today since she passed away. I went to lay a wreath at her grave."

"I miss Ritva very much," Disa said.

She put her fork down and sat quietly for a while.

Finally she said, "Do you know what she said the last time I saw her? She took my hand and told me that I should seduce you and make sure I got knocked up."

Joona laughed. "I can believe that!"

The sun sparkled in Disa's quiet, dark eyes. "I told her that I didn't believe that would happen. Then she told me I should leave you and never look back."

He nodded but was at a loss for words.

"And then you'd be all alone," Disa continued. "A large, lonely Finn."

He stroked her fingers.

"I don't want that," he said.

"Don't want what?"

"Don't want to be a large, lonely Finn."

"And I now want to use my teeth on you. Bite you hard. Can you explain that? My teeth always start to itch when I look at you," Disa said with a smile.

Joona reached out to touch her face. He knew he was already late to the meeting with Carlos Eliasson and the CID, but he kept sitting there across from Disa, making small talk and thinking at the same time that he should go down to the Nordic Museum to look at the Sami bridal crown.

While he was waiting for Joona Linna, Carlos Eliasson had told the National Criminal Investigation Department about the young woman who'd been found dead on a motorboat in the Stockholm archipelago, and Benny Rubin noted for the record that there was no rush to begin an investigation and that they should wait for the Coast Guard's findings.

Joona had come in a little later but had hardly taken part in the meeting when a call came from John Bengtsson of Routine Patrol.

Joona and John had a history together over the years. They'd played floorball more than a decade before. John Bengtsson was popular, but when he was diagnosed with prostate cancer, a lot of his friends had fallen away. Although he was now fully recovered, like other people who'd had a brush with death, he had a slight air of fragility, of a depth of understanding, about him.

Joona had stood in the hallway outside the conference room listening on the phone to John's slow recitation. His voice was filled with the tiredness that comes immediately after high stress. He described how he'd just found the general director for the National Inspectorate of Strategic Products hanging from the ceiling in his home.

"Suicide?" asked Joona.

"No."

"Murder?"

"Can't you just come over?" John asked. "I can't decide what I'm seeing. The body is hanging way too high above the floor, Joona."

He'd taken Nathan Pollock and Tommy Kofoed along. Joona had just explained that this was a suicide when the doorbell had rung at Palmcrona's home. In the darkness of the landing, a woman was standing and holding two plastic grocery bags in her large hands.

"So have you cut him down yet?" she asked.

"Cut him down?"

"Director Palmcrona," she replied matter-of-factly.

"What do you mean by that?"

"Excuse me, I'm just a housekeeper and I thought . . ."

Obviously she was troubled, and she turned away to start walking down the stairs. She was stopped in her tracks by the answer to her first question.

"He's still hanging there."

"I see." She turned toward him with a blank face.

Joona asked, "Did you see him earlier today?"

"No."

"How did you come to ask whether we'd taken him down, then? Did you see anything unusual?"

"A noose from the ceiling in the small salon," she answered.

"So you saw the noose?"

"Yes, indeed."

"But you weren't afraid that he might use it?"

"Dying's not a nightmare." She was holding back a smile.

"What did you just say?"

The woman just shook her head.

"How do you think he died, then?"

"I think he tightened the noose around his neck," she replied in a low voice.

"How did he manage to get the noose around his neck?"

"I don't know . . . maybe he needed help."

"What kind of help?"

Her eyes rolled toward the back of her head and for an instant, Joona thought she was going to faint. Instead, she steadied herself with a hand on the wall and then she met his gaze.

Softly, she said, "There are always helpful people around."

the needle

The police station's swimming pool is large and blue, almost completely still. Lit from below, its light dances across the walls and ceiling of the natatorium, and all that breaks the stillness is the steady movement of Joona Linna swimming laps, one after the other.

While he swims, idle thoughts tumble over and over in his head: Disa's face when she told him her teeth itched when she looks at him.

Joona touches the edge of the pool, turns underwater, and kicks off again. He doesn't realize he's picking up speed when the memory of Carl Palmcrona's apartment on Grevgatan comes to him. Once again, he sees the hanging body, the pool of urine, and the flies on the body's face. The dead man had been wearing his coat and shoes and yet had taken the time to turn on music.

Actions both impulsive and yet planned, not that unusual when it comes to suicide.

Joona's swimming even faster now, picking up more speed as he kicks off another lap. He sees himself walking back through Palmcrona's hallway and opening the door after the unexpected ringing of the doorbell. The tall woman in the darkness of the landing. The impression of her large hands. The fact she was hiding behind the door.

Breathing heavily, Joona pulls up to the edge of the pool and steadies himself, resting his arms on the plastic grille over the gutter. His breathing slows but he can feel the heavy increase of lactic acid in his shoulder muscles. A group of policemen in bathing suits walk into the pool area carrying two rescue dummies: one a child and the other an overweight adult.

Dying's not a nightmare. The large woman had smiled when she said that.

Joona heaves himself out of the pool. He's filled with nervous tension. The Carl Palmcrona case won't leave him alone. For some reason, the empty, light-filled room keeps coming back into his mind: the languid violin music and the slow buzzing of the flies.

Joona knows in his gut that it *is* a suicide and is not a case for the CID. Still, he feels the urge to run back to the apartment, to take another look and examine it minutely to make sure he's missed nothing.

Initially he'd thought that shock had confused the housekeeper, fogged her mind, and made her suspicious, causing her to speak in that strange, disjointed way. Now Joona tries thinking in reverse. Maybe she wasn't confused at all. Maybe she wasn't shocked in the least but was answering his questions as clearly as she could. Edith Schwartz had hinted that Carl Palmcrona may have had help with the noose: that there were helpful hands, helpful people. In any case, she'd insinuated he was not alone in meeting his death. He was not the only person responsible.

Something is not right.

But he can't put his finger on why he thinks that.

Joona walks through the door to the changing room and unlocks his locker. He picks up his cell phone and calls Nils Åhlén, "The Needle."

"I'm not done yet," The Needle says instantly.

"It's about Palmcrona. What was your first impression, even if—"

"I'm not done yet."

"Even if you're not done—"

"Come by on Monday."

"I'm coming over now."

"At five o'clock, me and the missus are going to check on a sofa at the furniture store."

"I'll be there in twenty-five minutes," Joona says, and disconnects the phone before The Needle can protest again that it's too soon.

After Joona has showered, dressed, and come out of the changing room, he can hear the laughter from the children's swimming class.

He wonders what's behind the death of a man as important as the general director for the National Inspectorate of Strategic Products. When it came to the export of military equipment in Sweden, this was the one person who made all the final decisions regarding Sweden's export of arms, and now he's found hanged.

What if I'm wrong? What if he really was murdered? Joona says to himself. *I have to talk to Pollock before I go see The Needle. Maybe Pollock and Kofoed have had a chance to look at the material evidence by now.*

Joona strides through the hallway, runs down a staircase, and calls his assistant, Anja Larsson, to see if Nathan Pollock is still at the station.

all about hand-to-hand combat

Joona's thick hair is still wet as he opens the door to Lecture Hall 11 where Nathan Pollock is lecturing a special training group on handling hostage situations and rescue operations. Projected on the wall behind Pollock is the anatomy of a human body, and seven weapons are lined up on a table. They range from a small silver SIG Sauer P238 to a matte-black automatic carbine from Heckler & Koch equipped with a 40 millimeter grenade thrower. Pollock is demonstrating an attack technique on a young police officer. He holds a knife close to his body, then suddenly rushes the officer and marks his throat. He turns back to the group.

"The problem with a cut like this is that the enemy can still scream. He can still move, and since only one artery is cut, it'll take some time for him to bleed to death," Pollock tells them.

He walks up to the young officer again and puts his arm around the officer's face so that his elbow covers the officer's mouth.

"If I do this instead, I can cover the scream, control his head, and slice open both arteries with one cut."

Pollock lets the young officer go just as Joona Linna enters the room. The young officer wipes his mouth and returns to his seat. With a big grin, Pollock tries to wave Joona over, but Joona shakes his head.

"I just need a word with you," Joona says quietly.

A few of the police officers swivel their heads as Pollock walks over to

Joona and shakes hands. The shoulders of Joona's jacket are dark from the water dripping from his hair.

"Tommy Kofoed took shoe prints from the Palmcrona scene," Joona says. "I must know—did he find anything else unusual?"

"I didn't realize there was a rush on it," Nathan says. He also keeps his voice low. "Of course we photographed all the impressions on the foil, but we haven't had time to analyze the results. I absolutely have no overview yet—"

"But you saw something," Joona states.

"It seems that maybe . . . when I entered the photos into the computer . . . there could have been a pattern . . . it's too early—"

"Just tell me what you think—I have to run."

"It looked like two different sets of shoe prints in two circles around the body," Nathan tells him.

"I'm going to see The Needle. Why don't you come with me?" Joona asks.

"Right now?"

"I have to be there in twenty minutes."

"Damn, I can't." Nathan gestures to the class. "I'll keep my phone on in case you have to get back about something."

"Thanks," Joona says, and turns toward the door.

"Hey . . . could you just say hi to this gang for a second?" Nathan asks.

The entire class has already turned to look at them. Joona waves.

Nathan raises his voice. "May I introduce Joona Linna? He's the one I was telling you about. I'm trying to talk him into giving you some insight into hand-to-hand combat."

The room is silent and everyone is staring at Joona.

"Most of you know more about hand-to-hand combat than I do," Joona says with a small smile. "But one thing I do know is when you're in a fight for your life, no rules apply. It's not a game—it's a real fight."

"Listen up," Nathan says, his voice hard.

"In a real fight, you'll only win if you keep thinking. Be flexible. Take advantage of anything and everything that comes your way," Joona continues calmly. "Maybe you're in a car or on a balcony. Maybe in a room filled with tear gas. Maybe there's broken glass covering the floor. There could be weapons all around. Is it a short fight? Or will you have to conserve your strength? Don't waste time with fancy jump kicks or be cool with round kicks."

A few laugh.

"And accept the idea of pain. When you're in close combat without a weapon, you may have to take a real pounding to win as quickly as you can." Joona finishes. "That's about it . . . I really don't know much more than that about this stuff."

He bows his head faintly and turns to leave the lecture hall. Two of the officers clap. The door closes and the room falls silent. Nathan Pollock is smiling to himself as he comes back to the table.

"I originally meant to save this for another class," he says as he taps on the computer. "This film is a classic—it's the hostage drama from Nordea Bank headquarters on Hamngatan nine years ago. There are two robbers. Joona Linna has already gotten the hostages out. He's also already taken down one of the robbers, the one who had an Uzi. There'd been a violent firefight. The other robber is hiding and still has a knife. They had spray-painted all of the security cameras, but missed one. Anyway, I'll play it in slow motion because the whole thing happens in just a few seconds."

Pollock clicks again, and the film starts in slow motion. It's a grainy video shot from directly overhead and showing the interior of the bank. At the bottom right of the image, a counter ticks off the seconds. Joona moves smoothly sideways with his arms out, holding his pistol high. It almost looks like he's underwater, his movements are so slow. The robber is hiding behind the open door to the safe. He holds a knife. Suddenly he rushes out with long, fluid strides. Joona points his service pistol toward the robber, directly at his chest. The robber doesn't hesitate. Joona is forced to pull the trigger. "The pistol clicks but a faulty bullet is lodged in the barrel," narrates Pollock.

The grainy film flickers. Joona retreats as the man with the knife leaps at him. The whole thing is spooky and silent. Joona ejects the magazine and reaches for a new one. There is no time. Swiftly he reverses the useless gun until the barrel becomes an extension of his forearm.

"I don't get it," says a female officer.

"He's transforming the pistol into a *tonfa*," Pollock explains.

"What's that?"

"It's a kind of stick or baton. American police use something similar.

Obviously, your reach is lengthened and if you must strike, the impact is intensified."

The man with the knife has reached Joona. Almost in slow motion, he strikes at Joona's abdomen, the blade glittering in a half arc. His other arm is up and turns with his body. Joona does not look at the knife at all. He moves straight into the robber and instantly strikes him in the throat, right under the Adam's apple, with the shaft of his gun.

As if in a dream, the knife falls slowly, swirling to the ground. The man goes to his knees, clutching his throat, and then falls forward.

the woman who drowned

Joona Linna is in his car, driving toward the Karolinska Institute, the medical research center in Solna, a suburb north of Stockholm. He's thinking about Carl Palmcrona's hanging body, the tight laundry rope, the urine on the floor.

To the picture in his mind, Joona adds two sets of shoe prints on the floor circling the dead man.

This case is not over.

The department of forensic medicine is in a redbrick building set among the well-tended lawns on the large campus of the Karolinska Institute.

Joona swings into the empty visitors' parking lot. He sees that the chief medical officer, Nils Åhlén, The Needle, has driven his white Jaguar over the curb and right onto the manicured lawn next to the main entrance.

Joona waves at the woman sitting in reception, who answers with a thumbs-up. He continues down the hallway, knocks at The Needle's door, and goes right in. As usual, The Needle's office is completely barren of anything extraneous. The blinds have been drawn but sunshine still filters in between the slats. The light is bright on white surfaces but disappears into the gray areas of brushed steel.

As if to match his environment, The Needle wears white aviator glasses and a white polo shirt underneath his lab coat.

"I just put a parking ticket on a white Jaguar outside," Joona says.

"Good for you."

Joona pauses in the middle of the room, his serious gray eyes darkening.

"So how'd he really die?"

"You're talking about Palmcrona?"

"Right."

The telephone rings and The Needle hands the autopsy report to Joona.

"You didn't need to come all the way here to find that out," The Needle says before he picks up the phone.

Joona sits down on a white leather chair. The autopsy on Carl Palmcrona's body is complete. Joona flips through the file and eyes a few entries at random:

74. Kidneys weigh 290 grams together. Surfaces are smooth. Tissues are gray-red. Consistency is firm and elastic. Renal capsule is clear.
75. The ureters have normal appearance.
76. The bladder is empty. Mucous membrane is pale.
77. The prostate is normal size. Tissues are pale.

The Needle pushes his glasses up his narrow, hooked nose and finishes his phone call. He looks up.

"As you see," he says, yawning, "nothing unusual. Cause of death is asphyxiation, that is, suffocation . . . but with a successful hanging we're not talking about your typical meaning of suffocation. Rather, here we have closure of artery supply."

"So the brain dies when the flow of oxygenated blood is stopped."

The Needle nods. "That's right. Artery compression, bilateral closure of the carotids. It happens unbelievably quickly, of course. Unconsciousness within seconds—"

"But he was alive before the hanging?" Joona asks.

"Right."

The Needle's narrow, smooth face is gloomy.

"Can you determine the drop?"

"I imagine it was a matter of decimeters. There aren't any fractures of the cervical vertebra or at the base of the skull."

"I see . . ."

Joona is thinking of the briefcase with Palmcrona's shoe prints. He opens the file again and flips to the external examination: the investigation of the skin of the neck and the measurement of the angles.

"What's bothering you?"

"Could the same rope have been used to strangle him before the hanging?"

"Nope."

"Why not?"

"Well, first of all there is just one line and it's perfect." The Needle starts to explain. "When a person is hanged, the rope or line cuts into the neck and it—"

"But a killer might know that," Joona says.

"But it's practically impossible to reconstruct . . . you know, with a successful hanging, the line around the neck is like the point of an arrow with the edge on the upward side, right at the knot—"

"Because the weight of the body tightens the loop."

"Exactly. And for the same reason the deepest part must be precisely across from the edge."

"So hanging was the cause of death."

"No doubt about it."

The tall, thin pathologist gently gnaws his lower lip.

"But could he have been forced to kill himself?" Joona asks.

"There are no signs of it on the body."

Joona shuts the file, drums on it with both hands, and thinks about the housekeeper's statement that other people had been involved in Palmcrona's death. Was it just confused rattling on? But what about the two sets of shoe prints Tommy Kofoed had found?

"So you're absolutely sure of the cause of death?" Joona stares into The Needle's eyes.

"What did you expect?"

"I expected this," Joona says slowly, tapping the autopsy. "Exactly this. But still, something's not right."

The Needle smiles thinly.

"Take it and use it as bedtime reading."

"Fine," Joona agrees.

"Still, I'm sure you can just let go of this one . . . it's nothing more dramatic than a suicide."

The Needle's smile disappears and he drops his gaze. Joona's eyes are still sharp and focused.

"You're probably right."

"Of course I'm right," The Needle replies. "And I can speculate a little more if you want . . . Palmcrona was probably depressed. His fingernails were ragged and dirty. He hadn't brushed his teeth for several days and he hadn't shaved."

"I see."

"You can take a look at him if you'd like," The Needle prompts.

"No, that's not necessary," Joona answers and slowly stands up.

The Needle leans forward, a note of expectancy in his voice as if he'd been waiting for this moment.

"Something more exciting came in this morning. Do you have a few minutes?"

The Needle stands up as well, and gestures Joona to follow him along the hall. A light blue butterfly has managed to get into the building and it flutters in front of them.

"Has the other guy quit?"

"Who?"

"The other guy who worked here, the one with the ponytail . . ."

"Frippe? No way in hell we'd let him quit. He has a few days off. Megadeth was playing the Globe yesterday. Entombed was the lead-in act."

They walk through a dark room between autopsy tables of stainless steel, hardly noticing the strong smell of disinfectant. They continue walking to a much cooler room where bodies are being stored in chilled lockers, waiting to be examined by the department of forensic medicine.

The Needle opens the door and turns on the ceiling lamp. The fluorescent light flickers once or twice before it's fully on and can illuminate the white-tiled room and the long autopsy table covered in plastic. The table has double sinks and gutters for drainage.

The Needle uncovers the body lying on the table.

It is a beautiful young woman.

Her skin is tanned and her long hair winds in a thick, shimmering mass across her forehead and shoulders. She seems to look into the room with an expression of both doubt and amazement. There's an almost mischievous tilt to the corners of her mouth, as if she had been a person who easily smiles and laughs. However, any light in those large, dark eyes has long gone. Small brownish yellow specks are starting to appear.

Joona moves closer for a better perspective. She can't be more than nineteen or twenty years old. Not that long ago, she'd been a child still sleeping in bed with her parents. Then she was an adolescent schoolgirl and now she's dead.

A line, like a smile painted in gray, curves for about thirty centimeters across the woman's collarbone.

"What's this?" Joona points at it.

"No idea. Maybe from a necklace or the top of a blouse. I'll take a closer look later."

Joona peers more closely at the quiet body. He sighs at the familiar wave of melancholy he feels when he faces death, the colorless vacuum.

Her fingers and toes had been painted with a light, almost beige, rose.

"So what's the story?" Joona finally asks after a minute of silence.

The Needle gives him a serious look and light reflects from his glasses as he turns back to the body.

"The Coast Guard brought her in," he relates. "They found her sitting on the bunk down in the forward cabin of a large motorboat. It was abandoned and drifting in the archipelago."

"She was already dead?"

The Needle looks at him and his voice becomes almost melodic.

"She drowned, Joona."

"Drowned?"

The Needle nods, and his smile almost vibrates.

"She drowned on a boat that was still afloat," he says.

"I assume someone found her in the water and brought her on board."

"If that was the case, I wouldn't waste your time."

"So what's going on?"

"There are no marks of water on the body itself—I've sent her clothes to be analyzed, but I know the National Forensic Laboratory won't find a thing."

The Needle falls silent and flips through his preliminary report. He sneaks a look at Joona to see if he's at all curious. Joona stands completely still and then his expression shifts. Now he looks at the corpse with an expression that is awake and alert. He takes up a pair of latex gloves and pulls them on. The Needle is happily content to see Joona leaning over the body to lift her arms, first one, then the other, for closer examination.

"There's no trace of violence on her," The Needle almost whispers. "I don't understand it at all."

11

in the cabin

The glistening white motorboat is docked at the Coast Guard harbor on Dalarö Island, tied up between two police boats.

Joona Linna drives through the tall steel gates leading to the harbor area, then carefully along the gravel road, past a small garbage truck and a lifting frame with a rusty winch. He parks, gets out of the car, and walks closer, to get a good look at the boat.

A boat has been found adrift and abandoned, Joona thinks. *On the bunk in the forecabin sits a girl who drowned. The boat is not filled with water, but the girl's lungs are. Brackish salt water.*

From a distance, Joona can see the bow is heavily damaged, with deep scratches running along the side from a major collision. The paint is scraped off, and fiberglass dangles in thin shreds.

He calls the Coast Guard.

"Lance," a perky voice replies.

"Am I speaking with Lennart Johansson?" Joona asks.

"That's me."

"I'm Joona Linna from the National Criminal Investigation Department."

There's silence on the other end. Joona can hear the sounds of waves lapping.

"That pleasure boat you found," Joona says. "I'm wondering if it was taking on water."

"Why do you ask?"

"The bow is damaged."

Joona begins to walk again, heading toward the boat as he listens to Lennart say, dismissively, "Dear Lord, I wish I had a crown for every drunk who's trashed a—"

"I need a look at it," Joona says.

"Let me brief you on what usually goes down," Lennart Johansson says. "A group of drunken teenagers from . . . who knows, maybe Södertälje . . . steal a boat, pick up a few chicks, drive around listening to music and partying, and then they ram into something. There's a big bang as they crash and the girl lands in the water. The guys turn the boat around to find her, pull her on board, and when they realize she's dead, they panic and take off." He falls silent and waits for a reaction.

"Not a bad theory."

"Okay," Johansson says happily. "If you agree, you don't have to make the trip out here to Dalarö Island."

"Too late," Joona says, and heads straight to the Coast Guard boat.

A Combat Boat 90 E is one of the two boats next to the pleasure boat. A man, about twenty-five, with a bare, tanned chest stands on deck, a phone to his ear.

"Suit yourself," he says in English. He switches back to Swedish. "You have to call ahead for any sightseeing."

"I'm here now. And I believe I'm looking right at you, if you're the one standing on one of the Coast Guard's shallow-draught—"

"Do I look like a surfer?"

The grinning young man looks up and scratches his chest.

"Pretty much," Joona answers.

They each put their phones away and walk toward the other. Lennart Johansson buttons up a short-sleeved uniform shirt as he walks down the gangplank.

Joona gestures "hang loose." Johansson's white teeth shine in a big smile.

"I go surfing any time there's more than a ripple. That's why they call me Lance."

"I get it," Joona says drily.

The two walk over to the boat and stop on the dock by the gangway.

"It's a Storebro 36 Royal Cruiser," Lance says. "A good boat, but obviously it's come down a bit. Registered to Björn Almskog."

"Have you contacted him?"

"No time yet."

They take a closer look at the damage to the boat's bow. It looks recent, since there's no algae mixed with the fiberglass shreds.

"I've called a technician—he'll be here soon."

"She's gotten a proper kiss," Lance says.

"Who's been on board since it was found?"

"Nobody," Lance answers quickly.

Joona smiles and waits patiently.

"Well, I have, of course. And Sonny, my colleague. And the ambulance guys who removed the body. Our own forensic technician, though he used protective mats and clothing."

"Is that everyone?"

"Plus the guy who found the boat."

Joona doesn't answer but looks down into the shimmering water and thinks of the girl lying on the table in The Needle's autopsy room.

"Is your technician completely finished?" he finally asks.

"He's done with the floor and he's filmed the scene where she was found."

"I'm going on board."

A narrow, well-used gangplank stretches between the dock and the boat. Joona climbs on board and then stands for a while on the rear deck. He slowly looks around, letting his eyes focus on each object one by one. This scene will never be the same again, fresh and new. Each detail he registers might be one that makes a crucial difference. Shoes, an overturned lounge chair, a bath towel, a paperback that has yellowed in the sun, a knife with a red plastic handle, a bucket with a rope, beer cans, a bag of charcoal for grilling, a tub with a wet suit, bottles of sunscreen and lotion.

He looks in through the large window and makes out the salon with the steering console and the decor of lacquered wood. From a certain angle, fingerprints shine on the glass doors when the sunlight passes over them: finger marks from hands that have pushed the door open and pushed the door shut or held on when the boat was in motion.

Joona steps into the little salon. The afternoon sun glistens on the varnish and chrome. There's a cowboy hat and sunglasses on the sofa, which is covered with marine-blue pillows.

Outside, the water laps against the hull.

Joona lets his gaze wander from the dull floor in the salon and down the narrow stairs toward the bow. It's as dark as a deep well down there. He sees nothing until he turns on his flashlight. The light shines down the glossy, steep passageway with an icy, dim light. The red wood shines as wet as the inside of a body. Joona continues down the creaking steps and thinks about the girl. He imagines her sitting alone on the boat, then deciding to take a dive from the bow. She hits her head on a stone, gets water in her lungs, but nevertheless manages to get back on board, takes off her wet bikini, and puts on dry clothes. Perhaps she feels tired and goes to her bed, not realizing that her injury is serious, a damaged blood vessel that leaks into her brain.

But in that case, The Needle would have found traces of the brackish water somewhere on her body.

This scenario is wrong.

Joona keeps going down the stairs, passes the galley and the head, and goes toward the large berth.

There's a lingering sense of her death in the boat even though her body has been moved to the pathology department in Solna. The impression is the same no matter where he looks. It's as if everything here stares back at him, as if it has had its fill of screaming, fighting, and sudden silence.

The boat creaks and appears to tilt toward the side. Joona waits for a second and listens before continuing into the forecabin.

June light streams through the small windows near the ceiling onto a double bed with a pointed head, formed along the bow. This is where she was sitting when she was found. A sport bag is open on the floor and a dotted nightgown has been unpacked. Just inside the door, there's a pair of jeans and a thin cardigan. The owner's shoulder bag hangs from a hook. The boat rocks again and a glass bottle rolls across the deck above Joona's head.

Joona photographs the shoulder bag from various directions. The flash makes the room shrink as if the walls, ceiling, and floor were coming closer together for a moment.

Joona carefully lifts the bag from its hook and carries it with him up the stairs, which moan under his weight. He hears a metallic clink from the outside. When he reaches the salon, he sees an unexpected shadow in front of the glass doors and takes a step back into the stairwell, into the shadows and darkness.

an unusual death

Joona Linna stands stock-still, just two feet from the dark stairwell. From this angle, he can make out the lower edge of the glass doors and some of the rear deck. A shadow falls over the dusty glass; then a hand appears. Someone is moving very slowly. A split second later, Joona recognizes Erixson's face. Sweat is dripping from it as Erixson puts gelatin foil over the area beside the door.

Joona carries the shoulder bag into the salon. Carefully, he turns it upside down and empties it onto the hardwood table. He flips a red wallet open with his pen. There's a driver's license in the scratched plastic pocket. He looks more closely and sees a beautiful yet serious face revealed in the flash of an automatic photo booth. She's sitting slightly back as if she's looking up at the observer. Her hair is black and curly. He recognizes the girl on the autopsy table at the pathologist's: the straight nose, the eyes, the South American features. "Penelope Fernandez," he reads. Somehow it sounds familiar.

In his mind, he sees again the pathology lab and the naked body on the table in that tile-covered room, the girl's relaxed expression, the face beyond sleep.

Outside, Erixson's moving the bulk of his huge body one decimeter at a time as he takes up fingerprints along the railing: painting with magnetic powder, lifting the prints with tape. He dries off a wet area, carefully drops SPR solution on it, and then photographs the impressions that slowly are revealed. The entire time, he sighs as if every movement is torture and he's just used up the last of his strength.

Joona peers along the deck and sees the bucket and its rope next to a gym shoe. From below, the earthy smell of potatoes reaches his nose.

He looks back down at the driver's license and the tiny photograph. He looks at the young woman's mouth and her slightly parted lips. A niggling thought comes; something is not quite right.

He feels that he's seen something important and was just about to put his finger on it when it slides away.

Joona startles as the phone in his pocket vibrates. He pulls it out and sees The Needle is calling.

"Joona," he answers.

"This is Nils Åhlén, chief medical officer, in Stockholm."

Joona can't help smiling. They've known each other for twenty years and he'd recognize The Needle's voice whether he introduced himself or not.

"Did she hit her head?" Joona asks.

"No," The Needle answers, surprised.

"I thought that she might have hit her head on a stone."

"No—nothing like that. She drowned. That's the cause of death."

"You're absolutely sure?"

"I've observed froth inside her nostrils, mucosal tears in the throat, most likely due to strong gag reflexes, and there are bronchial secretions in both the trachea and the bronchi. The lungs have the typical appearance found in a drowning. They're filled with water and have gained weight and, well . . ."

Silence falls between them. Joona hears a scraping sound as if someone is shifting a metal pedestal.

"There's a reason you called," Joona says.

"Yes, there is."

"Can you tell me about it?" Joona asks patiently.

"She had a high concentration of tetrahydrocannabinol in her urine."

"Cannabis?"

"Right."

"But that's not what caused her death."

"Hardly," The Needle says with suppressed excitement. "I expect you are on the boat right now reconstructing events . . . and there's a piece of the puzzle you might not know."

"Her name is Penelope Fernandez."

"How nice to meet her," mumbles The Needle.

"What was the piece of the puzzle?"

"Well . . ." The Needle's breath is audible in the receiver.

"Tell me."

"It's still not a normal death."

The Needle falls silent again.

"What did you notice?"

"Nothing in particular. It's just a feeling . . ."

"Bravo," says Joona. "You're beginning to sound like me."

"I know, but . . . It's clear that this could be a case of *mors subita naturalis*, that is, a hasty but natural death . . . There's nothing to contradict this, but if this is a natural death, it's a very unusual natural death."

They end the call but The Needle's words echo in Joona's head. *Mors subita naturalis.* There is something mysterious about Penelope Fernandez's death. She was not found in the water and lifted on board; then she would have been lying on the deck. But perhaps the person who found her wanted to treat the body with respect. But why not just carry her to the sofa in the salon? Of course she might have been found by someone who loved her and wanted to put her in a setting where she would have been comfortable—in her own room and her own bed.

Perhaps The Needle was wrong. Maybe she had been rescued, helped on board, helped to her room. Perhaps her lungs had already been seriously injured and she was beyond saving. Perhaps she was feeling ill and wanted to lie down and be left alone.

But why no trace of seawater on her body or clothes?

There's a freshwater shower on board, Joona thinks, and tells himself it's time to search the rest of the boat and take a good look at the berth in the stern, the bathroom, and the galley. There is still quite a bit to examine before the entire picture can become clear.

When Erixson stands up and moves his enormous body, the boat rocks again.

Joona's attention is again drawn to the bucket with the rope. It's next to a tub where a wet suit had been flung. A pair of water skis is lying along the railing. Joona's eyes wander back to the bucket. The rope tied to the handle. The round zinc edge of the washtub shines like a crescent moon in the sun.

A realization washes over him and, with icy clarity, Joona is able to picture what took place. He waits, and lets his heart calm back down. He lets the entire scenario repeat in his mind once more and he is now completely sure it's correct.

The woman named Penelope Fernandez was drowned in the washtub.

In his mind, Joona sees again the mark he'd noticed in the pathology lab: the mark on the skin over her collarbone, the one that reminded him of a smile.

She was murdered and then she was put down on the bed.

Now his thoughts whirl as adrenaline rushes through his system. She was drowned in the brackish water and then carried onto her bed.

Not a common killing. Not a common killer. A voice wells up from deep inside him, becoming more and more clear. More and more demanding. It repeats four words, louder and faster each time. *Leave the boat now! Leave the boat now!* Joona peers at Erixson through the window. He's putting a swab into a paper bag, sealing it with tape, and marking it with a ballpoint pen.

"Peek-a-boo." Erixson smiles.

"Let's go ashore," Joona says calmly.

"I don't like boats because they keep moving all the time, but I've just started with—"

"Take a break," Joona says.

"What's gotten into you?"

"Just come with me and don't touch that cell phone."

They scramble ashore and Joona leads Erixson far away from the boat, as quickly as he can, before they stop. He feels a heat in his face while a kind of calmness spreads through his body—a weight in his legs and calves.

Quietly he says, "I believe there's a bomb on board."

Erixson plumps down on the edge of a cement piling. Sweat pours from his forehead.

"What are you talking about?"

"This is not normal, this murder," Joona says. "There's a risk that—"

"Who said anything about murder?"

"Just wait and listen to me," Joona says insistently. "Penelope Fernandez was drowned in that washtub on deck."

"Drowned? What the hell?"

"She was drowned in seawater in that washtub and then she was put on the bed," Joona says. "And I believe the next step was to sink the boat."

"But—"

"Because then the seawater in her lungs would be natural if she was found in a sunken boat."

"But the boat didn't sink," Erixson protests.

"That's what made me think. Logically there is an explosive on board the boat, which for some reason or another did not go off."

"It's probably in the fuel tank then, or the gas cylinders for the galley," Erixson says slowly. "Let's clear the area and call in the bomb squad."

the reconstruction

At seven that evening, five sour-faced men meet in Hall 13 at the department of forensic medicine at the Karolinska Institute. Detective Inspector Joona Linna intends to open a criminal investigation into the death
of the woman found in a drifting pleasure craft in Stockholm's archipelago. Although it's a Saturday, he's called his immediate superior
Petter Näslund and Chief Prosecutor Jens Svanehjälm for a reconstruction. He plans to convince them that this is truly a murder investigation.

One of the lighting fixtures in the ceiling is blinking on and off and
the cold light bounces off the walls of shining white tiles.

"I have to change the starter," The Needle says softly.

"You sure do," Frippe says.

Petter Näslund mutters something inaudible from where he's standing, pressed against the wall. The strong angles of his wide face seem to
move with the flickering light. Next to him, Jens Svanehjälm is waiting.
His boyish face reveals his irritation. He appears to be weighing the risk
of placing his leather briefcase on the floor or leaning against the wall in
his well-tailored suit.

The strong stench of disinfectant permeates the room. Strong lamps
with directable beams are mounted to the ceiling above a bench made
from stainless steel, which has two faucets and a deep sink. The floor is
covered with a light gray plastic mat. A zinc tub just like the one on the

boat sits in the middle of the bench and is already half filled with water, but again and again, Joona Linna carries more water to it from the faucet on the wall.

"It's not a criminal offense to be found drowned on a boat," Svanehjälm says sarcastically.

"Exactly," says Petter.

"This could just be an unreported drowning incident," Svanehjälm continues.

"The seawater in her lungs is the same the boat was in," says The Needle. "But there's no water on her clothes or on the rest of her body."

"That *is* odd," Svanehjälm agrees.

"There must be a rational explanation," Petter says with a wry smile.

Joona empties a last bucket of water into the tub, sets the bucket down, looks up at the other four men, and thanks them for taking the time to come.

"I know it's the weekend and everyone wants to be home," he begins. "Yet, I believe I've noticed something important."

"Of course, we always come when you tell us that," Svanehjälm says as he finally decides to put his leather briefcase on the floor between his feet.

"The suspect gets on the boat," Joona begins. "He goes down the stairs to the forecabin and sees Penelope sleeping. He returns to the afterdeck and begins to fill the tub using a bucket with a long rope attached."

"Five or six buckets at least," says Petter.

"And only when the tub is filled does he wake Penelope. He leads her up the stairs and across the deck and then he drowns her in the tub."

"Why? And who would do something like that?" asks Svanehjälm.

"I don't know yet. Perhaps it was to torture her with fake drowning, waterboarding—"

"Revenge? Jealousy?"

Joona cocks his head and says thoughtfully, "This person doesn't feel like your average killer. Perhaps the suspect wanted information from her or to force her to tell or confess to something until he finally held her under enough that she could no longer resist the urge to draw a breath."

"What does the chief pathologist say?" asks Svanehjälm.

The Needle shakes his head.

"If she'd been drowned," he says, "I would have found signs of force on her body, bruises and the like—"

"Can we all wait with the objections for a moment?" Joona says. "First I would like to show you how it happened. As I see it. How the events play out in my head. And then, once I'm finished, I would like us all to go and look at the body to prove my theory."

"Why can't you do things like everyone else? Just tell us," demands Petter.

The chief prosecutor warns, "I have to be home soon."

Joona looks at him with an ice-cold glint in his eyes—and a trace of a smile.

"Penelope Fernandez," he begins. "At first she was sitting on deck and smoking some pot. It was a warm day and she became tired and decided to take a nap. She goes to bed and falls asleep still wearing her denim jacket."

He gestures to Frippe, The Needle's young assistant who is waiting in the open door.

"Frippe here will help."

Frippe steps into the room with a big smile. His dyed black hair hangs in locks down his back. His worn leather pants are full of rivets, and he is carefully buttoning his jacket over his black T-shirt with its picture of the hard-rock group Europe.

"Watch me," Joona says softly. Behind Frippe's back he quickly grips both sleeves of Frippe's jacket in one hand while with the other he grabs his long hair.

"Now I have complete control," Joona says grimly. "And I guarantee there won't be a single bruise on him."

Joona levers the young man's arms higher behind his back. Frippe moans and leans forward.

"Take it easy!" he laughs.

"You're much larger than the girl, of course," says Joona. "Still, I believe I can dunk your head into the tub."

"Don't hurt him," says The Needle.

"I'll only ruin his hairstyle," says Joona.

"Not a chance," grunts Frippe.

It's a silent struggle. The Needle looks nervous and Svanehjälm appears troubled. Without too much effort, Joona forces Frippe's head underwater and holds him there for a slight moment, then lets him go and steps back. Frippe gets up, staggering, and The Needle hurries to him with a towel.

"You could have just told us how it went," The Needle says with irritation.

As Frippe towels off his hair, they troop together into the next room, into the strong smell of decay. One of the walls is covered with three rows of stainless-steel refrigerated boxes. The Needle opens box 16 and pulls out a drawer. The body of the young woman is lying on the narrow gurney. She's naked and has no color. A brown network of arteries can be seen on the pale skin of her neck. Joona points at the thin, curved line over her breastbone.

"Take off your shirt," Joona says to Frippe.

Frippe unbuttons his jacket and pulls off his T-shirt. On his chest they can see a light rose mark from the edge of the tub. It's curved like a smiling face.

"I'll be damned," Petter says.

The Needle steps nearer to peer closely at the roots of the woman's hair. He takes out a small pocket flashlight and aims it directly at the pale skin of her scalp.

"I don't need a microscope to see how someone has held her head tight by using her hair."

He turns off the flashlight and drops it back into his pocket.

"In other words . . ." Joona waits.

"In other words, you're right, of course," says The Needle, and claps his hands.

"Murder," Svanehjälm pronounces, sighing.

"Impressive," remarks Frippe as he catches some black hair dye that has run down his cheek.

"Thanks," says Joona, but he sounds distracted.

The Needle looks at him.

"What now, Joona?" he asks. "What do you see?"

"It's not her," Joona says.

"What?"

Joona looks up at The Needle and then points to the body before them.

"This woman is not Penelope Fernandez. This is someone else."

Joona meets the chief prosecutor's eyes. "This dead woman is not Penelope. I've seen Penelope's driver's license and it doesn't match. I'm absolutely sure."

"But what—"

"Perhaps Penelope Fernandez is also dead," Joona says. "We just haven't found her yet."

a party in the night

Penelope tries to breathe slowly, but the air tears at her throat. She slides down the cliff, ripping off sheets of moss as she squeezes between the branches of the spruce trees. She shakes with fright and creeps closer to the tree trunks, where the darkness of night is already gathering. As she thinks of Viola, she begins to whimper. Björn is ahead of her, already sitting perfectly still underneath the spruce trees, his arms wrapped tightly around himself. He's mumbling something over and over.

They've been running in panic, not looking, stumbling over objects, falling, getting up again, clambering over fallen trees. They've ripped open sores on their legs, their knees, their hands, but they've let nothing stop them.

Penelope has no idea how close their pursuer might be, if he's caught sight of them again or even decided to give up and go away. Perhaps he's found a spot to wait them out. They're fleeing for their lives, but Penelope has no idea why.

Perhaps it's all a mistake, she thinks. *A horrible mistake.*

She feels nauseous, feels like she's going to throw up, but swallows resolutely.

"Oh God, oh God," she whispers to herself. "We can't go on like this. We have to get help. They'll find the boat soon and then they'll come looking for us—"

"Shhh!" Björn shushes her, visibly, shockingly terrified.

Her hands tremble uncontrollably as images flash through her head. She blinks so that she won't have to see them, but the visions keep flashing back: Viola dead; eyes wide-open, face wet, sitting on the bed, hair dripping in streams.

Penelope knows instinctively that the man on the beach, yelling out to Björn at sea, was the one who killed her sister. She'd reacted the instant she'd understood. If she hadn't, they'd both be dead.

When they fled the boat, they'd carried nothing with them, not even a cell phone. Scrambling up the bank, Penelope had turned around only once to see the man in black tying the rubber boat to the pier.

Penelope and Björn had run, side by side, into the spruce forest, darting around trees and skirting outcroppings; Björn's voice was a series of painful gasps as the soles of his naked feet tramped over sharp brush. And when he'd seemed to slow down, Penelope had pulled him with her, knowing their pursuer was not far behind. All the while she could hear herself crying as she ran, in a voice she'd never heard before.

A thick branch whacked her thigh and brought her to a stop. Her breath ripped at her. She moaned and with shaking hands pushed her way under low-hanging branches with Björn close beside her. Her legs throbbed. She kept going straight ahead. She heard Björn behind her and kept plunging deeper into the dark forest without turning around.

From far outside herself, Penelope contemplated the fact that thoughts change when panic sets in. Fear is not constant. Now and then there's room for rational thought. It's like silencing a racket to discover a quiet space in your head, which gives you a clear overview of your situation. Then the noise returns and your thoughts race in circles until the only impetus is to run.

Penelope kept expecting to find people. There had to have been hundreds of people out and about on Ornö Island that evening. The south end of the island is developed; there had to be people there. There had to be help.

For a moment, Penelope and Björn hid between tightly spaced spruce trees, but after only a few seconds, their fear overwhelmed them and they began to flee again. Even as she ran, Penelope could feel the presence of her pursuer. She thought she could hear his long, swift strides. He wouldn't stop. If they couldn't find help, he would catch up.

The ground was rising again. Stones loosened underneath their feet and tumbled down the slope.

There *must* be people nearby. There *must* be a house. Hysteria swept through Penelope and she felt the need to just stop and scream as loud as she could. Silently, she ran on.

Björn coughed behind her, strangled for breath; coughed again.

What if Viola wasn't really dead? What if she just needed help? Somehow Penelope knew she was having these thoughts to ward off the terrible truth. Viola was dead, but thinking that was unbearable: an empty dark space she refused to comprehend and didn't even want to make the attempt to understand.

They kept climbing up another steep slope between yet more spruce trees, around more huge branches, lingonberry bushes, and craggy rocks. She used her hands to steady herself until she finally reached the crest. Björn was right behind her. He tried to tell her something, but instead just gasped for breath. He took her hand to start down the other side, which now sloped toward the western shore. They could see the light of water between the dark trees. It wasn't far.

Penelope slipped and slid over the edge of a small cliff. She fell freely and hit the ground hard. Struggling to get up, she wondered whether she'd broken something. Then she realized she was hearing music and laughter. She leaned against the damp cliff side for support so she could stand up. She wiped her lips and studied her bloody hand.

Björn reached her and pulled her along. He pointed. There was a party going on somewhere ahead of them. They took each other's hands and stumbled shakily to a run. Colored lights, strung on trellises around a wooden patio, twinkled between the dark trunks of trees.

They slowed to a cautious walk, looking carefully around.

People were sitting at a table outside a beautiful summerhouse painted Falun red. Penelope wondered if it was the middle of the night. The sky was still light, but dinner must have ended a while ago. Wineglasses and coffee cups were scattered about along with crumpled napkins and empty potato-chip bowls.

A few partygoers were singing together, while others refilled their glasses from boxes of red wine and chatted. Tendrils of wavy warm air still rose from the grill. Any children must have already been put to bed, snuggled in the house underneath cozy blankets. To Björn and Penelope, they seemed like denizens of another planet—a planet where calm, happy people lived safely together under a giant glass dome.

Only one person stood outside of that charmed circle. He lurked at the side, facing the forest as if he expected visitors. Penelope stopped dead and silently gripped Björn's hand. They dropped to the ground and crept behind a low spruce. Björn's eyes were scared and uncomprehending, but Penelope was absolutely sure what she'd seen. Their pursuer had read their minds and gotten ahead of them. He knew they couldn't resist the lights and the sounds of the party. Like moths to a flame, they'd be drawn here. So he'd waited. He'd want to catch them just inside the darkness of the trees. He hadn't worried about any screams. He knew the people at the party wouldn't think to investigate anything so strange until it would be too late.

When Penelope dared look up again, the man was gone. She shook from shock. Perhaps he'd changed his mind and believed he'd made a mistake. She searched around with her eyes. Maybe he'd gone somewhere else.

Hope had just started to creep into her mind. Then she saw him again, closer.

He was a dark form blending into a tree trunk not far from them.

He was calmly unpacking a set of black binoculars with green lenses.

Penelope pressed closer to Björn and fought her mindless instinct to leap up and start running again. Instead, she coolly watched the man as he lifted his binoculars to his eyes. He must have night-vision goggles or a heat sensor, she thought.

When the man's back was turned, Penelope pressed Björn's hand and, bent double, she pulled him away from the house and the music and back deep into the forest. After a while, she felt safe enough to straighten up. They began to run diagonally across a slope, a gently rounded reminder of the ancient glaciers that once ground northern Europe under ice. They kept going—through tangled bushes, behind a huge boulder, over a rocky crest. Björn grabbed a thick branch and hurried as carefully as he could down the slope. Penelope's heart thudded in her chest and her thigh muscles screamed. She tried to breathe quietly, but could not. She slid down a rocky cliff, pulling damp moss with her, and landed on the ground next to the deep shade of a spruce. She looked at Björn. All he had on were his knee-length swimming trunks. His body was a pale blur and his lips almost disappeared in his white face.

15

the identification

It sounds as if someone is bouncing a ball against the wall beneath Chief Medical Officer Nils Åhlén's window. The Needle is waiting with Joona Linna for Claudia Fernandez. They don't have much to say, so they keep quiet. Claudia Fernandez had been asked to appear at the department of forensic medicine early that Sunday morning to identify the body of a dead woman.

When Joona had to phone to tell her they feared her daughter, Viola, was dead, Claudia's voice sounded unnaturally calm.

"No, that can't be. Viola is out in the archipelago with her sister," she'd said.

"On Björn Almskog's boat?" Joona asked.

"Yes. I called Penelope and asked her to take her sister with them. I thought Viola needed to get away for a while."

"Was there anyone else on the boat?"

"Björn, of course."

Joona had fallen silent and waited a few seconds to force away the heaviness in his heart. Then he'd cleared his throat and said, very softly, "Mrs. Fernandez, I would like you to come to the department of forensic medicine's pathology office in Solna."

"Why?" she'd asked.

Now Joona is sitting on an uncomfortable chair in the office of the chief medical officer. Wedged in the corner of the frame of The Needle's wedding picture is a tiny photo of Frippe. From a distance they keep hearing the ball thud against the wall. It is a lonely sound. Joona remembers how Claudia Fernandez had caught her breath when she finally understood that her daughter might indeed not be alive. They'd arranged for a taxi to pick her up from her town house in the Gustavsberg neighborhood. She should arrive here any minute.

The Needle had tried for some small talk but gave up when Joona did not respond. Both of them wish this moment would soon be over.

Hearing steps in the hallway, they rise from their chairs.

To see the dead body of a loved one is merciless—everyone's worst fear. The experts say it is a necessary step in the process of grief. Joona has read that once an identification is made, there's a certain kind of liberation. One can no longer sustain wild fantasies that the person is still alive. These kinds of fantasies and hopes only lead to frustration and emptiness.

Those are nothing but empty words, Joona thinks. *Death is horrible and it never gives you anything back.*

Claudia Fernandez is now in the doorway. She's a woman of about sixty, frightened. Traces of worry are etched on her face. She huddles as if chilled.

Joona greets her gently.

"Hello. My name is Joona Linna and I'm a detective inspector. We spoke on the phone earlier."

The Needle introduces himself almost soundlessly as he briefly shakes the woman's hand and then turns away to shuffle through some folders and files. It must seem he is a cold person, but Joona knows he's deeply moved.

"I've been calling and calling, but I can't reach my girls," Claudia says. "They should—"

"Shall we go in?" The Needle interrupts, as if he hadn't heard her words.

Silently they walk through the familiar hallway. With each step Joona feels as if air is being squeezed from his body. Claudia is in no rush. She walks slowly a few paces behind The Needle, whose tall silhouette precedes them. Joona turns and tries to smile at Claudia, but then he has to turn away from the expression in her eyes. The panic, the pleading, the prayers—her attempts to make a bargain with God.

It feels as if she is being dragged in their wake as they enter the morgue.

The Needle mumbles something to himself in an angry tone. Then he bends down and unlocks the stainless-steel locker and pulls out the drawer.

The young woman's body is covered with a white cloth except for her head. Her eyes are dull and half closed, her cheeks a little sunken, but her hair is still a black crown about her beautiful face. A small, pale hand is half uncovered along her side.

Claudia Fernandez reaches out her hand, carefully touches the hand of her daughter, and begins to whimper. It comes from deep within, as if in this moment part of her is breaking to pieces.

She begins to shake. She falls to her knees. She holds her daughter's lifeless hand to her lips.

"No, no," she's crying. "Oh God, dear Lord, not Viola. Not Viola . . ."

From a few feet behind, Joona watches her shoulders shake as she cries; he hears her despairing wail crescendo and then gradually fall away.

She wipes at the tears streaming down her face, breathing shakily as she slowly gets back up on her feet.

"Can you positively confirm that this is Viola Fernandez?" The Needle says gruffly.

His voice stops and he quickly clears his throat, angry at himself.

Claudia nods her head and gently moves her fingertips over her daughter's cheek.

"Viola, Violita . . ."

She draws back her shaking hand and Joona slowly says, "I'm very, very sorry for your loss."

Claudia looks faint but reaches out a hand to the wall for support. She turns her face away and whispers to herself.

"We were going to the circus on Saturday. I bought tickets as a surprise for Viola . . ."

They all look at the dead woman: her pale lips and the arteries in her throat.

"I've forgotten who you are," Claudia says in confusion. She looks at Joona.

"Joona Linna," he says.

"Joona Linna," the woman says with a thick voice. "Let me tell you about my daughter Viola. She is my little girl, my youngest, my happy little . . ."

Claudia looks at Viola's white face and it seems as if she might fall to one side. The Needle pulls over a chair, but Claudia waves it away.

"Please forgive me," she says. "It's just that . . . my eldest daughter, Penelope, had to endure so many terrible things in El Salvador. When I think about what they did to me in that jail, when I remember how frightened Penelope was, how she'd cry and scream for me . . . hour after hour . . . but I couldn't answer her, I couldn't protect her . . ."

Claudia meets Joona's eyes and takes a step toward him. Gently he puts an arm around her, and she leans heavily against his chest, trying to catch her breath. She moves away again, not looking at her daughter's body, gropes for the chair back, and then sits down.

"My greatest joy was that Viola was born here in Sweden. She had a nice room with a pink lamp in the ceiling, toys and dolls. She went to school. She watched Pippi Longstocking on television . . . I don't know if you can understand, but I was proud that she never needed to be hungry or afraid. Not like us, not like Penelope and me. We wake up at night and are frightened that someone will come into our house and hurt us . . ."

She falls silent and then whispers, "Viola was happy, just happy . . ."

Claudia leans forward to hide her face in her hands as she weeps. Joona lays a hand gently on her back.

"I'll go now," she says, even though she's still crying.

"There's no hurry."

She manages to contain herself, but then her face twists again into tears.

"Have you talked to Penelope?" she asks.

"We haven't been able to reach her," Joona says in a low voice.

"Tell her that I want her to call me because—"

She stops suddenly. Her face turns pale. Then she looks up again.

"I just thought that she might not be answering me when I call because I . . . I was . . . I said some horrible things, but I didn't mean anything, I didn't mean anything—"

"We have already started a helicopter search for Penelope and Björn Almskog, but—"

"Please, tell me that she's alive," she whispers. "Tell me that, Joona Linna."

Joona's jaw muscles tense as he reassures her by the pressure of his hand and says, "I will do everything I can to—"

"She's alive, tell me that," Claudia whispers. "She must be alive."

"I will find her," Joona says. "I know that I will find her."

"Tell me that Penelope is alive."

Joona hesitates and then meets Claudia's black eyes as a few lightning sensations sweep through his heart. A number of unseen connections click in his mind, and suddenly he hears his own voice answer, "She's alive."

"Yes," Claudia whispers.

Joona looks down. He's not able to recover the thought behind the certainty he'd felt that prompted him to ignore caution and tell Claudia that her eldest daughter was still among the living.

the mistake

Joona follows Claudia Fernandez to the waiting taxi and helps her in. Afterward he stands motionless until the taxi disappears around a curve in the driveway. Only then does he dig in his pocket for his cell phone. When he realizes he must have forgotten it, he strides back to the forensic department and quickly enters The Needle's office, takes The Needle's phone, and sits in The Needle's chair. He dials Erixson's number and waits while the call goes through.

"Let people sleep," Erixson drowsily answers. "It's Sunday, you know."

"Confess that you're at the boat," Joona says.

"Yes, I am," Erixson confesses.

"So there was no explosive," Joona says.

"Not your average bomb, no. But you were still correct. This boat could have gone up at any second."

"What do you mean?"

"The power cables' insulation is seriously damaged in one spot because of crimping. Someone stuffed an old ripped seat cushion behind the cables, too. Very flammable. So it's not that the leads are making contact—that would trip the circuit breaker. But they are exposed. If you kept running the engine, eventually you'd cause a discharge, with an electric arc running between the two power cables."

"What happens then?"

"The arc would reach a temperature above three thousand degrees Celsius and it would ignite the seat cushion back there," Erixson continues. "Then the fire would find its way to the hose from the fuel pump, and *bang!*"

"A quick process?"

"Well, the arc could take ten minutes to form, maybe longer, but after that, everything would happen fast—fire, more fire, explosion—and then the broken boat would fill with water and sink, fast."

"So if the motor was started, there would soon be a fire and an explosion sooner or later?"

"Yes, but the fire wouldn't necessarily be considered arson."

"So the cables were damaged by accident and the sofa cushion just happened to be lying there?"

"Of course."

"But you don't believe that."

"Not for a second."

Joona pictures again the drifting boat. He clears his throat and says thoughtfully, "If the killer planned all this—"

"He's not your normal killer," Erixson finished.

Joona repeats the thought to himself once the conversation ends. Again he agrees. The average murderer is motivated by passion, by greed, by anger. Emotions are almost always involved even to the point of hysteria. Only later does he fumble to cover his tracks and fabricate an alibi. This time it appears the killer had followed a sophisticated strategy right from the start.

And still, something went wrong.

Joona stares into space, grabs a legal pad from The Needle's desk, and writes *Viola Fernandez* on the first page. He circles her name and then writes *Penelope Fernandez* and *Björn Almskog* beneath it. The women are sisters. Penelope and Björn are in a relationship. Björn owns the boat. Viola asks if she can come with them at the last minute.

Joona feels the road to finding the motive behind this murder is long. He's still internally convinced that Penelope Fernandez is alive. It's not just a wild hope or an attempt to give comfort. It's intuition. Based on what, he cannot say. He'd caught the thought in flight, but lost it again before he could capture it and pin it down.

If he followed the usual procedures put forth by the CID, suspicion would immediately fall on Viola's boyfriend or perhaps on Penelope and Björn since they were on the boat. Speculation would include alcohol and drugs. Perhaps a fight. Perhaps a serious drama stemming from jealousy. Before too long, Leif G. W. Persson would be sitting on a couch in a television studio explaining that the suspect was a close acquaintance and probably a boyfriend or ex-boyfriend.

What is the point behind making the fuel tank explode? Where's the logic behind this plan? Viola is already dead, drowned in the zinc tub on the afterdeck. The killer carries her downstairs and leaves her on the bed.

Joona realizes too many ideas are coming at once. He puts on mental brakes and begins to find structure in the evidence he's gathered, tries to find questions that still need answers.

He circles Viola's name again and starts over.

What he knows now is that she was drowned in a tub and placed on a bed in the forecabin and that Penelope Fernandez and Björn Almskog have still not been found.

But that's not all, he tells himself, and flips to a new page.

He writes the word "Calm" on the paper.

There was no wind and the boat was found drifting near Dalarö Island.

The boat's bow had been damaged in a serious collision. Joona expected the technicians had likely already found evidence, perhaps even making some plaster casts for possible matches.

Joona throws the legal pad against the wall and shuts his eyes.

"*Perkele*," he swears in Finnish.

Something has slipped through his fingers again. He had been just about to grasp it. He'd instinctively realized something, almost understood something, but then—it was gone.

Viola, he thinks. *You died on the afterdeck. Why were you moved after your death? Who moved you, the killer or someone else?*

If someone were to find her lifeless on the deck, that person would still try to bring her back to life. They'd call in an SOS alarm—that's what people do. And if they realized she was already dead and it was too late, that she wouldn't be coming back to life, then they wouldn't just leave her lying there. They'd want to carry her inside and put a blanket over her. However, a body is awkward to move, even with two people.

Yet the distance was hardly more than five meters, just in through the glass doors and down the stairs.

Even one person could manage that. It's possible.

But you don't carry her down the stairs and through the narrow hallway and then set her on the bed in the cabin.

Someone would only do that to stage some sort of setup: that she'd be found drowned on her bed in a water-filled boat.

"Exactly," Joona mumbles and stands up.

He looks out through the window and sees an almost blue beetle crawling along the white ledge. Raising his gaze, he sees a woman on a bicycle disappear behind the trees—and, suddenly, he recovers the missing element he'd dropped.

Joona sits back down and drums the table. It was not Penelope they'd found in the boat, but her sister, Viola. But Viola was not on her own bed. She was on Penelope's. The murderer made the same mistake I did, Joona thinks as shivers travel down his spine.

He thought he'd killed Penelope Fernandez. That's why he'd put her on the forecabin's bed. This is the only explanation that makes sense.

Joona jumps as the office door bangs open. It's The Needle, pushing it open with his shoulder and backing in with a long, flat box in his arms. On the front there's the image of large flames and the text proclaims *Guitar Hero.*

"Frippe and I are going to—"

"Quiet!" Joona barks.

"What's up?" The Needle asks.

"Nothing. I just have to think."

Joona gets up from the chair and strides out without another word, through the foyer, not even hearing the words said by the woman with the dazzling eyes in reception. He comes into the heat of the sun and stands quietly on the lawn by the parking lot.

A fourth person, unknown to either Penelope or Viola, killed Viola, Joona thinks. He mistook one sister for the other. This must mean that Penelope was alive when Viola was killed, or he wouldn't have made that mistake.

Perhaps Penelope really is still alive, Joona thinks. Or her body is somewhere in the archipelago, on an island or deep beneath the sea. But we can hope that she's still alive and if she is, we will find her very soon.

Joona strides quickly to his car even though he has no idea where he will go. He spots his cell phone up on its roof; he must have put it there when he locked the car door. He picks up the sun-warmed phone and calls Anja Larsson. No answer. He climbs in, automatically fastens the seat belt, but makes no next move. He just sits and tries to find the flaws in his reasoning.

The air is suffocating, but the heady aroma of the lilac bushes next to the parking lot eases its way into his nostrils and chases away the smell of decaying corpses from the pathology lab.

The cell phone in his hand rings. He looks at the display and answers.

"I've just talked to your doctor," Anja says.

"Why have you been talking to him?"

"Janush says that you've not come in to see him," she says accusingly.

"I really haven't had the time."

"But you're taking your medicine?"

"It tastes terrible," Joona jokes.

"But seriously . . . he called me because he was worried about you," she says.

"I'll talk to him."

"But not until you've solved this case, right?"

"Do you have a pen and paper?"

"Go ahead, ignore me," she says.

"The woman found on the boat is not Penelope Fernandez."

"It's Viola, I know. Petter told me."

"Good."

"You were wrong, Joona."

"Yes, I know—"

"Say it, Joona!" she laughs.

"I'm always wrong," he says.

There's a moment of silence between them.

"Don't joke about it," she says.

"Have you found out anything about the boat or Viola Fernandez?"

"Viola and Penelope are sisters," Anja replies. "Penelope and Björn are in some kind of relationship, and that's lasted four years so far."

"Yes, that's about what I've guessed."

"So I see. Do you want me to bother to continue?"

Joona doesn't answer. Instead, he leans his head back on the headrest and sees that the windshield is covered with some kind of tree pollen.

"Viola wasn't supposed to go on the boat with them," Anja continues. "But she'd had a fight with her boyfriend, Sergei Yarushenko, that morning, and when she called to cry on her mother's shoulder, it was the mother who suggested Viola go with her sister on the boat trip."

"What do you know about Penelope?"

"I've actually focused on the victim, Viola, since—"

"The murderer believed he was killing Penelope."

"What are you saying, Joona?"

"He made a mistake. He was going to hide the killing in a fake boating accident. He didn't realize he'd put Viola on her sister's bed."

"Since he'd mixed up the sisters."

"I need to know everything you have on Penelope Fernandez and her—"

Anja cuts Joona off. "She's one of my idols. She's a peace activist. She lives on Sankt Paulsgatan 3."

"We've put out a search bulletin on her and Björn Almskog," Joona says. "The Coast Guard is flying two helicopters in the area around Dalarö, but they should coordinate with the maritime police."

"I'll take a look at what's going on," Anja says.

"Someone should track down Viola's boyfriend, and also the fisherman who found the boat. We've got to get everything together as fast as we can—the evidence from the boat, the results from the National Forensic Lab—"

"Do you want me to give Linköping a call?" Anja asks.

"I'll talk to Erixson. He knows them and we're going together to look at Penelope's apartment."

"It sounds like you've taken over the investigation. Right?"

an extremely dangerous man

The skies are still bright, but the air is heavy and damp, as if a thunderstorm is looming.

As Joona Linna and Erixson park outside the old fishermen's supply shop, Joona's cell phone rings. It's Claudia Fernandez. He ducks into a shady spot before answering.

"You told me I could call," she says weakly.

"Of course."

"I know you tell this to everyone, but I thought . . . my daughter Penelope. I mean . . . I have to know if you find something, even if she . . ."

Claudia's voice fades away.

"Hello? Claudia?"

"I'm here. Sorry," she whispers.

"I'm a detective," Joona says. "I'm trying to find out whether there is criminal activity behind these events. The Coast Guard is searching for Penelope."

"When will they find her?"

"Well, they're flying over the area in helicopters right now. They're searching by sea and land. Since that takes longer, they start with the helicopters."

Joona hears that Claudia is muffling her crying.

"I don't know what I should be doing . . . I . . . I need to know what I can do or whether I should keep talking with her friends."

"The best thing you can do is stay home," Joona says. "Penelope might try to contact you and then—"

"She won't call me," says Claudia.

"I think she—"

"I've always been too hard on Penny. I'm always angry at her. I don't really know why. I . . . I don't want to lose her. I can't lose Penelope, I . . ."

Claudia's sobs are now loud in the receiver. She tries to control herself; fails. With a barely audible apology, she ends the call.

Right across from the fishermen's supply shop is Sankt Paulsgatan 3, where Penelope Fernandez lives. Joona walks over to Erixson, who is staring into a shop window. The shop used to display photos of the fisherman who caught the largest salmon in the Stockholm River that week. Now the windows are crowded with hundreds of Hello Kitty items. The entire shop provides an amazingly stark contrast to the dirty brown walls of the building's exterior.

"Little body, large head," Erixson says as Joona comes up to him. Erixson points at the Hello Kittys.

"They're rather cute," Joona admits.

"Me—I'm totally backward. Small head on a large body," Erixson jokes.

Joona gives him an amused glance as he opens the wide entrance door. They walk up the stairs and look at the nameplates, the illuminated buttons for turning on the ceiling lights, and the overflowing garbage cans. In the stairwell, it smells like sunshine, dust, and green soap. Erixson takes hold of the shiny wooden handrail so hard that its screws and mounting brackets creak as he climbs, panting, while trying to keep up with Joona. They make it to the fourth floor at the same time and look at each other. Erixson's face is quivering from the effort. He nods while wiping the sweat from his forehead and whispers to Joona, "Sorry about that."

"It's humid today."

There are stickers near the doorbell. Antinuclear, fair trade, and the peace symbol. Joona gives Erixson a brief glance, then puts his ear to the door. His eyes narrow.

"What is it?"

Joona presses the doorbell while still listening. He waits another moment before he pulls his picklock from his inner pocket.

"Maybe it was nothing," Joona says as he carefully jimmies the simple lock.

He eases open the door, then changes his mind and softly closes it again. He waves Erixson to the side. He's not sure why. They hear the melody from an ice-cream truck outside. Erixson frowns and taps his cheek nervously. Joona's arms feel cold, but then he calmly opens the door and steps inside. Newspapers, ads, and a letter from the Left Party litter the rug. The air is unmoving and smells stale. A velvet curtain hangs in front of a closet. There's a hissing sound, perhaps from the pipes, and somewhere something's ticking.

Joona has no idea why his hand is reaching for his holstered weapon. He touches it with his fingers where it's resting underneath his jacket, but leaves it there. His eyes go to the bloodred curtain and then to the kitchen door. He holds his breath as he tries to look through the ribbed, glass-paned door to the living room.

Joona takes another step although his instinct is to turn around and leave. He feels he should have called for reinforcements. A dark shadow glides across the other side of the glass. A wind chime made with hanging rods sways soundlessly. Joona sees the dust specks in the air change direction in an unfelt breeze.

He is not alone in Penelope's apartment.

There's someone in the living room. He can feel it. He casts one look at the kitchen door and then everything happens at once. A floorboard creaks; a series of rapid clicks keeps a rhythm all its own. The door to the kitchen is half open and in the gap between the hinges Joona spots movement. He presses against the wall as if he were in a train tunnel, his heart beating fast. Someone else is sneaking along in the dark hallway; Joona sees a back, a shoulder, an arm. The figure slides closer and then whirls around. The knife is like a white tongue. It's leaping up, piercing in an angle so unusual Joona can't parry the blade. Its sharp edge slices through his clothes, hitting the leather of his holstered weapon. Joona swings at the person but hits thin air. *Swish.* He hears the knife a second time and throws his body to the side. The blade has come from directly above this time. Joona hits his head on the bathroom door. A long sliver of wood curls down as the knife hits the door.

Joona slides down and simultaneously releases a wide kick. He connects, perhaps on the intruder's ankle. He rolls away, pulling out his pistol and releasing the safety in the same movement. The outer door is open now. Footsteps sound running down the stairs. Joona scrambles to his feet and is ready to chase after the man, but he stops. There's a humming sound behind him. He knows immediately what is going on and runs into the kitchen. The microwave is on. Behind its glass door, it's giving off sparks. The control knobs of the four burners on the old gas stove are turned fully open and gas is blasting into the room. With a feeling that the flow of time has slowed down, Joona leaps to the microwave. The timer clicks menacingly, the sparking sounds keep increasing. A spray can of insect poison is rotating inside the microwave.

Joona grabs the electric plug and yanks it out. The ticking stops. The gas hisses loudly until Joona turns off the stove. The chemical smell is nauseating. He yanks open the kitchen window and then looks in on the spray can in the microwave. Its belly is grotesquely swollen. Joona thinks it could still explode at the slightest touch.

He leaves the kitchen and quickly surveys the rest of the apartment. The other rooms are empty. The air is still heavy with gas.

Erixson's lying on the floor beside the stairwell, a cigarette in his mouth.

"Don't light that!" Joona yells.

With a smile and a weak wave of his hand, Erixson replies, "It's chocolate."

He coughs weakly and Joona can see that there's a pool of blood beneath him.

"You're bleeding," Joona says.

"No big deal," Erixson replies. "I'm not sure how he did it, but he sliced my Achilles tendon."

Joona calls for an ambulance and then crouches next to Erixson, whose face is pale and whose cheeks glisten from sweat. He looks nauseated.

"He cut me while he ran past. It was so quick . . . like being attacked by a fucking spider."

They fall silent. Joona remembers the lightning-fast movements behind the kitchen door and how the blade of the knife moved effortlessly, with a life of its own. He'd never seen anything like it before.

"Is she in there?" Erixson pants.

"No."

Erixson smiles, relieved. Then he's serious again.

"Was he going to blow the place to hell anyway?"

"Looks like it. He's good at getting rid of evidence," Joona answers sarcastically.

Erixson fumbles at the paper on his chocolate cigarette but drops it. He closes his eyes for a minute. By now his cheeks are ash-white.

"I take it you didn't see his face either," Joona says quietly.

"No," Erixson mumbles. "We saw something, though. There's always something we notice in spite of ourselves."

the fire

The medical crew from the ambulance reassures Erixson that they're not going to drop him.

"I can walk," Erixson protests and shuts his eyes.

His chin shakes each step down.

Joona goes back into Penelope Fernandez's apartment. He opens all the windows to clear the air and then sits down on the apricot-colored sofa. It is very comfortable.

If the apartment had exploded, it would have looked like an unfortunate accident caused by a gas leak. The case would have been closed.

Joona lets his memory expand. No fragment of observation ever completely disappears. It simply must be retrieved just like the seas heave flotsam and jetsam up onto the beach.

But what was it?

He had seen nothing. Just a quick, blurred movement and a knife blade.

That's what I saw! Joona realizes. *I saw nothing!*

This lack is exactly what is nudging his intuition.

We're dealing with a pro here, a contract killer, a hit man, a grob.

There aren't many in the world.

This was not the first inkling he's had, but now he's thoroughly convinced. The killer in the hallway is the same man who murdered Viola.

There was certainly time to do both. He'd planned to kill Penelope and sink the cruiser as if it were an accident; then he'd use the same method here. This is a killer who wants to remain invisible. He wants to kill under the radar of the police.

Joona looks around slowly. He tries again to assemble the parts of the puzzle into a whole.

He hears children playing in the apartment above his head. They're rolling marbles over the floor. They'd have been in the middle of an inferno right now if Joona hadn't been able to pull the plug in time.

This was a cold-blooded, driven attack, Joona thinks, and the man behind it was not some hate-filled right-wing activist. Penelope Fernandez might be involved in the peace movement, sure, and those groups did, ironically, resort to violence sometimes. But this man was different: a highly trained professional at a level well above any of the amateur groups.

So why were you here? Joona wonders. *What does a hit man have to do with Penelope Fernandez? What is she mixed up in? What's going on beneath the surface?*

Joona reviews those unusual knife movements. The technique was obviously meant to circumvent the usual police and military defensive training. His skin prickles as he realizes that the first cut would have sliced into his liver if he hadn't carried his pistol under his right arm. The second cut would have gone straight into his brain if he hadn't thrown himself backward.

Joona gets up from the sofa and walks into the bedroom. He studies the well-made bed and the crucifix over the headboard.

A hit man believed he'd killed Penelope, and his intention was to make it seem like an accident . . . but the boat never sank.

Either the killer was interrupted or he left the scene of the crime intending to return and complete his assignment. He must never have intended that the Coast Guard would find the boat adrift with the drowned girl on board. Something had gone wrong or the plans had to be drastically changed. Maybe he was given new orders. At any event, a day and a half after killing Viola, he was here in Penelope's apartment.

You must have had a strong reason to come here. What was your motive behind this major risk? Is there something here that connects you or your client to Penelope?

You did something here. You got rid of fingerprints or you erased a hard drive or destroyed an answering machine or you came to get something.

That's what you wanted, but then I showed up and wrecked your plan.

Or maybe your plan was to destroy something in the fire? That's a possibility, Joona thinks.

Joona wishes he had Erixson with him now. He needs a forensic technician; he doesn't have the right tools and might even destroy evidence if he searched the apartment on his own. He could contaminate DNA or miss invisible evidence.

Joona walks to the window and looks down at the street. He sees empty tables by a sandwich café.

He really must head back to the police station and talk to his boss, Carlos Eliasson. He must ask to be assigned as the leader of the investigation and call in another forensic technician now that Erixson will be on sick leave.

Joona's telephone rings just as he's made the decision to play by the rules and go talk to both Carlos and Jens Svanehjälm and put together an investigative group.

"Hi, Anja," he says.

"I want to go to the sauna with you," Anja says.

"Why the sauna?"

"Well, why not? Can't we take a sauna together? You could show me how real Finns use the sauna."

"Anja," he replies slowly, "I've lived almost my entire life in Stockholm."

Joona starts walking through the hallway to the outer door.

"I know, I know. You're a Swede with Finnish heritage. How boring is that? Why couldn't you be from El Salvador? Have you read any of Penelope Fernandez's opinion essays in the newspaper? You should see her—the other day she scolded the entire Swedish weapons export industry on television!"

Joona can hear Anja's light breaths in the receiver as he leaves Penelope Fernandez's apartment. There are bloody marks on the stair from the ambulance crew's shoes. A shiver runs down his back as he remembers his colleague sitting there, legs splayed, as the color drained from his face.

Joona believes the hit man is still under the impression he killed

Penelope Fernandez, so he thinks that part of his contract is done. The other half was to get into the apartment for some reason. When the killer figures out Penelope's still alive, he'll be back on the hunt in a hurry.

"Björn and Penelope were not living together," Anja is saying.

"I figured that out," he replies.

"Even so, they could still be in love—just like you and me."

Joona walks into strong sunshine. The air has grown heavier and even more humid.

"Can you give me Björn's address?"

He hears Anja's fingers fly over the keyboard. Small clicking sounds.

"Almskog, Pontonjärgatan 47, third floor."

"I'll go there before I—"

"Wait a second!" Anja said. "Not possible. Listen to this . . . I've just cross-checked this address . . . there was a fire in the building on Friday."

"Björn's apartment?"

Anja replies, "Everything on that floor is gone."

the house

The darkness of night is giving way to morning, even in the forest. Penelope and Björn move back toward the beach together but angle farther south, away from the house where the party had been. Away from their pursuer.

As far from their pursuer as they possibly can go.

Spotting another house between the trees, they start to run again. It's about half a kilometer away, maybe even a little less. They hear the roar of a helicopter overhead somewhere but the sound fades as it moves on.

Björn looks dizzy; Penelope fears he won't be able to keep running much longer. His bare feet are raw.

A branch breaks behind them. Perhaps underneath a human boot.

Penelope begins to run as fast as she can through the forest.

As the trees thin out more, she can see the house again. It's just one hundred meters away. Lights in the window reflect on the red paint of a parked Ford.

A hare leaps up and jumps away over moss and twigs.

Panting and terrified, Penelope and Björn run up the gravel driveway and clamber up the stairs to the house. They spring inside.

"Hello? We need help!" Penelope screams.

The house is warm from yesterday's sunshine. Björn, bare-chested and white with cold, is limping and leaves tracks of blood on the floor as he limps in. Penelope hurries from room to room, but the house is empty. The people who live here probably attended last night's party and are sleeping it off at the neighbors', Penelope realizes. She goes to the window and, hiding behind the curtains, peers outside. There's no movement in the forest or over the lawn. Perhaps the man has lost their trail. Perhaps he's still waiting at the other house. She returns to the hallway where Björn sits on the floor examining the open wounds on his feet.

"We have to find you a pair of shoes."

He looks up at her as if he no longer understands human speech.

"It's not over. You have to find something to put on your feet."

Björn slowly begins to rummage in the closet and pulls out beach shoes, rubber boots, and old bags.

Penelope creeps past the windows in search of a phone. She looks on the hall table, in the briefcase by the sofa, in the bowl on the coffee table, and among the keys and papers on the kitchen counter.

She hears something outside. She freezes to listen.

Maybe it was nothing.

The first rays of the morning sun shine through the windows.

Crouching low, she hurries into the large bedroom, pulls open dresser drawers. Tucked among the underwear, she finds a framed photograph, a studio portrait of a man, a wife, and two teenage daughters. All the other drawers are empty. Penelope yanks opens the closet and pulls out a black hoodie for herself and an oversized sweater for Björn.

She hears the faucet run in the kitchen and hurries there. Björn is leaning over the sink, cupping handfuls of water. He's found a pair of worn-out sneakers a few sizes too large.

This is crazy, Penelope thinks. There must be people all around here; we have to find someone who can help us.

Penelope hands Björn the sweater when someone knocks on the door. Björn smiles, surprised, and pulls it on while mumbling something about their luck turning. Penelope wipes her hair back from her face, and is almost at the door when she sees the silhouette through the frosted glass.

She stops abruptly and observes the shadowy form in the windowpane. Her hand no longer reaches out to open the door. She knows that stance; that head and shoulders. That's the man in black.

All the air rushes from her lungs. She backs toward the kitchen slowly, her body tense and ready to run. Staring at the glass pane, she can see the blurred outline of a face—a face with a small chin. She feels dizzy, stumbles backward over bags and boots, and reaches to steady herself against the wall.

She finds Björn next to her, holding a carving knife with a wide blade. His cheeks are pale and his mouth is half open. He's staring at the pane of glass, too. Penelope backs into a table as the door handle slowly turns down. Suddenly she races into the bathroom, blasts on the water, and yells loudly, "Come in! Door's open!"

Björn jumps and his pulse pounds in his head. He holds the knife out in front, ready to attack, when he sees the door handle ease back up. Their pursuer has let go. The silhouette disappears. A few seconds later, they hear footsteps crunching on the gravel path around the house. Björn looks stiffly to the right. Penelope emerges from the bathroom and Björn points to the window in the TV room. They move away into the kitchen as the man crosses the wooden deck. The footsteps reach the veranda door. Penelope tries to put herself in the killer's head. Are the angle and the light enough to show the shoes tossed out of the closet and Björn's bloody footprints? The wooden deck creaks again near the back stairs. Björn and Penelope creep along the floor and then roll right next to the wall underneath the window. They try to lie still and breathe silently. They can hear that the man has reached the kitchen window, can hear his hands touch the windowsill. They realize he's peering inside.

In the reflection of the window in the oven door, Penelope can see him look from side to side. If he stares at the oven, she thinks, he'll see them too.

The face in the window disappears and they hear steps on the wooden deck yet again. This time, the steps are continuing along the paved path toward the front of the house. As the front door is opened, Björn dashes to the kitchen. He quietly sets the knife on the counter as he turns the key in the lock, pushes the door open, and rushes out.

Penelope follows at his heels. They're running through the garden in the cool morning air, across the lawn, past the compost pile and into the forest. Fear forces Penelope to keep up her stride as it lashes the panic in her chest. She ducks underneath thick branches and leaps over low bushes and rocks. Soon she hears Björn's panting beside her. And behind them, she senses their pursuer: a man attached to them like a dark shadow.

He's following them to kill them.

She remembers a book she read. A woman from Rwanda was telling how she'd managed to survive the genocide by hiding in the woods and running every day. She ran the entire time the killings were going on. Her former friends and neighbors were hunting her with machetes. *We imitated the antelopes,* she'd written. *We who survived in the jungle lived by imitating the flight of the antelopes from their hunters. We ran in unexpected ways, split apart and kept changing directions to confuse our pursuers.*

Penelope knows that she and Björn should be smarter. They're running without a plan, which will help their pursuer but not them. She and Björn are not clever. They want to go home, they want to find help, they want to contact the police. Their pursuer knows all this. He understands them and knows they want to find safety in the company of other humans or find a way to reach the mainland.

Penelope snags her shorts on a branch and rips a hole in them. She staggers a few steps but keeps going. She feels the pain as a burning loop around her leg.

They must not stop. She tastes blood in her mouth. Björn stumbles through a thicket. They have to circle a muddy, water-filled gap left by an uprooted tree.

In her flight next to Björn, a memory springs up unbidden. She had been as frightened then as she is now. It was in Darfur. She remembers the look in people's eyes. Some eyes showed people so traumatized they could not go on. Others refused to give up the fight and kept going. What should have been children came to Kubbum one night. They held loaded guns. She would never forget the fear she felt that night.

the security service

The main office of Sweden's Security Service, Säpo, is on the fourth floor of the National Police Board headquarters. Its main entrance is on Polhemsgatan. The room smells of dust and warm lightbulbs, and pale light falls into the room from a small window facing the courtyard. A whistle can be heard from the exercise yard of the jail, located on the roof of the building. The head of the department of security is Verner Zandén. He's a tall man with a pointed nose, coal-black eyes, and a deep bass voice. He sits now on a chair behind his desk with his legs wide apart, and he's holding up a calming hand. Standing in this unusually depressing room is a young woman named Saga Bauer. She's an investigator and her group's antiterrorism expert. Saga Bauer is just twenty-five years old. Stripes of green, yellow, and red cloth are braided into her long blond hair. She looks like a wood sprite standing in the stream of light in a dark forest. She carries a large-caliber pistol in a shoulder holster under her unzipped exercise hoodie. NARVA BOXING CLUB has been printed on it.

"I've led this entire effort for more than a year," she's pleading. "I've been on stakeout for twenty-four hours at a time—"

"This is something entirely different," her boss says with a smile.

"Please, please . . . You can't just bypass me again!"

"Who says I'm doing that? A technician from CID is seriously wounded and an investigator has been attacked. That apartment could have exploded and—"

"I know. I need to get over there now—"

"I've already sent Göran Stone."

"Göran Stone? I've been here for three years and I haven't closed a case yet! This is my field of expertise! Göran knows nothing at all about—"

"He did a good job with the underground tunnel case."

Saga swallows hard and then she replies, "That was also my case. I found the link to—"

"But it got dangerous and I still believe I made the right call."

Saga's cheeks turn red. She struggles to collect herself. "I can do this. This is what I've been trained for—"

"Yes, but I've made a different call."

Verner sighs and props his feet up on the wastebasket next to his desk.

"You know my record. Affirmative action had nothing to do with my being accepted here," Saga says, as calmly as she's able. "I wasn't part of a quota. I was top of my class in all the tests. I was best at sharpshooting. I have investigated two hundred and ten different—"

"I just don't want anything to happen to you," Verner says softly, and his coal-black eyes meet hers.

"But I'm not a doll, I'm not a princess, or some elf!"

"But you are so . . . so . . ."

Verner lifts his hands helplessly.

"All right, what the hell, let's do it. You be the lead preliminary investigator. But Göran Stone is part of it and I want him to keep an eye on you."

"Thanks," she says, relieved.

"But this is a big deal. Remember that," he warns. "Penelope Fernandez's sister has been killed execution-style and Penelope is missing—"

"And we've noted increased activity among the left-wing extremist groups," Saga says. "We want to know if the Revolutionary Front is behind the theft of explosives in Vaxholm."

"The most important thing is if there is an immediate threat," Verner emphasizes.

"Right now the radicals are sounding more threatening," Saga continues, a little too eagerly. "I've just been in contact with Dante Larsson at Military Intelligence and Security, and he says there will probably be acts of sabotage this summer."

"Right now just concentrate on Penelope Fernandez," Verner demands.

"Of course," Saga answers swiftly. "Of course."

"The technical investigation might be a cooperative effort between the National Criminal Investigation Department and us, but, basically, keep them out of it."

Saga nods and waits a moment before she asks one last question.

"I want to bring this investigation to its conclusion. It's important to me because—"

"Right now, you're in the saddle," he says. "But at this moment we don't know where it's leading or where it will end. We don't even know how it began."

the incomprehensible

Along Rekylgatan in the town of Västerås, there's a shiny white apartment building. The people in the area enjoy being close to Lillhagen School, the soccer fields and tennis courts.

A young man is leaving from Door 11. He's carrying a motorcycle helmet. His name is Stefan Bergkvist and he's almost seventeen years old. He attends an automotive vocational school and lives with his mother and her partner. He has long blond hair and sports a silver ring in his lower lip. He's wearing a black T-shirt, saggy jeans ripped at the cuffs from being walked on, and skate shoes.

In no hurry, he saunters to the parking lot. He hangs his helmet on the bar of his motocross cycle and slowly drives down the sidewalk next to the building. He continues alongside the double train track, then underneath the Norrleden viaduct and into a large industrial area. He finally stops near a construction shed covered in silver-and-blue graffiti.

Stefan and his friends like to meet here. They compete on their own motocross track that they built along the train-track embankment. They drive over various sidings and then circle back along Terminal Road. They started coming here after they stumbled upon a key to the construction shed buried in thistles by the back wall. The shed hadn't been touched for ten years or more, forgotten after all the renovation work.

Stefan climbs off his motorcycle, retrieves the hidden key, and unlocks the padlock underneath its cap. He pushes aside the steel boom and shoves open the wooden door to the shed, closing the door behind him. He checks the time on his phone and sees that his mother has called. He doesn't realize that he's under surveillance from across the train tracks. A sixty-year-old man idles near a Dumpster that belongs to a nearby industrial building. He's wearing a gray suede jacket and light brown trousers.

Stefan walks over to the small kitchen and picks up a bag of chips lying in the sink. He pours the last crumbs into his palm and licks them up.

Light enters the shed from two windows covered with bars. The glass is dirty.

Stefan is waiting for his friends. He flips through an old magazine found among others scattered on a drawing table. On the front cover, a headline screams: JUST THINK! PEOPLE PAY ME TO LICK MY PUSSY!

The man in the suede jacket saunters from his spot and passes the high lattice poles with their looping electric lines. He crosses the brown grass on the embankment and walks over its double train tracks. He continues until he reaches Stefan's motorcycle. He releases the kickstand and quietly wheels the motorcycle to the front.

He glances around once before he lays the motorcycle on its side and shoves it with his foot until it blocks the door. He opens the gas tank and lets the gasoline run out. It leaks underneath the shed.

Stefan is still flipping through the magazine. He looks at the faded photos of women in jail. A blond woman is sitting with her legs open, showing her pussy to a jailer. Stefan is immersed in the picture until he's interrupted by a rustling sound outside. He thinks he hears someone walking around and closes the magazine quickly.

The man in the suede jacket has pulled out the red gasoline can stashed by the boys in the brush next to the shed. He now begins to empty it all around the perimeter. Only when he reaches the back does he hear the shouts from within. The boy is banging on the door and is trying to get it open. He hears the boy's footsteps before the boy's face appears at one of the dirty windows.

"Hey, open the door! This isn't a joke!" the boy says in a high voice.

The man in the suede jacket continues around the shed, emptying the last of the gasoline. Then he puts the container back where it had been hidden.

"What are you doing?" the boy yells.

He then throws his whole body against the door and tries to kick it open, but it doesn't give. He tries to call his mother on his cell phone. Her phone is off. His heart is thudding with panic as he goes from one filthy window to the next.

"Have you lost your mind?" he yells.

As the boy recognizes the stinking smell of gasoline vapor, terror seizes his body and his stomach cramps.

"Hey! Hello?" he yells with fear in his voice. "You *know* I'm in here!"

The man takes a match from his pocket.

"What do you want? Please! Tell me what you want!"

"It's not your fault," the man says. "But a nightmare must be reaped." He hasn't raised his voice at all. He strikes the match.

"Let me out!" the boy screams.

The man throws the match into the grass soaked in gasoline. It makes a sucking sound, as a sailboat's sail does when it fills with wind. Light blue flames burst up with such force that the man has to step backward. The boy is screaming for help. The fire quickly circles the shed. The man takes a few more steps backward. He feels the heat on his face; he hears the terrible screams.

In a few seconds, the whole shed is ablaze. The glass panes behind the bars shatter from the heat along the walls.

The boy's screams are even higher when the heat ignites his hair.

The man walks calmly away. He crosses the train tracks again and then stands by the industrial buildings to watch the torch that had once been an old shed. A few minutes later, a freight train arrives from the north, rolling slowly along its tracks, wheels now scraping and creaking as the row of brown wagons passes the high flames. As the man disappears along Stenby Road, the wind catches his suede jacket, lifting it high behind him. Underneath, he is completely dressed in black.

the forensic technicians

Although it's the weekend, the head of the National Criminal Investigation Department is in his office. He's never been particularly welcoming to unexpected visitors. There's a BUSY sign in red, lit up on his door, which is shut.

Joona knocks on it as he pushes it open.

"I have to know the minute the maritime police find anything," Joona says.

Carlos Eliasson pushes a book across the desk. "Both you and Erixson have been attacked. That's traumatic. You need a break. You need to take care of yourselves."

"We do take care of ourselves."

"They've finished the helicopter search," Carlos says.

Joona stiffens.

"Finished! How much area did they cover?"

"I don't know."

"Who's in charge of the operation?"

"We have nothing to do with it," Carlos says. "It's under the direction of the maritime police."

Joona says sharply, "It would be awfully nice to know whether we're dealing with one murder or three."

"Joona, you're not on this. I've handed it over to Jens Svanehjälm.

We're putting together a team with Säpo. Petter Näslund and Tommy Kofoed will be on it from our side and—"

"What's my job?"

"To take the week off."

"No."

"Then you get to teach a week at the Police Training Academy."

"No."

"Don't be so obstinate," Carlos says.

"Fuck you."

"Fuck *me*?" Carlos Eliasson exclaims. "I'm your *boss*."

"Maybe Penelope Fernandez and Björn Almskog are still alive," Joona argues roughly. "*His* apartment is burned out; *hers* would have been if I hadn't gotten there on time. I believe the killer is looking for something they have and I believe he drowned Viola trying to get it out of her—"

"Thank you very much," Carlos barks. "Thank you for your input. We have . . . no, give me a minute here. I know that you're finding this hard to accept, but there are other police officers than you, Joona. And most of them are highly competent, I assure you."

"I agree," Joona says slowly, a sharp edge to his voice. "And you ought to look out for them, Carlos."

Joona studies the brown spots on his shirtsleeves. Erixson's blood.

"What are you implying?"

"I've met the killer. I think we'll lose some men before this is done."

"I know he surprised you," Carlos says more softly. "And I know this has been tough."

"All right, then," Joona says gruffly.

"Tommy Kofoed will be in charge of the investigation and I'll call Brittis at the Police Training Academy. She will welcome you as a guest teacher all next week," Carlos concludes.

As Joona leaves the police station, the heat hits him hard. Pulling off his jacket, he senses someone coming up behind him. Someone has emerged from the shadows of the park. Joona turns and sees that it's Claudia Fernandez.

"Joona Linna," she calls in a tense voice.

"Claudia, how are you doing?" he asks gravely.

Claudia Fernandez's eyes are bloodshot and her face looks tortured.

"Find her. You must find my girl," she says, and thrusts a thick envelope at him.

Joona opens it. It's stuffed with money. He pushes it back to Claudia, but she refuses.

"Please, take my money. It's everything I have," she says. "But I'll find more. I'll sell the house. Just find her."

"Claudia, I can't take your money," he says quietly.

"Please."

"We are already doing everything we can."

Joona puts the envelope back in Claudia's hands. She holds it away from her body. She murmurs that she will return home and wait next to the phone. Then she holds him back and tries to explain. "I told her that she was no longer welcome in my home . . . she won't call me."

"You had an argument. That's not the end of the world, Claudia."

"But how could I ever have said such a thing?" She hits her forehead with her fist. "What kind of a person says that to her own child?"

"Sometimes words just slip out . . ."

Joona's voice dies away. He forces away fragments of memory that have been stirred up.

"I can't stand it," she says quietly.

Joona takes Claudia's hand in his and repeats that he's doing everything he can.

"Of course you must get your daughter back," he whispers to her.

She nods, and they break apart to walk away in different directions. Joona hurries down Bergsgatan and squints at the sky as he heads to his car. It's sunny, but also hazy and still extremely humid. Last summer he would have been sitting at the hospital, holding his mother's hand. They spoke to each other in Finnish, as they usually did. He told her that they'd take a trip to Karelia as soon as she was feeling better. She had been born in a small Karelian village, one of the few not burned down by the Russians during the Second World War. His mother had replied that Joona ought to go to Karelia with someone special instead.

Joona buys a bottle of Pellegrino at Il Caffè and drinks it all before he climbs back into his overheated car. The steering wheel is hot to the touch and the seat almost burns his back. Instead of heading over to the Police Training Academy, he returns to Sankt Paulsgatan 3 and to Penelope Fernandez's apartment. He recalls the remarkable speed and precision of movement, as if the knife his assailant had used had come alive.

The entrance is cordoned off with blue-and-white police tape marked DO NOT CROSS and CRIME SCENE in bold letters.

Joona flashes his badge to the uniformed officer on duty, then shakes his hand. They've met before but never worked together.

"Hot today."

"You're telling me," the officer replies.

"How many technicians on the scene?" Joona asks, nodding toward the stairwell.

"One of our guys and three from Säpo," the officer answers cheerfully. "They've trying to find DNA from the perp."

"They're not going to find any," Joona says, almost to himself, as he starts up the stairs.

Standing in front of the apartment door on the fourth floor is Melker Janos, an older officer whom Joona remembers from his own training days as a stressed and unpleasant superior. At that time, Melker was rising in his career, but then came a bitter divorce and periodic alcohol abuse, which resulted in his step-by-step demotion until he landed back on patrol.

When he sees Joona, he greets him sourly and opens the door for him with an exaggeratedly servile gesture.

"Thanks," Joona says. He doesn't wait for a response.

Tommy Kofoed is just inside the door, moving around hunched and morose. He doesn't even reach Joona's chest anymore, but when their eyes meet, Kofoed's face breaks into a wide grin.

"Joona, great to see you. I thought they were sending you over to the Police Training Academy."

"I took a wrong turn."

"How wonderful!"

"Have you found anything?"

"We've secured all the shoe prints in the hallway," Tommy replies.

"Yes, they'll all match my shoes." Joona grins as they shake hands.

"And the attacker's," Kofoed protests. "He was moving around in an awfully peculiar way, wasn't he?"

"Right."

There are mats all over, protecting the floor from evidence contamination. A camera has been set up on a tripod and the lens is focused on the floor. A strong lamp with an aluminum reflector lies in the corner, its cord wrapped around the base. The technicians are scanning for invisible shoe prints using raking light, a kind of light which shines parallel to the floor, then they lift the prints electrostatically. They've marked the intruder's path from the kitchen through the hall.

Joona doubts they will connect these prints with his assailant. The man would have certainly destroyed any shoes, gloves, and clothes he was wearing. He's probably burned them.

"Tell me, how did he run, exactly?" asks Kofoed as he points to the markings. "There . . . there . . . across there . . . and then nothing before here . . . and here."

"You've missed a shoe print," Joona says with a small smile.

"What the hell?"

"There." Joona points.

"Where?"

"On the wall."

"What the fuck!"

A faint shoe print can be seen about seventy centimeters above the floor, outlined on the light gray wallpaper. Tommy Kofoed calls another technician over and asks him to take a gelatin print.

"Can I walk on the floor now?" Joona asks.

"Sure. Just keep off the walls," a frustrated Kofoed replies.

24

the object

In the kitchen, there's a man wearing jeans and a light brown blazer with leather patches on the elbows. He's stroking his blond mustache, talking loudly and pointing at the microwave oven. As Joona walks inside, he observes a technician in a mask and protective gloves pack the misshapen spray can into a paper bag, wrapping the open end of the bag twice. Then he tapes the bag shut and writes on it.

"Joona Linna, right?" the man with the mustache says. "If you're as good as they say, you ought to come work for us."

They shake hands.

"Göran Stone, Säpo," the man says contentedly.

"Are you in charge of the initial investigation?" asks Joona.

"Yes, I am. Or rather, formally, it's Saga Bauer. For the sake of statistics," he adds and grins.

"I've met her. She seems capable—"

"Isn't that right?" Göran Stone laughs out loud and then snaps his mouth shut.

Joona glances out the window. His mind is back to the drifting boat. What kind of contract had the killer been given, and why? He knows it's much too soon to draw any type of conclusion, but still, a tentative hypothesis is not a bad thing. Joona leaves the kitchen and heads for the bedroom. The bed is made. The cream bedcover is smoothed. Saga

Bauer from Säpo is standing in front of a laptop on the windowsill while also talking on her cell phone. Joona remembers her from a counterterrorism seminar.

Joona sits down on the bed and tries to reorder his thoughts yet again. Three people on a boat. He visualizes Penelope and Viola standing before him and in his mind he places Björn next to them. All three of them could not have been on the boat when Viola was killed, otherwise the killer would have gotten the right person. At sea he would have just killed all three, put them on their beds, and sunk the boat. So they were not at sea. They'd docked the boat somewhere.

Joona stands up again and walks into the living room. He lets his eyes wander over the flat-screen TV on the wall, the red plaid blanket folded over the arm of the sofa, the modern table with copies of *Ordfront* and *Exit* fanned on top.

He walks over to a bookshelf that covers an entire wall. He stops and thinks about the boat. He visualizes the apparently crimped cables in the engine room, which were supposed to have generated an electric arc within a few minutes; the seat cushion stuffed behind the cables in order to catch fire more easily; the loop in the rerouted fuel line. Why hadn't the boat sunk? They had probably not run the engine long enough.

These were not coincidences: Björn's apartment is set on fire. The same day, Viola is murdered, and if the boat had not been abandoned, there would have been an explosion in the fuel tank. Then the killer tries to ignite a gas explosion in Penelope's apartment.

Björn's apartment. The boat. Penelope's apartment.

He's searching for something either Penelope or Björn possesses. He started by searching Björn's apartment and when he didn't find what he was looking for, he set the apartment on fire. Then he followed the boat and when he'd searched it and couldn't find what he was looking for, he tried to force Viola to talk. When she couldn't reveal anything useful, he headed to Penelope's apartment.

Joona borrows a pair of latex gloves from a box and goes back to the bookshelf. He peers at the layer of dust in front of the books and sees there is none in front of some of the volumes. He concludes that someone has pulled out those books recently, perhaps sometime during the past several weeks.

"I don't want you here," Saga Bauer says behind him. "This is my investigation."

"I'll be going," he says softly, "but there's one thing I have to find first."

"Five minutes," she says.

He turns to look at her. "Can you have these books photographed?"

"Already done," she snaps.

"From above so you can see the dust," he says, not troubled at all.

She realizes what he's getting at. She doesn't change her expression, but simply takes a camera from a technician and photographs every shelf she can reach before she tells Joona that he can look at the books on the five lower shelves.

Joona takes out Karl Marx's *Das Kapital* and looks inside. Flipping through it, he notices the underlined passages and notes written in the margins. He looks at the gap between the books but sees nothing. He replaces the book. Then his eyes range over a biography of Ulrike Meinhof, a worn-out anthology called *Key Texts of Political Feminism*, and the collected works of Bertolt Brecht.

Joona looks at the next shelf down. Three books have obviously been taken out of the bookshelf recently since there's no dust in front of them. One of them, *The Cleverness of Antelopes*, is a collection of witness reports from the genocide in Rwanda. Another is Pablo Neruda's poetry collection *Cien sonetos de amor.* The last is *The Roots of Swedish Racial Ideas in the History of Ideas.*

Joona flips through each one. When he reaches *The Roots of Swedish Racial Ideas in the History of Ideas,* a photograph falls out. It's a black-and-white picture of a serious young woman with braided hair. He recognizes Claudia Fernandez. She can't be more than fifteen years old, and the resemblance to her daughter is remarkable.

Who would keep a photograph of one's mother in a book on racial biology? Joona wonders to himself as he turns the photograph over.

On the backside of the photo, someone has written a line: *Don't go far off, not even for a day.* It's in pencil.

Joona takes out Neruda's poetry collection again. He flips through it until he finds the entire verse:

No estés lejos de mí un solo día, porque cómo,
porque, no sé decirlo, es largo el día,

y te estaré esperando como en las estaciones
cuando en alguna parte se durmieron los trenes.

The photograph should have been in the Neruda collection.

If the killer had been looking through the books, this photo could have fallen out.

He was standing right here, Joona thought. *He was looking at the dust in front of the books just as I am doing now and he was quickly flipping through the ones pulled out the past few weeks. He notices a photograph has fallen out of one of the books and is on the floor. He automatically picks it up and sticks it back, but into the wrong book.*

Joona closes his eyes.

That's what happened, he thinks. *The hit man was looking through the books.*

If he knows what he's looking for, then the object must be small enough to be hidden between the pages of a book.

What could it be?

A letter? A will? A photograph? A confession? Maybe it was a CD or a memory stick or a SIM card?

the child on the staircase

Joona leaves the living room and peeks into the bathroom, now in the process of being photographed in minute detail. He continues along the hallway and out the door of the apartment. He stops in front of the tight grillwork that covers the elevator shaft.

There's a nameplate on the apartment door next to the elevator. Nilsson. Joona knocks and waits. Finally, he hears footsteps from inside. A plump woman of around sixty opens the door a crack and looks out.

"Well?"

"Hello, I'm Joona Linna, a detective inspector, and I—"

"But I told you before, I didn't see his face."

"Have the police already visited you? I didn't know that."

She opens the door wider and two cats hop down from the telephone table to disappear deeper in the apartment.

"He was wearing a Dracula mask," the woman says impatiently, as if she's said this a number of times before.

"Who?"

"Who?" the woman repeats, muttering, and goes inside her apartment.

After some time she returns with a yellowed newspaper clipping.

Joona takes a look at the twenty-year-old article describing a flasher who wore a Dracula mask and who groped women living in the Södermalm district.

"He wasn't wearing a stitch down there—"

"But this is not—"

"Not that I was looking, of course," she continued. "But I've already talked to you about this over and over again."

Joona looks at her and smiles. "I actually intended to ask you about something completely different."

The woman's eyes widen. "Well, why didn't you say so?"

"I was wondering if you know your neighbor, Penelope Fernandez, who—"

"She's like a grandchild to me," the woman says. "So sweet, so kind, so pleasant—"

She stops herself short. "Is she dead?"

"Why do you ask?"

"Because the police only come over to ask unpleasant questions," she replies.

"Did you notice any unusual visitors during the past couple of days?"

"Just because I'm old, doesn't mean I pry into other people's business."

"No, I mean, perhaps you might have noticed something."

"I have not."

"Has anything else unusual happened lately?"

"Absolutely not. That girl is hardworking and dutiful."

Joona thanks her for her time saying he might come back with a question some other time. Then he moves aside so the woman can shut the door.

There are not many more apartments on the fourth floor. He begins to climb the stairs. Halfway up, he finds a child sitting on the steps. It looks like a boy approximately eight years old. His hair is short and he's wearing jeans and a worn Helly Hansen sweater. He has a bag with a bottle of Ramlösa mineral water. Its label is almost worn completely away. He also has half of a French roll.

Joona pauses in front of the child, who is looking at him in a shy way.

"Hello there," Joona says. "What's your name?"

"Mia."

"My name's Joona."

Mia is a girl. Joona notices she has dirt on her chin and around her tiny neck.

"Do you carry a gun?" she asks.

"Why do you ask?"

"You told Ella that you were from the police."

"That's right. I'm a detective inspector."

"So you have a gun?"

"Yes, I do," Joona says. "Would you like to shoot it off?"

The girl looks at him astonished.

"You're joking."

"Yes, I'm joking," Joona says with a smile.

The child laughs.

"Why are you sitting on the staircase?" he asks.

"I like it. You can hear stuff."

Joona sits down next to the child.

"What kind of stuff have you heard?" he asks calmly.

"Right now I just heard you were from the police and I heard Ella lying to you."

"What was she lying about?"

"That she likes Penelope," Mia says.

"She doesn't like Penelope?"

"She sticks cat poop through Penelope's mail slot."

"Why would she do something like that?"

"I dunno." The girl shrugs her shoulders and fiddles with the bag on her lap.

"Do you like Penelope?"

"She says hi to me."

"But you don't know her?"

"Not really."

Joona looks around. "Do you live in the stairwell?"

The girl gives a slight smile back. "No, I live on the second floor with my mom."

"But you like to hang out on the stairs."

Mia shrugs. "Most of the time."

"Do you sleep here sometimes?"

The girl picks at the label on the bottle. "Sometimes."

"Last Friday," Joona says slowly. "Early in the morning, Penelope left home. She took a taxi."

"No luck," the girl says quickly. "She missed Björn by, like, a second. He got here right after she left. I told him that she just left."

"What did he say?"

"No big deal, he said. He was just going to pick something up."

"Pick something up?"

Mia nods.

"Sometimes he lets me borrow his phone so I can play games on it. But he was in a hurry. He just went inside and came right back out. Then he locked the door and ran down the stairs."

"Did you see what he picked up?"

"No."

"What happened after that?"

"Nothing. I went to school. Quarter to nine."

"And after school, in the evening. Did anything happen then?"

Mia shrugged. "Mom was gone so I was inside and I ate some macaroni and cheese and watched TV."

"What about yesterday?"

"Mom was gone again so I was home."

"So you didn't see anyone coming or going?"

"No."

Joona takes out one of his business cards and writes a telephone number.

"Look at this," he tells Mia. "Here are two good telephone numbers. One is my own number."

He points at the number on the card, which is also imprinted with the police insignia.

"Call me if you need help or if someone is doing something mean to you. And the other number is the Child Hotline. See, I've written it down: 0200-230-230. You can call them whenever you want and talk about anything you want."

"Okay," Mia whispers as she takes the card.

"Don't throw that card away, now, the minute I turn my back," Joona says. "Keep it, because even if you don't want to call someone now, you might want to later on."

"When he came out, Björn had his hand on his stomach," Mia said. She demonstrated.

"Like he had a tummy ache?"

"Yeah. Just like he had a tummy ache."

26

Joona knocks on the other doors, but all he finds out is that Penelope was a quiet and somewhat shy neighbor who took part in the annual cleaning days as well as the yearly meetings, but not much else. Once he's done, he slowly climbs the stairs back to the fourth floor.

The door to Penelope's apartment is open. A Säpo technician has just dismantled the lock from the outer door and bagged the bolt in plastic.

Joona goes in but stays in the background to watch the forensic investigators work. He's always enjoyed hanging around to see how systematically they photograph everything, collect evidence, rigorously note every aspect of what they find. It's ironic how the investigation itself will destroy the crime scene, contaminating layer by layer, even as it progresses. No piece of evidence or a key to reconstructing what has happened must be lost.

Joona lets his gaze wander over Penelope Fernandez's tidy apartment. Why had Björn Almskog come here? He had arrived the minute Penelope left. Joona could almost picture him hiding outside the entrance to the building waiting for her to leave.

Perhaps it was a coincidence, but maybe he did not *want* to run into her.

Björn had hurried in, met the child sitting on the stairs with no time to speak to her, explaining he just had to pick something up, and had only stayed a few minutes.

Perhaps Björn *did* pick up something, just as he told the little girl. Perhaps he'd forgotten the key to the boat or something else that fit in a pocket.

Perhaps he *left* something behind instead. Perhaps he only had to take a look at something or make sure of a piece of information or write down a telephone number.

Joona walks into the kitchen and looks around.

"Have you checked the fridge?" he asks.

A young man with a goatee looks up, surprised, at Joona.

"Are you hungry?" he asks in a strong Dalarna accent.

"It's a good place to hide something," Joona replies drily.

"We haven't gotten to it yet," the investigator says.

Joona returns to the living room. He notes that Saga is still off in a corner of the room talking on her cell. Tommy Kofoed is placing a strip of tape with picked-up fibers onto OH film. He looks up.

"Finding anything unexpected?" Joona asks.

"Besides a shoe print on the wall?"

"Nothing else?"

"The important stuff is at the lab in Linköping."

"Can we get their results in a week?"

"If we give them enough hell, sure," Tommy says, shrugging. "Right now I'm going to look at the cut from the knife blade and make a mold of the edge."

"Don't bother," Joona says.

"So you were able to see the blade? Was it carbon steel?"

"No, the blade was a lighter color. Perhaps sintered tungsten carbide. Some people prefer it. But, actually, nothing's going to really help."

"What won't help?"

"This entire crime scene investigation," Joona says. "We won't find DNA or fingerprints. Nothing will lead to the suspect."

"So what should we do?"

"I believe the killer came for something here. And I believe he was interrupted before he could find it."

"So maybe it's still here?"

"Entirely possible," Joona replies.

"But you have no idea what it could be."

"It fits inside a book."

Joona's granite eyes meet Kofoed's brown ones. Göran Stone from Säpo is photographing the bathroom door, the edges of the door, the frame, and the hinges. Then he sits down on the floor to photograph the bathroom's white ceiling. Joona reaches to open the living-room door, about to ask Göran to take a photo of the magazines in the living room, when the flash goes off. The brightness startles him. Things go black for a second. Four white points prick the darkness and then a light blue iridescent palm print emerges. Then they're gone. Joona looks around, unable to determine where they'd been.

"Göran!" Joona calls loudly, his voice penetrating through the thick glass door. "Take another picture right there!"

Everyone freezes in the apartment. The man by the outer door shoots Joona a curious look. The tech guy with a Dalarna accent sticks his head into the hallway from the kitchen. Tommy Kofoed takes off his face mask and scratches his neck. Göran Stone is still sitting on the floor, now looking very interested.

"Like you did just now," Joona says. "Take a photo of the ceiling."

Göran shrugs and lifts his camera to take another photo of the bathroom ceiling. There's a flash, and Joona's pupils shrink in protest. Tears come to his eyes. He closes them and still sees a black triangle. He realizes that it is a glass pane in the door transformed into a negative image.

The middle of the square shows four white spots and next to them floats a light blue palm print.

He knew that's what he'd seen.

Joona blinks and walks close to the door. The remains of four pieces of tape form a square, and right next to it is the palm print.

Tommy Kofoed steps up next to him.

"A handprint," he says.

"Can you lift it?" Joona asks.

"Göran," Kofoed says. "We need a picture of this."

Göran gets up and is humming as he stands by the door, camera ready. He peers at the handprint.

"Yes, somebody was here and wasn't too clean either," he says contentedly as he takes four pictures.

Then Göran moves aside and waits as Tommy Kofoed treats the palm print with cyanoacrylate to bind the salt and moisture. Then he uses Basic Yellow 40.

Göran waits a moment and then takes two more pictures.

"Now we got you!" Kofoed whispers to the print as he carefully lifts it with a stiff sheet of plastic.

"Can you check it out right away?" Joona asks.

Tommy Kofoed carries the print to the kitchen. Joona remains behind to inspect the pieces of tape left on the glass pane. Caught under one is the torn corner of a piece of paper. Whoever left the palm print had no time to be careful but just ripped the paper free.

Joona takes a closer look at the ripped corner. It's not normal paper, he realizes immediately. It's shiny paper—the kind photographs are printed on.

A special photograph had been taped up here to be looked at over and over. Then someone was in such a hurry, they couldn't take the time to be careful but just ran up to the door, leaned on the glass with one hand, and ripped the photo off with the other.

"Björn," Joona says.

Björn came here to get this photograph. He wasn't holding his stomach because he had a stomachache but because he was hiding a photograph underneath his jacket.

Joona turns his head to the side so he can study the palm print in the reflection. He can barely make out the thin lines of the palm.

The papillary lines of a human's palm or fingers will never change or grow old and are totally individual. Compared to DNA, even the fingerprints of identical twins differ.

Quick steps come stamping up behind him.

"Stop whatever you're doing right now, damn it!" Saga Bauer snarls. "This is *my* investigation! You're not even fucking supposed to be here!"

"I only want to—"

"Shut the fuck up, Joona Linna!" she shouts. "I was on the phone with Petter Näslund! There's nothing for you to do here and you don't even have permission to be here!"

"I know. I'll leave soon," he says soothingly as he turns his gaze back to the glass pane.

"Damn it, Joona!" she says, but curiosity has taken over a bit and her voice is calmer. "You can't just come in here and start messing with pieces of tape!"

"There was a photograph taped to the glass," he answers, unperturbed. "Someone has pulled it off. Leaned over to steady himself with his hand while he pulled off this photograph."

She still looks at him with irritation, and Joona notices a white scar that cuts straight through her left eyebrow.

"I am perfectly capable of running this investigation," she reiterates with clenched teeth.

"Chances are the print came from Björn Almskog," Joona replies as he starts toward the kitchen.

"Wrong direction, Joona."

He ignores her and walks right in.

"This is my investigation!" she yells futilely at his back.

The technicians have set up a work station in the middle of the room. Two chairs, a table with a computer on it, a scanner, and a printer. Tommy Kofoed is standing behind Göran Stone, who is connecting his camera to the computer. They've entered the palm print and are doing the initial fingerprint comparison.

Saga comes in right behind Joona.

"What do you see?" Joona asks them, not paying attention to Saga.

"Don't you speak to him!" Saga says quickly.

Tommy Kofoed looks up. "Don't be ridiculous, Saga," he says. "Sorry, this isn't our guy. This *is* from the boyfriend, Almskog."

"Lucky he's already in the suspect register," Göran Stone says.

"What do you have on him?" Joona asks.

"Rioting and harming an officer," Göran replies.

"The worst kind of criminal," Tommy jokes. "He probably took part in a demonstration."

"You think that's funny," Göran growls. "Not everyone on the force finds left-wing shenanigans and sabotage amusing."

"Speak for yourself," Kofoed replies.

"The search-and-rescue effort speaks for *itself*," Göran says with a grin.

"What's that all about?" Joona asks. "I haven't been able to follow the operation—what's happened?"

the extremists

When Joona Linna slams open the office door, Carlos Eliasson, head of CID, jumps and dumps too much fish food into the aquarium.

"Why is there no ground search?" Joona demands harshly. "There are two lives at stake and we don't have any boats out looking?"

"The maritime police make their own decisions, as you well know," Carlos replies coolly. "They've covered the area by helicopter and have decided that the two are either dead or they don't want to be found . . . neither of which demands an all-out rush to search further."

"They have something the killer wants to get his hands on and I actually believe—"

"It's useless to guess, Joona. We don't know what happened. Säpo happens to believe these two young people have gone underground and by now could be on a train to Amsterdam—"

"Cut it out," Joona says forcefully. "You can't listen to Säpo when—"

"It's their case."

"Why? Why is it their case? Björn Almskog has no criminal record at all unless it's become a felony to disturb the peace! These accusations mean absolutely nothing! Nothing at all!"

"I was talking to Verner Zandén and he's already told me that Fernandez has some connections to left-wing extremist groups."

"That may be so, but I'm absolutely certain there's more going on here. This murder is about something else entirely."

"Of course! Of course you're absolutely certain!" Carlos yells back.

"I can't put my finger on it yet, but the killer I met in Penelope's apartment was a real pro and not some kind of—"

"Säpo believes that Penelope and Björn were planning some kind of sabotage."

"You're telling me that Penelope is a terrorist?" Joona asks, incredulous. "Have you read what she's written? She's a complete pacifist."

"Yesterday a member of the Brigade was caught by Säpo as he was making his way to Penelope's apartment."

"I have no idea what kind of organization the Brigade is supposed to be."

"It's a militant movement on the left, loosely connected to the Antifascist Faction and the Revolutionary Front, but it's freewheeling. They're close to the ideology of the Red Army Faction and want to be as operative as Mossad."

"Though you know that's not true," Joona says.

"Maybe you don't *want* it to be true, but so what?" Carlos says. "Meanwhile, we will search further for those two. We're going to chart the currents and determine the direction the boat was drifting so we can start dragging the water or maybe send some divers down."

"Well, good," Joona mutters.

"All that's left is to decide if or why they were killed, or else why they went into hiding."

Joona opens the door to the hallway. He stops and turns toward Carlos again. "What happened to that man from the Brigade?"

"He was released," Carlos answers.

"Did they find out why he was there?" Joona asks.

"He was just dropping by."

"Dropping by." Joona sighs. "That's all Säpo found out?"

"You are *not* going to start investigating the Brigade," Carlos says with new worry in his voice. "I hope you understand me?"

Joona leaves and pulls out his cell as he strides down the hallway. Behind him, he can hear Carlos yelling *"That's an order!"* and *"Don't tread on Säpo's toes!"* Joona keeps going. He finds Nathan Pollock's number.

Nathan picks up.

"What do you know about the Brigade?" asks Joona as the elevator doors open.

"Säpo has been trying to infiltrate and keep an eye on all the militant left-wing groups in Stockholm, Gothenburg, and Malmö for the past few years. I don't think the Brigade is all that dangerous, but Säpo seems to believe they have weapons and explosives. At any rate, most of their members have been to reform school and have been convicted of violent crimes."

The elevator is rushing down.

"From what I understand, Säpo hauled someone in for trying to enter Penelope Fernandez's apartment. Someone with a direct connection to the Brigade."

"His name is Daniel Marklund," Nathan replies. "He belongs to the inner circle."

"What do you know about him?"

"Not much," Nathan answers. "He has a suspended sentence for vandalism and hacking."

"Why Penelope's place?"

The elevator stops and the doors open.

"Don't know. He had no weapon," Nathan tells him. "Demanded a lawyer when we started asking questions. He answered nothing and was let go later the same day."

"So we know nothing."

"Nothing."

"Where can I find him?" Joona asks.

"He has no home address. According to Säpo, he lives with other members of the inner circle at the Brigade's main headquarters near Zinkensdamm."

the brigade

While Joona Linna walks purposefully to the garage underneath Råd-hus Park, he thinks about Disa, and desire for her wells up from deep within him. He wants to touch her slender arms, smell her soft hair. He finds a strange kind of peace listening to her talk about her archaeological discoveries: shards of bone not connected to any crime and the remains of humans who finished their lives many centuries ago.

Joona decides to call her. He's been much too busy lately. He continues down into the garage and between the parked cars. There's a flicker of movement behind one of the concrete pillars. Someone is waiting beside his Volvo. The figure is partially hidden by a garbage truck—he can almost make it out. Nothing can be heard over the loud racket from the large fans.

"That was fast!" Joona yells.

"Teleporting," replies Nathan Pollock.

Joona stops, closes his eyes, and presses his fingers against his temples.

"Headache?"

"I haven't been sleeping much."

They get into the car and close the doors. Joona turns the ignition key and a tango by Astor Piazzolla comes from the speakers. Pollock turns the volume up a bit: it sounds like two violins echoing each other.

"You didn't get this from me, you know," Nathan says.

"Right."

"I've just heard from Säpo that they are going to use Marklund's attempt to break into Penelope's apartment as an excuse for conducting a raid of the Brigade's headquarters."

"I've got to get to Marklund before that happens."

"Then you'd better hurry."

Joona backs out, turns, and drives up the ramp.

"How much of a hurry?" He turns left onto Kungsholmsgatan.

"They're on their way now."

"Show me the entrance to the Brigade's headquarters and then you can head back to the station and pretend you don't know anything," Joona says.

"What's your plan?"

"Plan?"

Nathan laughs.

"Well, the *plan* is to find out why Marklund went to Penelope's apartment," Joona explains. "Maybe he knows something about what's going on."

"But—"

"It's no coincidence the Brigade tried to break into her apartment just now. That's what I believe. Säpo thinks that the extreme left is planning some kind of attack, but—"

"They always think that. It's their job," Pollock says, smiling.

"Anyway, I'm going to talk to Daniel Marklund before I drop this case."

"Even if you get there before Säpo's boys, do you think the Brigade wants to talk to you?"

waiting for the swat team

Saga Bauer presses thirteen bullets into the magazine and then shoves it into her large black Glock 21. Säpo is about to storm the Brigade's head-quarters.

Saga is in a minivan parked at Hornsgatan, just outside the Folk Opera. She's with three colleagues; all are dressed in civilian clothes. In fifteen minutes they'll head over to Nagham Fast Food and wait for the SWAT team.

For the past month, rumors have come back to Säpo that left-wing extremists are on the move. Perhaps it's more than rumors, but Säpo's best strategists have now decided many of these groups have joined forces to plan something really big, perhaps some explosive sabotage. Given the recent theft of explosives from a military facility on Vaxholm Island, they believe it's a real possibility.

The strategists have also connected the murder of Viola Fernandez and the attempt to blow up Penelope Fernandez's apartment to this planned attack.

Säpo believes the Brigade to be the most militant and violent of the left-wing fringe groups. Daniel Marklund belongs to their innermost cir-cle, and Säpo's logic follows that since he tried to break into Penelope Fernandez's apartment, he might be the assailant who attacked Detec-tive Inspector Joona Linna and his technician.

Göran Stone is smiling as he puts on his heavy protective vest.

"Let's go get those fucking cowards!"

Anders Westlund laughs but can't hide his nervousness. He says, "Shit, I hope they resist. I really want to take out one of those communists!"

Saga Bauer is replaying the memory of Daniel Marklund being caught outside Penelope Fernandez's apartment. Verner Zandén had assigned Göran Stone to the interrogation. Stone had come on strong to startle something out of Marklund, but that strategy had backfired. Marklund had requested legal representation and then clammed up.

The car door opens and Roland Eriksson slides in carrying a bag of marshmallow banana candy and a can of Coca-Cola.

"Damn, I'm jittery. I'll shoot the second I see a gun," Roland says, and they can hear the stress in his voice. "Things can go so fast and the only chance you have is to shoot them first—"

"We will follow my plan," Göran Stone says firmly. "But if shooting breaks out, you don't have to aim for the legs."

"Shove it right into their mouths," Roland yells.

"Take it easy," Göran says.

"My brother's face—"

"We know all about it, Roland, shut the fuck up," Anders says. He's also very nervous.

"A firebomb right to the face!" Roland repeats in a loud voice. "Eleven operations later and he can—"

"Can you handle this?" Göran asks sharply.

"Sure, what the fuck!"

"Are you sure?"

"I'm fine," Roland answers quickly. He looks out of the window and scrapes his thumbnail sharply over the lid of his tin of snuff.

Saga Bauer opens the door slightly to let some air into the van. She accepts this is the right time for a raid and there's no reason to wait. Even so, she still wants to understand the connection to Penelope Fernandez. What was her role in the Brigade? And why was her sister killed? Too much was still not clear. She desperately wants to talk with Daniel Marklund again, look him right in the eye and ask a few direct questions. She'd tried to bring this up with her boss. She wants answers before they go in on this raid. Especially if there is a question about who will be alive afterward.

This is still my investigation! she thinks angrily as she climbs out of the van into the suffocating heat of the sidewalk.

"The SWAT team will go in here and here." Göran Stone stabs his finger on an architectural drawing of the building. "We're here and maybe we'll have to get in through this theater—"

"Where the hell did Saga Bauer go?" Roland asks.

"Maybe she got her period and needed a Tampax!" Anders says with a smirk.

the pain

Joona Linna and Nathan Pollock park on Hornsgatan and quickly scan a bad printout of the picture of Daniel Marklund. Then they get out, make their way through the heavy traffic on the street, and enter the door of a small theater. The Tribunal Theater is an independent theater group—with income-pegged ticket prices. Plays from *Oresteia* to *The Communist Manifesto* have been performed within its walls.

Joona and Nathan continue swiftly down the wide staircase and over to the combined bar and box office. A woman with a silver ring in her nose and straight hair dyed black smiles at them. They nod in a friendly way but walk right past her without a word.

"You guys looking for someone?" she yells as they start walking up a metal staircase.

"Yes," Pollock says, but his voice is low.

They enter a messy office crowded with a copier, a desk, and a bulletin board from which newspaper clippings hang down. A thin man with matted hair and an unlit cigarette dangling from his mouth sits in front of a computer.

"Hi there, Richard," Pollock says.

"Who are you?" asks the man absentmindedly as he returns his gaze to his screen.

They continue past the actors' dressing rooms—past racks of carefully hung costumes and makeup stations. A bouquet of roses droops on one of the tables.

Pollock takes a quick look around and then points. They walk up to a steel door with a stenciled sign: ELECTRICAL ROOM.

"It's supposed to be in here," Pollock says.

"In the electrical room of a theater?"

Pollock doesn't answer but picks the lock as fast as he can. They look inside a cramped space with an electrical meter, a cupboard for props, and stacks of boxes. The ceiling light doesn't work. Joona clambers over paper bags filled with old clothes. There is a new door behind some extension cords hung across the ceiling. Joona pushes it open and finds a hall with bare cement walls. Nathan Pollock follows him. The air is stagnant and it smells like garbage and damp dirt. In the distance, they can hear the faint backbeat of music. On the floor, there's a flyer featuring Che Guevara with a lit fuse at the top of his head.

"The Brigade's been hiding out here several years now," Pollock says softly.

"I should have brought some cake for our little visit," Joona replies.

"Promise me you'll be careful."

"The only thing I worry about is whether Daniel Marklund will be here."

"He'll be here. He's almost always here."

"Thanks for your help, Nathan."

"Maybe I should go in with you anyway?" Pollock asks. "You'll have only a few minutes before Säpo storms the place. It could get dangerous."

Joona's gray eyes narrow. "I'm just dropping in for a little chat."

Nathan starts heading back to the theater and coughs as he closes the steel door behind him. Joona stands alone in the empty hallway for a moment. He draws his pistol and checks that the magazine is full before he slides it back in his holster. He starts to walk toward another steel door at the other end of the hall.

He loses a few precious seconds as he picks the lock.

Someone has scratched "The Brigade" in tiny letters, not more than two centimeters high, into the blue paint on the door.

Joona presses down the handle and the door slowly opens. He's met by loud, screeching music; it sounds like an electronically reprocessed version of Jimi Hendrix's "Machine Gun." The shrieking guitars have a dreamlike, surging beat. They drown out everything.

Joona closes the door behind him and keeps going, half running, into a space filled with junk. Mounds of books and magazines reach the ceiling. Although it's dark in the room, Joona can tell the heaps of books are not just random but have been created as a kind of labyrinth leading to other doors. He quickly makes his way through it to a dimly lit area. The path forks there and he keeps going to the right, but swiftly backtracks. He thinks he saw hasty movement out of the corner of his eye. He's not sure, though.

Joona walks on, squinting to see something more. A bare bulb sways at the end of its ceiling cord. Over the music, Joona suddenly hears a roar. Someone is screaming behind walls that dampen the sound. Joona stops, walks back, and looks into a thin passage where a stack of magazines have slid down and now are scattered across the floor.

Joona's head is starting to hurt. He thinks he should have had something to eat. He should have taken something with him. A few pieces of dark chocolate would have been enough.

He steps over the magazines and reaches a spiral staircase leading down to the floor below. He can smell sweet smoke in the air. Holding tightly to the rail, he tries to sneak down as quietly as possible, but he cannot silence his shoes on the metal steps. On the lowest rung, he stops before a velvet curtain that has been drawn shut. He puts his hand on his holstered pistol.

The music is fainter here.

A plastic clown lamp with a red bulb for a nose is in the corner, and more red light leaks through a gap in the curtain. Joona tries to get a glimpse through it, but the gap is too small. He hesitates, then steps quickly through the curtain and into the room. His pulse thuds and his headache pounds as he sweeps the space with his eyes. On the cement floor, there's a double-barreled shotgun and an open box of cartridges. The shells have lead slugs, the kind that would leave considerable damage. Sitting on an office chair is a young, naked man, smoking; his eyes are shut. This can't be Daniel Marklund, Joona thinks. A blond girl with bare breasts lounges on a mattress, leaning back against the wall, an army blanket around her hips. She meets Joona's gaze, blows him a kiss, and then, unconcerned, takes a sip of beer from a can.

From behind the only open door comes another scream.

Joona keeps his eye on the two as he picks up the shotgun, points the opening of the barrels down, and then steps hard on the barrels until they're bent.

The woman puts down her beer can and scratches her armpit absent-mindedly.

Joona gently lays the shotgun back on the floor. He continues past the woman and into a hallway with a low ceiling of chicken wire and fiberglass. Heavy cigar smoke hangs in the air. Intense lamplight shines right in his face, and he shields his eyes with his hand. The end of the hallway is obscured by strips of white industrial plastic. Blinded, Joona can't see what's going on. He can glimpse movement and he can hear an echoing voice filled with fear and terror. Someone close at hand suddenly screams loudly. It's a deep-throated scream followed by rapid gasps. Joona makes it past the blinding lamp and now can see into the room behind the thick plastic.

Veils of smoke swirl through the air. A short, muscular woman in black jeans and a hoodie stands before a man dressed only in underwear and socks. His head is shaved, and on his forehead, there's a White Power tattoo. He's bitten his tongue and blood runs down his chin, throat, and thick stomach. "*Please,*" he begs.

The woman raises a smoking cigar overhead, then brings it down, pressing its glowing end right onto the tattoo. The man screams. His thick stomach and hanging breasts shake. He's pissing himself. A dark spot spreads over his blue underwear and the urine runs down his naked legs.

Behind the curtain of protected plastic, Joona has pulled out his gun. He tries to spot if anyone else is in the room but he can't see. He's about to yell . . . then his gun falls from his hand to the floor.

It clatters against the concrete and slides to a stop next to the plastic. Joona looks down at his own hand, seeing it shake, and in the next moment, feeling the horrendous pain flood in. He loses all sight and feels only a heavy, breaking movement inside his forehead. He throws out a hand against the wall in an attempt to stay upright. He fears he's about to lose consciousness. Still, he can hear the voices behind the curtain.

"Just admit what the fuck you did!" the woman with the cigar is yelling.

"I don't remember," the neo-Nazi cries.

"What did you do?"

"I bullied some guy."

"Confess exactly what you did!"

"I burned his eye out."

"That's right! You used a cigarette to burn out the eye of a ten-year-old boy!"

"Yes, but I—"

"What did he do to you?"

"We followed him from the synagogue and down to . . ."

Joona doesn't notice that what he's grabbed is a fire extinguisher, a big one, and it's coming down with him. He no longer has any sense of time or of where he is. The pain in his head and a fierce ringing in his ears is all he knows.

the message

Behind the dark veils of pain, Joona can feel her hand on his back.

"What's going on?" asks Saga Bauer in a low voice. "Are you hurt?"

He tries to shake his head but is in too much pain to speak. It feels as if a hook is being drawn through his brain: down through the skin, the cranium, the brain membranes, and the heavy, floating brain fluid.

He drops to his knees.

"You've got to get out of here," says Saga.

He feels her lifting his face but he can't see anything. His entire body is bathed in pearls of sweat that pour from his armpits, his neck, his back.

Saga is hunting through his clothes. She thinks he's having an epileptic fit and is trying to find some kind of medicine in his pockets. Joona realizes she's opening his wallet and looking for the sign of a flame, the symbol for epileptics.

The pain starts to recede. Joona wets his mouth with his tongue. He looks up. His jaws are tense and his whole body aches from the migraine attack.

"You guys can't go in there yet," he whispers. "I have to—"

"What the hell happened here?"

"Nothing." Joona picks his gun up from the floor.

He gets to his feet and staggers as fast as he can through the plastic curtains and into the room. It's empty. An emergency exit sign is lit on the other side. Saga has followed him and she questions him with a look. Joona opens the emergency door and sees a steep half set of stairs leading to a steel door at street level.

"*Perkele*," he swears in Finnish.

"Talk to me!" Saga says angrily.

Joona always pushes the direct cause of his illness as far from his consciousness as possible. There was an incident many years ago . . . it keeps giving him this pulsing pain, this pain so severe that he almost passes out. But he refuses to think about the incident.

What the doctor says is that this is an extreme form of migraine with a physical cause. The antiepileptic drug Topiramate is the only medicine that seems to help. Joona is supposed to take it daily, but when he's working and needs a clear head, he stops. Not only does it make him tired, it dulls his mind. He knows he's playing a game of roulette. Without the medication, he might manage for weeks without a migraine, yet another time he'll be hit by one after only a few days.

"They were torturing a guy . . . a neo-Nazi, I think, but—"

"Torturing?"

"With a cigar," he answers as he turns around and heads back into the hallway.

"What happened?"

"I . . . couldn't . . ."

"But Joona," Saga says tentatively. "Maybe . . . if you've got a physical problem, you shouldn't be working . . . operatively, that is . . ."

She puts her hand to her face.

"What a shitty situation," she whispers.

Joona walks toward the room with the clown lamp and hears Saga's footsteps behind him.

"And why in the hell are you even here?" she asks to his back. "Säpo's SWAT team is going to raid this place any moment. If they see that weapon in your hand, they'll shoot first and ask questions later . . . it'll be dark, there'll be tear gas—"

"I have to speak to Daniel Marklund," Joona says stubbornly.

"You're not supposed to even know about him!" she exclaims as she follows him up the spiral staircase. "Who told you about him?"

Joona starts down another hallway, but stops when he sees Saga gesture a different way. He follows her, but pulls out his gun when she starts
to run. They both turn a corner, and Joona hears her yell something.

Saga has come to a halt in a room with five computers. In one corner
stands a man with dirty hair and a beard. He matches the picture of
Daniel Marklund in Joona's mind. His lips look dry. He's licking them.
He holds out a Russian bayonet knife in one of his fists.

"Police," Saga says, flashing her ID. "Put down the knife."

The young man shakes his head and waves the knife in the air in
front of him, flashing the blade in different directions.

"We just need to speak with you," Joona says as he holsters his gun.

"So speak."

Joona walks closer, looking into the young man's frightened eyes, totally ignoring the knife being waved directly at him. He ignores its sharp-
ened point.

"Daniel, you're really not good at this," he says with a smile.

Joona can smell the scent of gun grease on the blade.

Daniel is waving the bayonet knife in faster circles and wears a look
of concentration. He growls, "Don't think only Finns are good at—"

Lightning fast, Joona grabs the young man's wrist, twists it, and takes
away the knife. He gently puts it down on the table.

The room is silent. The men look at each other, and then Daniel
Marklund shrugs.

"Usually I only deal with the computers," he says apologetically.

"They're going to raid us any moment," Joona says urgently. "Tell us
why you went to Penelope Fernandez's place."

"Just dropping by to say hi."

"Daniel," Joona says darkly. "This knife business could lead you to a
prison term. But right now I have more important things on my plate.
Don't waste my time."

"Does Penelope belong to the Brigade?" Saga asks quickly.

"Penelope Fernandez?" Daniel Marklund smiles. "She's against us.
She's made that perfectly clear."

"So what's the connection?" Joona asks.

"What do you mean, she's against you?" Saga puts in. "Is there a power
struggle going on?"

"Doesn't Säpo know anything?" asks Daniel with a tired smile. "Penelope Fernandez is a complete pacifist. She's a firm believer in democracy. So she doesn't like our methods—but we like her."

He sits down on a chair in front of two computers.

"Like her?"

"We respect her."

"Why?" asks Saga. "Why should you—"

"You guys really don't know how much some people hate her, do you? Why don't you just Google her name? People have said some really brutal things about her, and there are always people who go too far."

"What do you mean, 'go too far'?"

Daniel gives them a testing look. "You do know she's disappeared, don't you?"

"Yes," Saga replies.

"That's good," he says. "Though I really don't expect the police to make much effort to find her. That's why I went over to her place. I wanted to check her computer to see who might be behind this. I mean, there was a group, the Swedish Resistance, who sent a message to their members this past April telling them to kidnap 'the communist whore Penelope Fernandez' and make her into a sex slave for the movement. But take a look at this."

Daniel Marklund clicks a few keys on one of his computers and turns the screen to Joona.

"This one is connected to the Aryan Brotherhood."

Joona takes a quick glance through a vulgar chat page about Aryan penises and how they are supposed to execute Penelope.

"But I don't think these groups are involved," Joona says.

"Not them? Then who? The Northern Brotherhood?" Daniel speculates, now eager to help. "You need to get going! It's not too late!"

"How do you know?"

"You guys are always so slow. This time I caught a message on her mother's answering machine. That's got to give you an edge. You're not too late yet."

"You caught what?" Joona asks.

"She tried to call her mother yesterday morning," the young man answers as he scratches through his dirty hair.

"Penelope called?"

"Yes, it was her."

"What did she say?" Saga asks breathlessly.

"Säpo doesn't have a monopoly on listening in to phone calls." Daniel gives a crooked smile.

"What did Penelope say?" Joona repeats, raising his voice.

"People are after her," Daniel says.

"Exactly what did she say?"

Daniel gives Saga Bauer a glance and asks, "How much time do we have left?"

Saga looks at her watch. "Three or four minutes. Maybe."

"Then listen to this," Daniel says as he clicks a few keys on the second computer.

There's a hiss in the speakers and then there's a click and Claudia Fernandez's voice-mail message comes on. Three brief tones are heard followed by crackling noises due to a very bad connection. Underneath all the noise, one can hear a faint voice. A woman's voice. It's hard to make out what she says. A few seconds later, a man yells, "Get a job!" Then the connection is gone.

"Let me try again with the filters on," Daniel mumbles.

"We're running out of time," Saga warns.

Daniel moves a dial, looks at crossing sound curves, and replays the recording.

"This is Claudia Fernandez. I can't answer the phone right now, but please leave a message and I'll call back as soon as I can."

The three tones sound different this time. The crackling is now a weak, metallic crinkling in the background.

And Penelope's voice is clear.

"Mamma, I need help. People are after me—"

"Get a job!" a man's voice says, and then it's silent.

real police work

Saga Bauer looks at her watch and says they have to go. Daniel Marklund makes a halfhearted joke about manning the barricades, but there is fear in his eyes.

"We're going to hit you hard," Saga says. "Hide that knife. Don't make any resistance. Give up at once, hands high, and don't make any sudden moves."

She and Joona leave the tiny room.

Daniel watches them go, and still sitting in the desk chair, dumps the bayonet knife into the wastebasket.

Joona and Saga wend their way through the labyrinthine headquarters of the Brigade and exit onto Hornsgatan. Saga rejoins Göran's task force. They're gathered in Nagham Fast Food and are chowing down on french fries. Their eyes are shining and hard as they wait for orders.

It comes two minutes later as fifteen heavily armed security police pour from four black trucks. The SWAT team forces all the entrances open and floods the inside with tear gas. Once they trample in, they find five young people sitting on the floor with their hands over their heads. They're led outside cuffed with plastic strips.

The security police take the Brigade's weapons into custody: one old military pistol, a Colt, as well as a decorative rifle, a shotgun with its barrels bent, and a carton of cartridges. Additionally four knives and two throwing stars. They were fairly poorly armed.

Driving along Söder Mälarstrand, Joona picks up his cell phone and calls his boss. After two rings, Carlos answers, pressing the Talk button with his pen.

"How do you like the Police Training Academy, Joona?" he asks.

"Not there."

"I know, since—"

"Penelope Fernandez is still alive." Joona interrupts him. "She's running for her life."

"Who says so?"

"She says so. She left a message on her mother's answering machine."

Carlos's end of the connection falls silent. Then he draws a deep breath.

"Okay. She's alive. All right . . . what else do we know? She's alive, but—"

"We know that she was alive thirty hours ago at the time she made the call," Joona says. "And that someone is after her."

"Who?"

"She wasn't able to say, but—if it's the same man I ran into, we absolutely don't have any time to lose."

"You've said you believe this man is a professional killer."

"I'm absolutely sure of that. The man who attacked Erixson and me was a professional hit man . . . a *grob*."

"A *grob*?"

"Serbian for 'grave.' These guys are expensive. They usually work alone. They're well paid to follow orders precisely."

"It all seems a bit far-fetched."

"But I'm right," Joona says doggedly.

"You always say that, but how has Penelope gotten away from this kind of killer? It's been two days," Carlos says.

"If she's still alive, it's because his priorities have shifted."

"You still think he's searching for something?"

"Yes," Joona replies.

"What is it?"

"Don't know for sure, but maybe a photo . . ."

"Why do you think so?"

"That's my best theory at the moment." Joona quickly relates what he found at Penelope's apartment: the books taken out of the shelf, the picture with the lines of poetry, Björn's quick visit and how he held his hand over his stomach when he was leaving, the palm print on the glass door, the bits of tape, and the corner of a photograph.

"So you think the killer is after that photo?"

"I believe he started in Björn's apartment. When he didn't find what he was looking for, he poured out gasoline and turned the neighbor's iron on high. The alarm went to the fire department at five after eleven that morning and before they could even get the fire under control, the entire floor had been destroyed."

"That evening he kills Viola."

"He probably assumed that Björn had taken the photograph on the boat so he followed them, went on board, drowned Viola, and then searched the entire boat with the intention of sinking it afterward. Something made him change his mind. He left the archipelago, returned to Stockholm, and searched through Penelope's apartment—"

"You don't think he found the photograph, do you?" asks Carlos.

"Either Björn has it on his person or it is hidden at a friend's place or in a safe-deposit box. Any place at all, really."

Silence on the line. Joona can hear Carlos breathe deeply.

"But if we find it first," Carlos says, thinking out loud, "and this killer finds out we have it, then all of this is over."

"That's right," Joona says.

"Because . . . if we on the force, we the police, see it, then it's not a secret anymore. It will cease being something to kill over."

"I only hope it's that easy."

"Joona, I can't . . . I can't take this case away from Petter, but I presume—"

"—that I'll be busy lecturing at the Police Training Academy," Joona says.

"That's all I need to know," Carlos says with a laugh.

On the way to Kungsholm, Joona checks his voice mail and finds a number of messages from Erixson. In the first, Erixson says he can keep working from the hospital. Thirty minutes later, he asks if he can't be part of the work on the ground, and twenty-seven minutes later he yells that he's going crazy without anything to do. Joona calls him and after two rings, he hears Erixson's tired voice go "*Quack.*"

"So I'm too late?" Joona asks. "You're already crazy?"

Erixson hiccups as a reply.

"I don't know what you know," Joona says. "But we're in a big rush. Yesterday morning Penelope Fernandez left a message on her mother's answering machine."

"Yesterday?" Erixson was immediately alert.

"She said someone was chasing her."

"Are you on the way here?" Erixson asks.

There's noise on the line and Erixson asks someone to leave him alone. Joona hears a woman's strict voice telling him it's time for physical therapy and Erixson hissing back that he's on a private call.

Erixson pumps Joona for information, and Joona obliges. He explains that Penelope and Björn were not together in the apartment on Sankt Paulsgatan the night before Friday. She was picked up by taxi at exactly 6:40 a.m. and was driven to the television station to be part of a debate. A few minutes after the taxi left, Björn entered the apartment. Joona tells Erixson about the palm print on the glass door, the tape, and the corner ripped from a photograph. He says he's convinced that Björn had waited for Penelope to leave the apartment so he could get the photo quickly without her knowledge.

"And I believe that the person who attacked us is a hit man and he was looking for that photograph when we surprised him."

"Maybe so," Erixson whispers.

"It wasn't his priority to kill us. He just wanted to get out of the apartment," Joona says.

"Otherwise we would be dead."

"We can conclude that the hit man doesn't yet have this photograph," Joona continues. "If he'd found it on the boat, he wouldn't have bothered with Penelope's apartment."

"And it's not at her place because Björn had already taken it."

"My theory is that his attempt to blow up the place means that the man behind all this doesn't really need the photo in his hand, he just wants it destroyed."

"But why would such a photograph hang on the door of Penelope's living room? And why is it so damned important?" asks Erixson.

"I have a few theories," Joona says. "Most likely Björn and Penelope took a photograph of something and left it in plain sight because they didn't realize that it was documenting evidence and what that evidence really meant."

"That's right," Erixson chortles.

"As far as they knew, the photo wasn't something they needed to hide, let alone that someone would murder for it."

"But then Björn changes his mind."

"Maybe he figured something out. Maybe he realized that it's dangerous and that's why he went to get it," Joona says. "There's still a great deal we don't know. Now we've just got to slog along through routine police work."

"Exactly!" Erixson exclaims.

"Can you gather everything you can find—all the telephone calls made this past week? All text messages? All bank withdrawals? All that stuff: receipts, bus tickets, meetings, activities, working hours—"

"I sure as hell can!"

"On the other hand, maybe you should just forget about all that," Joona says. "Isn't it time for your physical therapy?"

"Are you pulling my leg?" Erixson says, hardly able to hold back his indignation. "What is physical therapy anyway but hidden unemployment?"

"But you really ought to rest," Joona teases. "Maybe another tech guy—"

"I'm flipping out just sitting here!"

"You've only been on sick leave for six hours."

"I'm climbing the walls!"

the search

Joona is driving east toward Gustavsberg. *I ought to call Disa*, he thinks. Instead, he calls Anja.

"I need Claudia Fernandez's address."

"Mariagatan 5," she replies immediately. "Not far from the old porcelain factory."

"Thanks."

Anja stays on the line.

"I'm waiting," she says, her voice teasing.

"What are you waiting for?" he asks softly.

"For you to tell me that we have ferry tickets to Finland. We'll rent a cottage with a wood-fired sauna next to the water."

"Sounds good," Joona says hesitantly.

The weather is now gray and hazy and extremely humid as Joona parks his car in front of Claudia Fernandez's house. Joona steps out and smells the bitter scent of currant bushes and elf-cap moss. He stands still for a moment, lost in a memory. The face he's conjured up fades as he rings the doorbell. The nameplate looks like it came from a woodshop class. "Fernandez" is in letters childishly burned into the wood.

The doorbell's melodic ring echoes inside the house. He waits. After a few moments, he hears approaching footsteps.

Claudia has a worried expression as she opens the door. Seeing Joona, she steps back into the hallway knocking a coat loose from its hanger.

"No," she whispers. "Not Penny—"

"Claudia, please, I don't have bad news," Joona says quickly.

Claudia can't stay upright and collapses to the floor among the shoes, underneath the coats. She breathes like a frightened animal.

"What's happened?" she asks in a fearful voice. Joona bends forward, down to her.

"We don't know much yet, but yesterday, Penelope tried to call you."

"She's alive," Claudia whispers.

"So far," Joona answers.

"Thank you, dear Lord. Thank you, thank you!" Claudia whispers again.

"We caught a message on your answering machine."

"On my . . . no, that's not possible," she says as she gets up with his help.

"There was a lot of static. We needed an expert to recover her voice," Joona explains.

"The only thing I heard, there was a man who told me to get a job!"

"That's the one," Joona says. "Penelope is speaking first, but it's barely audible."

"What does she say?"

"She says she needs help. The maritime police want to organize a search-group chain."

"But to trace the phone—"

"Claudia," Joona says soothingly. "I must ask you a few questions."

"What kinds of questions?"

"Why don't we sit down?"

They walk through the hallway and into the kitchen.

"Joona Linna, may I ask you something?" she says timidly.

"You can ask, but I might not be able to answer."

Claudia puts coffee cups on the table for them both. Her hand shakes slightly. She sits across from him and stares at him for a long time.

"You have a family, don't you?" she asks.

It's dead quiet in the light-filled, yellow-painted kitchen.

Joona finally fills the silence. "Do you remember the last time you were at Penelope's apartment?"

"Last week. A Tuesday. She helped me hem a pair of pants for Viola."

Claudia's mouth trembles.

"Think carefully, Claudia," he says, leaning forward. "Did you see a photograph taped up on her glass door?"

"Yes."

"What did the photo show?" Joona asks, trying to keep his voice calm.

"I don't know. I didn't pay attention."

"But you're sure you saw a photograph?"

"Yes." Claudia nods.

"Perhaps there were people in the picture?"

"I don't know. I thought it had something to do with her job."

"Was the picture taken inside or outside?"

"No idea."

"Try and picture it in your mind."

Claudia shuts her eyes. She shakes her head. "Sorry, I can't."

She looks down, thinks, and shakes her head again. "The only thing I remember thinking is that it was odd that she'd hung that photo on her door because that's not particularly attractive."

"Why do you think it had something to do with her job?"

"I don't know," Claudia whispers.

Joona's cell phone rings inside his jacket. He picks it up, sees that it's Carlos, and answers, "I'm here."

"I just talked to Lance at the maritime police on Dalarö. He says they've arranged an organized search starting tomorrow. Three hundred people and almost fifty boats have agreed to join."

"That's good," Joona says. He watches Claudia get up and walk into the hall.

"And then I called Erixson to see how he was doing," Carlos says.

"He seems to be doing okay," Joona says neutrally.

"Joona, I have no idea what you're up to, but Erixson warned me that you're about to be right again."

Once the call is finished, Joona follows Claudia out into the hall. She's put on her coat and is pulling on rubber boots.

"I heard what that man said on the phone," Claudia says. "I can help look. I can look all night if—"

She opens the door.

"Claudia, you must let the police handle this."

"My daughter called me and needs my help."

"I know it's hard to sit and wait—"

"But, please, can't I go with you? I won't be in the way! I can make food and answer the phone so you won't have to worry about that."

"Is there anyone who can stay here with you? A relative or a friend?"

"I don't want anyone else here! I just want my Penny!"

dreambow

Erixson holds a map on his lap as well as a large folder he acquired by getting a messenger to deliver it to his hospital room. He's cooling himself with a whirring face fan while Joona pushes him in his wheelchair through the hospital corridors.

His Achilles tendon has been sutured, and instead of a cast, his foot is fixed inside a special boot with toes pointing down. He mutters that all he needs is a ballet shoe on the other foot and he'll be ready to perform *Swan Lake*.

Joona nods in a friendly way toward two elderly ladies sitting on a sofa and holding hands. They giggle, whisper to each other, and then wave at him as if they were schoolgirls.

"On the same morning they headed out on the boat," Erixson was saying, "Björn bought an envelope and two stamps at Central Station. He had a receipt from Pressbyrån in his wallet, which we found on the boat. I forced the security company to send along the tape from the security camera. It really does look like he's mailing a photograph, just as you've said all this time."

"So who is he sending the photograph to?" asks Joona.

"We can't read the address on the envelope."

"Maybe to himself."

"But his apartment is so burned out he doesn't even have a door," Erixson says.

"Call the post office and ask them."

As they enter the elevator, Erixson starts some strange swimming movements with his arms. Joona looks at him calmly but doesn't ask any questions.

"Jasmin tells me it's good for me," Erixson explains.

"Who's Jasmin?"

"My physical therapist. She looks like a sweet little cupcake, but she's hard as nails: *Keep quiet, stop complaining, sit up straight.* She even called me a little potbelly." Erixson smiles shyly as they step into the hallway.

They turn into a room set aside for meditation. It has a simple altar with a smooth wooden cross hung on a meter-long stand above it. There is also a tapestry on the wall, a Christ figure surrounded by a series of light-colored triangles.

Down the hall, Joona pulls from a storage closet a large set of flip charts and markers that he'd stashed earlier. Back in the meditation room, he sees Erixson has already pulled down the Christ tapestry and draped it over the cross that's now propped in a corner.

"All that we know is that at least one person is willing to kill for this photograph," Joona says.

"Yes, but why?"

Erixson pulls out a glue stick from his supplies and adheres Björn Almskog's bank-account withdrawals to the wall. He also sets up lists from each phone call, copies of bus tickets, receipts from Björn's wallet, and notes from the voice mails they'd collected.

"This photograph must reveal something so important someone is desperate to keep it a secret," Joona says, as he takes out a marker and begins to write a timeline on the largest flip chart.

"Right," Erixson answers.

"Let's just stop him by finding this photo," Joona says.

06:40 Penelope takes a taxi from her apartment
06:45 Björn arrives at Penelope's apartment
06:48 Björn leaves the apartment with the photograph
07:07 Björn mails the photograph from the Pressbyrån at Central Station

Erixson rolls up to look carefully at each point while he peels the wrapper and foil from a chocolate bar.

"Penelope Fernandez leaves the television studio and calls Björn ten minutes later," he says, pointing to the list with the phone calls. Her strip of transportation coupons is stamped ten thirty. Her little sister, Viola, calls Penelope at ten forty-five. Penelope is probably already with Björn at the marina on Långholmen."

"But what does Björn do in the meanwhile?"

"That's what we need to find out," Erixson says contentedly and cleans his fingers with a white handkerchief.

Erixson rolls his wheelchair along the wall and points to another strip of transportation coupons.

"Björn leaves Penelope's apartment with the photograph. He takes the subway and at seven minutes after seven he buys the envelope and two stamps."

"And mails the letter," says Joona.

Erixson clears his throat and continues. "The next piece of evidence is a transaction on his Visa card. He pays twenty crowns to Dreambow Internet Café on Vattugatan at seven thirty-five."

"Five minutes after seven thirty," Joona says as he writes this on the chronology.

"Where in the hell is Vattugatan?"

"It's a fairly small street," Joona says. "It's in the old Klara Quarter."

Erixson nods and continues. "I'm guessing that Björn continues on the same stamp to Fridhemsplan. After that we have a phone call from his landline in his apartment. It was an unanswered call to his father, Greger Almskog."

"We'll have to ask his father about it."

"The next piece of evidence is a new stamp on the coupon strip for nine o'clock. Apparently, he took the number 4 bus from Fridhemsplan to Högalindsgatan on Södermalm. From there he went to the boat at Långholmen Harbor."

Joona fills in the last notes on his paper and then steps back to take a good look at the timeline of that morning.

"So Björn is in a real hurry to get that photograph," Erixson says. "But he doesn't want to run into Penelope so he waits until she's left, rushes inside, takes it off the glass pane, leaves the apartment, and heads to Central Station."

"I want to look at all the security tapes," says Joona.

"After that, Björn heads to a nearby Internet café, stays there about half an hour at most, and then goes—"

"That's it," Joona says.

"What's it?"

"Both Björn and Penelope already have Internet access at home."

"So why'd he go to an Internet café?"

"I'll head there now," Joona says, already walking out of the room.

deleted data

Detective Inspector Joona Linna turns onto Vattugatan from Brunke-
berg Square behind the City Theater. He parks, gets out, and hurries through an anonymous metal door and down a steep cement
walkway.

It's quiet at the Dreambow Internet Café. The floor has been freshly
scrubbed. The scent of lemon and plastic hangs in the air. Shiny Plexi-
glas chairs have been pushed below the small computer tables. Nothing
moves except the patterns on the monitors. A plump man with a pointed
black goatee leans against a high counter, sipping coffee from a mug
with the inscription "Lennart means Lion." His jeans are baggy and a
shoelace hangs untied from one of his Reeboks.

"I need a computer," Joona says before he's even reached the man.

"Get in line," the man jokes as he makes a sweeping gesture toward
the empty seats in the room.

"I need a specific computer," Joona continues. "A friend of mine
was here this past Friday morning and I need to use the same computer
he did."

"I don't know if I can give out—"

Joona bends over and ties the man's loose lace. "It's extremely important."

"Let me take a look at Friday's log," the man says, an embarrassed flush coming to his cheeks. "What's his name?"

"Björn Almskog," Joona says.

"He used number five, the one in the corner," the man says. "I need to see your ID."

Joona hands over his police ID, and the man looks confused as he writes it all down in the log.

"Go ahead and start surfing."

"Thanks," Joona says in a friendly way as he walks over to computer number 5.

Joona takes out his cell phone and places a call to Johan Jönson, a young man in the CID's department for cyber crimes.

"Just a mo," answers a ragged voice. "I've just swallowed a piece of paper . . . an old tissue . . . I blew my nose and at the same time breathed in to sneeze and . . . no, I really don't have the energy to explain everything. Who am I talking to?"

"Joona Linna, detective inspector with the National Criminal Investigation Department."

"Oh, damn. Hi, Joona, what a surprise."

"You're already sounding better."

"Yes, I've swallowed it."

"I need to see what a guy was doing on a computer this past Friday."

"Say no more!"

"I'm in a hurry. I'm sitting in an Internet café."

"Are you on the same machine he used?"

"Right in front of me."

"Much easier. Much easier. Try to find History. It's probably been erased. That's what they do after each user, but there's always something left on the hard drive. All you have to do is . . . or really, the best thing to do is to take the thing away and bring it along to me so I can go through the hard drive with a program I've designed for—"

"Meet me in a half an hour in the meditation room at Saint Göran's Hospital," Joona says as he unplugs the computer, takes it under his arm, and heads toward the exit.

The man with the coffee mug stares at him, astonished, and tries to block him.

"Hey, wait! The computer can't leave the premises!"

"It's under arrest," Joona says in his friendliest manner.

"What's it suspected of?"

The man's pale face stares at Joona as Joona waves at him with his free hand and walks out into the bright sunshine.

the connection

The parking lot in front of Saint Göran's Hospital is hot and the air is thick and muggy.

Inside the meditation room, Erixson easily maneuvers his wheelchair around what has truly been converted into a base of operations. Erixson has accumulated three phones, which now all ring at once.

Joona carries in the computer and puts it on a chair. Johan Jönson is already there. He looks to be about twenty-five years old. He wears an ill-fitting black tracksuit, has a shaved head and thick eyebrows that grow straight across his face. He comes up to Joona shyly. He shrugs off the shoulder strap of his red computer bag, and shakes Joona's hand.

"*Ei saa piettää*," he says, while he pulls out a thin laptop. Erixson pours some Fanta from his thermos into small, unbleached paper cups.

"Usually I put the hard disk in the freezer for a few hours if it's wobbly," Johan says. "Then I plug in an ATA/SATA contact. Everyone has a different method. I have a pal over at Ibas who uses RDR and he doesn't even meet his clients in person—he just sends all the shit over an encrypted phone line. Usually you can save most stuff, but I don't want to just get most of it—I want it all! That's my way, getting each and every crumb, and then you need a program like Hanger 18 . . ."

Johan Jönson throws his head back and pretends to laugh like a mad scientist: "MWA-HA-HAH!"

"I've written it myself," he continues. "It works like a digital vacuum cleaner. It picks up everything and arranges it according to time down to every microsecond."

He sits down on the altar rail and connects the two computers. His own computer clicks faintly. Typing commands at a furious pace, he studies his screen, scrolls down, reads some more, and types in a new set.

"Is this going to take a while?" Joona asks after a few minutes.

"Who knows?" Johan replies. "Not more than a month."

Johan swears to himself and writes a new command and then observes the blinking numbers.

"I'm just joking," he says after a while.

"I realized that."

"In about fifteen minutes we'll know how much can be retrieved," Johan continues. He looks down at the piece of paper where Joona has written the time and date for Björn Almskog's café visit.

"The history is usually erased in batches, which can be difficult . . ."

Fragments of old graphics pass over the sun-bleached screen. Johan shoves a piece of snuff underneath his lip without paying any attention to it. He wipes his hands on his pants and waits with half his attention on the screen.

"They've done a good job cleaning this one," he says. "But you can't erase everything. There are no secrets anymore . . . Hanger 18 finds places no one knows exist."

Johan's computer begins to beep and he writes something down as he reads through a long table of numbers. He writes something else and the beeping stops at once.

"What's that?" Joona asks.

"Not much. It's just hard to get through all the modern firewalls, sandboxes, and faked virus protection. It's amazing that a computer can even work at all with all these preventive measures."

Johan shakes his head and licks a bit of snuff away from his upper lip.

"I've never even had one antivirus program and—hey, look out." He interrupts his own lecture.

Joona comes closer to look over Johan's shoulder.

"What do we have here? What do we have here?" Johan says in a singsong voice.

He leans back and rubs his neck as he starts writing with his other hand. He presses ENTER and smiles to himself.

"Here we are."

Joona and Erixson stare at the screen.

"Just give me a second . . . this is not easy. It's coming out in small bits and fragments."

Johan hides the screen with his hand and waits. Slowly letters and pieces of graphics appear.

"Look here, the door's opening . . . now we'll be able to see what Björn Almskog was up to."

Erixson puts the brakes on his wheelchair and leans far forward so he can see the screen.

"Damn it all, this is just a few dashes."

"Look in the corner.".

"Okay. He's used Windows," Erixson says. "Very original."

"Hotmail," Joona says.

"Logging in," says Johan Jönson.

"Now things are getting interesting," says Erixson.

"Can you see a name?" Joona asks.

"It doesn't work like that; you can only move through time," Johan says as he scrolls down.

"What's that?" Joona points.

"Now we're in the folder for sent mail."

"Did he send something?"

On the screen there are graphic fragments of advertisements for cheap trips to Milano, New Y k, Lo dn, P ris. Farthest down in the corner, a light gray tiny number, a time: 07:44:42 a.m.

"Here we have something," says Johan Jönson.

Other fragments are appearing on his screen:

```
rec I contact ith
```

"Ads to connect with people." Erixson grins. "I've tried those, and they never work . . ."

He falls silent at once. Johan has carefully scrolled past incomprehensible graphic garbage and stops. He pushes back from his machine with a big grin.

Joona takes his spot and peers at the monitor to read what's at the center of the screen:

```
Carl Palmcr
Ck ph graf. Rec I contact withi
```

Joona feels hair rising on the back of his neck. *Palmcrona*, he thinks again and again as he writes down what he sees on the screen. He tries to think clearly and breathe calmly. The small stab of an oncoming migraine comes and then goes.

Erixson stares at the screen and swears to himself.

"Are you absolutely sure Björn Almskog wrote this?" Joona asks.

"No doubt about it," replies Johan Jönson.

"Absolutely sure?"

"If he was at this computer at this point in time, he wrote this e-mail."

"So it is definitely from him," Joona tells himself, wanting to make sure, but his thoughts already zoom away.

"What the fuck," Erixson whispers.

Johan Jönson scans the address field fragments scattered over the screen: "crona@isp.se." He drinks Fanta straight out of the thermos. Erixson leans back into his wheelchair and closes his eyes for a moment.

"Palmcrona," murmurs Joona again, his voice tense in concentration.

"This is fucking crazy," Erixson says. "What the hell does Carl Palmcrona have to do with all this?"

Joona silently walks out the door, concentrating on his thoughts and leaving his colleagues behind. He walks quickly down the stairs and out of the hospital into strong sunshine. He hurries across the parking lot to his black car.

collaborating units

Joona Linna heads straight to Carlos's office, full of the news about Carl Palmcrona. To his surprise, the door to Carlos's office is wide open. Carlos is looking out the window.

"She's still standing there," he says.

"Who?"

"The mother of those girls."

"You mean Claudia Fernandez?" Joona asks as, in turn, he goes to look out the window.

"She's been standing there for an entire hour."

Joona can't see her. A father in a dark blue suit is walking past. He's wearing a king's crown on his head and holding the hand of a little girl dressed in a pink princess dress. But then, almost directly across from the National Police Board, he sees a slumped woman next to a dirty Mazda pickup truck. It's Claudia, staring intently at the foyer of the police building.

"I went outside and asked her if she wanted someone in particular. I thought maybe you'd forgotten a meeting with her."

"No," Joona says quietly.

"She said she was waiting for her daughter, Penelope."

"Carlos, we have to talk."

But before Joona can say anything, there's a light knock at the door and Verner Zandén, the head of Säpo's department of security, comes in.

"Nice to see you again," the tall man says as he shakes Carlos's hand. Verner greets Joona, then looks around the room and behind his back.

"Where the hell did Saga go?" he asks in a deep bass voice.

Saga Bauer slowly steps through the door. The tension in her thin body almost seems to reflect the silvery shimmer of Carlos Eliasson's aquarium.

"I didn't realize you hadn't kept up." Verner smiles benevolently.

Carlos turns to Saga but he looks uncertain, as if he can't decide how to interact with a young woman who looks so much like . . . like an elf, he thinks. He decides to simply take a step back and open his arms in a welcoming gesture.

"Welcome," he says, a strange shrill tone in his voice. .

"Thanks," she says.

"You've already met Joona Linna."

Saga just stands still. Her hair is a shimmering mass down to her waist, but her eyes are hard and her jaw is clamped shut. The sharp scar through one of her eyebrows glimmers chalk-white on her face.

"Please feel right at home," Carlos says, and he almost sounds pleasant.

Saga sits down stiffly next to Joona. Carlos sets a shiny paper folder on the conference table. It is titled "Strategies for Collaborating Units." Verner lifts his hand jokingly as if he were a schoolboy asking permission to speak before his deep bass fills the room.

"Formally, the entire investigation is in Säpo's hands. However, without the services of the National Criminal Investigation Department and Joona Linna, we wouldn't have had this breakthrough."

Verner points at the folder and Saga's face turns bright red.

"Perhaps this is not such a 'breakthrough,'" she mumbles.

"What?" Verner says loudly.

"All Joona found was a palm print and a piece of a photo." .

"And you . . . along with him, yes, you found out that Penelope Fernandez is still alive and someone is hunting her. Of course it's not just Joona alone . . ." He tries to soothe her.

"This is sick," Saga yells and shoves all the paperwork onto the floor.

"How the hell can you guys sit here and heap praise on him! He wasn't even supposed to be there! Someone even spilled the beans about Daniel Marklund—"

"But he did find out," Verner says.

"But this is all highly classified! What the fuck!"

"Saga," Verner says in rebuke. "You were also not supposed to be there!"

"True! But if I hadn't, everything would have—"

She stops herself short.

"Can we continue more calmly now?" Verner asks.

Saga looks at her boss before she turns to Carlos and says, "Forgive me. I'm sorry I lost my temper."

She bends down and begins to pick up the papers from the floor, her forehead still covered with angry red dots. Carlos tells her to leave them, but Saga picks them all up, shuffles them into their proper order, and puts them back on the table.

"I'm really very sorry," she says again.

Carlos clears his throat and says tentatively, "We hope that you might come to appreciate Joona's contribution. Perhaps enough to allow him to join your investigation."

"No! Seriously," Saga turns to her boss. "I don't want to seem so negative, but I don't see why you're making such a big deal about him. We would have found all the evidence he did. You talk about break-throughs, but I don't think that—"

"I agree with Saga," Joona says slowly. "I'm sure that eventually you would have found it all without my help."

"Maybe so," Verner says.

"Is that it, then?" Saga asks, keeping her voice under control as she stands up.

"But then there's one thing that you don't yet know," Joona continues calmly. "Björn Almskog secretly contacted Carl Palmcrona on the same day Viola was killed."

The room falls completely silent. Saga slowly sinks back into her chair. Verner leans forward and visibly collects his thoughts before he clears his throat. "So, Carl Palmcrona's suicide and the murder of Viola Fernandez might be connected?" he asks in his booming bass.

"Joona?" Carlos asks.

"Yes, I believe there's a connection between these two deaths."

"This is much bigger than we thought," Verner says, almost in a whisper. "This is very big . . ."

"Good work, Joona!" Carlos exclaims with a forced smile.

Saga Bauer has crossed her arms tightly across her chest. She's looking at the floor and the small red spots are reappearing on her forehead.

"Joona," Carlos says carefully, "I can't go over Petter's head, so he'll still be in charge of our own investigation, but I can let you work on loan to Säpo."

"What do you think, Saga?" Joona asks softly.

"Perfect," Verner answers immediately.

"It's up to me," Saga answers defiantly. "I'm still the one in charge of this case."

She gets up and leaves the room at once.

Verner excuses himself and hurries after her.

There's an icy glitter in Joona's gray eyes.

Carlos is still in his chair. He clears his throat yet again and says, "She's young and you have to try . . . I mean . . . be nice, watch out for her."

"I believe she is entirely capable of taking care of herself," Joona replies.

· *saga bauer*

Saga Bauer is distracted, thinking about Carl Palmcrona, and she barely manages to move her face, even slightly. She's seen the hit coming from the side, but too late. A low hook that passes over her left shoulder and hits her ear and chin. She's rocked. Her head protector has slipped to the side again and she can hardly see a thing. Still, she knows the next blow is on its way and sinks her chin and protects her face with both hands.

It's a hard hit followed by one to her upper ribs. She stumbles backward onto the rope. The referee rushes over but Saga has already figured a way out of the trap. She moves to the side and toward the middle of the ring and at the same time she is weighing her opponent: Svetlana Krantz from Falköping, a wide woman around forty years old with sloped shoulders and a Guns N' Roses tattoo. Svetlana is breathing with her mouth open and is hunting Saga with elephantine steps; she believes she's on the way to a knockout.

Saga dances softly backward, whirling like an autumn leaf over the ground. Boxing is so easy, she thinks, and a wave of joy fills her chest. She stops and smiles so broadly that her mouth guard almost falls out. She knows Svetlana is her match, but she had planned to win on points and not a knockout. However, when Svetlana's boyfriend howls that Svetlana should turn the blond cunt's face into mush, Saga changes her mind.

Svetlana is moving too quickly around the ring. Her right hand is eager, almost too eager. She is so convinced that she's going to beat Saga that she's no longer concentrating. She's already decided to end the match with one or more direct right-hand blows. She's thinking that Saga is already so groggy she won't be able to land a punch. But Saga Bauer is not weakened. Instead, she zeroes in on her concentration. Saga dances a bit in place as she waits for her opponent to rush forward. She holds her hands over her face as if in defense only. At the perfect moment, Saga executes a surprising shoulder-and-foot combination so that, stepping to the side, she glides away from her opponent's line of attack. Saga is now beside her and uses all her momentum for one blow—right into Svetlana's solar plexus.

She feels the edge of Svetlana's breast shield through her glove as Svetlana's body simply folds in half. Saga's next blow glances off Svetlana's head, but the third is a clean, hard uppercut right to the mouth.

Svetlana's head snaps backward. Sweat and snot spray out. Svetlana's dark blue mouth guard flies away and her knees give out. She falls straight to the mat and rolls over once, remaining still for a second before she starts to move again.

After the match, Saga Bauer pads around the women's dressing room feeling the tension run out of her body. There's a taste of blood and tape in her mouth. She'd had to use her teeth to undo the fabric tape around her glove's lacing. She looks at herself in the mirror and wipes away a few tears. Her nose is throbbing. She'd been thinking of other things during the match: her conversation with her boss and the head of the National Criminal Investigation Department and the decision that she was supposed to work with Joona Linna.

Inside her locker door is a sticker with the name Södertälje Rockets and a picture of a rocket that looks like an angry shark.

Saga's hands shake as she pulls off her shorts, pelvic protection and underwear, a black tank top, and the bra with the breast shield. Shivering, she steps into the showers and turns on the stream of water. Water pours over her neck and back. She forces her mind to think of things other than Joona Linna as she spits blood-tinged saliva into the floor drain.

There are about twenty women in the dressing room when she returns. A round of KI aerobics must have just let out. Saga doesn't notice them stop and stare at her in disbelief.

Saga Bauer is astonishingly beautiful, beautiful in a way that makes people weak in the knees. Her face is perfectly symmetrical and free of makeup, her eyes remarkably large and sky blue. Even with her pumped-up muscles and recent bruises, at five feet seven she's finely shaped; most of the women in the dressing room would take her to be a ballet dancer, not an elite boxer or an investigator with Säpo's security department.

Or they'd see her as an elf or a fairy princess, like Tuvstarr the valiant princess, able to stand fearlessly before the huge, dark troll in the paintings of the legendary artist John Bauer. John Bauer had two brothers: Hjalmar and Ernst. Ernst was Saga's great-grandfather. She never met him, but she still remembers well the tales her grandfather told about his own father's grief when his brother John, wife Esther, and their baby son drowned one November night on Lake Vättern just a few hundred meters from the harbor of Hästholmen. Three generations later, John Bauer's painting seems to have miraculously come to life in Saga.

Saga Bauer knows that she's a good investigator, even though she's never brought an investigation to its conclusion. She's used to having her work pulled out from under her or being excluded after weeks of hard work. She's used to being overprotected and overlooked for dangerous assignments. Used to it. But that doesn't mean she likes it.

She did very well at the Police Training Academy; after that, she went to the Security Service to be trained in counterterrorism and there rose to the rank of investigator. She's worked on both investigative and operational duties, and all the while, she's never neglected continuing education and she's always kept to a tough physical-training routine. She runs daily, boxes at least twice a week, and not a week goes by where she fails to make the shooting range with her Glock 21 and an M90 sharpshooter rifle.

Saga lives with a jazz musician, a pianist named Stefan Johansson, whose group won a Swedish Grammy for their sorrowful, improvisational album *A Year Without Esbjörn*. When Saga gets home from work or training, she'll lie on the sofa, eating candy, watching a movie with the sound off, while Stefan plays the piano for hours at a time.

Leaving the gym, Saga spots her opponent waiting by the concrete plinths.

"I just wanted to congratulate you and say thanks for a good match," Svetlana says.

Saga stops. "Thanks."

Svetlana turns red. "You're amazingly good."

"So are you."

Svetlana looks toward the ground and smiles.

Garbage is caught in the twigs of square-cut bushes meant to decorate the entrance of the parking lot.

"You taking the train?" Saga asks.

"Yeah, I guess I better start walking."

Svetlana picks up her bag, but then stops. She wants to say something else but has trouble letting it out. "Saga . . . hey, I'm sorry about what my guy said," she finally says. "I don't know if you heard . . . but he's not coming to any more of my matches."

Svetlana clears her throat and then starts walking again.

"Wait a minute," Saga says. "If you'd like, I can give you a ride to the station."

farther away

Penelope cuts across the slope at an angle. She slips on the loose stones, slides; her hand shoots out to balance her and it gets cut. She cries out; pain shoots from her wrist. Her shoulders and back burn too. She can't stop coughing. She forces herself to look behind, into the forest, between the tree trunks; she dreads catching sight of their pursuer again.

Björn helps her up, muttering something as he does. His eyes are bloodshot and haunted.

"We can't stay still," he's whispering.

Where is the pursuer? Is he close-by? Has he lost them? Not that many hours ago, they were lying on a kitchen floor while he was looking in the window. Now they're running up through a spruce thicket. They can smell the warm scent of the pine needles and they keep going, hand in hand.

There's a rustling and, crying out in fear, Björn takes a sudden step to the side and gets a branch in the face.

"I don't know how much longer I can take this," he says, panting.

"Don't think about it."

They slow to a walk. It is hard to ignore the pain in their knees and feet. Through brushwood and rotting piles of leaves, they keep going, down into a ditch, up through weeds, and finally they find themselves on a dirt track. Björn looks around and whispers to her to follow. He starts running south, toward the more inhabited area of Skinnardal. It can't be far. She limps a few steps and then begins to run after him. The track curves around a grove of birches and, once past the white trunks, they suddenly see two people. There's a woman barely out of her teens, dressed in a short tennis dress, talking to a man standing by a red motor-cycle.

Penelope zips up her hoodie and sucks in air through her nose to steady her breath.

"Hi," she says.

They're staring at her. It's easy to see why: she and Björn are bloody and dirty.

"We've had an accident," she says. "We need to borrow a phone."

Tortoiseshell butterflies flutter over the goosefoot and horsetail grow-ing in the ditch.

The man nods and hands his phone to Penelope.

"Thanks," Björn says, although he keeps his eyes glued on the road and into the forest.

"What happened?" the man asks.

Penelope doesn't know what to say. Tears begin to stream down her cheeks.

"An accident," Björn says.

"Oh my God," the woman in the tennis dress hisses to her boyfriend. "She's that bitch."

"Who?"

"The bitch on TV the other day who was criticizing our Swedish exports."

Penelope doesn't hear. She tries to smile engagingly at the young woman as she taps out Claudia's number. But her hands are shaking too hard and she hits the wrong number. She has to stop and try again. Her hands shake so fiercely she's afraid she'll drop the phone. The young woman is whispering into her boyfriend's ear.

She plants herself in front of Penelope. "Tell me something. Do you think that hardworking people, people working sixty hours a week, are supposed to pay for people like you to just say whatever the hell you want on some television program?"

Penelope can't comprehend why the young woman is so angry. She's unable to concentrate on her question. Her thoughts whirl as she anxiously scans the area between the trees while she hears the signal go through. The ringing crackles. It sounds far away.

"So real work's not good enough for you?" The woman is really working herself up.

Penelope pleads with Björn with her eyes to help her out here and calm the woman down. She sighs as she hears her mother's voice on the answering machine.

"This is Claudia Fernandez. I can't answer the phone right now, but please leave a message and I'll call back as soon as I can."

Tears run down her cheeks and her knees are about to buckle. She's so tired. She holds up her hand toward the woman in a plea.

"We paid for our phones with our own money we earned ourselves," the young woman says. "You do the same. Pay for your own damn phone . . ."

The line is breaking up. Penelope moves away in search of a better signal but it only gets worse. It cuts out and she's not sure she's even gotten through as she starts to speak.

"Mamma, I need help. People are after us—"

The woman yanks the phone from Penelope's hand and tosses it back to the young man.

"Get a job!" he yells.

Penelope sways in shock. She watches the woman climb onto the motorcycle behind the man and wrap her arms around his waist.

"Please!" Penelope calls after them. "*Please—*"

Her voice is lost in the roar of the motorcycle as it speeds away, spitting gravel. Björn and Penelope start to run after them, but the motorcycle disappears down the track to Skinnardal.

"Björn," Penelope says as she stops running.

"Keep running," he yells.

She's out of breath. This is a mistake, she thinks. He stops and looks at her. Then he starts walking away.

"Wait! He understands how we think!" she yells after him. "We have to outwit him!"

Björn walks more slowly and then turns to look at her. He keeps on walking backward.

"We've got to get help," he pleads.

"Not yet."

Björn slowly comes to a stop and then returns. He takes her by the shoulders.

"Penny, I'm sure that it's only ten minutes or so to the first house. You can do it. I'll help—"

"We have to get back in the woods," Penelope says. "I know that I'm right."

She pulls off her hair band and throws it on the road in front of them and heads back into the woods, away from habitation.

Björn looks behind him down the road, then reluctantly follows Penelope. Penelope hears him behind her. He catches up and takes her hand. They're now running side by side but not all that fast. A small inlet of water bars their way. They wade across for approximately forty meters, the water coming up to their thighs. Out of the water, they start to jog again in shoes that are completely soaked.

Ten minutes later, Penelope slows down. She stops, takes a deep breath, lifts her gaze, and looks around. Somehow she no longer senses the cold presence of their pursuer. Björn asks, "When we were in the house, why'd you yell for him to come in?"

"He'd have just come inside anyway—but he didn't expect a voice."

"Still—"

"Up to now, he's been one step ahead of us," she continues. "We've been scared and he knows how fear makes people stupid."

"Still, even stupid people don't say, 'Come on in,'" Björn says, and a tired smile crosses his face.

"That's why we can't head toward Skinnardal. We have to zigzag, change our direction all the time, keep deep in the forest, and head toward nothing at all."

"Right."

She observes his exhausted face and his white, dry lips.

"I think we have to think it out now. Try new ideas. I believe that we have to . . . instead of heading for the mainland . . . we have to keep going farther out into the archipelago and away from the mainland."

"No one in their right mind would do that."

"Can you keep going?" she asks softly.

He nods and they begin to move again, farther into the forest, farther away from roads, from houses and people.

the replacement

Axel Riessen unbuttons the cuff links from his stiff shirtsleeves and puts them in the bronze bowl on his dresser. The cuff links were an inheritance from his grandfather, Admiral Riessen. This design is civilian, however, a heraldry design consisting of two crossed palm leaves.

Axel studies himself in the mirror next to the closet door. He loosens his tie and then walks to the bed and sits down on the edge. The radiator hisses and he thinks he can make out snatches of music coming through the wall.

The music is coming from his younger brother's apartment in their shared family mansion. One lone violin, Axel thinks as his mind gathers the fragments he's heard into a whole. It's the Bach Violin Sonata in G Minor, the first movement, an adagio, but played much more slowly than conventional interpretations. Axel hears not only the musical notes but also every single overtone as well as an accidental bump against the body of the violin.

His hands long to take up a violin. His fingers tremble when the music changes tempo. It's been a long time since he's let his fingers play with the music, running over the strings and up and down the fingerboard.

When the telephone rings, the music in his head falls silent. He gets up from the bed and rubs his eyes. He's very tired and hasn't slept much for the past week.

Caller ID reveals that the call is coming from Parliament. Axel clears his throat before he answers in a calm voice.

"Axel Riessen."

"I'm Jörgen Grünlicht. As you may know, I'm the president of the Government Panel for Foreign Affairs.

"Good evening."

"Please excuse me for calling so late."

"I was still awake."

"They told me you might be," Jörgen Grünlicht says. He hesitates before continuing. "We've had an extra board meeting just now where we decided to try to recruit you for the post of general director for the ISP."

"I understand."

There's silence on the other end. Grünlicht adds hastily, "I assume you know what happened to Carl Palmcrona."

"I read about it in the newspaper."

Grünlicht clears his throat and says something that Axel can't understand before Grünlicht raises his voice again. "You are already aware of our work and—if you accept our nomination—could get up to speed fairly quickly."

"I'd have to resign my UN post," Axel replies.

"Is that a problem?" Grünlicht's voice seems worried.

"No, not really—I've been taking some time off anyway."

"We'll be able to discuss the terms, of course . . . but there's nothing that's off the table," Grünlicht says. "You must already know we would like you on board. There's no point in keeping that a secret."

"I need to think about it."

"Can you meet us tomorrow morning?"

"You're in a hurry."

"We'll take, of course, the time needed," Grünlicht replies. "But it must be said that after what happened . . . there have been hints from the economics minister about a matter already delayed—"

"And that would be?"

"Nothing unusual, just an export permit. The preliminary report was positive and the Export Control Committee has completed its work, the contracts have been signed. Unfortunately, Palmcrona wasn't able to sign it."

"His signature was required?"

"Only the general director can approve exports of defense matériel or products of dual usage," Jörgen Grünlicht explains.

"But can't the government approve certain business transactions at times?"

"Only once the general director of the ISP has decided to turn the matter over to the government."

"I understand," says Axel.

For eleven years, Axel Riessen served as a war matériel inspector in the old system for the Foreign Office before being assigned to the United Nations Office for Disarmament Affairs. At fifty-one, he still looks youthful. His hair, flecked with gray, is still thick. His features are regular and friendly, and the tan he picked up recently on vacation in Cape Town gives him a healthy glow. It had been an exceptional vacation: he'd sailed solo along the breathtaking, rugged coast.

Axel walks to his library and settles into his reading chair. He closes his eyes and starts to reflect on the fact that Carl Palmcrona is dead. He'd read the obituary in the morning edition of *Dagens Nyheter*. It was not clear what had happened, but he'd gotten the impression the death was unexpected. Palmcrona had not been ill, that much was clear. He thinks back to some of the times they'd met through the years and recalls when they'd worked together on how to combine the Military Equipment Inspection Committee with the Governmental Strategic Export Control Committee. In the end, a new agency would emerge: the National Inspectorate of Strategic Products.

And now Palmcrona is dead. Axel remembers the tall, pale man with his military air and a sense of loneliness about him.

Axel starts to worry. The rooms are too quiet. He stands up and looks around the apartment, listening for sounds.

"Beverly?" he calls in a low voice. "Beverly?"

She doesn't answer and fear rises in his mind. He walks quickly through the rooms and heads for the hallway to put on his coat when he hears her humming to herself. She is walking barefoot over the rugs in the kitchen. When she sees his worried face, her eyes widen.

"Axel," she says. "What's wrong?"

"I was just worried that you'd left," he mutters.

"Out into the dangerous world." She smiles.

"I'm just saying there are people you can't trust out there."

"I don't trust them," she says. "I just look at them. I look at their light. If it shines around them, I know that they're nice."

Axel never knows what to say when she says things like that, so he just tells her he's bought some chips and a big bottle of Fanta.

It seems as if she's stopped listening. He tries to read her face, to see if she is restless or depressed or closed off.

"So are we still going to get married?" she asks.

"Yes," he lies.

"It's just that flowers make me think of Mamma's funeral and Pappa's face when—"

"We don't need to have flowers," he says.

"Though I like lilies of the valley."

"Me, too," he says weakly.

She reddens contentedly and he hears her pretend to yawn for his sake.

"I'm so sleepy," she says as she leaves the room. "Do you want to go to sleep?"

"No," Axel says, but only to himself.

Parts of his body want to stop dead, but he gets up and follows her, clumsily and strangely slow, over the marble floor that leads along the hallway, up the stairs, through two large rooms, and finally into the suite where he retires in the evening. The girl is skinny and short and doesn't even come up to his chest. Her hair is frizzy. She shaved it last week, but it's begun to grow out again. She gives him a quick hug and he can smell the odor of caramel from her mouth.

sleepless

It's been ten months since Axel Riessen met Beverly Andersson, and that only came about because of his acute insomnia. Ever since he experienced a traumatic event thirty years ago, he's had difficulty sleeping. As long as he took sleeping pills, he was able to manage, but he slept a chemical sleep without dreams and without real rest. At least he slept.

Eventually he had to keep increasing the dosage. The pills caused a hypnotic noise that drowned out his thoughts, but he loved his medication and he usually mixed it with expensive, well-aged whiskey. One day, after twenty years of high consumption, Axel's brother found him unconscious in the hallway, blood flowing from both nostrils.

At Karolinska Hospital, he was diagnosed with severe cirrhosis of the liver. The chronic cell damage was so serious that, after the usual medical tests, he was placed on the waiting list for a liver transplant. He was in blood group O and his tissue type was unusual, so the number of possible donors was fairly slim.

His younger brother could have donated a partial liver if he hadn't suffered from such severe arrhythmia that his heart could not have endured an operation.

The hope of finding a liver donor was nearly nonexistent, but if Axel refrained from drinking and using sleeping pills, he would not die. As long as he took regular doses of Konakion, Inderal, and Spironolakton, his liver functioned and he lived a normal life.

Except that he never slept more than an hour or two at night. He was admitted to a sleep clinic in Gothenburg and underwent a polysomnography and had his insomnia officially diagnosed. Since medication was out of the question, he was given advice about meditation, hypnosis, self-suggestion, and sleep techniques. None of this helped.

Four months after his liver collapsed, he was awake for nine days straight and had a psychotic episode.

He had himself voluntarily admitted to the private psychiatric hospital Saint Maria Hjärta.

There he met Beverly. She was just fourteen years old.

As usual, Axel had been lying awake and it was about three in the morning. It was totally dark outside. She just opened his door. She was like an unhappy spirit who walked all night through the hallways of the psychiatric hospital. Perhaps all she was looking for was a person she could be with.

He was in bed, sleepless and disconsolate, when the girl came into his room and stood in front of him without a word. Her long nightgown brushed against the floor.

"I saw there was light in this room," she whispered. "You're giving off light."

Then she crawled into his bed. He was still sick from lack of sleep and he didn't know what he was doing. He grabbed her tiny body hard, too hard, and pressed her to him.

She said nothing. She just lay there.

He buried his face in the back of her neck. Then he fell asleep.

It was as though he had plunged deep into the waters of sleep and found dreams. He slept only a few minutes that first time. Every night after that, she came to his room. He would hold her tightly and then, covered with sweat, he'd fall asleep.

His psychological instability slowly dissipated like condensation from a mirror. Beverly stopped wandering through the hospital hallways all night.

Axel Riessen and Beverly Andersson left Saint Maria Hjärta Hospital with a silent and desperate agreement. Both of them understood that this close-knit arrangement had to be a secret. As far as the outside world could see, Beverly Andersson was temporarily housed in one of the apartments in Axel Riessen's mansion until a student apartment opened up.

Beverly Andersson is now fifteen and had been diagnosed with a borderline personality disorder. She has no sense of boundaries between herself and other people. She also has no self-defense mechanism.

In past eras, girls like Beverly might be locked up in mental institutions permanently or they might be forced to undergo sterilization or a lobotomy to control their lack of morals and unrestrained sexuality.

Girls like Beverly often still follow the wrong people home and trust people who are not worth their trust.

Beverly is lucky she found me, Axel Riessen would reassure himself. *I am not a pedophile, do not want to harm her or make money off her. I just need her next to me so I can sleep. Without sleep, I'll be destroyed.*

She often talks about their getting married once she's old enough.

Axel Riessen lets her spin her fantasies of marriage because it makes her happy and calm. He convinces himself that he's protecting her from the outside world, but he also knows that he's using her. He's ashamed, but can't figure out any other alternative. He's afraid of returning to relentless insomnia.

Beverly walks out of the bathroom with a toothbrush in her mouth. She nods toward the three violins hanging on the wall.

"Why don't you ever play them?" she asks.

"I can't," he replies with a smile.

"Are they just going to hang there? Why don't you give them to someone who can play them?"

"I like these violins. Robert gave them to me."

"You hardly speak about your brother."

"We have a complicated relationship."

"I know he makes violins in his workshop," she says.

"Yes, that's what he does . . . he also plays in a chamber orchestra."

"Maybe he can play for us at our wedding?" she asks as she wipes toothpaste from the corner of her mouth.

Axel looks at her and hopes that she doesn't pick up on the mechanical way he answers as he says, "What a good idea."

He feels exhaustion flowing over him like a wave, over his body and his brain. He walks past her and into the bedroom and sinks down on the edge of the bed.

"I'm very sleepy. I . . ."

"I feel very sorry for you," she says in total seriousness.

Axel shakes his head.

"I just need to sleep," he says. All at once, he feels as if he'll burst into tears.

He stands up again and picks out a nightgown in pink cotton.

"Please, Beverly, why don't you wear this one?"

"Sure, if you want me to."

She pauses to look at a large oil painting by Ernst Billgren. A fox is wearing clothes and sitting in an armchair in some upper-middle-class home.

"I hate that picture," she says.

"You do?"

She nods and starts to undress.

"Can't you change in the bathroom?" he asks.

She shrugs and as she pulls off her pink top, Axel moves away so that he won't see her nude. He walks over to the painting of the fox, looks at it, then takes it down to set it, facedown, on the floor.

Axel's sleep is stiff and heavy, his jaw clenched. He's held the girl very tightly. Suddenly he startles awake and lets her go. He sucks in air like a drowning man. He's sweating and his heart is pounding from fear. He turns on the lamp on the nightstand. Beverly sleeps as relaxed as a child, mouth open and a little sheen on her forehead. Axel starts to think about Carl Palmcrona again. The last time they'd met, they mingled with the nobility at a meeting in Riddarhuset. Palmcrona had been drunk and aggressive. He'd gone on and on about the UN weapon embargoes and finished his tirade with those strange words: *If everything goes to hell, I'll pull an Algernon so I won't reap my nightmare.*

Axel turns off the lamp and lies down again while he tries to understand what Palmcrona meant by saying "pull an Algernon." What was he talking about? What kind of nightmare was he thinking about? And did he really say that strange *I won't reap my nightmare?*

What *had* happened to Carl-Fredrik Algernon? It was a mystery in Sweden. Up until his death, Algernon had been the military-equipment inspector for the Foreign Office. One January day he'd had a meeting with the CEO of Nobel Industries, Anders Carlberg. He'd told Carlberg that their investigation had turned up information that one of the members of the conglomerate had smuggled weapons to countries in the Persian Gulf. Later that same day, Carl-Fredrik Algernon had fallen in front of a subway train in Central Station in Stockholm.

Axel's thoughts slip away and become increasingly blurred, circulating around accusations of arms smuggling and bribery concerning the Bofors Corporation. He sees a man in a trench coat falling backward in front of an oncoming train.

The man falls slowly, his coattails flapping.

Beverly's soft breathing catches him up, calms him, and he turns toward her to wrap his arms around her again.

She sighs as he pulls her closer to him.

Sleep comes to him in the softness of a cloud. His thoughts fade away.

For the rest of the night, he still sleeps restlessly and wakes again at five in the morning. He's been holding on so tightly to Beverly, his arms are cramped. Her stubbly hair tickles his lips. He wishes desperately that he could take his sleeping pills instead.

national inspectorate of strategic products

At seven in the morning, Axel walks out onto the terrace he shares with his brother. He has that eight o'clock meeting with Jörgen Grünlicht in Carl Palmcrona's old office at the National Inspectorate of Strategic Products.

The air is already warm but not yet humid. His younger brother, Robert, has opened the French doors to his apartment and come out to sit on a lounge chair. Robert hasn't shaved yet and just lies there with his arms hanging limply. He's staring up into the chestnut tree's foliage, still damp from the morning dew. He's wearing his worn-out silk bathrobe, the same one their father used to wear every Saturday morning.

"Good morning," Robert says.

Axel nods without looking at his brother.

"I've just repaired a Fiorini for Charles Greendirk," Robert says in an attempt at conversation.

"He'll be happy, I'm sure," Axel says. He sounds down.

"Something bothering you?"

"Yes, a bit," Axel admits. "I might be changing jobs."

"Well, why not?" Robert says, though his thoughts are already elsewhere.

Axel looks at his brother's kind face with its deep wrinkles, and at his bald head. So many things could have been different between them.

"How's your heart?" he asks. "Still pumping away?"

Robert puts his hand on his chest before he answers. "Seems to be."

"That's good."

"What about your poor old liver?"

Axel shrugs and turns back into his apartment.

"We're going to play Schubert this evening," his brother calls out.

"How nice."

"Maybe you could . . ."

Robert falls silent and looks at his brother. Then he changes the subject.

"That girl in the room upstairs—"

"Her name is Beverly."

"How long is she going to be living here?"

"I don't know," Axel says. "I've promised her that she can stay until she finds a student apartment."

"You always want to rescue birds with broken wings."

"She's not a bird, she's a human being," Axel says.

Axel opens the tall French doors to his own apartment and watches the reflection of his face glide past on the curved glass surfaces as he steps inside. Once behind the curtain, he silently observes his brother. He watches Robert get up from his lounge chair, scratch his stomach, and walk down the stairs from the terrace to the small garden and workshop. As soon as Robert is gone, Axel returns to his room and gently wakes up Beverly, who is still asleep with her mouth wide open.

The National Inspectorate of Strategic Products is a government agency that was established in 1996 to take over responsibility for all matters concerning arms exports and dual-usage items. Its offices are on the sixth floor of a salmon-pink building located at Klarabergs Viaduct 90. After riding up in the elevator, Axel sees that Jörgen Grünlicht is already waiting for him, nodding impatiently. Grünlicht is a tall man with a blotchy face: irregular patterns of white patches contrast with his reddish skin.

Grünlicht slips his identification card in and keys in the code to admit Axel. They walk to Carl Palmcrona's office. It's a corner suite with two huge windows overlooking a cityscape of southbound roads behind

Central Station and across from Lake Klara and the dark rectangle of city hall.

Despite its exclusive location, there's something austere about the ISP offices. The floors are laid with synthetic carpet and the furniture is simple and neutral in pine and white—its neutrality almost an intentional reminder of the morally dubious nature of arms exports, Axel thinks with a shudder. This is the national agency entrusted with the responsibility of making sure that Swedish weapons do not wind up in war zones and dictatorships. But Axel can't help feeling that under Carl Palmcrona's directorship, the ISP began to drift off course. It was less inclined to cooperate with the United Nations, and more likely to behave like the proactive Export Council. Axel is not a pacifist. He is well aware that arms exports are vital for Sweden's balance of trade. But he believes that the Swedish neutrality policy must be protected as well.

He looks around Palmcrona's office. Being there so soon after his death feels macabre.

A high-pitched whine is being emitted from the light system in the ceiling. It sounds like an inharmonious overtone from a piano. Axel remembers he once heard the same overtone on a recording of John Cage's first sonata.

Closing the door behind them, Grünlicht asks Axel to take a seat. He appears tense in spite of his welcoming smile.

"Good that you could come so quickly," he says, handing over the folder with the contract.

"Of course."

"Go ahead and read through it," Grünlicht says as he sweeps his hand over the desk.

Axel sits in a straight-backed chair and puts the folder back down on the desk. He then looks up.

"I'll take a look at it and get back to you next week."

"It's a very good contract, but this offer won't last forever."

"I know you're in a rush."

He looks at Grünlicht's pale, expectant face.

Axel knows there is no one in this country with a track record that can equal his own. This is perhaps the greatest argument for him to take the position. If he says yes, it will enable him to prevent some idiot from getting control over arms exports. He can stay committed to limiting the spread of weapons—and stay in Sweden with Beverly.

Grünlicht leans forward and says, with a shadow of guilt in his voice, "I know I'm pushing you, Axel, and I'm sorry for that. But the situation is a bit urgent. Palmcrona left several urgent matters hanging, and the companies are about to lose their deals, and—"

"Why doesn't the government take over for the time being?"

"Sure," Grünlicht says with a thin smile. "They can certainly take over, but they would still need advice, preferably from you."

Silence fills the room. It's as if feathers were falling all around them.

"I hear what you're saying," says Axel slowly. "But I'm still . . ."

Grünlicht slides the folder directly in front of Axel. "I just got off the phone with the prime minister. He asked if you were on board. You really should look at the agreement we've produced for you. It's a pretty—"

"I believe you," says Axel, "but you should know that I've been sick."

"Who has not?"

"I mean, I have—"

"We know all about it," says Grünlicht.

Axel lowers his eyes. "Of course."

"But we also know that the problems are a thing of the past. ISP is an authority based on trust. You have worked against the flow of weapons to war zones, and that is precisely what ISP stands for. There is only one name at the top of the government's list—and it is yours."

As Axel reaches for the agreement, he wonders if it is possible that they know everything about him—except for Beverly.

Opening the folder, he tries to push away the gut feeling that this is a gold-plated trap.

He reads through the contract carefully. It's very good, almost too good. Often he feels a slight blush as he reads through it.

"Welcome aboard," Grünlicht says, as he hands Axel a pen.

Axel thanks him and signs his name. He stands up, turns his back to Grünlicht, and looks out the window. The three crowns of city hall are erased by the haze.

"Not a bad view, is it? Better than mine from the Foreign Office," says Grünlicht over his shoulder.

Axel turns toward him as he continues.

"You've got three cases at the moment. The one with Kenya is under the greatest time pressure. It's a big, important piece of business. I advise you to look at it right away. Carl has already done the preliminary work, so . . ."

Grünlicht falls silent and pushes another document toward him. He watches Axel closely with a strange gleam in his eye. Axel has the feeling that if Grünlicht could, he'd put the pen in Axel's hand and hold it there while he signs.

"You'll be a fine replacement for Carl."

Without waiting for an answer, Grünlicht heads out of the door. "Meeting with the expert group this afternoon at three," he calls as he goes.

Axel is left standing alone in the room. A heavy silence descends around him. He sits back down at the desk and begins to glance through the document that Carl Palmcrona had left unsigned behind him. It seems perfectly well-prepared. It deals with the export of one and a quarter million units of 5.56 x 45 millimeter ammunition to Kenya. The Export Control Committee had voted for a positive recommendation. Palmcrona's preliminary decision had also been positive. Silencia Defense AB was a well-known, established firm. But without this last step of the general director's signature on the permission form, the actual export could not take place.

Axel leans back and suddenly Palmcrona's mysterious words come back to him: *I'll pull an Algernon so I won't reap my nightmare.*

a cloned computer

Göran Stone smiles at Joona Linna, removes an envelope from his brief-case, opens it, and holds out a key in his cupped palm. Saga Bauer stands right next to the elevator, looking downcast. All three of them are out-side the apartment of Carl Palmcrona at Grevgatan 2.

"Our technicians come tomorrow," Göran says.

"Do you know what time?" asks Joona.

"What time, Saga?" asks Göran.

"I believe—"

"Believe? You should know exactly," Göran says.

"At ten o'clock," Saga says in a low voice.

"And did you give them my orders to start with the Internet and tele-phone system?"

"Yes, I—"

Göran silences her with a wave of his hand as his phone rings. He takes a few steps down the stairs to answer, stepping into a niche next to the window with reddish brown panes.

Joona turns to Saga and asks quietly, "Aren't you in charge of this case?"

Saga shakes her head.

"What happened?" he asks.

"Don't know," she says in a tired voice. "It always happens this way. Counterterrorism isn't even Göran's specialty."

"So what are you going to do about it?"

"There's nothing to do . . ."

She falls silent as Göran finishes his phone call and returns to where they're standing. Saga suddenly holds out her hand for the key to Palmcrona's door.

"I want the key," she says.

"What?"

"I'm in charge of this investigation," she states firmly.

"What do you say about all this?" Göran says jokingly as he smiles at Joona.

"This is nothing against you, Göran," Joona says. "But I was just in a meeting with the higher-ups and I accepted an offer to work under Saga Bauer—"

"Oh, she can come along," Göran says hastily.

"As the one in charge of the investigation," Saga says again.

"Are you guys trying to get rid of me—or what the hell is this all about?" Göran says, looking both surprised and injured.

"Well, you can come along, if you want," Joona answers calmly.

Saga takes the key from Göran's hand.

"I'm going to call Verner," Göran says as he heads back down the stairs.

They listen to his footsteps and then how he speaks to his boss. The tone rises and his voice sounds increasingly upset until they hear him yell *"Fucking cunt!"* until it echoes.

Saga tries to stifle a smile as she turns to focus on the job. She puts the key in the lock, turns it twice, and opens the heavy door.

The police tape banning access to the apartment has been removed now that there no longer is any suspicion of a crime having been committed. The investigation was halted as soon as Nils Åhlén's autopsy report was concluded. As Joona had suspected, it confirmed a suicide: Carl Palmcrona hanged himself using a laundry line made into a noose and hung from the ceiling lamp of his home. The crime scene investigation was broken off and no analysis was performed on any evidence sent to the National Forensic Laboratory in Linköping.

But now it had been revealed that the day before, Björn Almskog had sent him an e-mail.

Later that same evening, Viola Fernandez had been killed on Björn Almskog's boat.

Saga and Joona walk into the hallway and notice there's been no mail delivery. They walk through the large rooms. Sunlight floods in through the windows and the smell of green soap lingers in the air. The red tin roof of the building across the street reflects the light, and from the bay window they can see the shimmering waters of Nybroviken Bay.

The forensic technician's protective mats have been removed and the floor underneath the ceiling lamp in the empty salon has been scrubbed.

They step lightly across the creaking parquet floor. There seems to be no lasting impression of Palmcrona's suicide. Now the place appears merely uninhabited. Joona and Saga both feel that the large rooms, almost empty of furniture, are now filled with a quiet sense of peace.

"The housekeeper's still taking care of the place," Saga says as she realizes what's behind the change.

"Exactly," Joona says and then smiles. The housekeeper has been there to clean the apartment, air out the rooms, carry in the mail, and change the linens.

Both of them understand that this is not unusual after a sudden death. People refuse to accept that their lives are going to change. Instead, they keep on with the old routine.

The doorbell rings. Saga looks a little concerned, but she follows Joona back to the hallway. The outer door is opened by a man with a shaved head and dressed in a black, baggy tracksuit.

"Joona told me to toss my hamburger aside and get over here pronto," says Johan.

"This is Johan Jönson from our computer tech division," Joona explains.

"Joona drive car," Johan says with an exaggerated Finnish accent. "Road swerve, Joona no swerve."

"Saga Bauer is an investigator with Säpo's security department," Joona continues.

"We work, we no talk, right?" asks Johan Jönson.

"Cut that out," says Saga.

"We have to look at Palmcrona's computer," Joona says. "How long will it take?"

They start walking toward Palmcrona's home office.

"You want to use it as evidence?" asks Johan.

"Yes," says Joona.

"So you want me to copy the data?" asks Johan.

"How long will it take?" Joona repeats.

"You'll have time to tell a few jokes to our colleague from Säpo," Johan answers without moving.

"What the hell is wrong with you?" Saga asks, irritated.

"By the way, are you dating anyone?" Johan asks with a shy smile.

Saga looks Johan straight in the eye and makes a definite nod. Johan looks down and mumbles something before he quickly follows Joona into Carl Palmcrona's office.

Joona borrows a pair of protective gloves from Saga and flips through the mail in the in-box on the desk but doesn't see anything special. There's not much to see. A few letters from the bank and the accountant, some information from the governmental offices, test results from a back specialist at Sophia Hospital, and the minutes of the spring condo association meeting with ballot results.

They go back into the room where soft music had surrounded the hanging body. Joona sits down on a Carl Malmsten sofa and carefully waves his hand across the narrow ray of ice-blue light emanating from the music system. At once, the music of a single violin starts streaming through the speakers. A fragile melody sounds in the highest register, but carrying the temperament of a nervous bird.

Joona looks at his watch and then leaves Saga by the music system to walk back to the home office. Johan Jönson is no longer there. He's sitting with his own computer at the kitchen table.

"Did it work?" asks Joona.

"What?"

"Could you copy Palmcrona's data?"

"Of course. This is an exact copy," Johan answers as if the very question is incomprehensible.

Joona walks around the table to look at the monitor.

"And his e-mail?"

Johan opens the program.

"Ta-da!" he says.

"We'll go through everything from the past week," Joona continues.

"Let's start with the in-box."

"Yes, let's."

"Do you think Saga likes me?" Johan asks.

"No," Joona says.

"Love often begins with an argument."

"So try pulling her hair." Joona grins and then he points at the screen.

Johan opens the in-box and smiles.

"Jackpot!" he says in English. "*Voitto!*" he adds in Finnish.

Joona sees three messages from skunk@hotmail.com.

"Open them," he says.

Johan clicks on the first one and instantly Björn Almskog's e-mail covers the entire screen.

"Jesus Christ Superstar," whispers Johan in English.

the e-mails

Saga Bauer comes up behind Joona and Johan as they read the e-mail through again.

"Find something?" she asks.

The men nod and keep reading.

"Let's see the next," Joona says, and Johan eagerly clicks on another e-mail from skunk@hotmail.com. They read it through twice, and repeat the routine one last time as Saga tries to read over Joona's shoulder.

"So you can see," says Joona at last, "on the second of June, Carl Palmcrona received a blackmail letter sent by Björn Almskog from an anonymous e-mail address."

"So that's what this is about: blackmail," Saga says.

"But I'm not sure that's the whole story," Joona replies.

He then reports what he has found out about Carl Palmcrona's final days.

On June 2, Palmcrona and Gerald James of the Technical-Scientific Advisory Committee had gone to the munitions factory of Silencia Defense in Trollhättan. That morning, he'd received an e-mail from Björn Almskog, but had probably not read it until evening, because he did not reply until six twenty-five. In his reply, Palmcrona warns the extortionist of terrible consequences.

At lunchtime the next day, not having heard back from Björn, Palmcrona sends a second e-mail to Björn, this time saying that he's resigned to the consequences he'd warned of earlier. It was at that point that he'd probably attached the noose to the ceiling lamp and had asked his housekeeper to leave him in peace. Once she'd gone, he'd turned on the music, walked into the smaller salon, placed his briefcase on end, climbed onto it to put the noose around his neck, and then kicked the briefcase away.

It was after Palmcrona's death that Björn's second e-mail arrived in Palmcrona's in-box, and the day after that, a final e-mail.

Joona sets the five e-mails in sequence on the table, so that he and Saga can read through the entire correspondence.

The first e-mail from Björn Almskog is dated Wednesday, June 2, at 11:37 a.m.:

Dear Mr. Palmcrona

    I am writing to inform you that I've come into
possession of an awkward original photograph. It shows
you sitting in a private box and drinking champagne
with Raphael Guidi. Since I understand that this
photograph could bring trouble to you, I am willing
to sell it to you for the sum of one million crowns. As
soon as you place the money in transit account 837-9
222701730, the photograph will be sent to your home
address and all correspondence will be deleted.
    Greetings from a "skunk"

The reply from Carl Palmcrona is dated Wednesday, June 2, at 6:25 p.m.:

    I do not know who you are, but I do know you have no
idea what you are getting yourself into. You must have
absolutely no clue.
    I warn you, therefore, that this is a very serious
matter and I ask that you send me this photograph
before it is too late.

On Thursday, June 3, at 2:02 p.m., clearly not having heard from Björn, Palmcrona sends a second reply:

```
It is already too late. We are both dead men.
```

Björn sends a response to that two hours later:

```
All right, I'll do as you ask.
```

And Björn Almskog sends a third e-mail the following day, Friday, June 4, at 7:44 a.m.:

```
Dear Mr. Palmcrona
    I've sent the photograph. Forget I even tried to
contact you.
    Greetings from a "skunk"
```

After reading through the e-mails twice, Saga looks up at Joona.

"So Björn Almskog wants to sell a compromising photograph to Palmcrona. It's obvious that Palmcrona believes him but also that the photograph is much more dangerous than Björn imagined. Palmcrona warns Björn that he's not going to hand over any money and even seems to believe the mere existence of this photograph threatens both their lives."

"So what do you think happened next?" asks Joona.

"Palmcrona waits for an answer by e-mail or by regular mail," Saga says. "When there's no reply, he sends his second message warning that they both will die."

"And then Palmcrona hangs himself," says Joona.

"When Björn shows up at the Internet café and reads Palmcrona's second e-mail—'It is already too late. We are both dead men'—he gets scared and replies he'll do just what Palmcrona asked."

"Without knowing that Palmcrona is already dead."

"Right," Saga says. "It is already too late and anything Björn can do now will be in vain."

"He seems to panic after receiving Palmcrona's second e-mail. He gives up any idea of blackmail and now just wants to get out."

"But the problem is, the photograph in question is taped to Penelope's door."

"So he doesn't have a chance to get at it until she leaves for the TV studio," Joona continues. "He waits outside, watches Penelope leave in a taxi, rushes in, sees the little girl on the stairs, gets into the apartment, rips the photo from the glass door, takes the subway, mails the photo to Palmcrona, and then sends Palmcrona an e-mail. Then he goes to his apartment on Pontonjärgatan 47, packs for the boat trip, takes the bus to Södermalm, and hurries to his boat anchored at Långholmen Harbor."

"So what makes you think that this is bigger than common blackmail?"

"Because Björn's apartment was completely destroyed by a fire barely four hours after he'd left it," Joona replies.

"I've stopped believing in coincidences when it comes to this investigation," Saga says.

"Me, too," Joona says with a grin.

They look at the correspondence again and Joona points at Palmcrona's two e-mails.

"He must have contacted someone between his first and second e-mail," he says.

"The first is a warning," Saga says. "The second one says it's already too late and they're going to die."

"I believe that Palmcrona called someone for advice when he received the blackmail letter. He was scared to death, but he was hoping to get help," Joona says. "Only when he realizes that there's no help to be had does he write the second e-mail where he tells Björn that they will both die."

"We'll have to put someone on his telephone lists," Saga says.

"Erixson's already on it."

"What else?"

"Who's the person mentioned in Björn's first e-mail?" Joona says.

"Raphael Guidi?"

"Do you know about him?"

"He was named after the archangel Raphael," Saga says. "He's an Italian businessman who deals in weapons contracts for the Middle East and Africa."

"Weapons contracts," Joona repeats.

"Raphael has been in the business for thirty years and he's built a private empire. There have been rumors, of course, but never anything concrete. Interpol's looked but never found anything on him."

"Would it be unusual to find Palmcrona in Raphael's company?"

"Not at all," she replies. "It's part of his job. But toasting something in champagne? I don't know."

"But you wouldn't kill someone, murder someone, because of that," Joona says.

"No."

"That photograph must reveal something else, something much more dangerous."

"If Björn mailed it, it must have arrived here, in the apartment," Saga says.

"I looked through the mail in his in-box but—" Joona cuts himself off mid-sentence. Saga gives him a look.

"So, what is it? What are you thinking?"

"There are only personal letters in the box. No ads. No bills," he says. "The mail had already been sorted when it arrived here."

riding down the highway

The housekeeper, Edith Schwartz, has no telephone. She lives forty-six kilometers north of Stockholm just outside of Knivsta. Joona is in the passenger seat next to Saga, who's driving at a reasonable clip down Sveavägen. They leave Stockholm's central area at Norrtull and get on the highway near Karolinska Hospital.

"Säpo has finished going through the crime scene at Penelope Fernandez's apartment," Saga is telling him. "I've gone through all the material, and based on that, it's perfectly clear she has no connection to left-wing groups. On the contrary, she's distanced herself from them and is an avowed pacifist. She actively argues against their methods. I've also gone through what little information we have on Björn Almskog. He works at Debaser, which is a club located at Medborgarplatsen. He's not politically active but was arrested once at a street party organized by Reclaim the City."

They quickly pass between the flickering black fence posts along North Cemetery and Haga Park's wall of greenery.

"I've also looked through our archives," Saga continues. "Everything we have on both the left-wing and right-wing extremists in Stockholm. It took me most of the night. Of course, most of this is classified as top secret, but there's one thing you need to know: Säpo made a mistake here. Neither Penelope nor Björn have ever been involved in sabotage or anything remotely resembling sabotage. They're almost laughably innocent."

"So you're dropping that angle?"

"Like you, I'm convinced that we're investigating something in another league entirely, far above either left- or right-wing local extremists . . . a league that's perhaps even beyond Säpo and the National Criminal Investigation Department for that matter. I'm talking about Palmcrona's death. Connect that with the fire in Björn's apartment and Viola's murder . . . this is something else again entirely."

Saga falls silent. Joona thinks back to the housekeeper's strange manner as she looked at him and asked if he'd cut Palmcrona down yet.

He'd said to her, "What do you mean by that?"

She'd said, "Excuse me, I'm just a housekeeper and I thought . . ."

He'd asked her if she'd seen anything unusual.

"A noose from the ceiling in the small salon," she'd answered.

"So you saw the noose?"

"Yes, indeed."

Of course she did, Joona thinks as he watches the highway unroll before them. "Yes, indeed," she'd said. The housekeeper's forceful expression—in words and manner—reverberates in his head. So does the look she gave him when he'd told her she would have to go down to the police station to give a statement. He'd thought that would alarm her, but it hadn't at all; she'd just nodded.

They're now passing Rotebro. Joona was involved in an old case there in which they'd dug up ten-year-old remains in a garden while looking for Erik Maria Bark's son, Benjamin. It had been winter then. Now wildflowers and greenery soften the rust-brown railroad tracks and brighten the way around the parking lot and on toward the town houses and larger homes.

Joona decides to call Nathan Pollock at the National Criminal Investigation Department. After a few rings, he hears Nathan's nasal voice.

"Nathan here."

"You and Tommy found circles of footprints beneath Palmcrona's body."

"That investigation was shut down," Nathan answers as Joona hears him typing on a computer.

"Right, but now—"

"I already know," Nathan said. "I've just talked to Carlos and he told me about the new developments."

"So can you take another look?"

"I'm already doing that," Nathan says.

"Sounds good. When will you have some results?"

"Now," Nathan replies. "They're from Palmcrona and his house-keeper, Edith Schwartz."

"Nobody else?"

"No one."

Saga is keeping a steady speed of 140 kilometers an hour. They're heading north on European Route 4.

Earlier that morning, Joona and Saga had gone to the police station to listen to the recorded interrogation of Edith Schwartz while simulta-neously following John Bengtsson's handwritten notes.

Joona reviews the questions and answers in his memory. After the standard formula statements informing Edith that there was no suspi-cion of a crime, they requested whether she could shed some light on the reasons behind Carl Palmcrona's death. Silence. Then Joona and Saga could hear the sounds from the ventilation system, the creaking of a chair, and the scratching of a pen on a sheet of paper. John Bengtsson had decided that due to Edith Schwartz's apparent disinterest, he would let her speak first.

At least two minutes passed before she spoke. Two minutes is a long time to sit before a police officer's desk while a tape is running.

Finally, she asked, "Did Director Palmcrona take off his coat?"

"Why do you ask that?" John Bengtsson replies in a friendly manner.

She said nothing. Another half minute went by. Finally, John ended the silence by asking, "Was he wearing his coat the last time you saw him?"

"Yes, he was."

"Earlier, you told Detective Linna that you'd seen a noose hanging from the ceiling."

"That's correct."

"What did you think he was going to use the noose for?"

She did not answer.

"How long was the noose hanging there?"

"Since Wednesday," she said calmly.

"So you saw the noose hanging from the ceiling on the evening of June second, went home, returned the next morning, the third of June, saw the noose still hanging there, met Palmcrona, left the apartment, and then returned on the fifth of June at two p.m. when you met Detective Linna."

The notes state she shrugged her shoulders at this point.

"Could you tell us something about those four days?" he asked.

"I come to Director Palmcrona's apartment every morning at six. I am only allowed to use my key early in the morning, since Palmcrona sleeps until six thirty. He keeps regular hours and he never sleeps in, not even on Sunday. I grind the coffee beans in the hand grinder, cut two slices of brown bread, and spread extra salted margarine on them before I place two slices of truffle-filled liver pâté and pickles along with one slice of cheddar cheese to one side. I set the table with starched linen and the summer porcelain. I must remove all advertisements and the sports section from the morning papers and place them, folded, on the right side of his plate."

With minute detail she ran through the entire preparation of Wednesday's ground-veal patties in cream sauce as well as her preparations for Thursday's lunch.

When she got to the point where she returned to the apartment with food for the weekend and rang the doorbell, she fell silent again.

"I understand that this might be difficult for you," John Bengtsson said after some more time had passed. "But I've been listening to your every word for quite a while. You have gone through Wednesday and Thursday but not once have you said anything that might touch on Palmcrona's unexpected death."

She said nothing.

"I ask you to search your memory again," John Bengtsson said with great patience. "Did you know that Carl Palmcrona was dead when you rang the doorbell?"

"No."

"Did you or did you not ask Detective Linna whether he had been cut down yet?" John asked, irritation creeping into his voice.

"Yes, I did."

"Had you already seen him dead?"

"No, I had not."

"But what the hell!" John's irritation burst forth. "Can't you just tell me what you know? What made you ask whether we'd taken him down or not? You were the one who asked that! Why did you ask if you didn't even know that he was dead?"

John Bengtsson noted that he'd unfortunately allowed himself to be provoked by the woman's stolid avoidance of direct answers and that after he'd cursed, she'd closed up like a clam.

"Are you accusing me of a crime?" she asked coolly.

"No."

"Then I believe that we're finished."

"We would really like your help . . ."

"I remember nothing else," she said as she got up from the chair.

Joona looks at Saga. Her eyes are fixed straight ahead.

"I'm thinking about the interview with the housekeeper," he says.

"Me, too."

"John got fed up with her attitude and thought she was contradicting herself. He assumed that she knew that Palmcrona was dead when she rang the bell and we answered."

"Right," Saga says, still not taking her eyes from the road.

"But she was speaking the simple truth. She really did not know that he was dead. She believed he might be, but wasn't sure," he continues. "That's why she said no to his statement."

"Edith Schwartz sounds like an unusual woman."

Joona says, "I believe she's trying not to lie but still keep something secret from us."

the photograph

Neither Joona nor Saga believe they'll be able to get anything important from Edith Schwartz, but perhaps she can reveal where the photograph might be. They need it to solve this case.

Saga turns west onto Route 77 underneath the highway viaduct on the way to Knivsta, then almost immediately turns off onto a small gravel road paralleling the highway.

Low spruce forests line fallow fields. The masonry edge of a manure pool has broken and its tin roof is hanging lopsidedly.

"We should be there," Saga says with a glance at the GPS.

They slowly roll up to a rusty boom and stop. As Joona gets out, he hears the dull drone of traffic on the highway. Twenty meters along, they can see a one-story house of dirty yellow brick. Decorative shutters are screwed on, and moss covers asbestos cement sheeting on the roof.

As they approach the house, they hear an unusual whirring sound. They glance at each other and move cautiously toward the outer door of the house. A rattling noise is coming from out back; then they hear the metallic whine again, coming closer. Racing around the house comes a German shepherd, mouth gaping wide. He slams to a stop a meter away from Saga, jerked back onto his hind legs by a long leash. He shuffles back a little, crouches, and begins to bark. He tosses his head from side to side to set himself free. As he jumps, the leash slides along a wire line with a whining, rattling sound.

The dog turns to rush at Joona but is choked back again. He barks dementedly but stops the second he hears a voice from inside the house.

"Nils!" a woman commands.

They hear the floor creak inside and a moment later the door opens. The dog scurries back behind the house and the whirring sound disappears with him.

"We need to talk to you," Joona says.

"I've already told the police everything I know," she replies.

"May we come inside?"

"No."

Joona glances past her into the dark interior of the house. The hall is littered with pots and pans, plates, a gray vacuum-cleaner hose, clothes, shoes, and a rusty crayfish pot.

"We can stay outside," Saga says reassuringly.

Joona glances at his notes. It's routine to go over details from an interrogation to catch any discrepancies or even catch someone out in a downright lie they no longer remember correctly. "What did Palmcrona have for dinner on Wednesday?"

"Ground-veal patties in cream sauce," she says.

"With rice?" asks Joona.

"With potatoes," she replies. "Always boiled potatoes."

"At what time did Palmcrona return to his apartment on Thursday?"

"At six in the evening."

"What were your duties when you left Palmcrona's apartment on Thursday?"

"He gave me the evening off."

Joona looks directly into her eyes and decides there's no point in beating around the bush. He goes straight to the point.

"Did Palmcrona fix the noose already by Wednesday evening?"

"No," says Edith.

"That's what you told our colleague, John Bengtsson," Saga said.

"That's incorrect."

"Your interview was recorded," Saga wants to say, but she finds herself so irritated, she decides to keep quiet.

"Did you ask Palmcrona any questions about the noose?" Joona asks.

"We never discussed private matters."

"But isn't it odd to just leave a man with a noose hanging from his ceiling?" asks Saga.

"Well, what could I do? Stay around and watch him?" Edith replies with a small smile.

"That's true," Saga agrees calmly.

For the first time, Edith inspects Saga. Without embarrassment, she runs her eyes from Saga's fairy-tale hair caught back in a colorful headband to her clear face and down to her jeans and running shoes.

"Well, I must say, I find this a bit confusing," Saga says. "You told our colleague that you saw the noose on Wednesday, but just now, you said the opposite."

Joona checks his notebook for Saga's earlier question.

"Edith," Joona says, "I believe I understand what you've said."

"That's good," she replies.

"Concerning the question of whether Palmcrona hung up the noose on Wednesday, you said no—because Palmcrona wasn't the one who put it up."

The old woman gives Joona a hard look. Then she says firmly, "He tried, but he couldn't do it. His back was too stiff from his operation last winter . . . so he asked me to."

Silence falls again. The trees surrounding them are completely still in the heat of the day.

"So you were the one who tied a laundry line into a noose and hung it from the ceiling?" Joona asks.

"He tied the knot and held the ladder when I climbed up," she says.

"Then you put the ladder away, went back to your normal duties, and went on home after washing up the dishes from Wednesday's dinner," Joona says.

"That's right."

"You came in the following morning," he continues. "You began the day as usual by making his breakfast."

"Did you know that he wasn't already hanging from the noose yet?" Saga asks.

"Well, I took a peek into the small salon," Edith answers.

The shade of a sarcastic smile appears for a split second on her closed face.

"You've already told us that he'd eaten breakfast as he usually did, but that he didn't go to work Thursday morning either."

"He was in the music room for at least an hour."

"Was he listening to music?"

"Yes, he was."

"Right before lunch, he placed a call," Saga says.

"Well, that I don't know. He went into his office and closed the door, but before he came to eat his lunch of boiled salmon, he asked me to order a taxi for two o'clock."

"Was he planning to go to Arlanda Airport?"

"Yes, he was."

"And at ten minutes to two, someone called him?"

"Yes, he'd already put on his coat and he answered the hall phone."

"Did you hear what he said?" Saga asks.

" 'It's not a nightmare to die,' " replies Edith.

"I've asked you what he said," Saga repeats.

"Now you'll have to excuse me," Edith says shortly and begins to close the door.

"Just a second," Joona says.

The movement of the door stops and Edith frowns at him through the gap without reopening it.

"Did you sort Palmcrona's mail today? Do you have it here?" Joona asks.

"Of course."

"Please bring us everything that's not an advertisement," Joona requests.

She nods, walking into the house, leaving the door ajar, and returns with a blue bowl filled with mail.

"Thank you," Joona says as he takes the bowl.

Edith closes the door completely and they hear her locking it behind her. A few seconds later, they hear the whirring of the dog's tether again.

They hear his aggressive barking behind them as they walk to the car and climb in.

Saga starts the engine, then puts the car into gear and turns it around. Joona puts on protective gloves to sort through the letters in the bowl and then pulls out a manila envelope with a handwritten address. He opens it carefully and just as carefully slides out the photograph for which at least two people have died.

the fourth person

Saga Bauer pulls onto the shoulder of the road and parks. The grass in the ditch is so tall it brushes the passenger-side window. Joona Linna remains absolutely still as he contemplates the photograph.

There's something fuzzy on the upper edge of the picture, but in general, it is perfectly sharp. Probably the camera was hidden and the photograph taken secretly.

There are four people sitting in the large box of a concert hall. Three men and one woman. Their faces are clearly visible. Only one person is turned away, but even that face is not hidden.

There's champagne in a chiller and the table has been set so they can converse and eat and still listen to the music.

Joona recognizes Carl Palmcrona right away. He holds a champagne flute. Saga can identify two of the other people.

"That one is Raphael Guidi, the weapons dealer mentioned in the blackmail letter," she says as she points to a man with thin hair. "And the one looking away is Pontus Salman, the head of Silencia Defense."

"Weapons," Joona says.

"Silencia Defense is a well-known company."

Under the spotlight, onstage behind the men, a string quartet can be seen: two violins, a viola, and a cello. The musicians are all men. They sit in a half circle, their faces calm in concentration. It's hard to tell if their eyes are closed or slightly open, whether they are looking at their music or simply following the different parts.

"Who is the fourth person, the woman?" Joona asks.

"Let me think and it'll come to me," Saga replies as the wheels turn in her mind. "I do recognize her, but . . . damn . . ."

Saga's voice fades as she stares at the woman in the picture.

"We have to find out who she is," Joona says quietly.

"Right."

Saga starts the car and, at the same time she bumps back onto the road, she has the answer. "That's Agathe al-Haji," she says. "She's the military adviser to President Omar al-Bashir."

"Sudan."

"Right."

"How long has she been his adviser?"

"Fifteen years or so. I can't really remember."

"So what's going on in this picture?" Joona muses.

"I have no idea. I mean . . . the fact that the four of them are meeting is not so strange. Perhaps they are discussing business proposals," Saga speculates. "These kinds of meetings happen all the time. This could be a first encounter. You meet, explain your intentions, and maybe ask for ideas, even a preliminary decision, from Carl Palmcrona."

"And his positive reaction could mean that the ISP will most likely give export permission in the end?"

"Exactly. It would be a good indication."

"Does Sweden usually export war matériel to Sudan?" asks Joona.

"No, I don't think so," she answers. "We should ask an expert. I believe that China and Russia are the largest exporters to Sudan, but I'm not so sure anymore. There was a peace pact made in Sudan in 2005 and I imagine that the export market was opened after that."

"So what does this picture tell us? Why would Carl Palmcrona take his own life because of it? I mean, they met in public in a concert-hall box."

In silence they keep driving south on the dusty highway while Joona goes over the photograph again and again, turns it over, notices the torn corner, and thinks.

"So this actual photograph cannot be dangerous to anyone," he states.

"Not if you ask me."

"Did Palmcrona take his own life because he realized that the person who took this picture could expose something? Maybe the photograph is just a warning? Maybe Penelope and Björn are more important than the picture?"

"We don't know a damn thing." .

"Yes, we do," Joona says. "The problem is that we don't know how to connect the dots. We're still guessing at the orders for this hit man. It looks like he was only trying to find this photograph to destroy it and that he killed Viola because he thought she was Penelope."

"Perhaps Penelope took the shot," Saga suggests. "Even so, this killer wasn't content with just her murder."

"Exactly. We don't know which one comes first: Is the picture a link to the photographer, who is the true threat? Or is the photographer the link to the photograph, the primary threat?"

"The first attack was on Björn's apartment."

They say nothing for a few minutes. They've almost gotten back to the police station when Joona takes another close look at the photograph. The four people in the box, the food, the four musicians onstage, the instruments, the heavy curtain, the champagne bottle, the champagne flutes.

"Looking at this photograph," Joona says, "I see four faces. One of them must be behind the murder of Viola Fernandez."

"Right. Palmcrona is dead, so we can probably exclude him. So that leaves three . . . and two of them are out of our reach, so we can't question them."

"We've got to interview Pontus Salman," Joona says.

48

the bridal crown

It is difficult to find a real human at Silencia Defense AB. All outside lines lead to the same labyrinth of automated menus and recorded information. Finally, Saga decides to bypass it all with the number 9 and the star key. She is connected to the company secretary. She ignores this person's questions and goes right to what she wants. The secretary says nothing for a moment and then tells Saga that she must have gotten the wrong number and that everyone has gone out for lunch.

"Please call back tomorrow morning between nine and eleven and—"

"Tell Pontus Salman to be ready for a visit from Säpo at two this afternoon," Saga says in a loud, firm voice.

"I'm sorry," the secretary says. "He's in meetings all day."

"Not at two o'clock," Saga answers sweetly.

"Yes, his appointment book says that—"

"Because at two o'clock, he is meeting with me," Saga says.

"I will forward your request."

"Thank you very much," Saga replies. She meets Joona's eyes across the desk.

"Two o'clock?" he confirms.

"Yes, indeed."

"Tommy Kofoed would like a look at that photo," Joona says. "Let's stop by his office after lunch, before we head out."

―――――

While Joona is having lunch with Disa, the technicians at the National Forensic Laboratory are enlarging the photograph.

The face of one person in the box is specifically being blurred so as to be unrecognizable.

Disa is smiling to herself as she removes the inset from the rice cooker. She holds it out to Joona and watches him as he moistens his hands to check if the rice is cool enough to form into small patties.

"Did you know that Södermalm used to have its own Calvary?"

"Calvary like Golgotha or cavalry like horses?"

"A place for executions." Disa nods as she opens Joona's kitchen cabinet, finds two glasses, pours white wine into one and water into the other.

Disa looks relaxed. Her freckles have turned darker and she's put her disheveled hair into a loose braid. Joona washes his hands and takes out a new kitchen towel. Disa goes up to him and puts her arms around his neck. Joona answers her embrace by putting his face next to hers and breathing in the scent of her hair even as he feels her hands gently caressing his back and neck.

"Let's go ahead," she whispers. "Let's try."

"Maybe," he says in a low voice.

She holds him tightly, very tightly, and then she eases from his arms.

"There are times I get really mad at you," she mutters as she turns away.

"Disa, I am who I am, but I—"

"I am very happy that we're not living together," she says, and then she leaves the kitchen.

He hears her lock herself in the bathroom and wonders whether he should follow and knock on the door, but he also knows that she really wants to be left alone, so he just continues making lunch. He picks up a piece of fish, places it on his palm, and then spreads a line of wasabi onto it.

A few minutes later, Disa comes back. She stands in the doorway and watches him finish making the sushi.

"Do you remember," she says, laughing, "how your mother always took the salmon off the sushi and fried it before she put it back on the rice?"

"Of course."

"Should I set the table?"

"Please."

Disa carries plates and chopsticks to the big room, stops next to the window, and looks down at Wallingatan. A grove of trees lights up the view with its green late-spring leaves. Her eyes wander over the pleasant area all the way to Norra Bantorget where Joona Linna has been living for the past year.

She sets the off-white dinner table, returns to the kitchen to take a sip of wine. The wine has lost the crispness from being chilled. She dismisses the sudden urge to sit down on the lacquered wooden floor under the table and have lunch, eating with their hands as if they were still children.

Instead, she says, "I've been asked out."

"Asked out?"

She nods and feels she wants to be a little bit mean, even though she doesn't really.

"Tell me about it," Joona says calmly as he carries the tray with sushi to the table.

Disa picks up her glass and says in an easy tone, "It's just that there's a man at the museum who's been asking me out to dinner for the last six months."

"Do people still ask people out to dinner these days?"

Disa smiles somewhat crookedly. "Are you jealous?"

"I don't know. Maybe a little," Joona says as he walks over to her. "It's always pleasant to be asked out to dinner."

"That's right."

Disa pushes her fingers through a bit of Joona's thick hair.

"Is he good-looking?"

"Actually, yes he is."

"How nice."

"But you know that I really don't want to." Disa smiles.

He doesn't answer and turns his head away.

"You know what I want," Disa says softly.

Joona's face is now a little pale. She sees a sheen of sweat on his forehead. He slowly turns his face back to her. His eyes have darkened until they're as black and hard as an abyss.

"Joona?" she asks. "Forget about it. I'm sorry—"

It looks like Joona starts to say something and begins to take a step when his legs buckle.

"Joona!" Disa cries and knocks her glass off the table as she hurries to his side. She holds him closely and whispers that it will be over soon.

After a few minutes, Joona's face relaxes bit by bit from its tight expression of pain.

Disa gets up to sweep the broken glass off the floor. Then they sit at the table and eat in silence.

After a while, Disa says, "You're not taking your medicine."

"It makes me sleepy. I have to think. It's important to think clearly right now."

"You promised me that you'd continue with it."

"I will, I will," he reassures her.

"It's dangerous not to. You know that," she whispers.

"As soon as I've solved this case, I'll start taking it again."

"What if you never solve it?"

At a distance, the Nordic Museum appears to be a fancy image carved in ebony, despite being built of sandstone and limestone. It's a Renaissance dream of elegance with its many towers and pinnacles. The museum was planned as an homage to the sovereignty of the Nordic peoples, but by the time it was inaugurated one rainy day in the summer of 1907, the union between Sweden and Norway had dissolved and the king was dying.

Joona walks swiftly through the enormous great hall of the museum and stops only after he's climbed the stairs. He collects himself, then walks slowly past the lighted display cabinets. Nothing there catches his eye. He keeps going, his thoughts bound in memories and the sadness of loss.

The guard has seen him coming and has set a chair out for him next to one particular display case. Joona Linna takes his seat and lifts his eyes to the Sami bridal crown before him. The eight points of the crown are like linked hands, and the crown shines softly in the light behind the thin glass. Inside himself, Joona can hear a voice, and he sees a face smiling at him as he sits behind the wheel of his car. He is driving. It rained that day, but now the sun is reflecting in the puddles on the road so brightly, it's as if they're lit by fires below. He turns toward the backseat to make sure that Lumi has been buckled in properly.

The bridal crown appears to have been made from light branches of leather or braided hair. He drinks in its promise of love and joy and remembers how his wife looked: her serious smile, her sand-colored hair brushing her face.

"How are you doing today?" the guard asks.

Joona looks up at the guard in surprise. The man has been working here for many years. He's middle-aged with stubble on his cheeks and tired eyes.

"I really don't know," Joona replies as he gets up from the chair.

the blurred face

Joona Linna and Saga Bauer are in the car on their way to the interview with Pontus Salman in Silencia Defense's main office. They're bringing the photograph that the technicians at the National Bureau of Investigation have enlarged. Quietly they travel south on Highway 73, which runs like a dirty track down to Nynäshamn.

Two hours ago, Joona had been looking again at the four people sitting in the box: Raphael with his calm face and balding pate; Palmcrona with his weak smile and steel-framed glasses; Pontus Salman with his placid, almost boyish demeanor; and Agathe al-Haji with her wrinkled cheeks and intelligent, heavy gaze.

"I have an idea," Joona had said slowly, catching Saga's eye. "If we could reduce the picture quality and touch it up so that Pontus Salman is no longer identifiable . . ."

He falls silent as he follows his internal train of thought.

"What would we achieve?" asks Saga.

"He doesn't know that we have a sharp original picture—right?"

"How could he? He'd expect us to make the photo more in focus, not the opposite."

"Exactly. We've done all we could to identify the four people in the picture and we've figured out three. The fourth is somewhat turned away and the face is too blurry."

"You're thinking we should give him the chance to lie," Saga says. "To claim that he wasn't there and that he hasn't met Palmcrona, Agathe al-Haji, and Raphael."

"If he denies he was there, then the meeting itself was the secret."

"And if he starts to lie, we have him in a trap."

They pass Handen and then turn off at the Jordbrolänken exit. They roll into an industrial area surrounded by silent forest.

The head office for Silencia Defense is located in a dull-gray impersonal concrete building. Joona takes a good look at it, with its black-tinted windows. He thinks again about the four people in the photo, which unleashed a chain of violence leading to a dead young girl and the sorrow of her mother. Perhaps Penelope Fernandez and Björn Almskog are also dead by now because of this picture. Joona steps out of the car and his jaw tightens. Pontus Salman, one of the people in this enigmatic photograph, is inside this building right now.

The original photograph is safely in the hands of the National Forensic Laboratory in Linköping. Tommy Kofoed has created a copy that appears old and worn like the original. One corner is missing and tape remains are seen on the others. Kofoed has rendered Pontus Salman's face and hand blurry so that it appears that Salman was moving at the moment the photograph was taken.

Salman will think that he's in luck—he alone is unrecognizable. Nothing connects him to the meeting with Raphael Guidi, Carl Palmcrona, and Agathe al-Haji. The only thing he needs to do is deny that it's him. It's not a crime to not recognize oneself in a blurry picture and to not remember meeting certain people.

They start toward the entrance.

If he denies it, we've caught him in a lie and we know he wants to keep something secret.

The air is oppressively hot and humid.

Saga nods seriously at Joona as they walk through the shiny, heavy entrance doors.

And if Salman starts to lie, Joona thinks, *we'll make sure he continues to lie until he's so entangled he can't get free.*

The reception area is large and cold.

When Pontus Salman looks at the photograph and says that he can't identify the people in it, we'll say that it's unfortunate that he can't help us, Joona continues to think. *We'll get ready to leave and then we'll stop and ask him to take one more look with a magnifying glass. The technician has left a signet ring visible on the hanging hand. We'll ask Pontus Salman if he recognizes the clothes, the shoes, or the pinkie ring. He'll be forced to lie again, and then we will have reason to bring him in for questioning and press him harder.*

Behind the reception desk, there is a lighted red emblem emblazoned with the company name and a serpentine logo encircled by runes.

"'He fought as long as he had a weapon,'" Joona says.

"Can you read runes now?" asks Saga skeptically.

Joona points at the sign with the translation as he walks to the reception desk. A pale man with thin, dry lips is ensconced behind the desk.

"Pontus Salman," Joona says shortly.

"Do you have an appointment?"

"Two o'clock," Saga says.

The receptionist shuffles through some papers, flips to one, and reads.

"Yes, that's right," he says as he raises his eyes. "Unfortunately, Pontus Salman sends his regrets. He cannot make this meeting."

"We received no notice of a cancellation," Saga says. "We must talk to him—"

"I am very sorry."

"Please call him. Tell him we're here," Saga says.

"I'll try, but I believe . . . he's in a meeting."

"On the fourth floor," Joona inserts.

"The fifth," the receptionist corrects automatically.

Saga sits down in one of the reception chairs. The sun streams in through the windows and spreads like fire in her hair. Joona remains standing as the receptionist lifts his phone to his ear and taps a number. The busy signal sounds and the receptionist shakes his head.

"Hang up," Joona says. "We'll just surprise him instead."

"Surprise him?" the receptionist repeats uncertainly.

Joona simply walks to the glass door beyond the reception desk and opens it.

"You don't even need to tell him we're coming," Joona says. Saga gets up from the chair and follows Joona.

"Wait!" the man calls out. "I'll try to—"

They keep walking through the hallway and into an open elevator. They punch the button for the fifth floor. The door closes and the elevator moves silently upward.

Pontus Salman is waiting for them when the doors open. He is about forty years old and there is a worn, tired look to his face.

"Welcome," he says drily.

"Thanks."

Pontus Salman looks them over.

"A detective and a fairy-tale princess," he says.

As they follow Salman through a long hallway, Joona runs through their plan in his mind.

Joona feels a cold shiver down his back—as if Viola Fernandez is opening her eyes right then in her cold box, watching him expectantly.

The hallway is lined with dark-tinted glass, creating an aura of timelessness. The office itself is fairly large and contains a desk of elm wood and a light gray sofa group around a black glass coffee table.

They each take one of the stuffed chairs. Pontus Salman smiles cheerlessly and forms a steeple with his hands. Then he asks, "Why are you here?"

"You know that Carl Palmcrona of ISP is dead?" asks Saga.

Salman nods. "I heard it was a suicide."

"Our investigation into that is not yet finished," Saga says in a friendly manner. "We're following up on a photograph we found. We want to find out who these people are around Palmcrona."

"Three of them are clear, but one person is blurry," Joona says.

"We'd like some of your employees to take a look, too. Perhaps someone will recognize him. One hand, for instance, is a little sharper."

"I understand," Salman says and purses his lips.

"Maybe someone can tell who it is from the context," Saga says. "It's worth a try."

"We've visited Patria and Saab Bofors Dynamics," Joona says. "None of them knows."

Pontus Salman's tired face shows nothing at all. Joona wonders to himself if Salman takes pills to keep calm and self-confident. There's something remarkably lifeless in his eyes—a lack of expression and contact—as if something inside has slid away, leaving him with no connection to anything at all.

"You must think this is important," Salman says, crossing one leg over the other.

"Indeed we do," Saga says.

"May I see this unusual photograph?" Pontus Salman asks in his easy but impersonal manner.

"Besides Palmcrona, we've identified the weapons dealer, Raphael Guidi," Joona says. "We've also identified Agathe al-Haji, who is the military adviser for President al-Bashir . . . but no one recognizes this fourth person."

Joona takes out the folder, and then hands over the photograph in its protective plastic cover. Saga points to the blurred person. Joona watches her concentrate on Salman to register every nuance, every nervous signal in his body if he lies.

Salman moistens his lips and, even though his cheeks turn pale before he smiles, he taps the photograph and says, "But that's me!"

"It's you?"

"Yes," he says with a laugh, revealing small, childlike front teeth.

"But—"

"We had a meeting in Frankfurt," he continues with a pleased smile. "We were listening to a wonderful . . . well, I don't remember what they were playing . . . maybe Beethoven . . ."

Joona tries to understand this unexpected confession. He clears his throat.

"You're absolutely sure?"

"Of course," Salman says.

"Well, that solves that puzzle," Saga says warmly with no hint of their miscalculation.

"Maybe I should get a job at Säpo," Salman jokes.

"If I may ask, what was this meeting about?" asks Joona.

"I can talk about it now." Salman laughs and looks directly at Joona. "This photo was taken in the spring of 2008. We were discussing a shipment of ammunition to Sudan. Agathe al-Haji was negotiating on behalf of the government. The area needed to stabilize after the peace agreement in 2005. The negotiations were fairly far along, but all our work went up in smoke in the spring of 2009, of course. We were shaken, yes, you understand . . . and since then, we've had no contact with Sudan."

Joona looks at Saga since he has no idea what happened in the spring of 2009. Saga is wearing a neutral expression, so he decides to ask another question.

"How many meetings did you have?"

"Just the one," he answers. "And even I can see how it appears odd that the director of ISP is accepting a glass of champagne."

"You think?" Saga asks.

"There was nothing to celebrate. But perhaps he was just thirsty," Salman says with a smile.

the hiding place

Penelope and Björn have no idea how long they've remained hidden within this deep crevice on the face of a cliff. They simply couldn't run any farther. Their bodies were beyond exhausted and they'd taken turns sleeping and keeping watch.

In the beginning, it seemed as if their pursuer had anticipated every move they'd made, but now the sense of his immediate presence was gone. For some time, he'd been noticeably quiet. That clammy feeling on their backs, the chilling sensation of someone running right behind them, had disappeared the moment they made the unpredictable choice of heading for the center of the forest and away from humankind and the mainland.

Penelope is uncertain if her mother's answering machine caught any of her words. *But soon someone will find Björn's boat,* she thinks. *After that, the police will start looking for us.* All they need to do is stay hidden long enough from their pursuer.

Although the rounded rock surface above is covered in moss, the crevice in the cliff is bare stone and in many spots clear water is dripping. It had been hot when they first found this spot, and they had lapped the water and decided to stay for the rest of the day. Toward evening, as the sun sank behind the shadow of the trees, they'd fallen asleep.

Dreams and dozing memories are mixed in Penelope's mind. She hears Viola play "Twinkle, Twinkle Little Star" on her tiny violin with stickers on the fingerboard to show where the fingers should go. She watches Viola put on pink eye shadow and pinch her cheeks in front of the mirror.

Penelope gasps when she wakes up.

Björn is sitting wide awake with his arms around his knees and trembling.

This is the dawn after the third night and they can't bear it any longer. They are hungry and weak. They leave their hiding place and begin to walk.

It's almost morning when Penelope and Björn come to the water's edge. The sun's red rays form glowing streaks along the long veils of clouds. The water is still in the morning calm. Two mute swans glide beside each other on the surface, paddling quietly away.

Björn extends his hand to lead Penelope to the water. His legs wobble with fatigue. He slips, then steadies himself on a rock as he gets back up. Penelope looks stiffly straight ahead with an empty gaze as she takes off her shoes, ties the laces together, and hangs them around her neck.

"Come on," Björn whispers. "We're just going swimming. Don't think about it. Just keep swimming."

Penelope wants to ask him to wait. She's not sure she can do this, but he's already wading into the water. She shivers and looks out toward the island opposite them and farther out in the archipelago.

She wades in and feels the cold water around her calves and then her thighs. The bottom under her feet is rocky and slippery but soon disappears deeper underwater. She has no time to hesitate but glides into swimming as she follows Björn.

Her arms ache and her clothes drag on her as she starts to swim to the far shore. Björn is already way ahead.

It's a major effort. Every stroke feels unendurable as every muscle cries out for rest.

The island of Kymmendö is a sandy beach on the other side. Penelope kicks with exhausted legs, fighting to stay afloat. The first rays of sun over the treetops are blinding. They hurt her eyes and she stops swimming. She's not cramping up but her arms can do no more; they're giving up. In just a few seconds, her wet clothes start to drag her below the surface before her arms obey her commands again. When she breaks the surface and gasps for air, she's terrified. Adrenaline pumps through her body and she sucks in more air, but she has lost her direction. She sees only ocean. Desperately she treads water and swirls around just keeping herself from wild screams. Finally she spots Björn's bobbing head, barely above the surface of the water, about fifty meters ahead. Penelope starts to swim again, but she's not sure she'll ever make it to the other island.

The shoes around her neck hinder her strokes and she tries to get rid of them, but the laces tangle in her crucifix. Then the thin chain of her crucifix snaps and everything sinks to the bottom of the sea.

She swims onward, feeling her heart pound in her chest. It takes a moment or so to realize she can see Björn staggering up onto land. He's looking back for her when he should be finding cover. For all they know, their pursuer could be on the north shore of Ornö Island, searching for them through his binoculars.

Penelope slows down more and more. She feels the weight and the slowness in her legs as the lactic acid spreads through them. She can barely swim at all. Björn looks fearful. He wades back into the water toward her. She is almost ready to give up, but takes one stroke after another. At last she feels the ground beneath her feet. Björn is in the water beside her and he wraps his arm around her and pulls her close and then up onto the pebble-filled sandy beach.

"Hide," Penelope whispers hoarsely.

He helps her past the beach and in among the spruce trees, until they can no longer see the ocean. They fall down on some moss and blueberries and hug, as much to warm themselves as to comfort each other.

"We can't keep this up," Penelope says through chattering teeth, her face pressed into his chest.

"We'll help each other."

Eventually they get back up, steadying each other, and walk again on stiff legs in silence as they make their way east. Twenty minutes later, they emerge on the other side of the island. The sun is high in the sky now; the air is getting warmer. Penelope stops short when she sees a tennis ball lying in the high grass of a meadow. Its greenish-yellow color is completely foreign to her. She glances up and sees the tiny red house. It's almost completely hidden behind a tight hedge of lilac bushes. The curtains in all its windows are closed and there's a hammock without pillows in the arbor; the lawn is overgrown and a broken branch from the old apple tree lies across the path of gray paving stones.

"Nobody's home," Penelope whispers.

They sneak closer, prepared to hear a dog bark or someone yell. They spy through the gaps between the curtains and continue around to the front and try the door. It's locked.

"I'll break a window," Björn says. "We have to rest."

Next to the wall, there's a clay pot holding a tiny bush with narrow pale green leaves. Penelope smells the sweet scent of lavender. She bends down to pick up one of the stones from the pot. This stone is plastic and underneath it, there's a little lid. She opens it and takes out the key before she puts the fake stone back.

Inside, the hall floor is made of pine. Penelope feels her legs shake. They're about to give way. The wallpaper is a plush medallion pattern. Penelope is so tired and hungry that the house appears unreal—a gingerbread house from a fairy tale. Covering the walls are framed photos. Björn and Penelope recognize many faces from popular Swedish television programs: Siewert Öholm, Bengt Bedrup, Kjell Lönnå, Arne Hegerfors, Magnus Härenstam, Malena Ivarsson, Jacob Dahlin.

They walk through the house, past the living room and into the kitchen. They cast a look around with worried eyes.

"We can't stay here," Penelope whispers.

Björn goes to the refrigerator and opens the door. The shelves are filled with fresh food. The house is not abandoned after all. Björn grabs some cheese, a log of salami, a quart of milk. Penelope finds a baguette and a box of breakfast cereal in the pantry. They rip the bread apart and pass the cheese back and forth between them as they eagerly bite off chunks. Björn gulps milk straight from the carton. It runs from the corners of his mouth down his throat. Penelope gnaws the salami and follows that with handfuls of breakfast cereal. Taking the milk carton from Björn, she swigs so much she chokes, then drinks some more. They grin nervously at each other, moving away from the window as they devour the food before finally slowing down.

"Let's find some warm clothes before we have to leave again," Penelope says.

As they search the house, they feel the warmth of the food expanding inside. Their blood seems to flow more freely, even as their stomachs ache.

There's a wall-size wardrobe with mirrored doors in the master bedroom. Penelope rushes forward and pushes half of the door to one side.

"What's this?"

There are gold jackets, black glittering cummerbunds, a golden tuxedo, and a medium-length fluffy fur coat. Penelope's eyebrows lift as she rummages through banana hammocks of all kinds: see-through, tiger-striped, camouflage, and stretch-fabric G-strings.

She slides open the other wardrobe door and finds simpler clothes: sweaters, jackets, pants. She searches quickly and pulls out some items. Unsteadily, she takes off her soaked clothes.

She catches sight of her naked self in the mirror. She's black and blue all over and her hair dangles in black strings. Her face is marked with scratches and bruises across her cheekbones. Blood still seeps from one of the gashes on her thigh and her hip is scraped from the fall down the cliff.

She pulls on a pair of pin-striped trousers and a T-shirt with the saying "Eat more oatmeal!" and a hoodie over that. The hoodie is so long, it hangs to her knees. She warms up enough so that her entire body wants to relax. She suddenly bursts into tears, but stops them, smudging away the tears from her cheeks. She goes into the hall to look for shoes. There she finds a pair of blue sailor boots that fit. Back in the bedroom, Björn, even though he is wet and muddy, has pulled on a pair of lilac velour pants. His feet look horrible. They are covered with dirt and wounds; he leaves bloodstains wherever he walks. He pulls on a blue T-shirt and a narrow-cut blue leather jacket with wide lapels. Penelope begins to cry again, her tears now streaming out in waves. She can no longer hold them back. It's as if all the anguish and terror are now making their way out.

"What's going on?" she sobs.

"I have no idea," Björn whispers.

"We haven't even seen his face. What does he want from us? What the hell does he want? Why is he after us? Why does he want to hurt us?"

She jerks the sleeve of her sweater across her face.

"I think," she says, "I mean . . . what if . . . what if Viola has done something bad, something stupid? You know her boyfriend, Sergei, the guy she broke up with, he must be connected to something criminal . . . maybe . . . all I know is that he worked as a bouncer."

"Penny—"

"I'm just saying, Viola, she's so . . . maybe she's done something wrong."

"No, it's not her," Björn whispers.

"What do you mean? We don't know anything! You don't have to comfort me."

"There's something I have to—"

"He . . . the man who was after us . . . maybe he just had something to tell us. No, I know, that's ridiculous . . . I mean, I don't know what I mean."

"Penny," Björn says seriously. "Everything that's happened is my fault."

He looks at her. His eyes are bloodshot, and his cheeks burn red against his pale skin.

"What are you saying now?" she asks in a deadly quiet voice.

He swallows awkwardly before he explains.

"I've done something incredibly stupid, Penny."

"What? What have you done?"

"That photograph," he answers. "It's all because of that photograph."

"Which photograph? The one of Palmcrona and Guidi?"

"That's the one. I got in touch with Palmcrona," Björn answers honestly. "I told him I wanted money for the picture, but—"

"You didn't," she whispers.

Penelope stares at him and instinctively steps backward, managing to knock over the bedside table with its water glass and clock radio.

"Penny—"

"No! No! No! Just shut the hell up!" she's screaming. "I don't get it! What the fuck are you trying to tell me? You can't mean it . . . you couldn't have . . . have you lost your mind? You tried to blackmail Palmcrona? Where was your mind?"

"Listen to me! I regretted it at once. I know it was wrong! He got the picture. I mailed him the picture."

The room falls silent. Penelope tries to comprehend what Björn has told her. Confused thoughts circle through her mind, and she fights to understand Björn's confession.

"That picture belonged to me," she says slowly. She's still trying to control her thoughts. "It might be extremely important. Maybe an incredibly important photograph. I was given it in confidence. Someone may be able to explain—"

"I needed money. I didn't want to have to sell my boat," Björn whispers. He looks like he's about to cry.

"I still don't get it—you mailed the picture to Palmcrona?"

"But I had to, Penny. I know it was yours and that it was wrong to send it, but I had to give him the picture."

"But I've got to get it back!" she says desperately. "Don't you understand? What if the person who sent it to me wants it back? This is big. It's dealing with Swedish arms exports. This isn't about your money or lack of it . . . this has nothing to do with you or me . . . this is way beyond just us, Björn."

Penelope looks at him in despair. Her voice rises until she's practically shrieking.

"This is about the lives of human beings! You betrayed me." With those words her voice falls heavily. "I am so angry with you, I could hit you. This is something I just can't deal with now."

"But, Penny, I didn't know," he whines. "How was I supposed to know? You never tell me anything. All you said was this picture would embarrass Palmcrona. You never said—"

She interrupts him. "What does that matter?"

"I only thought—"

"Shut the fuck up!" she screams. "I don't want to listen to your idiotic excuses! You tried to blackmail someone—you're a greedy little bastard! I don't know you at all. And you sure as hell don't know me!"

She falls silent and they stand facing each other. A seagull screams as it flies over the water and then there are other seagulls adding their screams as complaining echoes.

"We have to get out of here soon," Björn says without energy.

Penelope nods and then they hear the click as the outer door opens. Instinctively they move together deeper into the bedroom. They hear the heavy footsteps of a man. Björn tries to open the French doors, but they're locked. Penelope tries unlatching the windows, but she already knows it's way too late.

the winner

"What the hell are you doing here?" the man in the doorway demands in a hoarse voice.

Penelope understands immediately that he's the owner of the house—not their pursuer. He's short, broad, slightly chubby. His face seems familiar, as if he's someone she once knew.

"Are you drug addicts?" he asks with interest.

His face clicks into place. They've broken into Ossian Wallenberg's house. He was a beloved television celebrity, last on the air ten years ago. He hosted many popular variety shows: *Golden Friday, Up the Wall, Lion Evening*. And he had contests on his shows: games, and prizes, and special guests. Every *Golden Friday* ended the same way. Ossian would lift up his guest. He'd be smiling and his face would turn red. Penelope remembered that as a child, she'd once seen him pick up Mother Teresa. The delicate old woman had looked completely terrified. Ossian Wallenberg was known for his golden hair, his extravagant clothes—and his studied viciousness.

"We've been in an accident," Björn says. "We have to notify the police."

"I see," Ossian says indifferently. "I only have a cell phone here."

"That's okay. Please, we need to borrow it. We're desperate."

Ossian takes out his cell phone, looks at it, and then closes it again.

"What are you doing?" Penelope practically yells.

"I do whatever I want to do," Ossian replies.

"Look, we really need to borrow your phone," she says.

"Then you'll need my PIN number." Ossian smiles.

"What game are you playing?"

Ossian leans on the doorjamb and observes them for a while.

"Just think, a pair of drug addicts have found their way to little old me."

"We're not—"

"No one cares," says Ossian.

"Let's go," Penelope tells Björn.

But Björn seems incapable of moving. His cheeks and lips are white and he supports himself with one hand on the wall.

"Sorry that we broke into your house," he says. "We'll pay for everything we took. But really, we have to use your phone right now. Like she said, it's a desperate situation—"

"And what's your name?" Ossian interrupts, smiling.

"Björn."

"You're looking handsome in my jacket, Björn, but why not the tie as well? I've got a tie that matches the suit perfectly."

Ossian walks to his wardrobe and takes out a blue leather tie. Playing along, Björn submits to having it tied around his neck.

"You should call the police!" Penelope says. "Tell them that two drug addicts have broken into your house and you caught them in the act."

"That's no fun," Ossian replies.

"So what do you want?" Penelope asks desperately.

Ossian steps back and studies his intruders.

"I don't like her," he says to Björn. "But you, on the other hand, you have style. My jacket really looks good on you. Let her keep that ugly sweater, right? She looks like Helge the Owl. She doesn't even look Swedish. She looks like a—"

"Cut it out," Björn says.

Ossian walks close to Björn and shakes his finger in his face.

"Be good," he teases.

"I know who you are," Penelope says.

"I'm glad," Ossian says with a smile.

Björn looks at her and then back at Ossian. Penelope collapses onto the edge of the bed and tries to breathe calmly.

"Wait a minute," Ossian says. "I know you, too . . . I've seen you on TV. I recognize you."

"I've been on some political debates—"

"And now you're dead." Ossian smiles.

Her entire body tenses. What strange words. She tries to understand what he's talking about while she looks for a way to escape. Now Björn slides down along the wall to the floor, completely white and unable to say a word.

"If you don't want to help us," Penelope says, "then we'll just leave and find someone who will."

"Of course I want to help you! Of course!"

Ossian walks out into the hallway and returns with a grocery bag from which he takes a carton of cigarettes and an evening newspaper. He tosses the paper on the bed and leaves for the kitchen with the cigarettes. On the front page, Penelope sees a picture of herself, a larger picture of Viola, and one of Björn. Over Viola's picture is the word DEAD and over their pictures is the word MISSING.

BOAT DRAMA—THREE FEARED DEAD! screams the headline.

Penelope can see her mother in her mind's eye: terrified and broken by sorrow—perhaps completely frozen, her arms wrapped around her body, just as she'd done when they had been arrested.

The floor creaks as Ossian returns.

"Let's play a game!"

"What are you talking about?"

"I'm really in the mood for a game! A competition!"

"A competition?" Björn whispers uncertainly.

"You can't tell me that you don't know what a competition is?"

"Of course, but—"

Penelope studies Ossian and realizes they're in a precarious position. No one knows that they're still alive. He could even decide to kill them, since everyone else believes they're already dead.

"He's testing his power over us," Penelope says.

"Will you hand over your phone and your PIN number if we play?" asks Björn.

"Only if you win," Ossian answers, and smiles at them with glittering eyes.

"What happens if we lose?" asks Penelope.

the messenger

Axel Riessen walks to his kitchen window and looks out over the rose-bushes, past the iron fence, down the street, and toward the wide staircase of Engelbrekt Church.

The instant he'd signed his name to the employment contract, he'd taken over all of the late Carl Palmcrona's duties and responsibilities.

It felt very good, it felt right. *First thing I do,* he told himself, *is begin a collaboration with the United Nations as regards the Convention on the Prohibition of Chemical Weapons.*

He smiles to himself and marvels at how life can take strange turns. Then he remembers Beverly. His stomach flutters with worry. One time she'd told him that she was going to the store, but four hours later, she still hadn't returned. He'd gone out to search for her. He'd finally found her sitting in a wheelbarrow outside of the Observatory Museum. She was confused, smelled like alcohol, and her underwear was missing. Someone had stuck gum in her hair.

She said she'd run into some boys in the park.

"They were throwing stones at an injured dove," Beverly explained. "So I thought that I'd give them my money so they'd stop. But I only had twelve crowns. That wasn't enough. They wanted me to do something else instead. They told me they would stomp the dove to death if I didn't."

She became quiet and tears came into her eyes.

"I didn't want to do it, but I felt so sorry for the dove."

Axel takes out his cell phone and calls Beverly's number.

As the signal roams, he looks down the road, past the building that once housed the Chinese embassy, and down to the dark house where the Catholic network Opus Dei has its main headquarters.

His own building is an enormous mansion he and his brother, Robert, share. It is situated on Bragevägen in the middle of Lärkstaden, an exclusive district between Östermalm and Vasastan. All the houses there look alike, as if they were children produced from the same family.

The Riessen residence has two apartments, one on each side. Each one is three stories tall and is completely separate from the other.

Their father, Erloff Riessen, has been dead for twenty years. He was the Swedish ambassador to France and then England, while his brother, Torleif Riessen, had been a famous pianist who'd performed at Symphony Hall in Boston and the Grosser Musikvereinssaal in Vienna. The noble house of Riessen always ran to two professions, diplomats and classical musicians, and the two were strangely similar: they demanded absolute obedience and submission.

The father and mother, Erloff and Alice Riessen, decided on a logical agreement: from childhood Axel should devote himself to music while his younger brother, Robert, would be trained in his father's profession as a diplomat. This arrangement was turned upside down when Axel made the greatest mistake of his life. He was seventeen years old when he was forced to leave the music profession. Instead, he was sent to a military academy while Robert now trained as the family musician. Axel accepted his punishment, even thought it was fair, and since that day, he vowed never to pick up the violin again.

Axel's mother never again spoke with him.

After nine rings, Beverly answers the phone, coughing.

"Hello?"

"Where are you?" Axel demands.

"I'm—"

She must have turned her face from the receiver because he couldn't understand her next words.

"I can't hear you," he says, even more frightened. His voice is sharp and forced.

"Are you angry with me?"

"Just tell me where you are," he pleads.

"You're going on and on!" she says and laughs. "I'm here in my apartment, of course. Are you all right?"

"I was just worried."

"Silly, I was just about to watch a show on Princess Victoria."

She hangs up and he feels that ongoing worry. There is a vague tone to her voice.

He looks at the phone and wonders if he should dial her again. He jumps when the phone starts to ring.

"Riessen."

"Jörgen Grünlicht here."

"Hello," Axel says with a little surprise in his voice.

"How was your meeting with the team?"

"It was fairly fruitful," Axel replies.

"You made Kenya the priority, I hope."

"As well as the final user certificate from the Netherlands," Axel says. "There was a lot on the table and I'm waiting to decide where I stand. I need to research a little more—"

"But Kenya," Grünlicht says. "Have you signed the export form yet? Pontus Salman is on my back wondering why it's still held up. You understand that this is a damned big piece of business already way behind schedule. ISP had given them a positive preliminary decision and they've gone ahead with production, a damned large shipment already sent from Trollhättan to the docks in Gothenburg. The owner is sending a container ship from Panama tomorrow. They'll unload their cargo during the day and then the next day they can load the ammunition."

"Jörgen, I understand all this. I've gone over the paperwork and sure . . . I'll sign it, but I've just started this job and I need to be thorough."

"I, myself, went through the whole business," Jörgen says in a brusque manner. "There's nothing unclear about it."

"No, but—"

"Where are you now?"

"I'm at home," Axel says, even more mystified.

"I'll send the paperwork by messenger," Jörgen says shortly. "The messenger will wait while you sign it. Then we won't lose any more time."

"That's not really necessary. I'll look at it tomorrow," Axel protests.

Twenty minutes later, Axel goes to the door at the persistent ring of the messenger sent by Jörgen Grünlicht. He's greatly troubled by Grünlicht's obstinacy. On the other hand, there doesn't seem to be any reason to delay this piece of business.

the.signature

Axel opens the door and greets the bike messenger. The warm evening air sweeps into the house along with the pounding music from the end-of-the-year party at the School of Architecture.

Axel takes the folder and yet feels awkward about signing the contract in front of the messenger. He feels he would look like he's caving in under a bit of pressure.

"Just a minute," he says and gestures for the messenger to wait in the hallway.

Axel walks through his side of the house, through the library, and into the kitchen, past its granite counters, the glossy black cabinets, and up to the double-door refrigerator with its ice machine. He takes out a mini-bottle of mineral water and drinks straight from it as he loosens his tie. He sits on a high stool next to the bar counter and opens the folder.

Everything is neat, tidy, and appears to be in order. Every appendix is in its proper place: the opinion of the Export Control Committee, the classification, the preliminary decision, the copies for the Foreign Office, and the tender notice. He scans the document concerning export permission and flips to the line where the general director for the National Inspectorate of Strategic Products is supposed to sign his name.

A chill shivers through his body.

This is really big business. It appears to be a routine matter only delayed by the tragic suicide of Carl Palmcrona, but it is clear that it seriously affects his country's trade balance. He understands that Pontus Salman's situation is so precarious that this delay might drive his company under if drawn out much longer.

But while he understands this, Axel also understands that he is being pressured to approve export of ammunition to Kenya without being given the opportunity to personally weigh the decision.

Axel makes a decision and immediately feels much better.

He'll devote his attention to this matter over the next few days—and only then will he sign the approval.

He *will* sign, he's pretty sure of that, but he can't sign now. He doesn't care if they get angry or upset. He is the person who must make the decision: he is now the general director for the National Inspectorate of Strategic Products.

He doodles a smiley face and draws a one-word dialogue bubble on the signature line.

Axel returns to the hall wearing a stern expression and hands the folder back to the messenger. Then he goes upstairs and into the salon. He's wondering if Beverly is really upstairs or if she didn't dare tell him that she had sneaked out.

What if she sneaks out and then disappears?

Axel picks up a remote for his music system and selects a mix of David Bowie's earliest work. His music system looks like a shiny sheet of glass. It's wireless and the speakers are completely invisible and set into the walls.

He goes to the elaborate liquor cabinet, opens its embossed doors, and considers the gleaming bottles. He hesitates before he picks up a numbered whiskey bottle of Hazelburn from the Springbank Distillery, one located in Scotland's Campbeltown region. Axel once visited the area and had marveled at the hundred-year-old barrels. They were well worn, painted in clear red, and still in use. He pulls out the cork and breathes in the scent of the whiskey: deep earth and dark like a thunderstorm. Then he pushes in the cork again and slowly returns the bottle to the cabinet. The music system is playing a song from *Hunky Dory*. David Bowie sings:

But her friend is nowhere to be seen.
Now she walks through her sunken dream,
To the seat with the clearest view,
And she's hooked to the silver screen.

The door to his brother's apartment slams shut. Axel looks out
through the enormous panorama windows with their view of the overgrown garden. He wonders if Robert is going to stop by and at the same
moment, he hears the knock on his door.

"Come in," Axel calls out.

Robert marches in looking disturbed.

"I realize that you play that crap in order to drive me crazy, but—"

Axel smiles and starts to sing along:

Take a look at the Lawman,
Beating up the wrong guy.
Oh man! Wonder if he'll ever know:
He's in the bestselling show . . .

Robert does a few dance steps and walks over to the open liquor
cabinet. He takes a look at the bottles.

"Go ahead and help yourself," Axel says drily.

"Could you take a look at my Strosser—can I turn off the music for a
moment?"

Axel shrugs. Robert hits STOP.

"The Strosser is finished?"

"I was up all night," Robert says with a broad smile. "I attached the
strings early this morning."

There's a moment of silence between them. A long time ago, their
mother had been adamant that Axel would be a famous violinist. Alice
Riessen had been a professional musician and played for ten years as
second violin in the Stockholm Opera's chamber music orchestra. She'd
openly favored her firstborn son.

Everything fell apart when Axel, at the Royal College of Music, had
become one of the three finalists in the Johan Fredrik Berwald Competition for young soloists. It would have been a straight shot from there
into the world's elite.

But after the competition, Axel had entered the Military Academy in Karlberg. Robert had enrolled in the Royal Swedish Academy of Music. He never became a star violinist. On the other hand, he plays in a chamber orchestra and now owns a renowned atelier where he takes orders for stringed instruments from around the world.

"Show me your violin," Axel says after a while.

Robert nods and goes to get the instrument. It's a beautiful violin with a fiery-red lacquer and a bottom of tiger-striped maple.

He stands before his brother and begins to play a trembling strain from a Béla Bartók piece inspired by a journey through the Hungarian countryside. Axel has always liked Bartók, who as an open opponent of Nazism was forced to flee his native land. Axel admires Bartók's ability to be deeply thoughtful yet able to create short bursts of pure joy. *Or to write melancholy folk music amid the ruins of a great catastrophe*, Axel thinks as Robert finishes the piece.

"It sounds very good," Axel says. "But you should move the sound post slightly as there's a dead spot that—"

Robert's face shuts down.

"Daniel Strosser said that he wanted . . . a sound like this," Robert says. "He wants the violin to sound like a young Birgit Nilsson."

"Then you should absolutely move the sound post," Axel says with a smile.

"You don't understand! I just wanted you to—"

"Otherwise it's an excellent instrument," Axel hurries to add.

"You hear the sound—dry and sharp and—"

"I'm not saying it's a bad violin," Axel continues impassively. "I'm only saying that there's a spot in the sound that is not alive—"

"Alive? This is a Bartók performer buying this violin," Robert says. "We're talking about Bartók, and that's not the same thing as David Bowie."

"Maybe I heard wrong," Axel responds quietly.

Robert opens his mouth to answer when there's a knock on the door. It's Robert's wife, Anette.

She opens the door and smiles when she sees Robert holding his violin.

"So you were trying out the Strosser?" she asks expectantly.

"Yes," Robert says harshly. "But Axel doesn't like it."

"That's not true," Axel says. "I'm sure his customer will be perfectly satisfied. What I was saying might just be a figment of my imagination—"

"Oh, Robert, don't listen to him," Anette says with irritation. "What does he know?"

Robert now just wants to leave and take his wife with him to avoid a scene, but she turns to Axel.

"Confess that you just imagined a fault," she demands.

"There is no fault in it. Just an adjustment of the sound post that—"

"And when was the last time you played? Thirty years ago? Forty? You were nothing more than a child then. You owe Robert an apology."

"Let it go," Robert says.

"Say you're sorry," Anette demands.

"All right. I'm sorry," Axel says. He feels his cheeks flush.

"You don't want Robert to have the fame his new violin deserves."

"I'm sorry."

Axel turns his stereo back on very loud. *Ziggy Stardust* drops into rotation. The music sounds like two guitars that haven't been tuned properly and a singer who is searching for the right note: *Goodbye love, goodbye love . . .*

Anette mutters something more about Axel's lack of talent, but Robert tells her to just shut up as he pulls her out of the room. Axel raises the volume even higher and the drums and bass guitar turn the music around: *Didn't know what time it was and the lights were low oh oh. I leaned back on my radio oh oh.*

Axel shuts his eyes and feels how they burn in the dark. He is already very tired. There are times when he can sleep for half an hour and at other times he can't sleep at all, even when Beverly is in bed next to him. At those times, he wraps himself in a blanket and goes to sit on the glassed-in veranda with its view of the beautiful old trees in the garden. He will sit there until the dampened light of dawn appears. Of course, Axel understands completely what is wrong with him, and he closes his eyes and thinks back again to the day when his whole life changed.

54

Penelope and Björn study each other with tired, serious eyes. Through the closed door, they can hear Ossian Wallenberg singing "Do You Want to See a Star?" like Zarah Leander as he's rearranging the furniture.

"We can take him on," Penelope whispers.

"Maybe so."

"We've got to try."

"And what then? Are we going to torture him to get his PIN number?"

"I think he'll give it to us once we're in control," Penelope says.

"What if he doesn't?"

She sways from exhaustion as she walks to the window and begins to loosen the hooks. Her fingers are tender and swollen. Her fingernails are broken and embedded with dirt and clay and scabs.

"Maybe we can head farther up the beach," she says.

"Good," he says. "Go ahead."

"I'm not going to leave you behind."

"I can't keep going, Penny," he says, and he doesn't look at her. "My feet—I can't run anymore. At the most, maybe I could walk for another half hour."

"I'll help you."

"Maybe there's no one else with a phone on the whole island. We don't know. We haven't the slightest idea."

"I don't want to be part of his disgusting—"

"Penny, we have to contact the police. We have no choice: we have to use his phone."

Ossian throws open the door with a grin. He's wearing a leopard-patterned jacket with only a loincloth beneath. Ceremoniously he leads them to an enormous sofa. The curtains are still closed and he's moved the other furniture to the side to open a big space in the living room for him to move freely. The little man steps into the spotlight formed by two floor lamps, stops, and turns.

"Ladies and gentlemen! Time flies when you have fun on a Friday evening!" he announces, winking. "We've reached the competition segment of our show and tonight we welcome this evening's special guest, known from her appearances on television. She's a shitty communist and she has an underage lover. This is a truly mismatched couple, if you ask me. A hag and a young man with a well-sculptured torso."

Ossian winks again, and flexes his arm for the imaginary camera.

"Everybody ready?" he calls, jogging in place. "Do you have your approval buttons? I present: Truth or Consequences! Ossian challenges— the Hag and the Cutie!"

He spins an empty bottle on the floor. It rotates a few times and points to Björn.

"Cutie!" Ossian calls, smiling. "Cutie is the first man to play! Here's the question! Are you ready to tell the whole truth and nothing but the truth?"

"Absolutely," Björn says with a sigh.

A drop of sweat falls from the tip of Ossian's nose as he opens an envelope and reads out loud, "Who do you think about when you're making love to the Hag?"

"Very funny," says Penelope.

"Will you give me the phone if I answer?" asks Björn.

Ossian pouts like a child and shakes his head.

"No, but if our audience believes you, you'll get the first digit of the PIN number."

"And if I choose Consequence?"

"You'll compete with me and the audience will decide," Ossian says. "Time is running out. Tick, tock, tick, tock. Five, four, three, two . . ."

Penelope watches Björn in the wash of the strong lamplight: his dirty face, his stubble, his greasy hair. His nostrils dark with dried blood and his eyes so exhausted and bloodshot.

"I think about Penelope when we have sex," Björn says.

Ossian boos and makes a disgusted grimace as he jogs in the lamplight.

"You're supposed to tell the truth," he shrieks. "That's not even close! No one in the audience would ever believe that you think about the Hag when you're sleeping with her. That's one, two, three negative points for the Cutie!"

He spins the bottle again and it stops almost at once, pointed toward Penelope.

"Oh, oh, oh!" Ossian yells. "A special case! What does this mean? That's right! Consequence directly! Direct to go! I'll open the box and see what the Hippo has to say!"

Ossian picks up from the table a tiny hippopotamus made of dark lacquered wood. He holds it to his ear as if he's listening and he nods.

"You mean the Hag?" he asks. He listens again. "I understand, Mr. Hippo! Yes indeed, thank you so very much!"

Ossian replaces the hippopotamus and turns to Penelope with a smile.

"The Hag will compete with Ossian! The area is Striptease! If you can turn on the audience better than Ossian can, you'll get all the numbers of the PIN code—otherwise the Cutie will have to kick you in the ass as hard as he can!"

Ossian jumps up and down in front of his music system and hits a button so that the song "Teach Me Tiger" comes on.

"One time I lost this competition against Loa Falkman," Ossian says in a stage whisper while he swings his hips in time to the music.

Penelope gets up from the sofa and takes a step forward. She stands there wearing sailor boots, the pin-striped trousers, and the hoodie.

"So you just want me to take off my clothes," Penelope says. "Is that what this is all about? You just want to see me naked?"

Ossian stops singing and his mouth puckers in disappointment. He looks at her coldly before he replies.

"Do you believe I'd ever be interested in looking at a refugee whore's tiny cunt? That's easy enough to order on the Internet."

Ossian hits her hard. She sways and almost falls, but manages to keep her balance.

"You need to be polite when you're talking to me," he says seriously.

"All right," she mumbles.

A funny little smile distorts his mouth as he explains.

"I'm someone who often competes with celebrities from television . . . and I've seen you there, though I hurried to change the channel."

She looks at his excited, flushed face.

"You're not going to give us the phone, are you?"

"I promise I will. Rules are rules. You'll get it after I get what I want."

"You know we need help and you're using that to—"

"Yes, of course, I'm using it!" he screams.

"All right, then, let's say we strip for a while and then I get the phone."

Penelope turns away from Ossian and pulls off the sweater and T-shirt. Her scrapes and wounds are discolorations in the strong light. Her body is covered in bruises and dried dirt. She turns around but keeps her arms over her breasts.

Björn claps and whistles although he looks sad.

Ossian's face is sweaty, staring at Penelope. Then he stands in the lamplight in front of Björn. He rolls his hips and then whips off the loincloth and twirls it around. He lets it run between his legs before he throws it at Björn. Ossian kisses the air in front of Björn and makes an "I'll call you" gesture.

Björn claps and whistles louder and keeps clapping as he sees Penelope edging near the fireplace to pick up the iron poker from its rack. The ash shovel next to it sways and clangs slightly against the large tongs.

Ossian is dancing in glittery gold underwear.

Penelope holds the poker with both hands as she walks up behind Ossian, who is rolling his hips at Björn.

"Get on your knees, Cutie," Ossian whispers. "Get down and give it to me."

Savagely Penelope brings up the heavy poker between his legs as hard as she can. There's a loud smack and Ossian falls, screaming with an unearthly sound. He holds himself and writhes around on the floor, howling. Penelope walks over to the music system and gives it four vicious strokes, smashing it to bits while the music squeals to a stop.

Ossian is panting and moaning as he lies on the floor. Penelope walks over to him and he squints up at her with fearful eyes. She stands there looking impassively down. The heavy poker sways slightly in her right hand.

Penelope says calmly, "Mr. Hippo tells me that you'll give me the phone and the PIN number right now."

the maritime police

It's extremely humid in Ossian Wallenberg's summerhouse. Björn keeps getting up from a chair to look out the window at the ocean and the dock. Penelope is on the sofa with the phone in her hand, waiting for the police to call her back. They had taken her emergency call and had promised to call back once the maritime police boat got closer. Ossian is sitting in an armchair with a large whiskey glass in front of him. He watches them. He's taken painkillers and says, depressed, that he'll live.

Penelope keeps looking at the phone and notices that the signal is weaker but still strong enough to take a call. Anytime now they should be returning her call. She leans back. The humidity is suffocating. The T-shirt she's wearing is damp with sweat. She closes her eyes and begins to think about the time she was in Darfur: the oppressive heat as she traveled to Kubbum by bus in order to join Jane Oduya and her work with Action Contre la Faim.

She'd been on her way to the barracks, which was the organization's administration center, when she stopped. She'd glimpsed some children playing a strange game. It looked like they were putting clay figures in the road so that the passing vehicles would crush them. She walked closer. They laughed out loud whenever one of their clay figures was smashed.

"I killed another one! This one is an old man!"

"I killed another Fur!"

One of the children ran into the road and put out two clay figures. One was large and one was small. As a cart rolled past, the little one was crushed beneath its wheels.

"The kid died! That whore kid died!"

Penelope walked over to the children and asked them what they were doing. But they didn't answer, just ran away instead. Penelope stared down at the clay fragments left on the burnt-orange dirt road.

The name Fur had been given to the people in the area of Darfur. This ancient African tribe was now being slaughtered because of the Janjaweed terror.

For centuries the African people had been farmers, and there had always been conflict between the farmers and the remaining nomadic tribes; that conflict seemed to have gone on since the beginning of time. But now oil had been discovered under the ground in Darfur, and the African tribes that farmed this soil seemingly forever were being shoved aside. Oil production drove everything—including the genocide. On paper, the old civil war was over, but the Janjaweed continued systematic raids. They would kill the men, rape the women, and then burn down the village.

Penelope watched the Arab children run away, and then she gathered up the remaining clay figures. Someone called out "Penny! Penny!"

She jumped, fearful, but then turned to see Jane Oduya standing and waving to her. Jane was fat and short. She wore faded jeans and a yellow jacket. Penelope could hardly recognize her. Her face had aged so much in just a few short years.

"Jane!"

They hugged each other tightly.

"Don't talk to those children," Jane said. "They're like so many others. They hate us because we are black. I don't understand it. They just hate black skin."

Jane and Penelope walked toward the refugee camp. The odor of burned milk overlay the stench of latrines. The blue plastic UN tarps were everywhere and used for everything: curtains, windshields, blankets. Hundreds of the Red Cross's white tents shook in the wind coming across the open land.

Penelope followed Jane into the large hospital tent. Jane cast a glance through the plastic window to the surgical unit.

"My nurses have become good surgeons," she said. "They can now perform amputations and the easy operations on their own."

Two thin boys, about thirteen years old, brought in a large box with material for dressing wounds and set it down carefully. As they approached Jane, she thanked them and asked them to assist the women who were just arriving. The women needed water to wash their wounds.

The boys were soon back with water in two large plastic jugs.

"They used to belong to the Arab militia, but everything is quiet now. Without ammunition and weapons parts, equilibrium has set in. People have time on their hands and some have decided to help out here. We have a school for boys, many of whom used to be part of the militia."

A woman on a cot moaned. Jane went to her and stroked her face. She didn't seem to be more than fifteen years old but was greatly pregnant. One of her feet had been amputated.

An African man of about thirty, with a beautiful face and muscular shoulders, hurried over to Jane with a small white bottle.

"Thirty new doses of antibiotics!"

"Are you sure?"

He nodded, beaming.

"Good work!"

"I'm going to go and lean on Ross some more. He said that we might get a box of blood-pressure cuffs this week."

"This is Grey," Jane said. "He's actually a teacher, but I couldn't keep going without him."

Penelope extended her hand and met the man's laughing eyes.

"Penelope Fernandez."

"Tarzan," he replied as he gave her a gentle handshake.

"He wanted to be called Tarzan the minute he came here," said Jane, laughing.

"Tarzan and Jane." He smiled. "I'm her Tarzan."

"I finally agreed to let him call himself Greystoke," Jane said. "Everyone found Greystoke too hard to pronounce, however, so now he has to be content with the name Grey."

A truck honked outside the tent. They stepped quickly out. Reddish dust, kicked up by the tires, swirled in the air. On the bed of the truck lay seven wounded men. They'd been shot in a village farther west when a firefight broke out over a well.

Surgery took up the rest of the day. One of the men died. At one point, Grey stopped Penelope and held out a water bottle to her. Penelope shook her head, but he smiled calmly and said, "You have time to drink." She thanked him, drank the water, then helped him lift one of the wounded men onto a cot.

That evening, Penelope and Jane sat on the veranda of one of the living quarters of the barracks. The day had exhausted them. They'd eaten a late dinner. It was still fairly hot. They chatted and watched the road between the houses and the tents, watched the people going about the last chores of the day before nightfall.

Deep night brought an uneasy quiet. At first, Penelope could hear people going to bed: the rustling near the latrines and the small, almost silent movements in the darkness. Soon everything was totally quiet. Not even the sound of a crying baby.

"Everyone is still afraid that the Janjaweed will pass through here," Jane said as she collected the plates.

They went inside, locked the door, and barricaded it. They said good night, and Penelope headed to the guest room farthest down the hallway.

Two hours later, she woke with a jerk. She'd fallen asleep, fully dressed, on the guest bed. She lay still, listening to the powerful night, not remembering what had awakened her. Her heart had begun to calm when she suddenly heard a scream outside. Penelope stood to one side of the barred window to look out into the night. The moon shone down over the road. She could hear angry voices. Three teenage boys walked in the middle of the street; without a doubt, they belonged to the Janjaweed militia. One had a pistol. Penelope grasped that they'd been yelling about killing slaves, about an old African man who usually grilled sweet potatoes and sold them for two dinars apiece while sitting on his blanket outside the UN storehouse.

The boys had gone up to the old man and spat in his face. Then the thin boy had raised his pistol and shot the old man in the face. The *bang* had reverberated eerily between the buildings. That's what had jarred Penelope from her sleep. The boys had yelled, grabbed up some sweet potatoes, and eaten them while they kicked the rest into the dust beside the dead man.

They kept sauntering along the road, looking around. Then they headed for the barracks where Penelope and Jane lived. Penelope held her breath as she listened to them thump around the veranda, yelling excitedly as they banged on the door.

Penelope gasps for breath and opens her eyes. She must have fallen asleep on Ossian Wallenberg's sofa.

Thunder rumbles in the background. The skies have turned dark.

Björn is standing at the window. Ossian is sipping his whiskey.

Penelope looks at the phone—no one has called.

The maritime police should have been here by now.

The claps of thunder are approaching. The ceiling light goes out and the fan in the kitchen stops. The power is out. The patter of rain starts gently on the roof and shutters, then increases until it seems the skies simply burst open and let the rain pour down.

All cell-phone coverage disappears.

Lightning flashes and lights the room for a second. A crash of thunder follows it.

Penelope leans back to listen to the rain. She feels the cooler air streaming inside through the windows and starts to doze off again when she hears Björn say something.

"What?" she asks.

"A police boat," he repeats. "I see a police boat."

Penelope quickly leaps up and looks out. The seawater seems to boil from the massive downpour. The large, official-looking launch is already close and heading for the dock. Penelope glances at the phone. No reception yet.

"Hurry up," Björn says.

He tries to force the key in the lock of the French door. His hands are shaking. The police launch glides in next to the dock and blares a warning note.

"It doesn't work," Björn says. "This is the wrong key."

"Oh, dear, oh, dear," Ossian smirks. He takes out his key chain. "Why don't you try this one instead."

Björn fumbles with the door key, gets it into the lock, turns it, and hears the tumblers click open.

It's hard to see the police launch through the rain. It has already started to move away from the dock when Björn manages to open the door.

"Björn!" Penelope yells.

They can hear the motor thud and white water churns up behind the launch. Björn waves wildly and runs through the rain as fast as he can down the gravel pathway to the dock.

"Up here!" he yells. "We're over here!"

Björn doesn't even notice how drenched he's getting as he races down onto the dock. There is an underwater thud as the launch reverses its engines. Björn can barely make out the figure of a police officer in the wheelhouse. A new flash of lightning brightens the sky. It looks like the police officer is talking into his sea-to-shore radio. Rain pounds down on the roof of the launch and waves beat against the beach. Björn waves both arms. The launch turns back and bumps gently leeward-side against the dock.

Björn grabs onto the wet ladder and climbs aboard onto the foredeck, then clatters down a set of stairs to a metal door. The launch rocks in a swell. Björn staggers a second and then opens the door.

A sweet metallic smell fills the wheelhouse—oil and sweat.

The first thing Björn spots is a police officer, tanned from his work, lying on the floor with a bullet hole between eyes that are wide open. The pool of blood beneath him has dried almost black. Björn gasps, stunned, and looks around at a normal-looking clutter of belongings, magazines, raincoats. He hears a voice outside. It's Ossian: his voice carrying over the pounding engine. He's limping along the gravel pathway, a yellow umbrella over his head. Björn's blood pounds in his head. He's made a mistake. This is a trap. He fumbles for the door handle, dazedly seeing the splatter of blood on the inside of the windshield. The stairs to the sleeping quarters behind him creak and Björn fatally freezes, staring back at his nemesis. His pursuer wears a uniform. His face is alert, even curious. It's already much too late to flee, but Björn spots a screwdriver from above the instrument panel as a last-resort defense. The man climbs up casually, holding on to the railing, and blinks in the stronger light. He looks through the windshield to the beach. The rain pounds down. Björn stabs for his heart and stumbles, suddenly not comprehending what has just happened. The man's blow has numbed his arm from the shoulder down. It feels as if his arm no longer exists. The screwdriver clatters uselessly down and rolls behind an aluminum toolbox. The man now holds on to Björn's useless arm and pulls him forward. Then another blow folds Björn's body in on itself and he kicks Björn's feet out from under him. The killer guides his fall so that his face takes the full force of his momentum against the footrest at the steering wheel. Björn's neck is snapped by the collision. He feels nothing at all but does see strange sparks—small lights that jump about in darkness and then slow down and become more and more pleasant to watch. A quiver passes over his face, which he does not feel, and then he is dead.

the helicopter

Penelope stands at the window. The skies flash bright from lightning and thunder rolls over the sea. The rain pours down. Björn has disappeared into the wheelhouse of the police launch. She watches Ossian limp down toward the water, a yellow umbrella over his head. The metal door of the wheelhouse opens and a uniformed police officer steps out onto the foredeck, hops onto the dock, and ties up the boat.

Not until the policeman begins to walk up the gravel path does Penelope see who it is.

Her pursuer does not bother to answer Ossian's greeting. His left hand snakes out to clutch Ossian under the chin.

Penelope's phone drops from her hand unnoticed.

With professional ease, the man in uniform turns Ossian's face to one side, slides a dagger into his own right hand, turns Ossian's face farther awry, and then, in seconds, sends the dagger into Ossian's neck right above the atlas vertebra and directly into the brain stem. The yellow umbrella falls to the ground and rolls down the slope. Ossian is dead before his body touches the earth.

The man strides closer. A pale flicker of lightning illuminates his face and Penelope meets his eyes. Before the darkness falls again, she can see the worried expression on his face, his exhausted, sad eyes, and his mouth, disfigured by a deep scar. The thunder rolls. The man never pauses. Penelope stands by the window, absolutely paralyzed. Her breaths come quick, but she can't flee.

The rain batters the window frames and the glass panes. The world outside seems far away. Suddenly the man is silhouetted by a bright yellow light that seems to brighten the dock, the water, even the sky. As if a massive oak tree had sprouted from the boat behind him, a column of fire shoots up with a bellow. Metal scraps fly into the air. The cloud of fire grows and pulsates with an eerie, internal flickering. Its heat sets nearby brush, even the dock, afire. The explosion pounds against the house.

With shattered glass falling around her, Penelope is finally able to act. She whirls around, running so fast she just races up and over the sofa and down the hallway with all its signed portraits. Out the back door and over the ragged lawn. She slips but keeps going, through the pounding rain along the trampled path, around the grove of birches, and out onto a meadow. A family with children—all dressed in bright yellow rain gear, life vests, and carrying fishing poles—is braving the downpour. Penelope runs straight between them and down to the sandy beach. She's out of breath and feels she might faint. She has to stop, and yet she can't. Instead, she drops down behind a small wheelbarrow and vomits into the nettles. She whispers the Lord's Prayer. Thunder rumbles from far away. Shakily she rises to a crouch, wiping the rain from her face with her sleeve, to peer back across the meadow. The man is rounding the birch grove. He pauses next to the family group and they immediately point in her direction. She ducks, creeps backward, sliding down the shallow cliff to run close to the water. Her footsteps leave a white track behind her in the churned-up wet sand. A long pontoon bridge seems to offer the only distance she can reach, and she runs along it as far as she can. She hears the thud of helicopter blades and keeps on running. It takes only a quick glance to see her pursuer heading straight for her. At the far end of the bridge, a man is being winched down from the sky, from a rescue helicopter. He lands there, waiting for her. The water around him is whipped up in concentric circles from the wash of the helicopter's blades. Penelope runs straight to him. Quickly he fastens a harness to her, shouting instructions, and then circles his hand in a gesture to the aircraft above them. They are lifted free from the bridge, swept to one side close over the water as the line lifts them toward the helicopter. Penelope's view of the beach is almost immediately blocked by the encroaching spruce trees, but just before that moment, she sees her pursuer go down on one knee. He's setting down a black backpack and swiftly assembling something. He's out of her sight then; she sees only the tight tops of trees and the turbulent surface of the sea.

A short bang. She hears a crash overhead. The cable jerks and Penelope's stomach turns over as the man cabled to her yells something to the helicopter pilot. The helicopter swerves crazily. Horror sweeps over Penelope. The pilot has been shot. Instinctively, with no thought at all, she jerks at the security harness, wriggles free, and simply drops away.

She can see the helicopter stall in the air, tip to one side, and flip over. The cable with her rescuer still dangling on it is entangled in the large rotor. She plunges through the air, unable to look away. The machine rattles deafeningly, and, with a two-part bang, the enormous rotor blades are ripped from the axle. Penelope falls about twenty meters before she smacks into the water. She sinks down deep, semiconscious with the impact and the cold. It is a long time before she's able to move. Reaching the surface, her lungs react automatically and her body takes a deep breath. Almost without sight, she dully looks around. Then she begins to swim away from the island and out into the open sea.

thunderstorm

Joona Linna and Saga Bauer departed quietly from Silencia Defense after their short meeting with Pontus Salman.

Pontus Salman had ruined their trap by immediately identifying himself and pinpointing the date: 2008 in a concert hall in Frankfurt.

There had been discussion of a shipment of ammunition to Sudan, he'd explained, a plan well advanced before it was broken off in the spring of 2009. Salman seemed to assume that Joona and Saga were well aware of what had happened then.

He'd added that this had been the only meeting concerning Sudan and that now, of course, any continued business arrangements were out of the question.

"What was he talking about?" Joona asks. "Do you know what happened then?"

Before they've even swung out onto Nynäshamn, Saga has phoned Simon Lawrence at Säpo.

"I presume you're not calling me for a date," Simon says humorously.

"You're an expert on North Africa. What happened in Sudan in the spring of 2009?" Saga says.

"What's the context?"

"For some reason, after that time, Sweden can no longer export weapons to Sudan."

"Don't you read the newspapers?"

"Of course," she answers with gritted teeth.

"In March 2009, the International Criminal Court in The Hague indicted Sudan's president, Omar al-Bashir."

"An arrest warrant for the president?"

"That's right."

"That's big."

"The indictment includes the president's direct involvement in orders for plundering, rape, forced displacement, torture, murder, and genocide for all three ethnic groups in Darfur."

"Oh."

Simon Lawrence goes on to give Saga a short history lesson about events in Sudan before she finally hangs up the phone.

"So what's it all about?" Joona asks.

"The International Criminal Court in The Hague has an arrest warrant out for President al-Bashir," she says, and gives Joona a long look.

"I hadn't heard about that," says Joona.

"In 2004 the United Nations laid down a weapons embargo to the Janjaweed and other militia in Darfur."

They drive north on Nynäsvägen. The summer skies begin to turn dark and clouds are building.

"Go on," says Joona.

"President al-Bashir denies any connection to the militia. After the UN embargo, only direct exports to the Sudan government were allowed."

"Because there was no connection between the government and the militia."

"Exactly," Saga says. "Then, in 2005, a general amnesty was reached. The Comprehensive Peace Agreement. It was supposed to end the longest civil war in Africa. After that date, there was no reason for Sweden to stop weapons supplies to Sudan's army. Carl Palmcrona had to decide if these shipments were morally and legally a responsible thing to do."

"But the International Criminal Court thought differently," Joona says acridly.

"Yes indeed. They saw a direct connection between the president and the armed militia, and they demanded he be arrested for rape, torture, and genocide."

"What happened after that?"

"There was an election in April and al-Bashir remains the president. Sudan will not allow any arrest warrant to be served, so today it is absolutely forbidden to ship arms to Sudan and have any business with Omar al-Bashir and Agathe al-Haji."

"As Pontus Salman told us," Joona says.

"And that's why they broke off business connections."

"We have to find Penelope Fernandez," Joona says as the first raindrops hit the windshield.

They're now driving into a heavy thunderstorm that immediately obscures their vision. Rain sluices down, drumming on the roof of the car. Joona is forced to slow down to barely more than fifty kilometers per hour. It's totally dark, but at times lightning illuminates the sky. The windshield wipers swish at top speed back and forth.

Joona's cell phone rings. Petter Näslund snaps that Penelope has called SOS alarm twenty minutes ago.

"Why didn't you call me right away?"

"My first priority was to alert the maritime police. They're already on their way. I also sent a rescue helicopter."

"Good work, Petter," Joona says. Saga gives him a questioning look.

"I know you'll want to question them both as soon as possible."

"Right," Joona says.

"I'll call you as soon as I know anything more. What shape they're in."

"Thanks."

"The Coast Guard should be there by now . . . wait . . . something's happened. Hang on."

Joona hears Petter put down the phone. He's talking to someone, and his voice grows louder until he's yelling. He's yelling "Keep trying! Keep trying!" before Joona hears him pick up the phone again.

"I've got to go," Petter says.

"What's going on?" Joona asks.

A thunderclap rolls and fades away.

"We can't reach the officer on the boat. No answer. It's that idiot Lance; he's probably seen a wave he has to try."

"Petter," Joona shouts. "Listen! You need to work fast! That boat's been hijacked . . . and I believe—"

"Now you've gone too far!"

"Shut up and listen! Probably the guys on the boat are already dead. There may be only a few minutes to order a strike force. Take charge of this operation! Call CID on one phone and Bengt Olofsson on another and try to get two patrols from NI. Ask for backup from a Helicopter 14 from the nearest base."

the heir

A thunderstorm is rolling regally over Stockholm. The rain beats on the windows of Carl Palmcrona's large apartment. Tommy Kofoed and Nathan Pollock have begun the forensic investigation all over again.

It's so dark that they turn on the ceiling lamps.

In one of the full-length wardrobes in Palmcrona's dressing room, on the floor beneath a row of gray, blue, and black suits, Pollock unearths a black leather folder.

"Hey, Tommy," he yells.

Kofoed, in his usual hunched-over, melancholy posture, comes into the room. "What is it?"

Nathan Pollock taps the black leather folder lightly with his gloved fingers.

"I think I found something," he says simply.

They walk to the high window nook and Pollock undoes the clasp and opens the leather folder.

"What do we have here?" Kofoed whispers reverently.

Pollock lifts up the thin cover page with these few words on it: *Carl Palmcrona's Last Will and Testament.*

They read it in silence. The document is dated March 3, three years earlier. Palmcrona has bequeathed all he owns to one person: Stefan Bergkvist.

"Who the hell is Stefan Bergkvist?" asks Kofoed after they've finished reading. "Palmcrona has no relatives, and no friends either as far as I've found out."

"Stefan Bergkvist lives in Västerås . . . at least when this was written," Pollock says. "His address is Rekylgatan 11 and—"

Pollock stops and looks up.

"He's still a kid. According to his personal registration number, he's just sixteen right now."

The will had been drawn up by Palmcrona's lawyer at the firm of Wieselgreen and Sons. Pollock flips through the appendices that list Palmcrona's property. "There are four pension funds; one forest property, leased, of only two hectares; a partitioned farm in Sörmland, also on long-term lease; and the high-priced condominium on Grevgatan 2. The really large inheritance seems to be in a bank account at Standard Chartered Bank on the island of Jersey. Palmcrona sets its value at nine million euros."

"It looks like Stefan has become a wealthy kid," Pollock says.

"Yes indeed."

"But why? What's the connection?"

Tommy shrugs. "Who knows? Some people give everything to their dogs or their gym trainer."

"I'm going to call him."

"You mean, call the boy?"

"What else do you suggest?"

Nathan Pollock picks up his phone and taps in a number, asks to be connected to Stefan Bergkvist, living at Rekylgatan 11 in Västerås. He finds out that there is a Siv Bergkvist at the same address and guesses this is the boy's mother. Nathan looks out the window at the pounding rain and the gutters flowing over.

"Siv Bergkvist," a woman answers in a broken-sounding voice.

"My name is Nathan Pollock and I'm a criminal investigator. Are you the mother of Stefan Bergkvist?"

"Yes," she says in a whisper.

"May I speak to him?"

"What?"

"Please don't worry. I just need to ask him—"

"Go straight to hell!" she screams and slams down the phone.

Pollock redials the number but no one answers. He looks out the window, down at the road shining in the rain, and dials yet again.

"Micke here," a man's voice says in a reserved tone.

"My name is Nathan Pollock and I—"

"What do you want?"

Nathan hears the woman sobbing in the background. She says something to the man and he tells her he can take care of it.

"No, let me," she says.

Steps are heard as the telephone is handed over.

"Hello," the woman says softly.

"I really need—"

"Stefan is dead!" she screams shrilly. "You say you are a police officer and yet you say you need to talk to him! Why are you torturing me? It's just too much . . ."

She's sobbing into the receiver. Something crashes to the floor in the background.

"I'm so sorry," Pollock says softly. "I didn't know. I—"

"I can't take it any longer!" she sobs. "I can't!"

Steps are heard again and the man takes up the phone.

"This is enough," he says.

"Please wait a moment," Pollock says quickly. "Please tell me what happened. It's important . . ."

Tommy Kofoed, who has been catching Pollock's side of the conversation, sees him listen intently, then turn pale and run his hand over his silver ponytail.

when life gains meaning

Officers have gathered in the hallway of police headquarters until it is filled with nervous energy. Everyone waits for the latest reports. First, contact with the Coast Guard boat had been lost; then radio contact with the rescue helicopter had also gone dead.

At CID, Joona stands in his office, reading a postcard that Disa once sent him from a conference in Gotland. "I'm sending along a love letter from a secret admirer. Hugs, Disa." He guesses that she searched quite a while to find a postcard that would make him shudder so. He bites his lip as he turns the postcard over. SEX ON THE BEACH is printed over a picture of a white poodle wearing sunglasses and a pink bikini. The dog lounges in a deck chair and has a red drink beside it.

There's a knock on his door. Joona's smile disappears at the expression on Nathan Pollock's face.

"Carl Palmcrona willed everything he owned to his son," Nathan starts.

"I thought he had no relatives."

"His son is dead. He was sixteen years old. It appears there was an accident yesterday."

"Yesterday?" Joona repeats.

"Stefan Bergkvist survived Carl Palmcrona by just three days," Nathan says softly.

"What happened?"

"I don't really know. Something about his motorcycle," Pollock says. "I've asked for the preliminary autopsy report—"

"What do you have so far?"

"I've talked to his mother several times now. Her name is Siv Bergkvist. She lives with her partner, Micke Johansson. It appears that Siv was a substitute secretary for Palmcrona when he was working at the Fourth Navy Flotilla. They had a short relationship. She became pregnant. When she told him, he wanted her to get an abortion. Siv returned to Västerås instead, had the baby, and never told anyone the name of the father."

"Did Stefan know that his father was Carl Palmcrona?"

Nathan shakes his head and thinks back on the mother's words: *I told my son that his pappa was dead, that he had died before my little honeybee was born.*

Another knock on the door. Anja walks in and puts a report on the table. It's still warm from being printed out.

"An accident," Anja says grimly, without further explanation, and then leaves the room again.

Joona picks up the plastic folder and begins to read the report from the initial technical investigation. Death was not from carbon monoxide poisoning but as a direct result of burns. Before the boy died, his skin had swollen and split as if from deep cuts, and then all the internal musculature shrank. The heat had exploded the skull and the long bones. The coroner had put the cause of death as heat-related hematoma, due to the fact that the blood began to boil between the skull and the hard brain membrane.

"Unpleasant," Joona mutters.

Basically, nothing was left of the shed where Stefan Bergkvist's remains were found, which hindered the work of the fire investigators. The shed was now nothing more than a smoldering pyre of ashes, a few blackened pieces of metal, and a charred body in a fetal position next to what had been the door. Police based a preliminary theory of what had happened on the testimony of a single witness: the train engineer who'd called the fire department. He'd seen the burning motorcycle wedged next to the shed. Indications pointed to an accident in which sixteen-year-old Stefan Bergkvist had been trapped inside the old shed when his motorcycle had fallen over and blocked the door. The gas cap was not secure and gasoline had leaked out. The spark that led to the fire was still not accounted for, but the guess was that it was due to a cigarette.

"Palmcrona dies," Pollock says slowly. "He leaves his entire fortune to his son. Three days later, his son is also dead."

"Does the inheritance go to the mother, then?" Joona asks.

"Yes."

In silence they listen to the slow, halting steps in the hallway before Tommy Kofoed comes in.

"I've gotten into Palmcrona's safe," he says triumphantly. "Only this inside."

Kofoed holds up a beautifully bound book.

"What is that?" asks Pollock.

"It's a summary of his life," Kofoed says. "Very common among the nobility."

"So a kind of diary?"

Kofoed shrugs.

"Just a simple memoir not really meant for publication. Like a genealogy, it's meant to pass along another part of the family history. These pages are handwritten. It starts with a family tree and mentions his father's career and then a boring recitation of his school years, his diplomas, his military service, and his career . . . He'd made some bad investments and he needed money, so he sells some property and some other possessions. Everything in a very dry manner."

"What about his son?"

"At first, his relationship with Siv Bergkvist is described, short and sweet, as an 'unfortunate event,'" Tommy Kofoed answers. He takes a deep breath. "Soon, however, he begins to mention Stefan in his memoirs. All the entries for the past eight years are about his son. He follows his son's developments from a distance. He knows which school he's attending, what interests him, who he hangs out with. He says he's going to build up the inheritance again. It appears that he's saving everything he has for his son. Finally, he's decided to contact the boy when he turns eighteen. He hopes that his son will forgive him and that they will be able to get to know each other after all these years. That's the only thing he cares about . . . and now, they're both suddenly dead."

"What a nightmare," Pollock mutters.

"What did you say?" Joona looks up.

"I just said, I thought it's a nightmare come true," Pollock says, wondering why Joona's face is suddenly alive. "He does everything he can for his son's future and then it turns out that his son survives him by only three days. His son never even knew who he was."

a little more time

Beverly is already in his bed when Axel enters the bedroom. He's gotten only two hours of sleep the night before and now feels a little dizzy with fatigue.

"How long does it take for Evert to drive here?" she asks in a small, clear voice.

"It would take about six hours to get here," he replies succinctly.

She gets up and starts to the door.

"What are you doing?" Axel asks.

She turns around.

"I thought maybe he's sitting in the car waiting for me."

"You know that he doesn't drive to Stockholm," Axel says.

"I just want to look out the window and make sure."

"We can give him a call—should we call him?"

"I've already tried," she says.

Axel reaches out and brushes her cheek with his hand and she sits back down on the edge of the bed.

"Are you tired?" she asks.

"So tired I'm feeling sick," he replies.

"Do you want me to sleep in your bed tonight?"

"Yes, that would be nice."

"I believe that Pappa would like to talk to me tomorrow," she says softly.

Axel nods. "I'm sure it'll go well tomorrow."

Her large shining eyes make her look younger than ever.

"Come lie down," she says. "Lie down so you can sleep, Axel."

He blinks tiredly at her and then watches her lie down on her side of the bed. Her nightgown smells like freshly washed, pure cotton. As he lies down beside her, he wants to cry. He wants to tell her that he'll arrange psychiatric help for her. He'll help her out of this mess. Everything will get better. Everything always gets better.

He slowly clasps one of her upper arms and lays his other arm over her stomach. He hears her squeak as he pulls her closer to him. He presses his face into her neck, breathes moistly against her skin, and holds her tight. After a while, he hears her breathing soften. They lie completely still as their body warmth together brings sweat to their skin, but he does not let go of her.

The next morning Axel is up early. He's slept for only four hours and his muscles ache. He stands awhile at the window looking out over the dark outlines of the lilac hedge.

When he comes into his new office, he's still feeling frozen and tired. Yesterday he'd been one second away from signing his name to a dead man's contract. He would have put his personal honor into the hands of a man who'd hanged himself—trusted the judgment of a suicide and not his own.

He's glad he decided to wait, but regrets drawing the cartoon on the contract.

He knows he's obligated to approve the export of ammunition to Kenya in the next few days. He opens the report folder and begins to learn about Sweden's trade there.

One hour later, the door to Axel Riessen's office opens and Jörgen Grünlicht comes in. Without a word, he pulls a chair up to the desk and sits down. He opens the folder, takes out the contract, flips to the page where Axel's signature was supposed to be, and then meets Axel's eyes.

"Hi," Axel says quietly.

Jörgen Grünlicht can't help smiling. The cartoon face with spiky hair does resemble Axel Riessen and in the dialogue bubble from the figure's mouth the word "Hi!" had been written.

"Hello," Jörgen says.

"It was just too soon," Axel explains.

"I understand. I didn't want to pressure you, even if we're in a bit of a hurry," Jörgen says. "The trade minister was on my case again and Silencia Defense is ringing the phone off the hook. Still, I get you, you know. This responsibility is totally new to you and you . . . want to be especially thorough."

"That's right."

"And that's a good thing," he continues. "But you can send the agreement to the government instead if you're unsure about it."

"I'm not unsure," Axel replies. "I'm just not finished. That's all there is to it."

"It's just . . . from their perspective, things are going unreasonably slowly."

"I'm putting everything else aside for the moment and so far I can say that everything looks good," Axel replies. "I'm not telling Silencia Defense to wait before loading the freighter, but I'm just not finished yet."

"I'll let all parties involved know you are positive."

"Go ahead. I mean, if I don't find anything unusual, it's just—"

"You won't. I've done all the research myself."

"Well, then," Axel says softly.

"I won't disturb you anymore," Jörgen says. He gets up from the chair. "Any hint when you think you'll be ready?"

Axel glances down at the paperwork.

"Count on at least a few days. Maybe I'll have to look a little more into Kenya first."

"Of course." Jörgen Grünlicht smiles as he leaves the room.

always on his mind

Axel leaves the ISP office at ten o'clock in the morning to work from home. He puts all the paperwork needed into his briefcase. He still feels cold from being so tired, and now he's hungry as well. He drives to the Grand Hotel and picks up brunch for two people.

Axel carries the food into his kitchen. Beverly is sitting cross-legged on top of the kitchen table, right in the middle, and she's flipping through the bridal magazine *Amelia Brud & Bröllop*.

"Are you hungry?" he asks.

"I don't know if I want to wear white when I get married," Beverly says. "Maybe light rose . . ."

"I like white," Axel mumbles.

Axel prepares a tray and then the two of them ascend the stairs to the salon, where a red rococo sofa group is placed next to the large windows. As part of the grouping there's an eight-sided table from the eighteenth century. It shows how much that era appreciated intarsia; this motif shows a garden with peacocks and a musician, a woman playing the *erhu*.

Axel sets the table with the family china. It is imprinted in silver. He sets matching silver-gray napkins and heavy wineglasses beside the plates. He pours Coca-Cola into Beverly's glass and mineral water with slices of lime into his own.

Beverly's childish face has a tiny, chiseled chin above a fragile neck.

The entire curve of her head is clear under the fuzz of hair. She drinks the entire glass, then stretches her upper body indolently; a beautiful, innocent movement. Axel thinks that she'll do it exactly that way when she's an adult, maybe she'll stretch that way even as an old lady.

"Tell me more about the music," she asks him.

"Where were we?" Axel directs the remote toward his music system.

Alexander Malter's incredibly perceptive interpretation of Arvo Pärt's *Alina* comes out of the speakers. Axel sets his glass down on the table. The bubbles of the mineral water dance. Axel wishes with all his heart that it were champagne in that glass, champagne to go with this food. He wishes for another heart's desire—sleeping pills to get through the night.

Axel pours more Coke into Beverly's glass. She looks at him in thanks. He stares right into her large, dark eyes and doesn't notice that he's over-pouring until the Coke starts spreading over the table. The entire Chinese landscape darkens as if its sun is covered by a cloud. The liquid film shimmers over the park with its peacocks.

Axel stands up. He sees Beverly's reflection in the glass of the windows. The curve of her chin is so strong . . . and then he makes a sudden blinding connection. He realizes all at once that she resembles Greta.

How could he not have seen this before?

All he wants to do now is run away, run from this room, run from this house. Instead, he forces himself to get a cloth to wipe up the spill until his heart has a chance to slow and return to its normal rhythm.

It's not as if the two women would ever be confused one for the other, but now he spots one reminder, one trait after the other that they both share.

Axel stops and wipes his mouth. His hand is trembling.

There is not a single day when he does not think of Greta. And every day he does his best to forget.

The day after the competition still haunts him.

It was thirty-four years ago, but in his mind, everything since has been darkened by that event. His life was so new then; he was just seventeen, but all the bright hopes had come to an end.

sweet sleep

The Johan Fredrik Berwald Competition was northern Europe's most prestigious competition for young violinists. Many of the world's young virtuosi had come to be set directly in this blinding spotlight, but after six rounds before a closed jury, the number had been whittled down to just three. Now it was the final round, and the three violinists left would compete in the concert hall as part of a performance conducted by the legendary Herbert Blomstedt, and the music would be broadcast live on television.

In music circles, it was a sensation that two of the finalists, Axel Riessen and Greta Stiernlood, had both studied at the Royal College of Music in Stockholm. The other finalist was Shiro Sasaki from Japan.

For Alice Riessen, an uncelebrated professional musician, her son Axel's success was an enormous triumph. Especially now. She'd ignored the warnings from the school's principal about Axel's absences from classes, sometimes for an entire day, and that he was growing careless, wasn't concentrating.

Once Axel and Greta had reached the third round, they were granted permission to devote their time to rehearsal. The competition had brought them together, and, amazingly, each was happy about the other's success. Lately they'd been meeting at Axel's house for mutual support.

Axel and his younger brother, Robert, had the run of seven rooms on the top floor of the house in Lärkstaden. As a rule, Axel never practiced per se. Instead, he would find his way into a piece, exploring its undercurrent of sound as if in a new world. He loved to play and sometimes he was up long into the night playing his violin until even his toughened fingertips burned.

There was one day left before Axel and Greta would compete in the concert hall. Axel was sitting on the floor looking at the covers of his LPs spread out in front of his record player. He had three albums by David Bowie: *Space Oddity, Aladdin Sane,* and *Hunky Dory.*

His mother knocked on the door and came in with a bottle of Coca-Cola, two glasses with ice, and lemon slices. Axel was surprised to see her, but he thanked her, got up to take the tray, and set it on the coffee table.

"I thought you were practicing," Alice said as she looked around the room.

"Greta needed to go home and eat."

"You could still use this time for work."

"I'm waiting for her to get back."

"You know that the final is tomorrow," Alice said as she sat down on the floor next to her son. "I devote myself to practice eight hours a day and sometimes ten."

"I'm not even awake ten hours a day," Axel joked.

"Axel, you have the gift."

"Yes, Mamma."

"You say yes. But you don't understand. The gift is not enough. It's not enough for anyone."

"Mamma, I practice like crazy," he lied.

"Play for me," she requested.

"No," he said.

"I know you don't want your mother as a teacher, but let me help you just a little bit now when it really counts," Alice continued patiently. "The last time I heard you was two years ago at the Christmas concert. No one understood what you'd played."

"It was Bowie's 'Cracked Actor.'"

"A childish selection . . . but still a very impressive performance for a fifteen-year-old." She reached out to touch him. "But, see, tomorrow—"

Axel pulled away from his mother's hand.

"Stop nagging me."

"Can you at least tell me which piece you've chosen?"

"It's classical."

"Thank the Lord for that at least."

Axel shrugged and avoided his mother's gaze. When the doorbell rang, he raced down the stairs.

Twilight was starting to fall, but the snow reflected indirect light so that darkness could not engulf the house. Greta was at the bottom step, holding her violin case and duffel bag. Her cheeks were rosy from the cold, her striped scarf was wound close around her neck against it. Her hair was spread over her shoulders and sparkled from the snowflakes. She set her case on the dresser to hang up her coat and scarf. Then she took off her black boots and pulled out indoor shoes from her duffel bag.

Alice Riessen came down to the bottom of the stairs and held out her hands to her. Alice was exhilarated and her cheeks glowed with happiness.

"It's good that the two of you are helping each other practice," she said. "You have to be tough on Axel. Otherwise, he'll just be lazy," she scolded gently.

"I've noticed that." Greta laughed.

Greta Stiernlood was the daughter of an industrial giant who had great holdings in Saab-Scania and Enskilda Banken. She'd been raised by her father—her parents had divorced when she was a baby, and her father had erected a barrier against her mother ever since. Very early in her life—perhaps even before she was born—her father had decided she would be a violinist.

After the two of them climbed the stairs to Axel's music room, Greta went to the grand piano. Her shining hair curled to her shoulders. She was casually dressed in a Scottish plaid kilt, white blouse, dark blue cardigan, and striped socks.

She unpacked her violin, fastened the chin rest, wiped the rosin from the strings with a cotton cloth, tightened the bow, applied new rosin to it, set her music on the stand, and carefully tuned the instrument after its journey through the cold night.

Then she started to play. She played as she always did, with her eyes half shut as if concentrating on something inside herself. Her long eyelashes cast shadows over her serious face. Axel knew the piece well: the first movement of Beethoven's Violin Concerto in D Major—a serious, searching theme.

He smiled as he listened. He respected Greta's wonderful sense of music and the honesty in her interpretation.

"Nice," he said as she finished.

Greta changed the music and stretched her fingers.

"But I still can't decide . . . You know, Pappa wants me to play the Tartini Violin Sonata in G Minor. But I'm not so sure . . ."

She was silent, looking at the music, reading it, counting, and going over her memorization of the complicated legato.

"Can I hear it?" Axel asked.

"It sounds terrible," she said, blushing a little.

She played the last movement. Her face was tense, beautiful, and sad, but at the end, she lost the tempo just as the violin's highest notes were supposed to rise like a catching fire.

"Damn," she whispered, resting the violin under her arm. "I slowed down. I've been working like a beast but I have to give more to the six-teenths and the triplets, which—"

"Though I liked the swing, as if you were bending a large mirror toward—"

"I didn't play it correctly," she said, and blushed even deeper. "I'm sorry. I know you're trying to be nice, but it won't work. I have to play properly. It's crazy that on the night before the performance I'm still not able to make up my mind. Should I take the easy way out or put all my effort into the difficult piece?"

"You know both of them well, so—"

"No, I don't. It would be a big risk," she said. "Perhaps, though . . . I'd need a few hours, maybe three hours, and then I might risk the Tartini tomorrow."

"You shouldn't do it just because your father thinks—"

"But he's right."

"No, he's not," Axel said. He began to roll a joint.

"I know the easy piece well," she said. "But it might not be on a high enough level. It all depends on what you and Shiro Sasaki pick."

"You shouldn't think like that."

"How am I supposed to think? You've never let me see you practice even once. What are you planning to play—have you even picked out a piece?"

"The Ravel," he answered.

"The Ravel? Without even practicing?"

She laughed out loud.

"No, seriously, which piece?" she asked.

"Ravel's *Tzigane*—and that's the truth."

"I'm sorry, Axel, but that's a crazy choice. You know that yourself. It's too complicated, too quick, too reckless, and—"

"I'm going to play like Perlman, but without being in a hurry . . . because the piece shouldn't be rushed."

"Axel, it's supposed to be allegro," she said with a smile.

"Yes, for the hare that's being chased . . . but for the wolf, it should go a bit more slowly."

She gave him an exhausted look.

"Where did you read that?"

"Attribution"—he waved the joint—"Paganini."

"Well, then, I only have to worry about our Japanese competitor," she said as she tucked the violin back underneath her chin. "Since you never practice, you'll never be able to play the *Tzigane*."

"It's not as hard as people say," he replied as he lit the joint.

"No, indeed." She smiled as she started to play again.

After a while, she stopped and looked levelly at Axel.

"You're really going to play the Ravel?"

"Yep."

She was serious. "Have you lied to me and been practicing all this time? Maybe for four years? And not even telling me? Or what?"

"I decided this minute—the minute you asked."

She laughed. "How can you be such an idiot?"

"I don't care if I come in last," he said as he stretched out on the sofa.

"I care," she said simply.

"I know, but there'll be other chances."

"Not for me."

She started to play the Tartini. It was better, but she stopped. She repeated the complicated passage again and then once more.

Axel clapped his hands and then he put David Bowie's *The Rise and Fall of Ziggy Stardust and the Spiders from Mars* on the record player.

He put the needle over the LP and as the music started, he lay down, closed his eyes, and began to sing along:

Ziggy really sang, screwed up eyes and screwed down hairdo.
Like some cat from Japan, he could lick 'em by smiling.
He could leave 'em to hang.

Greta hesitated, put down her violin, walked over to him, and took the joint from his hand. She took a toke, another one, coughed, and handed it back.

"How can anyone be as dumb as you?" she asked as she touched his lips.

She bent over and wanted to kiss him on the lips, but her aim was off and she touched his cheek instead. She whispered "Sorry" and then kissed him again. They kept their lips together, searching and seeking. He drew off her cardigan and her hair sparked from static electricity. He received a little charge when he touched her cheek and snatched his hand back. They smiled nervously at each other and then they kissed again. He unbuttoned her white, stiffly ironed blouse and felt her tiny breasts through her simple bra. She helped him take off his T-shirt. Her long, lustrous hair smelled like the fresh air of snow and winter, but her body was as warm as newly baked bread.

They moved into his bedroom and sank deeply onto his bed. Her hands trembled as she unzipped and pulled off her skirt, and for a moment it seemed she would pull off her panties at the same time, but that's not what she had intended, and her hands kept them on as Axel pulled down her kneesocks.

"What's wrong?" he whispered. "Do you want to stop?"

"I don't know—do you?"

"No," he said.

"I'm just a little nervous," she said honestly.

"You're older than I am."

"Yes, you're still just seventeen—I'm robbing the cradle," she said, smiling.

Axel's heart pounded as he pulled down her panties. She lay still as he kissed her stomach, her small breasts, her throat, her chin, her lips. She opened her legs and he lay on her and felt how she slowly pressed her thighs against his hips. Her cheeks flushed bright red as he slid inside her. She pulled him close and stroked his back and neck and sighed every time he sank into her.

Once they finished, panting, there was a thin layer of sweat between their nude bodies. They lay wrapped in each other's arms, eyes closed, as they fell into a sweet sleep.

the johan fredrik berwald competition

It was light outside when Axel woke up on the day he would lose everything. He and Greta had not shut the curtains. They'd fallen asleep together in the bed and slept the entire night.

Axel slowly got up and looked down at Greta, who slept with a completely calm face and the thick blanket crumpled about her. He walked to the door and stopped next to the mirror and looked at his naked seventeen-year-old body for a while. Then he continued into the music room. He closed the door to the bedroom softly and walked over to the grand piano. He took his violin out of its case and tuned it. He put it to his chin, went to stand by the window, and looking out at the winter morning and the snow being blown from the roofs in long veils, he began to play Maurice Ravel's *Tzigane* from memory.

The piece begins with a sorrowful Romany melody, slow and measured, but then the tempo begins to increase. The melody echoes faster and faster in upon itself as a blistering, split-second memory of a summer night.

It's an extremely fast piece.

Axel was playing because he was happy. He wasn't thinking. His fingers ran and danced like eddies and ripples in a stream.

Axel started to smile. He was thinking of a painting his grandfather had in the salon. His grandfather had said it was the most apt and glowing version of *Näcken* by Ernst Josephson. As a child, Axel had loved the legends surrounding this mystical being whose violin music was so beautiful it lured people to their deaths, beautiful deaths drowning in the pool.

At that moment, Axel felt that he was just like the Näcke, a young man surrounded by water as he played. Except Axel was happy. That was the greatest difference between Axel and the Josephson painting.

His bow leaped over the strings at amazing speed. He didn't care that some of the bow's taut hair broke and danced in the air with the music.

This is how Ravel should be played, he thought. *Not exotically but happily. Ravel is a young composer, a happy composer.*

Axel let the final notes resonate in the body of the violin and then seem to whirl away like the light snow on the roof outside. He lowered his bow and was about to bow toward the snow outside when he realized that someone was behind him.

He turned and saw Greta in the doorway. She held the blanket around her body and her eyes were dark and strange as she looked at him.

Axel frowned at her stricken expression.

"What's wrong?"

She didn't answer. She swallowed loudly. A pair of large tears began to run down her cheeks.

"Greta, what's the matter?" he asked, insistently.

"You told me that you hadn't practiced," she said in a monotone.

"No, I . . . I . . ." he stammered. "I told you that I learned new pieces easily."

"Congratulations."

"What are you thinking?" he said, aghast. "It's not what you think!"

She shook her head.

"I can't believe I could have been so stupid," she said.

He set down the violin and bow, but she was already closing the bedroom door behind her. Axel snatched up a pair of jeans he'd left hanging on the back of a chair and pulled them on. Then he knocked on the door.

"Greta? May I come in?"

There was no answer, and with that, a black clump of worry settled in his stomach. In a little while, she came out of the bedroom fully dressed. She didn't even look at him as she put her violin in its case and gathered up her belongings to leave him alone.

The concert hall was full. Greta was the first to play. When she saw him, she looked away. She wore a blue velvet dress and a necklace with a heart pendant.

Axel sat alone in the dressing room and waited with half-closed eyes. It was absolutely silent. Only a small sound could be heard behind a dusty plastic fan guard. His little brother came into the room.

"Aren't you going to sit with Mamma?" Axel asked.

"No, I'm too nervous. I can't watch you perform. I'll just sit here and wait."

"Has Greta started yet?"

"Yes, it sounds good."

"Which piece did she choose? Was it Tartini's violin sonata?"

"No, something by Beethoven."

"That's good," Axel muttered.

They sat together silently and said nothing more. After a while, there was a knock at the door. Axel stood up and opened it. A woman told him that he would be next.

"Good luck," said Robert.

"Thanks," Axel said. He picked up his violin with its bow and followed the woman through the hallway.

Great applause sounded from the audience. Axel caught a brief glimpse of Greta and her father as they hurried into Greta's dressing room.

Axel walked close to the wings and had to wait through an introduction. When he heard his name, he walked into the center of the spotlight and smiled at the audience. A murmur arose when he announced his selection, the *Tzigane* by Maurice Ravel.

He put his violin to his chin and lifted his bow. He began to play the sorrowful introduction and then sped up the tempo to the impossible speed. The audience seemed to hold its breath. He could hear that he was playing brilliantly, but this time the melody didn't sparkle. His playing was no longer happy. It was as if he had become the Näcke, with a hectic, feverish sorrow. Three minutes into the piece, the notes were falling like rain in the night, and then he began to purposefully skip a few. He slowed, played off-key, and finally broke off the piece completely.

The concert hall was silent.

"I'm sorry," he whispered, and then he walked off the stage.

The audience clapped politely. His mother got up from her seat in the audience and followed him. She stopped him in the walkway.

"Come here, my boy," she said as she put her hands on his shoulders.

Then she stroked his cheek and her voice was warm as she said, "That was remarkable, the best interpretation I've ever heard."

"Forgive me, Mamma."

Her face stiffened, seemed to pull in on itself. "Never," she replied, and she turned away from Axel and walked out of the concert hall.

Axel went to the dressing room for his coat, but he was met by Herbert Blomstedt outside the dressing-room door.

"That was remarkable, my boy," he said in a very sad voice. "Until you began to pretend you could no longer play."

The house reverberated with silence when Axel returned home. It was already late at night. He trudged up to the top-floor apartment, in through his music room, and then to his bedroom. He shut the door behind him. He still heard the music in his head, how it had sounded until he began to drop notes, slow the tempo unexpectedly, break off the piece in the middle.

He had stopped. Over and over he had stopped.

Axel let himself down on the bed and fell asleep with his violin case beside him.

The next morning, he woke to the sound of the telephone.

Someone walked across the dining-room floor. It always creaked.

A moment later, there were steps on the stairs. His mother walked right into his bedroom without knocking.

"Sit up," Alice commanded.

Axel was frightened the moment he saw her. Her face was still wet from her tears.

"Mamma, please—"

"Be quiet!" she says in a low voice. "I've just gotten a call from your principal—"

"He's unhappy with me because—"

"Can you be quiet!" Alice yelled.

He stopped talking. She held a trembling hand to her mouth. New tears began to stream down her cheeks.

"It's about Greta," she finally was able to say. "She committed suicide last night."

Axel stared at her and tried to understand what she'd said.

"No! . . . Because I—"

"She was ashamed," Alice says. "They said she felt she let everyone down, that she should have practiced more. You promised to help. I knew it, though, I knew. She never should have come here, she . . . I'm not saying it's your fault, Axel, because it isn't. She was disappointed in herself because when everything was riding on her playing, she couldn't deal with it, and she couldn't bear that—"

"But, Mamma, I—"

"Be quiet," she said. "All of this is over."

Alice left. Axel got out of bed in a gathering fog. He swayed, but steadied himself. He took his beautiful violin out of its case and banged it violently against the floor. The neck broke and the bridge flopped over under the loose strings. Axel stamped on it and pieces of wood flew in all directions.

"Axel! What are you doing?"

Robert rushed into the room and tried to stop him. Axel pushed him away. Robert fell on his back against the wardrobe behind him, but he started back again.

"Axel, so you messed up, so what?" Robert said. "Greta did, too. I met her in the hallway and she'd also . . . everyone—"

"Shut up!" Axel screamed. "Don't ever say her name to me again!"

Robert stared while Axel continued to stamp on the wooden pieces until there was nothing left that resembled a violin. Robert then left the room.

Shiro Sasaki won the Johan Fredrik Berwald Competition. Greta had chosen the easier Beethoven piece, but she'd been unable to play it perfectly, a demand she had made upon herself. As soon as she'd gotten home, she'd locked herself in her bedroom and must have taken a huge amount of sleeping pills. She'd been found in bed the next morning when she'd been missed at breakfast.

Axel's memory sinks away as if it were a forgotten life down in the depths of the sea. He looks at Beverly. It's like Greta's big eyes looking back at him. He looks at the cloth in his own hand and the liquid on the table and the shining intarsia with the woman playing the *erhu*.

Light slides across the curve of Beverly's head as she turns to look at the violins hanging on the wall.

"I wish I knew how to play one," she says.

"Let's take a class together," he says, gently smiling.

"I'd like that," she answers in all seriousness.

He sets the cloth down on the table and feels the terrible exhaustion inside his body. The recording of the piano's echoing music fills the room. It's being played without a damper and the notes flow dreamily into one another.

"Poor Axel, you want to sleep," she says.

"I have to work."

"This evening, then," she says, and gets up.

64

Detective Inspector Joona Linna is at his desk at CID. He's reading Carl Palmcrona's memoir. Five years ago, Palmcrona recorded how he'd traveled to Västerås to watch his son graduate from elementary school. He'd stood at a distance as everyone gathered in the school yard and sang "Den blomstertid nu kommer" while standing in the rain holding umbrellas. Palmcrona described his son's white jeans and jacket, his long blond hair, and wrote that "the boy had a family resemblance in his nose and eyes, which made me want to cry." He'd driven back to Stockholm and wrote that his son was worth everything he'd done up to now and everything that he would ever do.

The phone rings. Joona picks it up immediately. It's Petter Näslund calling from the police bus on Dalarö.

"They've got Penelope Fernandez. I've just been in contact with the helicopter group, and they're flying back over Erstavik Bay right now," he tells Joona. His voice still sounds hunted.

"She's alive?" Joona asks, and is overwhelmed by a feeling of relief.

"She was swimming in the open ocean when they found her," Petter explains.

"How's she doing? Is she all right?"

"It appears so. They're heading toward Söder Hospital."

"Too dangerous," Joona says abruptly. "Fly her to the police station instead. We'll bring a team of doctors from Karolinska Hospital."

Petter says he'll contact the helicopters.

"What about the others?" Joona asks.

"It's complete chaos. We've lost people, Joona. It's crazy over here."

"What about Björn Almskog?"

"We haven't found him, but . . . right now we really know nothing, and it's hard to find out what went on."

"What about the killer?"

"We'll catch him. This is a small island. We've got men all over it along with help from the Coast Guard and the naval police."

"Good," Joona says.

"You don't think we'll get him?" Petter asks grimly.

"If you didn't catch him right away, he's probably slipped through."

"You're saying it's my fault?"

"Petter," Joona says quietly and softly. "If you hadn't been so fast on the uptake, Penelope would be dead, and without her, we'd have no leads at all."

An hour later, two doctors from Karolinska converge in a protected room deep underneath the National Police Board headquarters. Penelope lies unmoving in their care. They're bandaging her wounds, setting up an IV for rehydration and nutrition, and giving her tranquilizers.

Petter Näslund reports to Carlos Eliasson that the remains of their colleagues, Lennart Johansson and Göran Sjödin, have been found in the wreckage of the police launch along with another unidentified body, which is probably the remains of Björn Almskog. Ossian Wallenberg's body was found outside his house, and divers are on the way to the area where the helicopter crashed. Petter fears that all on board are lost.

The police have not caught the suspect, but Penelope Fernandez is still alive.

Flags are lowered to half-staff in front of the police station. Chief of Police Margareta Widding and the head of CID, Carlos

Eliasson, are holding a sorrowful press conference in the glass-enclosed pressroom. Detective Inspector Joona Linna does not take part in the press conference. Instead, he and Saga Bauer are on the elevator down to the lowest level of the building to meet Penelope Fernandez.

what eyes have seen

Five floors beneath the police station's most modern addition is an area with two apartments, eight guest rooms, and two sleeping areas. It has been created to guarantee security for leaders of the department during crises and catastrophes. For the past decade, the guest rooms have also been used for witness protection. The walls are a cheerful yellow, and pleasant-looking books line a nice bookshelf. It's obvious that the people staying in these rooms have plenty of time to read. There are no windows, but light behind a sheer curtain mimics one and tries to distract the mind from the thought of being deep underground in a bunker.

Penelope Fernandez lies on a hospital bed here, chilled. They tell her it's because the IV-drip speed into her arm is being increased.

"We're giving you liquids and nutritional supplements," Daniella Richards, the doctor, tells her. In a soft voice, Dr. Richards continues to explain what she's doing as she tapes the catheter to the inside of Penelope's elbow.

Penelope's wounds have been cleaned. Her injured left foot has been stitched and bandaged and the gash on her back has been washed clean and taped shut, while the deep wound on her hip got the eight stitches it needed.

"I now want to give you a bit of morphine for the pain."

"Mamma," Penelope says. "I want to talk to Mamma."

"I understand," the doctor replies.

Warm tears run along Penelope's cheeks and into her hair and ears. She hears the doctor ask the nurse to prepare an injection of 0.5 milliliters of morphine. The friendly Dr. Richards tells Penelope they will let her rest now, but if she needs anything, she can push the glowing red button.

"There's always going to be someone with you, if you want something or just for a bit of company," she says.

Now Penelope Fernandez can feel a sense of peace in the room. She closes her eyes as the morphine's warmth spreads through her body and pulls her down into sleep.

There's a slight crunch when a woman wearing a black niqab crushes two small figures of sun-dried clay under her sandaled foot. A girl and her little brother turn to fragments and dust. The veiled woman is walking along carrying a heavy load of grain and doesn't even notice what she's doing. Two boys whistle and point and cry out that the slave children are dead and soon only infants will be left. All the Fur will die.

Penelope forces the memory of Kubbum away, but before she can fall into sleep again, for an instant she feels the weight of the tons of stone, earth, clay, and cement above her. It feels as if she just keeps falling and falling and falling, falling into the center of the earth.

Penelope Fernandez wakes up abruptly. She can't open her eyes. The morphine has made her body too heavy. But she knows she's in a hospital bed in a protected bunker deep beneath the police station. She doesn't need to flee any longer. Her relief is followed by a massive wave of pain and sorrow. She doesn't know how long she's slept, or if she should just let herself drift off again. She opens her eyes anyway.

She blinks, but sees nothing. Not even the alarm button next to the bed is lit. There must have been a power outage. She's about to scream, but forces herself to be quiet when the door to the hallway clicks open. She stares into the darkness and hears her own heart pounding. Her body tenses and her muscles are ready to leap. Someone touches her hair. Almost unnoticeable. She lies completely still and feels someone do it again, stealthily, fingers twisting slowly into her locks. She is about to say a prayer when the person near her jerks her out of her bed by the hair. She screams as he throws her into the wall so that the framed pictures break and the IV stand falls over. She falls onto the floor surrounded by shards of glass. He keeps hold of her hair and pulls her back up, flips her over, and bangs her face against the bed's locked wheels. Then he pulls out a knife with a black blade.

Penelope wakes up. She's fallen out of bed. A nurse is rushing to her. All the lights are on and Penelope realizes that she's had a nightmare. She is helped back into bed, the nurse speaking calmly. Then rails are pulled up around the bed to keep her from falling out again.

The sweat on her body cools off after a while. She doesn't want to move. She is lying on her back with the alarm button clutched in her hand and she stares at the ceiling. There's a knock at the door. A young woman comes in. She has a colorful band braided into her long hair, and she looks at Penelope with a gentle seriousness. Behind her is a tall man with spiked blond hair and a friendly, symmetrical face.

"My name is Saga Bauer," the woman says. "I'm from the Security Service. This is my colleague, Joona Linna, from CID."

Penelope looks at them without expression and then looks down at her bandaged arms, all her scabs and bruises and the catheter in her arm.

"We're so sorry for all you've been through the past few days," the woman says. "And we can understand you might want to simply be left alone now. But we can't do that just yet. We need some information from you."

Saga Bauer pulls the chair from the tiny desk and then sits down beside the bed.

"He's still after me, isn't he?" Penelope asks.

"You're safe here," Saga answers.

"Tell me he's dead."

"Penelope, we must—"

"You couldn't stop him," she says weakly.

"We'll catch him. I promise," Saga says. "But you have to help us."

Penelope shuts her eyes.

"This must be so hard, but we do need a few answers," Saga continues softly. "Do you have any idea why this might be happening?"

"Ask Björn," she mumbles. "Maybe he knows."

"What did you say?"

"I said you have to ask Björn," Penelope whispers. She slowly opens her eyes. "Ask him. Maybe he knows."

Spiders and insects must have gotten on her body from the woods. They're running over her body. She tries to scratch her forehead, but Saga calmly stops her hands.

"He was hunting you," Saga says. "I can't even imagine how terrible it must have been. But did you recognize the person after you? Have you ever met him before?"

Penelope shakes her head so slightly it's hardly noticeable.

"We didn't think so either," Saga says. "But perhaps you can give us a good description of him, or something recognizable such as a tattoo or a special mark?"

"No," Penelope whispers.

"Then could you help our artist draw a picture of him? We don't need too much to begin a search through Interpol."

The man from CID comes closer, and his unusual gray eyes look like stones polished in a stream.

"I thought I just saw you shake your head," he says. His voice is also calm. "When Saga asked if you recognized him, you shook your head just a little, right?"

Penelope nods.

"Then perhaps you did see him," Joona says in a friendly way. "Perhaps you're not sure if you'd seen him before or not."

Penelope stares straight ahead and remembers how the killer moved so leisurely, as if he had all the time in the world, and still how everything happened so horribly fast. In her mind, she sees how he must have aimed up as she hung from the helicopter's lifeline. She sees him raise his weapon and fire. No hurry, no nervousness. Again she sees his face illuminated by the flash of lightning. How they looked right at each other.

"We understand that you must be frightened," Joona says. "But we—"

He stops speaking as a nurse comes into the room and tells Penelope that they're still trying to reach her mother.

"She's not home and she's not answering her cell phone."

Penelope moans and looks away, hiding her face in her pillow. The nurse places a comforting hand on her shoulder.

"I don't want to hear!" Penelope sobs. "I don't want to!"

Another nurse hurries in and says she will add just a bit more tranquilizer to Penelope's IV.

"Please, I must ask you to leave," the nurse says hastily to Saga and Joona.

"We'll be back soon," Joona says. "I know where your mother might be. I'll get her for you."

Penelope stops crying, but her breaths still come quickly. She hears the rustling noise as the nurse prepares the infusion and she thinks that this entire room reminds her of a jail cell. Her mother wouldn't want to come here. She bites her lip and tries to keep her tears back for a little while longer.

There are days when Penelope thinks she remembers her first years. The smell of steaming unwashed bodies. The cell where she was born. The wash of a flashlight beam across the faces of the prisoners. How she felt as her mother lifted her up over others to someone else before her mother disappeared with the guards. How a tune is hummed into her ear.

without penelope

Claudia Fernandez gets off the bus at Dalarö Beach Hotel. As she walks to the harbor, she can hear the sounds of helicopters and sirens fading into the distance. The search can't be over. They have to keep looking. A few police boats are moving out on the water. She looks around. There's no ferry at the dock and no cars waiting at the harbor.

"Penelope!" she screams right into the air. "Penelope!"

She realizes she must look insane, but without Penelope, there's nothing left on this earth for her.

She begins to walk along the water. The grass is dry and brown, with pieces of garbage everywhere. Seagulls screech in the distance. She begins to run, but soon can't keep it up and she starts to walk again. Empty cottages stand on the edge of a cliff. She stops next to a sign by a dock where the word PRIVATE is written in white letters. She turns onto the cement dock and looks toward the large cliffs. There's no one here, she thinks. She turns back toward the harbor. A man is walking along the gravel road and he waves to her. It's a dark figure with his coat flapping in the breeze. She blinks in the sunlight. The man shouts something. Claudia looks at him in confusion. He begins to walk more quickly, nears her, and only then does she recognize his friendly face.

"Claudia Fernandez!" he calls out.

"That's me," she replies, and waits for him to catch up to her.

"I'm John Bengtsson," he says as he reaches her. "Joona Linna sent me to find you. He told me that you'd probably come here."

"Why do you need me?" she says in a weak voice.

"Your daughter is alive."

Claudia looks into the man's face. He repeats those words.

"Penelope is alive," he's saying, and he gives her a big smile.

follow the money

Emotions are running high at the police station until the pitch is almost hate-filled. People compare the recent events to the police murders in Malexander in 1999 and the bestiality of the triple murders in Tumba two years before. The newspapers shout about the drama in the archipelago seas. They name the suspect "The Police Butcher," and journalists pounce on any lead, any possible source inside the station.

Joona Linna and Saga Bauer are going to brief a meeting of the department heads, Eliasson, Zandén, Näslund, and Rubin, as well as Nathan Pollock and Tommy Kofoed from the National Homicide Squad. They're on their way through the hallway and discussing what help Penelope Fernandez might be able to give.

"I think she'll be able to talk soon," Joona says.

"I'm not so sure. She could go the other way and just shut down completely," Saga says.

Anja Larsson has taken a step out of her office and stands in the hallway watching Joona and Saga mournfully. When Joona sees her, he gives her a big smile and waves, but he's gone past too quickly to see the heart she's formed with her thumbs and index fingers.

They shut the conference-room door behind them and greet everyone around the table.

"I want to start today by dismissing all suspicions of left-wing extremists being behind this," Saga begins.

Verner Zandén whispers something to Nathan Pollock.

"Am I right?" Saga says, raising her voice.

Verner looks up and nods.

"That's right," he says, clearing his throat.

"Why don't you start at the beginning?" Carlos asks Saga.

"Well . . . we are focused on an individual, Penelope Fernandez, who is a peace activist and the chairwoman for the Swedish Peace and Reconciliation Society. She has been in a long personal relationship with Björn Almskog, a bartender at the Debaser club on Medborgarplatsen. She lives at Sankt Paulsgatan 3 and he lives at Pontonjärgatan 47. Penelope Fernandez had a photograph taped to the glass door between her living room and the hallway."

Saga projects an image from her computer onto the screen that covers one wall of the room.

"This photograph was taken in Frankfurt in the spring of 2008," she says.

"We recognize Palmcrona," Carlos says.

"That's right," Saga says, and then points out the other people in the theater box. "This is Pontus Salman, the director of the weapons manufacturer Silencia Defense. This person is none other than Raphael Guidi. He's a well-known weapons dealer for many years, mainly in Africa and the Middle East. They call him the Archangel."

"And the lady in the group?" asks Benny Rubin.

"That's Agathe al-Haji," Saga says without smiling. "She's the military adviser to the government in Sudan and has close ties with President Omar al-Bashir."

Benny slaps the table and shows his teeth. Pollock gives him an irritated look.

"Is this usual?" asks Carlos. "Do people meet like this?"

"Yes, I believe so," Saga replies. "This meeting was supposedly about a shipment of ammunition going to the Sudanese army. It would have been completed, without a doubt, if the International Criminal Court in The Hague hadn't issued an arrest warrant for President al-Bashir."

"That was in 2009, wasn't it?" asks Pollock.

"It wasn't written up in the Swedish press," Saga says. "But the indictment pointed a finger at the president's direct participation in torture, rape, and genocide in Darfur."

"So the deal was scotched," Carlos says.

"Yes," says Saga.

"And what about that photograph? What's going on there? Nothing?" Verner asks.

"Penelope Fernandez must not have thought it was dangerous since she displayed it openly on her door," Saga says.

"And yet it must be important—since she had it there at all," Carlos says.

"We have no idea why. Perhaps it served as a reminder of how the world works," Saga speculates. "A few poor people fight for peace at the bottom of the barrel, while at the top the mighty clink their glasses and drink champagne over an arms deal."

"We hope to question Penelope Fernandez soon, but we're fairly sure Björn Almskog tried to deal behind her back," Joona continues. "Perhaps he knew nothing more about the photo than Penelope, or maybe he was just grasping at a chance to make money. But on the second of June, Björn uses an anonymous e-mail address in an Internet café to write a blackmail letter to Carl Palmcrona. The e-mail begins a very short correspondence: Björn writes he knows the photograph can be troublesome for Palmcrona and he's ready to sell it to him for a million crowns."

"Classic blackmail," Pollock mutters.

"Björn uses the word 'awkward' concerning this photograph," Saga continues. "This makes us believe that he does not understand how serious Palmcrona will find it to be."

"Björn believes he's in control," Joona says. "So he's amazed when Palmcrona turns around and warns *him*. Palmcrona explains darkly that Björn does not know what he's gotten himself into and then pleads with him to mail him the photograph before it's too late."

Joona drinks some water.

"What is the tone of the letter?" Nathan Pollock asks. "You say it's 'dark,' but is it also aggressive?"

Joona shakes his head as he passes out copies of the correspondence.

"No. Not aggressive. Rather, tinged with fear—for himself."

Tommy Kofoed reads the e-mails, nods, rubs his pockmarked cheeks, and writes something down.

"What happens next?"

"Before the housekeeper leaves that Wednesday, she helps Palmcrona fasten a noose to the ceiling fixture."

Petter has to laugh. "What? Why would she do that?"

"Because he'd had back surgery and couldn't reach up to do it himself," Saga replies.

"Well, then," Carlos says, and can't help a small smile.

"The next day at lunch . . . after the mail had been delivered, we believe," Joona continues, "Palmcrona calls a number in Bordeaux and—"

"We can't trace the number beyond Bordeaux," Saga adds.

"The number could have gone to an exchange and been sent on to another country, or even back to Sweden," Joona explains. "Anyway, wherever it went in the end, the conversation was only forty-three seconds long. Perhaps he just left a voice message. We presume he told about the blackmail letter and expected help.

"Shortly thereafter, just a few minutes later, Palmcrona's housekeeper uses Palmcrona's name to call for a taxi from Taxi Stockholm. It is to arrive at two o'clock for a trip to Arlanda Airport. Exactly one hour and fifteen minutes after the Bordeaux conversation, the telephone rings. Palmcrona has already put on his overcoat and his good shoes, but still answers the phone. The phone call comes from Bordeaux and from the same number. This conversation lasts two minutes. Palmcrona sends one last e-mail to his blackmailer warning him it is now too late. They both will die. He gives his housekeeper permission to leave for the day, pays the waiting taxi for his trouble, goes into his apartment, and doesn't even bother to take off his coat. He walks into the small salon, puts his briefcase on edge, climbs up, and hangs himself."

Everyone at the table is quiet.

"But the story doesn't end there," Joona says slowly. "Palmcrona's call has set things in motion. An international hit man is engaged. A professional killer is sent here to erase everything and get the photograph."

"How often . . . I mean in Sweden . . . do we have to deal with professional killers?" Carlos says with skepticism. "There would have to be a great deal of money involved here."

Joona looks at him without expression. "Correct."

"Palmcrona must have been frightened and just rattled off the contents of the blackmail letter including the bank account number Björn had given him," Saga says.

"With a bank account number, it's not difficult to find anyone," Verner mutters.

"At about the same time that Palmcrona is kicking away his briefcase, Björn Almskog is at the Dreambow Internet Café," Joona says. "He goes into his anonymous account and sees that he's gotten two messages from Palmcrona."

"Of course he's hoping that Palmcrona will come across with a million crowns," Saga says.

"Instead, he is greeted by Palmcrona's warning and then the short message that they're both going to die," adds Joona.

"And now they *are* both dead," Pollock sighs.

"We almost can't imagine how frightened Björn must have been," Saga says. "He's no professional blackmailer. He just took a chance at money when he saw it."

"What does he do then?" Petter watches them with his mouth slightly open. Carlos pours some water for him.

"Björn regrets what he's done and decides to send the photograph to Palmcrona and wash his hands of it," Saga says.

"But Palmcrona is already dead when Björn writes that he's giving up and sending the photograph to him," Joona says.

"And there's another problem. He doesn't actually have it. The photograph is in Penelope's apartment, taped to the glass door," Saga says. "And Penelope knows nothing about the blackmail attempt."

"He has to get the photograph without telling her anything," Tommy Kofoed says, nodding.

"We have no idea how he'd try to explain it," Saga says with a wry smile. "He was probably panicked, just wanted to put a stop to the whole thing, and hoped it would all blow over while they were hiding out on the boat in the archipelago."

Joona gets up and looks out the window. A woman carrying a child in her arms is pushing a stroller filled with grocery bags down on the sidewalk.

"The next morning, Penelope gets a taxi to the television studio for a debate," Saga continues. "As soon as she's left, Björn enters her apartment, tears down the photograph, runs to the subway station at Slussen, takes a subway to the Central Station, buys an envelope and some stamps at the Pressbyrån kiosk, and mails the photograph to Palmcrona. Then he runs to the Internet café and writes a note to Palmcrona to tell him that the photo has been sent. Björn then goes to his apartment and picks up his own and Penelope's luggage for the trip, and goes to his boat, which is docked at the motorboat club harbor at Långholmen. When Penelope is through, she takes the subway from Karlaplan and apparently goes directly to Hornstull to walk the last stretch to Långholmen."

"By now, the hit man has already ransacked Björn's apartment and started a fire that has destroyed the entire floor."

"But I've looked at that report," Petter objects. "The fire inspectors said it was caused by an iron that was left on in the neighboring apartment."

"I'm sure that's exactly how it happened," Joona says.

"Just as a gas explosion would be the official cause for the attempted fire in Penelope's apartment," Saga comments.

"The hit man's plan was to obliterate any trace," Joona continues. "When he did not find the photograph in Björn's apartment, he burns everything and heads next to Björn's boat."

"He's still searching for it," Saga adds. "He plans to kill them both and disguise the murders in a boating 'accident.'"

"What the hit man doesn't know is that there has been a change in plan. Penelope's sister, Viola, is also on the boat."

Joona falls silent and thinks about the dead woman in the morgue. Her young, vulnerable face. The red mark across her chest.

Joona continues. "I believe the young people anchor at one of the islands around Jungfrufjärden close to Dalarö. Before the hit man arrives, Penelope and Björn have gone ashore for one reason or another. When the hit man climbs aboard, he mistakes Viola for her sister. He drowns her in a tub and puts her in the bed of the main cabin. He has to wait for Björn, and while he does that, he must have searched for the photograph. Since it's not there, he occupies himself by completing the arrangement to have the boat explode. You have Erixson's report on that. We are not sure what happens next, but somehow Björn and Penelope escape."

"And the boat with Viola Fernandez on board is set adrift."

"We don't know how or where they run, but by Monday they're on Kymmendö."

Benny smiles. "At Ossian Wallenberg's place? He was a good television MC, but I always had the feeling he wasn't a good fit for this country."

Carlos clears his throat and pours more coffee.

"When the hit man realizes he's lost them, he goes to Penelope's apartment to continue the search for the photograph," Joona continues. "Erixson and I show up and foil his plan. Only when I'm facing him do I realize that we have a *grob*, an international hit man."

"We've decided he's able to tap into our police communications," Saga says.

"Is that how he found Björn and Penelope on Kymmendö?" asks Petter.

"We're not sure," Joona answers.

"He's very quick," Saga says. "Apparently he went to Dalarö to search for Björn and Penelope soon after he escaped from Penelope's apartment."

"Why do you assume this hit man is working alone?" asks Carlos.

"At this level, that's just how they do it," says Joona.

"So what happens next?"

"We're still reconstructing it," Petter says. "Somehow he managed to hijack the police launch and kill Lennart Johansson and Göran Sjödin. Then he drives the boat to Kymmendö, where Björn Almskog and Ossian Wallenberg are murdered. He blows up the launch. He follows Penelope and shoots down the Rescue Service helicopter."

"And disappears," Carlos sighs.

"But Petter Näslund acted so quickly that Penelope Fernandez was saved in the end," Joona says. He watches Pollock turn to Petter with interest.

"Of course, we've got to go through everything again in more detail," Petter says grimly. Nevertheless, there is an undernote of pleasure at having his actions recognized.

"Well, what about this photograph? There's got to be *something* there!" Carlos exclaims.

"It's just a fucking photograph," Petter says with a sigh.

"Seven people died because of it," Joona says gravely. "And more are going to die if we don't . . ."

Joona falls silent as he still looks out through the window.

"Maybe the photograph is a lock and we must hunt for the key," he says.

"What key?" asks Petter.

"The photographer," says Saga.

"Isn't Penelope Fernandez the photographer?" says Pollock.

"Perhaps," says Saga, drawing out the word.

"But?" asks Carlos.

"Where's any evidence for someone else?" Benny demands.

"Joona doesn't believe Penelope took that picture," Saga says.

"What the fuck!" Petter almost screams.

Carlos shuts his mouth firmly. He looks at the table and is smart enough to keep quiet.

"Penelope is still in a state of shock and we do not yet know her role in this," Saga says.

Nathan Pollock clears his throat and distributes copies of Carl Palmcrona's will across the table.

"Palmcrona has a bank account on the island of Jersey," he says.

"That wonderful tax haven." Petter Näslund nods. He takes his snuff out from beneath his lip. He wipes his thumb on the table without noticing Carlos's glance.

"Can we find out how much money he has in that account?" Verner asks.

"Officially, no," Joona says. "However, according to this will, he estimates he has nine million euros."

"His personal assets have taken a nosedive lately. It's hard to understand how he managed to accumulate so much lawfully in such a short time," Pollock states.

"Transparency International, the global agency fighting corruption, tells us they have nothing on Carl Palmcrona or anyone else in the ISP. Not even a rumor.

"Palmcrona's fortune was willed to a sixteen-year-old boy by the name of Stefan Bergkvist. As it turns out, he is Palmcrona's son. A son he'd never met in person—and a son who died in a freakish fire only three days after Palmcrona's suicide."

"The boy never knew who his father was," Saga adds.

"According to the preliminary police report, it is an accidental death," Carlos says.

"Of course. Accidental. But is there anyone in this room who believes it's just a coincidence that Palmcrona's son dies three days after Palmcrona's suicide?"

"No, a coincidence it is not," Carlos says.

"But that's just sick," Pollock exclaims. His cheeks flare red. "What motive would anyone have to murder a son Palmcrona never actually met?"

"What the hell is this all about?" Verner asks, rubbing his hands through his hair.

"Palmcrona keeps popping up again and again," Joona says. He taps the photograph on the face of the smiling man. "He's in the photograph. He's been blackmailed. He's found hanged. His son dies. He has nine million euros in the bank."

"The money is interesting," Saga says.

"We've looked at his life," Pollock says. "He has no other family, no other interests, doesn't invest in anything like stocks or—"

"So this accumulation of money in his bank account, it has to be connected in some way to his position as the general director of ISP," Joona says.

"Maybe he was involved in insider trading using a dummy front," Verner says.

"Or he took bribes," Saga says.

"Follow the money," Pollock whispers in English.

"Let's have a chat with his successor, Axel Riessen," Joona says, and gets ready to leave. "Anything odd or out of the way might be obvious to Riessen by now."

something to celebrate

Joona Linna and Saga Bauer hear whistles shriek and the insistent beating of drums when they reach the Royal Institute of Technology. A demonstration is heading down Odengatan. It seems to be about seventy young people carrying antifascist symbols and signs protesting Säpo's treatment of the Brigade's members. *"Säpo reeks of fascism, the state supports fascism!"* they chant in their bright young voices.

But the angry sounds disappear as Joona and Saga walk along idyllic Bragevägen, a gentle curve heading up to Engelbrekt Church. They'd contacted ISP to find that the general director was working from home that morning.

On the left side of the street, they soon see the Riessens' private palace. The façade is powerful with its dark, handcrafted brickwork, lead-lined windowpanes, carved woodwork, and the dull green of copper around the bay and chimney.

The outer door is equally imposing. A bronze plaque is affixed to the dark, shining wood to announce AXEL RIESSEN. Saga rings the doorbell. After a short time, a tall, tanned man opens the door. He has a friendly expression on his face.

Saga identifies herself as an inspector for the Security Service and explains their errand as briefly as possible while Axel Riessen examines her ID thoroughly. Then he looks up and says, "I doubt that I could be of much help to you, but—"

"It is always a pleasure to drop by," Joona says with courteous formality.

Axel gives him a surprised look, then smiles at Joona's pleasantry, appreciative of the joke. Dressed casually in dark blue trousers, a light blue shirt buttoned to the neck, and slippers, he shows them into the high-ceilinged entryway. It is filled with light.

"I suggest that we sit in the orangery. It's somewhat cooler there."

They find the apartment immense as they follow Axel past a mahogany staircase with dark wainscoting. They pass through two more large salons in a row to get to the orangery.

It is a glass room between the house and the garden. The high hedge right outside creates green shadows and a wall of flickering leaves. Scented herbs and scentless orchids fill copper pots lined up on benches and tiled surfaces.

"Please, make yourselves at home," Axel says, and gestures toward chairs around a table. "I was just about to take tea and crumpets and it would be pleasant to have some company."

"I haven't had crumpets since I was an exchange student in Edinburgh." Saga smiles.

"Well, then," Axel says contentedly, and leaves the room.

A few minutes later, he returns with a tray. He places the teapot, the napkins, the lemon wedges, and the sugar bowl in the middle of the table. The warm crumpets are covered by a linen cloth with a generous amount of butter nearby in a butter dish. Axel takes his time setting the table for them with care. He places teacups and saucers in front of them along with a linen napkin. Then he pours the tea.

They can hear soft violin music filtering through doors and walls.

"So tell me, what can I do for you?" Axel asks.

Saga carefully sets her cup and saucer down, clears her throat. "We have to ask you a few questions about ISP and we hope you'll be able to help us."

"Absolutely, but I must clear this first with a phone call," he says as he picks up his cell phone.

"Of course," Saga says.

"Please excuse me, but I've forgotten your name."

"Saga Bauer."

"May I please see your ID again, Saga Bauer?"

Saga hands it to him and he stands up and leaves the room. They can hear him speak for a few seconds, and then he returns, thanks them, and hands Saga her ID.

Saga starts her questions. "Last year, ISP issued export authorization for South Africa, Namibia, Tanzania, Algeria, and Tunisia. Ammunition for heavy machine guns, portable antitank guns, antitank rockets, grenade launchers—"

"And the JAS Gripen plane, of course," Axel adds. "Sweden has had a long working relationship with many of those countries."

"But never with Sudan?"

Axel meets her gaze with the hint of a smile. "Not to my knowledge."

"I mean before the arrest warrant was issued for President al-Bashir," she explains.

"I understand," he says strongly. "Otherwise it would be totally unthinkable. What we would call an absolute block, where there's nothing to discuss."

"You may have already had a chance to review many of your predecessor's—Carl Palmcrona's—decisions," Saga says.

"I have," Axel replies.

"Did you note anything odd?"

"What do you mean by 'odd'?"

"Decisions that appear strange to you," Saga says. She sips her tea again.

"Any reason for this question?" he asks.

"That's what we're asking you." She smiles.

"Then I'd say no."

"How far back in time have you been able to go?"

Joona listens to Saga's continuing questions regarding classification, preliminary permission, and export authorization of war matériel while he observes Axel Riessen's calm, attentive face. He hears the violin music again. It's now coming from outside, from the window open to the garden. It's a mazurka with high, sad notes. Then the violin stops, goes back to the beginning, and replays the piece.

Joona is listening to the music and thinking about the four people sitting in the private box. He touches his briefcase absentmindedly where he has the copy of the picture.

He thinks about Palmcrona and how he hung from the ceiling with a laundry line around his throat, about Palmcrona's will and Palmcrona's son.

Joona sees that Saga nods at something Axel is saying. A green shade passes over Axel's face, perhaps a reflection from the copper tray on the table.

Palmcrona understood the gravity of the situation immediately, Joona thinks. *All Björn Almskog had to mention in his blackmail letter was that Palmcrona was photographed in a private box with the arms dealer Raphael Guidi. Carl Palmcrona did not doubt the authenticity of the photograph for a moment.*

Maybe he already knew about its existence.

Or else Björn's knowledge made real a photograph he'd known nothing about.

Axel pours more tea for Saga. She is wiping a crumb from the corner of her mouth.

Something is not right here, Joona thinks.

Pontus Salman gave a definite date for the meeting. He did not find the photo troublesome.

So how did Palmcrona know the picture meant trouble?

Joona listens as Axel and Saga discuss how the initial situation of security policies will change when an embargo is imposed or lifted.

Joona makes a humming sound so they'll think he's following the discussion, but instead he concentrates on the meeting in the private box.

The table was set for four people and there were four people in the picture. This means that the fifth person, the one holding the camera, was not part of the party and would not be invited to sit down at the table with a champagne glass in his hand.

The fifth person probably has the answer to this riddle.

We'll have to get Penelope Fernandez to talk soon, Joona thinks. *Even if she is not the photographer, she might have the key; she might know who it was.*

His mind turns back to the people in the photograph: Carl Palmcrona, Raphael Guidi, Agathe al-Haji, and Pontus Salman.

Joona thinks back to their meeting with Pontus Salman. *He had pointed himself out right away. According to him, the only strange thing about the picture was that Carl Palmcrona was drinking champagne although they had nothing to celebrate. It was just a preliminary meeting.*

But maybe there was something to celebrate.

Joona's pulse quickens.

What if all four of them were about to toast an agreement with the champagne?

Pontus Salman had pointed himself out and given them so many details along with the place and the time.

The time, Joona thinks. *The time could be different.*

We have only Pontus Salman's word that the meeting happened in Frankfurt in 2008.

We need Penelope Fernandez's help.

Joona fiddles with the briefcase. *Would it be possible to identify the musicians in the background? Their faces are clear. Someone must recognize them.*

If we identify the musicians, we can pinpoint the time of the meeting. There are four people playing: a quartet.

Maybe the four of them have only played together once. That would fix the date beyond all doubt.

Of course, Joona thinks. *We should have gotten on this already.*

He intends to leave Saga and Axel Riessen to their discussion and return immediately to the police station. He wants to ask Petter Näslund if they'd considered the quartet of musicians as a way to find the exact date of the meeting.

He looks at Saga and watches her smile at Axel Riessen and then ask him about the American defense industry and their large corporations, Raytheon and Lockheed Martin.

Violin music can be heard again through the open window. It's a quicker piece this time. It stops suddenly and then there's the sound of two strings checked against each other.

"Who's playing?" Joona asks as he stands up.

"That's my brother, Robert," Axel says, somewhat surprised.

"I see—is he a professional violinist?"

"He's the pride and joy of the family . . . but these days he's primarily a violin maker. He has his studio on the grounds, here in the back."

"Would you mind if I go over to ask him a question?"

the string quartet

Joona walks with Axel out to the marble patio behind the house. The aroma from the lilac bushes is almost too heady. They continue to the studio, and Axel knocks. The violin stops. The door is opened by a middle-aged man whose thinning hair is belied by an extremely handsome, intelligent face. His body must once have been slim, but the passing years have left their mark.

"The police want to talk to you," Axel says in a no-nonsense tone. "You're suspected of disturbing the peace."

"I confess to everything," Robert says.

"Makes it easy," says Joona.

"Anything else?"

"We have a number of cold cases you could clear up, too." Joona smiles.

"I'm probably guilty of all of them," Robert replies, and he shakes hands with Joona.

"That's a relief," jokes Joona. "I'm Joona Linna from the National Criminal Investigation Department."

"What's this all about?" Robert is smiling.

"We're looking into a case of unexpected death. The previous general director of ISP. That's why I'm chatting with your brother."

"I know nothing more about Palmcrona than what's in the papers."

"May I come in for a moment?"

"Of course."

"I'll go on back to your colleague," Axel says, and closes the door behind Joona.

The ceiling of the studio has a steep slope, like an attic roof. A beautifully wrought wooden staircase leads down into the workshop, and the pleasant smell of freshly sawn wood, rosin, and turpentine rises to meet them. Everywhere violins hang in various stages of completion. Other construction gear is neatly collected: carefully chosen woods, scrolls, specialized tools for woodworking, planes as small as wine corks, bent knives, and much more.

"I heard your music through the window," Joona says.

Robert nods and gestures to a beautiful violin.

"It needed a little adjustment."

"You made it yourself?"

"Yes."

"It's unbelievably beautiful."

"Thanks."

Robert picks up the violin and hands it to Joona. The gleaming instrument is almost weightless. Joona turns it over and takes a deep sniff.

"The lacquer is a secret," Robert comments. He takes the instrument back and fits it in a case with wine-red lining.

Joona opens his briefcase and pulls out the plastic-encased photo and hands it to Robert.

"That's Palmcrona," Robert says.

"Yes, but do you happen to know the people in the background, the musicians?"

Robert looks at the picture again and nods.

"That's Martin Beaver," he says as he points. "Kikuei Ikeda . . . Kazuhide Isomura, and on cello that's Clive Greensmith."

"Are these musicians well-known?"

Robert can't help smiling at the question.

"They're a legend. This is the Tokyo String Quartet."

"The Tokyo String Quartet. Does that mean the same four people are in every performance?"

"Yes."

"Every time?"

"They've been together for a long time now. And doing very well."

"Anything particular or special about this photograph?"

Robert looks at the photograph very carefully.

"No," he finally says.

"They don't just play in Tokyo?" Joona asks.

"They play all over the world, but their instruments are owned by a Japanese endowment."

"Is that common?"

"Yes, especially with certain instruments," Robert answers. "These, the ones in this picture, are among the most precious instruments in the world."

"I see."

"It's the Paganini Quartet," Robert adds.

"The Paganini Quartet," Joona repeats as he stares at the photograph.

The wood gleams and the musicians' black clothes are reflected in the veneer.

"Stradivarius made them," Robert explains. "The oldest one is called Desaint, and it's a violin made in 1680—that's the one Kikuei is playing. Martin Beaver has the one that Count Cozio di Salabue presented to Paganini himself."

Robert hesitates, not wanting to bore Joona, but Joona nods for him to continue.

"Eventually all four instruments came into Niccolò Paganini's possession. I don't know how much you know about Paganini, but he was a virtuoso violinist and composer—he composed pieces that were considered ridiculous then because people, even musicians, thought they were impossible to play. Until Paganini himself took up the violin. After his death, it took one hundred years before any other violinist could approach his technique and play his pieces . . . and some of his techniques are still considered impossible. Yes, there are many legends about Paganini and his violin duels."

The room is silent. Joona takes another look at the photograph and the four men onstage in the background. He thinks about their instruments.

"So the Tokyo String Quartet often uses these particular instruments?"

"Yes. They play them in eight to nine concerts a month."

"Any ideas about when this photo might have been taken?"

"No more than ten years ago, at least, judging from Martin Beaver's looks. I've met him a few times."

"Perhaps where they're playing could give me the time?"

"This is the Alte Oper in Frankfurt."

"Are you absolutely sure?"

"I know they play there once a year," Robert says. "Sometimes twice or three times."

"*Perkele*," Joona mumbles in Finnish.

There must be some way to find out when this photograph was taken so if there's a hole in Pontus Salman's story we can find it.

Joona goes to replace the photo in his folder. Penelope is probably the only person who can shed any light on this.

Then he takes another look. He notes the principal violin, the placing of his bow, the elbow high . . . Joona's gray eyes look up into Robert's.

"Do they always play the same pieces on tour?"

"The same ones? No, I mean . . . they have been through all of Beethoven's quartets and that alone is a great variety. But they've played a number of other pieces as well: Schubert, Bartók. And Brahms, I know that. It's a long list . . . Debussy, Dvořák, Haydn, a great deal of Mozart and Ravel and on and on."

Joona is concentrating on his words and then he stands up to pace the studio before he stops and turns again toward Robert.

"I just thought of something," Joona says eagerly. "If you blew up this photograph and took a good look at the musicians' finger placement, their arm placement . . . would it be possible to determine which piece they're playing just from this photo?"

Robert opens and shuts his mouth, but then he smiles and picks up the photo again. In the spotlight on the Alte Oper stage, the Tokyo String Quartet members are seen clearly. Clive Greensmith's narrow face is unusually gentle, and his high forehead is glistening. And Kikuei Ikeda's little finger is high on the fingerboard, reaching for a high note.

"Sorry, I think that'd be impossible, it could be . . . any notes at all, but . . ."

"Say you had a magnifying glass . . . you can see the fingers, the strings, the necks of the instruments . . ."

"Sure, theoretically, but—" He sighs and shakes his head.

"Do you know someone who could help me?" Joona asks stubbornly.

"A musician or a professor at the Royal College of Music who might be able to analyze this photograph for us?"

"I wish I—"

"It's not possible, is it?" Joona asks.

"No, seriously, it isn't," Robert says, and shrugs. "If not even Axel could figure it out, no one can."

"Axel? Your brother?"

"Of course. You mean you haven't shown it to him?"

"No."

"Isn't that why you were talking to him?"

"No, you're the one who's the musician," Joona says, smiling.

"Go talk to him anyway," Robert says.

"Why should—"

Joona stops short, interrupted by a knock at the door. Saga Bauer steps in. The sunlight shines on her blond hair.

"Is Axel here?" she asks.

"No," Joona says.

"Another detective inspector?" asks Robert with a big grin.

"Säpo," Saga answers briskly.

The quiet lasts a moment too long. Robert is taking in Saga with his eyes as if he's fixated on her overlarge blue eyes and her neat rose mouth.

"I had no idea that Säpo had a division of elves," he says. He grins wider. Then he tries to become serious. "I'm sorry, I didn't mean to stare, but you do look like an elf, or a Bauer fairy-tale princess."

"Looks can be deceiving," Saga replies drily.

"I'm Robert Riessen," Robert says as he extends his hand.

"Saga," she says, and shakes his hand.

a feeling

Joona and Saga leave the Riessens' home and climb into the car. Saga's telephone vibrates. She looks at the text message and smiles to herself.

"I'm going to have lunch at home," she says. She blushes.

"What time is it?"

"Eleven thirty," she replies. "Are you going to keep working?"

"No, I'm going to go to the lunch concert at Södra Theater with a friend."

"Could you drop me off in Söder then? I live on Bastugatan."

"I'll drive you all the way home if you'd like," he says.

While Joona had been interviewing Robert, Saga had stayed with Axel. He was just starting a description of his UN career when he was interrupted by a call. Axel had looked at the display, excused himself, and left the room. After waiting fifteen minutes, she'd gone to Robert Riessen's studio. All three of them then looked for Axel before deciding he'd been called away from the house.

"What did you need to talk to Axel's brother about?"

"I just got a feeling . . ." Joona begins.

"Oh great," Saga mutters. "A feeling."

"You know . . . we showed the photograph to Pontus Salman," Joona continued. "He pointed himself out right away and then talked blah, blah, blah to the International Criminal Court's decision to indict—"

He stops talking as his phone rings. He searches for his phone without taking his eyes off the road and answers, "That was fast."

"The date is confirmed," Anja Larsson says. "The Tokyo String Quartet played at the Alte Oper in Frankfurt when Pontus Salman was there."

"I see," says Joona.

Saga watches as he listens to what Anja is saying, nods, thanks her, and hangs up.

"So Pontus Salman was telling the truth?" asks Saga.

"That we don't know."

"But the date is correct?"

"We only know that Pontus Salman went to Frankfurt and that the Tokyo String Quartet played at the Alte Oper . . . but Pontus Salman has been to Frankfurt often and the Tokyo String Quartet has also played at the Alte Oper at least once a year."

"Do you believe he lied about the date even though he knew we'd check it out?"

"No, but . . . well, I don't know. As I said, I just had a feeling," Joona says. "There's a good reason to lie if he and Carl Palmcrona were discussing business with Agathe al-Haji after the arrest warrant was issued."

"That would be a criminal offense, against international law. A weapons export directly to the militia in Darfur—"

"We believed Pontus Salman because he seemed so willing to help us, even pointing himself out," Joona says. "But because he told one truth doesn't mean that everything he says is true."

"So that's your feeling?"

"No, it was something in Salman's voice . . . when he said the only strange thing about the picture was that Carl Palmcrona didn't decline champagne . . ."

". . . since there was nothing to celebrate." Saga completes the thought.

"That's how he put it, but my feeling is that there *was* something to celebrate and they were toasting it with champagne. An agreement—"

"No facts to support what you've just said."

"But think about the picture for a second," Joona says stubbornly. "There's an atmosphere in that private box and . . . look at their faces, they're very happy about something."

"Even so, we can't prove it. We need Penelope Fernandez's help."

"What do her doctors have to say?"

"We'll be able to talk to her soon. But right now, she's mentally too exhausted."

"We have no idea what she can tell us," Joona says.

"No we don't, but what the hell *do* we have?"

"We have the photograph," Joona says. "We have the four musicians in it and perhaps we can tell the piece they were playing by their hand positions."

"Oh, Joona." Saga sighs.

"What?" he says, smiling.

"That's just fucking crazy—I hope you realize that."

"Robert said that theoretically it might be possible."

"Let's just wait until Penelope is a little better."

"I'll call," Joona says. He picks up his phone and calls the police station, requesting a connection to room U 12.

Saga looks at his impassive face.

"My name is Joona Linna and I—"

He stops talking and a large smile spreads across his face.

"Of course I remember you and your red cape," he says, and listens some more. "Yes, but . . . I almost believed you were going to suggest hypnosis?"

Saga can hear the doctor's laughing voice through the phone.

"No, but really—we absolutely, *absolutely* must talk to her."

His face takes a serious turn.

"I can understand her feelings, but can't you change her mind? All right, we'll just have to figure something else out . . . Bye."

He hangs up at the same time he turns onto Bellmansgatan.

"That was Dr. Daniella Richards," Joona tells Saga.

"What does she say?"

"She feels we can question Penelope in a few days. The big problem is we have to find a different place for her to live—she refuses to stay in that underground room. She says—"

"There's no more secure place."

"She refuses," Joona says simply.

"We've got to make it clear how dangerous the situation is."

"I believe she knows that better than we do."

seven million alternatives

In the Mosebacke Etablissement's restaurant, Disa and Joona are sitting across from each other. Sunshine fills the room through the enormous windows looking out over Gamla Stan, Skeppsholmen, and the glittering water. They are just finishing a lunch of fried Baltic herring with mashed potatoes garnished with lingonberries. They pour the last of the light beer into their glasses. In the background, on a raised platform, Ronald Brautigam performs on a black grand piano. The violinist, Isabelle van Keulen, is finishing the last stroke of her bow, her right elbow lifted.

The last note of the violin trembles, waiting for the piano, then finishes with a high, shivering sound as the music ends. After the concert, Joona and Disa walk out of the restaurant and onto Mosebacke Square. They pause for a moment, facing each other.

"What's all this about Paganini?" she asks. She pats Joona's collar into place. "The last time we were together, you talked about Paganini, too."

He gently catches her hand.

"I just wanted to see you—"

"Just so we can argue about you not taking your medicine?"

"No," he says seriously.

"Do you take it, then?"

"I'll start soon," he says a bit impatiently.

She says nothing more, meets his eyes for a second, then sighs and suggests they keep walking.

"At any rate, it was a very pleasant concert," she says. "Somehow I felt the music fit this soft light here, outside. I'd always thought Paganini was . . . well, you know, like a tightrope walker. Actually, I did have the chance to hear Yngwie Malmsteen play the Caprice no. 5 once at Gröna Lund."

"Ah, in the days when you and Benjamin Gantenbein were going out."

"We've just become Facebook friends after all these years."

They walk to Slussen hand in hand and head down Skeppsbron.

"Do you think you could tell what music a violinist is playing just by the finger positions?"

"Without hearing it, you mean?"

"On a photograph."

"Maybe. Perhaps you might get pretty close . . . it depends on how well you know the instrument," she replies.

"How close? How exact?"

"I'll ask Kaj if you think it's important," she says.

"Who's Kaj?"

"Kaj Samuelsson. He works in the music history department. He was a good friend of my father's and I used to practice driving with him."

"Can you phone him now?"

"Sure," Disa says, and then raises her eyebrows slightly. "You're not kidding. You really want me to call him this second."

"Yes," Joona says.

Disa drops his hand and pulls out her cell phone. She scrolls through her contact list and then calls the professor.

"Hi, Disa here," she says. "Am I interrupting your lunch?"

Joona can hear the sound of a man's voice coming from the phone. After a little small talk, Disa says, "By the way, I have a good friend here with some questions for you."

She laughs at something he says and then she asks directly, "Can you tell which note a violinist is playing . . . no, not that way . . . just by looking at the fingers?"

Joona observes Disa who listens, frowning. From Gamla Stan, he can hear the distant strains of march music.

"All right," Disa says. "You know what, Kaj, I think I'll just hand you over to him directly."

She hands the phone to Joona without saying a word.

"Joona Linna," he says.

"Ah, Disa talks about you a great deal," says Kaj Samuelsson. He sounds relaxed.

"A violin has only four strings," Joona begins. "Logically, there are only a limited number of notes that can be played."

"Where are you going with this?"

"The lowest note is the open G," Joona continues calmly. "And somewhere there must be the highest note that—"

"Yes, good reasoning," the professor says. "In 1636, the French scientist Mersenne published the *Harmonie universelle*. In that work, he posits that the best violinists can play one octave higher than the open string. This means the range can be from G to third E, which gives us altogether thirty-four notes in the chromatic scale."

"Thirty-four notes," Joona repeats.

"But if we go to musicians in the modern era, the range is greater due to new fingerings," Samuelsson continues. He sounds amused. "And you can begin to count on reaching third A and have a chromatic scale of thirty-nine notes."

"Keep going," Joona says, watching Disa, who has gone off to look at some odd, jumbled-looking paintings displayed in a gallery window.

"However, when Richard Strauss expanded Berlioz's *Grand Treatise on Instrumentation and Modern Orchestration* from 1904, fourth G became accepted as the highest possible note that could be reached by an orchestra violinist, which means forty-nine notes."

Kaj Samuelsson laughs to himself at Joona's impressed silence.

"Actually, we have yet to reach the highest possible note," the professor explains. "And in addition, we now have flageolets and quarter tones."

Disa and Joona are now strolling past a newly built replica of a Viking ship docked at Slottskajen as he speaks. They're nearing Kungsträdgården.

"What about a cello?" Joona asks impatiently.

"Fifty-eight," Samuelsson replies.

Disa is giving Joona a vexed look and points at an outdoor café.

"My real question is, if you were to look at a photograph of four musicians—two violins, one viola, and one cello—and if the image is clear, would you be able to tell, just from the placement of their fingers on the strings, which piece they're playing?"

Joona hears Kaj Samuelsson mumbling to himself on the other end.

"There are so many alternatives, thousands . . ."

Disa shrugs and keeps walking without looking at Joona.

"Seven million combinations," Kaj says at last.

"Seven million," Joona repeats.

There's silence on both ends of the phone.

"Yet on my photograph," Joona goes on, his voice stubborn, "you can clearly see the fingers and the strings so that many alternatives could be eliminated immediately."

"I'll gladly take a look at your photo," the professor replies. "But I would not be able to guess the notes, it's just not possible and—"

"But—"

"Imagine, Joona Linna," the professor continues happily. "Imagine you've actually figured out the approximate notes . . . How will you be able to tell from all the thousands of string quartets out there—Beethoven, Schubert, Mozart—which one is the correct composition?"

"I realize it might be impossible," Joona says.

"Seriously, it is," Kaj replies.

Joona thanks him for his time and goes to Disa, who is sitting on the rim of a fountain waiting for him. She lays her cheek on his shoulder as he sits down beside her. Just as he's putting an arm around her, he remembers Robert Riessen's words about his brother: *If not even Axel could figure it out, no one can.*

the riddle

While Joona is quickly walking up on the Bragevägen sidewalk, he hears children happily yelling on the grounds of the German School.

He rings Axel's doorbell and hears the melodious chime inside, but no one answers, and after waiting for a while, he decides to walk around the house. Suddenly he hears a screeching noise. He can see people standing in the shadow of a tree, and he pauses at a distance. A girl holding a violin stands on the marble patio. She looks about fifteen years old. Her hair is extremely short, and he can see some drawings she's inked on her arms. Axel Riessen is with her, nodding and listening carefully as she drags the bow across the strings. Her movements look awkward, as if she's holding the instrument for the very first time. Perhaps this is Axel's daughter, or even his grandchild, because he watches her with such a gentle, curious expression.

The bow crosses the strings at the wrong angle and elicits a hissing, whining sound.

"It's not in tune," the girl says as an excuse for the terrible noise.

She smiles and, with care, hands the instrument back to Axel.

"Playing the violin means listening," Axel says in a calm, friendly fashion. "The music is already inside you. You just release it into the world."

He sets the violin to his own shoulder and begins to play the introductory melody to "Séguedille" from Bizet's *Carmen,* then stops and holds out the violin to demonstrate.

"Now I'm going to tune these strings a little strangely, here . . . and here," he says, and he turns the pegs a few times in different directions.

"Why are—"

"Now the violin is completely out of tune," he continues. "And if I'd only learned how to play mechanically with exact fingering, then I would sound like this."

He plays "Séguedille" again, and it is so terrible it's almost unrecognizable.

"How pretty!" she says, joking.

"However, if you listen to the strings . . ." he says as he taps the E string. "Hear that? It's much too low, but that makes no difference at all. You compensate by moving your finger farther up the fingerboard."

Joona watches Axel Riessen put the violin back on his shoulder and play the piece again on the falsely tuned violin. He seems to use gymnastic fingering, but the piece is perfectly in tune.

"You're a magician!" The girl laughs and claps her hands.

"Hello," Joona says. He walks up and holds out his hand. Axel gathers the violin and bow together in his left hand and then shakes Joona's hand. The girl shyly does the same.

He looks at Axel with his mistuned violin.

"That's impressive."

Axel shakes his head.

"As a matter of fact, I haven't played for thirty-four years." His voice sounds stiff as he says this.

"Do you believe that?" Joona asks the girl.

She nods and then she says mysteriously, "Don't you see the glow around him?"

"This is Beverly," Axel says in a low voice. "Beverly Andersson."

Beverly gives Axel a big smile, and then she simply walks away between the trees.

Joona nods at Axel. "I need to talk to you."

"Sorry about earlier, when I took off like that," Axel says. He begins to retune the violin. "But something came up."

"Not to worry—I just came back."

Joona watches Axel, who, in turn, watches the girl pick some flowering weeds from the shaded lawn.

"Do we have a vase inside?" she calls out.

"In the kitchen," Axel replies.

She carries her tiny bouquet of dandelions—white balls of fluff—into the kitchen.

"That's her favorite flower," Axel says as he listens closely to the G string. He adjusts the peg slightly and then sets the violin on the mosaic table.

"I'd like you to take a look at this," Joona says, and he takes out the photograph from the folder.

They sit down at the table. Axel takes a pair of glasses from his front pocket and studies the photograph thoroughly.

"When was this taken?" he asks quickly.

"We don't know, but it was suggested this was in the spring of 2008," Joona replies.

"All right." Axel looks much more relaxed immediately.

"Do you recognize these people?" Joona asks calmly.

"Of course," Axel says. "Palmcrona, Pontus Salman, Raphael Guidi, and . . . Agathe al-Haji."

"I need your help in one specific area. Could you take a good look at the musicians in the background?"

Axel looks up at Joona speculatively and then down again at the photograph.

"The Tokyo String Quartet—they're very good," he says in a neutral voice.

"Well, the thing I'm wondering about is . . . I've been thinking about this picture and wondering if it is possible for a knowledgeable person to tell . . . just by looking at the picture . . . which piece they're playing."

"That's an interesting question."

"Would there be, even remotely, a possibility for an educated guess? Kaj Samuelsson didn't think so, and when your brother took a look, he said it was completely impossible."

Joona leans forward, his eyes smooth and warm in the shade.

"Your brother was adamant that if you couldn't solve this riddle, no one could."

A smile plays at the edges of Axel's mouth.

"He said that, did he?"

"Yes," Joona says. "Though I'm not sure what he meant by that."

"Nor am I."

"Still, take a close look at this picture. I have a magnifying glass—"

"You want to know when this meeting took place, don't you," Axel states in a suddenly grave tone.

Joona nods and takes a magnifying glass out of his briefcase.

"You should be able to see their fingers clearly," Joona says.

Joona sits back quietly and watches Axel minutely examine the photograph. He thinks if this had been taken in 2008, as they'd been told, his intuition had been wrong. But if these people had met after the arrest order in March 2009, the photograph was proof of criminal activity.

"Yes, I see the positions of their fingers," Axel says slowly.

"Could you guess which notes they're playing?" Joona asks expectantly.

Axel sighs, hands the photograph and the magnifying glass back to Joona, and then sings four notes aloud in a soft but clear voice as if it emanated from inside himself. Then he takes up the violin and plays two high, trembling notes.

Joona Linna stands up.

"And this is no joke—"

Axel Riessen looks directly into Joona's eyes and shakes his head. "No. Martin Beaver is playing a third C, Kikuei is playing a second C, Kazuhide Isomura has a rest, and Clive is playing a four-note pizzicato. That's what I sang, E, A, A, and C."

Joona writes this down. He asks, "How exact is your guess?"

"It's not a guess," Axel replies.

"Does this combination appear in many pieces? I mean, just by identifying these notes can you deduce the exact piece the Tokyo String Quartet is playing at this moment in this picture?"

"This combination is found in only one place," Axel replies.

"How do you know that?"

Axel turns away and looks away at a window in the house. Shadows of lacy leaves reflect on the glass.

"I'm sorry, please continue," Joona says.

"Of course, I have not heard every piece the quartet has played," Axel says with a shrug.

"But, again, you are sure this exact combination of notes is found in only one specific composition?" Joona asks again.

"I know of only one," Axel replies calmly. "Measure 156 in the first movement of Béla Bartók's Second String Quartet."

Axel picks up the violin and puts it to his shoulder.

"Tranquillo . . . this movement is so wonderfully peaceful, almost like a lullaby. Listen to the first voice," he says as he begins to play.

Axel's fingers move tenderly, the notes quiver, the music sings, light and soft. After four measures, he stops.

"Both violins follow each other. Same note, different octaves," he explains. "It's almost too beautiful, but then the cello's A-minor chord makes the violin's notes dissonant . . . even though they're not experienced as dissonant because they're harmonics, which . . ."

He stops talking and puts down the violin.

Joona watches him.

"So you're absolutely certain these musicians are playing Bartók's Second String Quartet?" Joona says quietly.

"Yes."

Joona, suddenly jittery, gets up and walks across the patio to stop by the lilac-bush hedge. This is everything he needs to determine the time of the meeting.

He smiles to himself, and immediately smoothes away the triumph with his hand. He turns back, takes a red apple from the bowl on the table, and meets Axel's questioning gaze.

"So yes, you're absolutely sure," Joona confirms again.

Axel nods and Joona gives him the apple. He turns aside to pull his cell phone from his jacket to call Anja.

"Anja, this is a rush—"

"We're going to take a sauna together this weekend," Anja replies.

"I need your help."

"I know." Anja giggles.

Joona tries to hide the tension in his voice.

"I need you to check the repertoire of the Tokyo String Quartet for the past ten years."

"I've already done that."

"Specifically what they played at the Alte Oper in Frankfurt during that time?"

"Yes, they went there annually, in fact."

"Have they ever played the Bartók Second String Quartet?" There's a pause as she checks her information.

"Yes, Opus 17. They've played it once."

"Opus 17," Joona repeats and meets Axel's eyes. Axel nods.

"What?" Anja asks.

"So when did they play that piece?"

"The thirteenth of November 2009."

"Are you absolutely sure?"

The people in the photograph met eight months after the arrest warrant for Sudan's president, Joona thinks. *Pontus Salman lied about the date. They met in November 2009. And all of this carnage has come from that—the brutal deaths of so many and perhaps even more in the future.*

Joona reaches out and absentmindedly brushes some lilac blossoms, and he can smell the barbecue on an outdoor grill in a yard somewhere. He thinks he must call Saga Bauer about this breakthrough.

"Was that it?" Anja says on the other end.

"Yes."

"Can you use the little word?"

"Oh, yes . . . *Kiitokseksi saat pusun,*" Joona says in Finnish. *As thanks, I'll give you a kiss.*

Joona ends the call.

Pontus Salman lied, Joona thinks again. *There were no exceptions or loopholes to a complete weapons embargo.*

But Agathe al-Haji wanted to buy ammunition. And the others wanted money. None of them could have cared less about human rights or international law.

Pontus Salman thought that one truth—openly pointing himself out in the photo—would obscure the big lie: the date they met.

Joona pictures Pontus Salman in his mind's eye: an oddly placid man with no emotions in his face.

Arms deals. Arms deals and the money they bring, the whisper in his head tells him. *All of this is due to weapons smuggling: the photograph, the blackmail attempt, the dead people.*

He pictures Saga Bauer standing up after their conversation with Salman. She'd left the marks of her five fingers on his desk as a silent testimony.

March 2009. That's when the International Criminal Court in The Hague issued an arrest warrant for Sudanese president Omar al-Bashir for direct involvement in the extermination of three ethnic groups in Darfur. At that moment, all the usual supplies of ammunition from the rest of the world stopped. Sudan's army still had their weapons—their machine guns and assault rifles—but they would be running low on, and soon be out of, ammunition. The strangled supply would strangle the militia in Darfur. Except these four—Carl Palmcrona, Pontius Salman, Raphael Guidi, and Agathe al-Haji—had chosen to put themselves above international law.

"What did you find out?" Axel asks as he stands up.

"What?" Joona is startled out of his thoughts.

"Could you determine the date of that meeting?"

"Yes."

Axel tries to catch Joona's eyes.

"And?" Axel persists.

"I have to go," Joona says.

"Did they meet after the arrest warrant for al-Bashir? They can't have! I have to know if that's what they've done!"

Joona looks directly into Axel's eyes. His eyes are calm and bright.

one last question

Saga Bauer lies on her stomach on the fluffy white rug. Her eyes are closed as Stefan slowly kisses her back. Her light hair spreads like a waterfall onto the floor. Stefan's face feels warm as it moves across her skin.

Keep going, she thinks.

His lips are light, tickling brushstrokes between her shoulder blades. She forces herself to keep still and shudders from pleasure.

Carl Unander-Scharin's erotic duet for cello and mezzo-soprano flows from the speakers of her music system. The voices of the woman and the cello cross rhythmically and repetitively like entwined trickles in a dark stream. Saga lies completely still, desire rising in her body. She is breathing through a half-open mouth and she licks her lips.

His hands glide over her waist, around her hips, and then effortlessly he lifts her buttocks.

No one I've ever met before has touched me so softly, Saga thinks as she smiles to herself.

She hears her own moan as she feels the touch of his tongue.

He carefully turns her body over. Impressions of stripes are left on her skin from the rug.

"Keep going," she whispers.

"Or you'll shoot me," he says.

She nods and smiles openly. Wisps of Stefan's black hair have curled around his face, and his narrow ponytail is hanging over one of her breasts.

"Come, come," Saga whispers.

She pulls his face down to hers and kisses him and her tongue meets his, warm and wet.

He quickly wriggles out of his jeans and lays down naked over her. She lifts her legs and feels him push inside. She moans a long moan and then breathes more quickly. They hesitate for a moment to marvel at the feeling of being beyond nearness. Stefan pushes softly. His narrow hips move carefully. Saga runs her fingers over his shoulder blades, his back, his buttocks.

Then the telephone rings. *Of course*, her thought snaps out. From the heap of clothes on the sofa, her cell phone sounds persistently with ZZ Top's "Blue Jeans Blues." It is well buried beneath her white linen chemise, underwear, and jeans pulled inside out.

"Let it ring," she whispers.

"It's your work phone," he says.

"Fuck it, it's not important," she mumbles and tries to hold him tight to her.

But he pulls out, gets to his knees, and searches through her jeans pockets while the phone nags insistently. Finally, he turns her jeans upside down and the phone falls out. It's stopped ringing. Then a small ding announces there's a message on the voice mail.

Twenty minutes later, Saga is running through the hallway of the police station, the tips of her hair still damp from her quick shower. Her body still vibrates, desirous and unsatisfied. Her underwear and jeans feel uncomfortable, and not quite right.

Anja Larsson's plump face pokes up over her computer, questioning, as Saga runs to Joona's office. He waits in the middle of the floor. His gray eyes give her a sharp glance and she feels a shudder of unease.

"Close the door," he says grimly.

She shuts it immediately and turns back to him. She's quietly panting.

"Axel Riessen remembers every single piece of music he's ever heard. Every note from every instrument in any symphony orchestra."

"And?"

"He knew immediately which piece the string quartet was playing. It was Béla Bartók's Second String Quartet."

"Okay, you were right. Now we know what they were playing, but we—"

"This photograph was taken in November 2009," Joona says sharply.

"So those devils ignored the embargo. They were doing a deal for arms," she says bitterly.

"Right."

"And they planned that the ammunition was to be siphoned into Darfur," she whispers.

Joona nods while the muscles in his jaw tighten. "Carl Palmcrona should never have been there. Not with Pontus Salman, not with anyone—"

"And here they are together, caught in a photograph," Saga says triumphantly. "Toasting a deal with Raphael Guidi and al-Haji."

"That's right." Joona meets Saga's summer-blue eyes.

"They say the really big fish always get away," Saga murmurs. "People have always said it . . . most people realize it . . . but it's true. The big ones almost always go free pretty much."

They silently gaze down at the photograph again. Four people in a private box. The champagne. The expressions on their faces. The musicians playing on Paganini's instruments at the Alte Oper. "Now we've figured out the first riddle," Saga says and takes a deep breath. "A dirty deal to get arms to Sudan."

"Palmcrona was there. The money in his account must surely have come from bribes," Joona says slowly. "But at the same time, Palmcrona did not authorize this deal. It would be impossible. He could never get it through—"

Joona is interrupted by the phone in his jacket. He answers, listens in silence, and then ends the call. He looks at Saga.

"Axel Riessen has figured out what's going on," Joona says. "He knows what the photograph means."

a perfect plan

A lone boy made of iron, fifteen centimeters high, sits with his arms wrapped around his knees. The statue is located in the back garden of the Finnish church in Gamla Stan. Axel Riessen is three meters away, leaning on the ocher wall, eating noodles from a carton. He waves with his chopsticks as Joona and Saga walk through the gate.

"Tell us what you've figured out," Joona says abruptly.

Axel nods, puts the carton of food down on the windowsill of the church, wipes his mouth with a paper napkin, and then takes time to shake hands with Joona and Saga.

"You said you understand what the photograph means," Joona repeats.

Axel looks down, takes a deep breath, and then begins to speak. "It's all about Kenya," he says. "The four people in the box are celebrating an agreement on a huge shipment of ammunition to Kenya."

He stops.

"Keep going," Joona prompts.

"Kenya is buying 1.25 million units of licensed, manufactured 5.56 x 45 millimeter ammunition."

"For automatic rifles," Saga says.

"Supposedly an export to Kenya," Axel says. "But they'll never see it. It will be diverted to Sudan and the militia in Darfur. It suddenly all came to me. Agathe al-Haji is the buyer's representative; therefore, it is for Sudan."

"How does Kenya fit in?" Joona asks.

"These four in the box meet after the arrest warrant was issued. Right? We know because of the date this composition is being played. An embargo is on Sudan . . . but not on Kenya. And Kenya is nearby, located just to the south."

"How can you be so sure?" Saga asks.

"Carl Palmcrona opted out of this tangle through suicide. This was his last job but he left it unfinished. He left it to me to carry out," Axel says bitterly. "And I've promised to sign the export authorization today."

"So it's the same business deal, just with the name of Sudan crossed out and Kenya put in," Saga says.

"It's watertight," Axel says.

"Or it was before someone photographed the meeting," Joona says drily.

"Before Palmcrona committed suicide, all the work was done. They believed he would sign the authorization," Axel tells them.

"And now they're really uptight to find out he hadn't done it." Joona smiles.

"Everything's left hanging," Saga says.

"I was brought in quickly," Axel says. "They practically forced a pen into my hand to make me sign the contract."

"But?"

"I wanted to make my own decisions."

"And you have."

"Right."

"And all the paperwork looked fine?" Saga asks.

"Yes . . . and I promised to sign and I would have, without a doubt, if I hadn't seen that photograph and connected it with the Kenyan deal."

They all stand quietly, contemplating the iron statue of the boy. It's the smallest public artwork in Stockholm. Joona leans forward and pats the boy's shiny head. The metal radiates warmth after a full day in the sun.

"They're already loading the container ship in Gothenburg Harbor," Axel says quietly.

"I've guessed as much," Saga says. "But without export authorization, then—"

"Then the ammunition cannot leave Sweden."

"They expect you to sign today?" Joona asks. "Can you delay it somehow? We've got to keep on with our investigation and releasing that cargo might hinder it."

"They're not going to just sit around and wait."

"Tell them that you're still going through the paperwork," Joona suggests.

"Well, I can do that, but it won't be easy. The deal's already delayed because of me, but I'll give it a shot," Axel says.

"Keep in mind your safety, too. Our investigation is important, but—"

Axel smiles and asks skeptically, "Do you think they'll threaten me?"

Joona smiles back gravely. "As long as they want a signature from you, you're not in danger. But if you block this, they'll lose an incredible amount of money. Just imagine what it's already taken to bribe people all the way from Sweden to Kenya."

"I can't delay the signature forever. Salman's been trying to reach me all day. These people know the field. You can't deceive them too long." Just then, Axel's cell phone rings.

He looks at the display and grimaces. "It's Pontus Salman again—"

"Pick it up," Joona says.

"All right," Axel says, and takes the call. They can all hear the staccato voice on the other end.

"I couldn't reach you," Salman says accusingly. "You know the ship is already loaded and waiting. It costs money to keep it in the harbor. The ship's owner has also tried to contact you. They haven't gotten the authorization form yet."

"I am so sorry," Axel says soothingly. He looks at Joona and Saga. "Unfortunately, I haven't had time to take one last look at—"

"I've talked to the government officials and they said you were going to sign today."

Axel blanks, his thoughts suddenly scattering. He's tempted to just hang up. Instead, he clears his throat, apologizes, and then he lies. "Something else came up that required my immediate attention. I had to put this aside for a moment—"

Axel can hear how false his voice sounds, and he had taken too long to answer. He was tempted again to simply tell the truth: that there would be no export authorization because he now knows the truth about the illegal deal.

"We understood this would be completed today," Salman says, not trying to hide his anger.

"You took a risk," Axel says.

"What are you telling me?"

"Without my authorization there can be no shipment—"

"But we have . . . *excuse me?*"

"You had permission to manufacture the ammunition and there's been a positive preliminary decision. But that's all."

"You understand there's a great deal at stake here," Salman says pleadingly. "What can I tell the ship's owner? Can you give us any idea at all about how long the delay will be? He needs to know how long he must stay in port. It's purely a question of logistics."

"I remain positive. But I still need to go through everything one last time. Then you'll get my decision," Axel says firmly.

the bait

Saga Bauer has been jumping rope for fifty minutes in the police station's gym when a worried colleague comes up to her and asks how she's doing. Her face is sweaty and serious, but her feet keep dancing as if unaware of the quickly passing jump rope.

"You're hard on yourself," he says.

"Nope," she replies, and keeps jumping.

Twenty-five minutes later, Joona comes down to the gym and sits on an incline bench next to a barbell.

"What a bunch of shit," she says, and she keeps jumping rope. "They're going to pump this ammunition into Darfur and we can't do a damn thing about it."

"Well, at any rate, we know what they're up to," Joona replies calmly. "We know that they're trying to go through Kenya and—"

"But what the hell can we do about it?" she asks as she jumps. "Arrest that bastard Pontus Salman? Contact Europol about Raphael Guidi?"

"We still have no proof."

"This is a big thing, much bigger than anyone realized. We certainly didn't want to have anything to do with something this huge," she reasons while the jump rope whirls around her and whacks the floor. "Carl Palmcrona is involved, Pontus Salman from Sweden . . . Raphael Guidi, he's a bigwig . . . and someone in Kenya's government, otherwise this whole deal wouldn't work . . . and probably someone in Sweden's government."

"We probably won't get everyone," Joona says.

"The smartest thing would be to drop the case," she says.

"So let's drop it."

She laughs at his joke as she keeps jumping with a serious expression.

Joona says thoughtfully, "Palmcrona has probably been taking bribes for years, but once he received Björn's blackmail letter, he realized the party was over . . . so he called someone . . . probably Raphael . . . but during the conversation he realized that he was expendable . . . and he was even a problem now that the photograph's existence was known. All the people investing in this deal wanted him gone. They were not about to lose their money and risk their situation because of him."

"So then he kills himself." Saga begins jumping even faster.

"He's out of the picture, so that leaves the photograph and the blackmailer."

"In comes the international hit man." Saga is beginning to be out of breath.

Joona nods while she jumps with raised knees.

"If Viola had not been on the boat at the last minute, he would have killed Björn and Penelope and sunk the boat," he says.

Saga does one last, fast burst and then stops.

"We would have . . ." she says, panting. "We would have written it off as an accident. The hit man would have gotten the photograph, cleaned out all the computers, left the country without a trace."

"Though I think that he's not the kind to be afraid of being discovered. He's practical," Joona says. "It's easier to solve the problem without getting the police involved, but solving the problem is what he's all about . . . otherwise, he wouldn't bother to burn the apartments. This draws attention. He's just being thorough and he prioritizes thoroughness above all."

Saga steadies herself with her hands on her thighs. Sweat drops from her face.

"Of course, we'd put the apartment fires and the boat accident together sooner or later," she says. She straightens up.

"But then it would be too late," he says. "The hit man's job is to erase the evidence and eliminate the witnesses."

"But now we have the photograph and Penelope," Saga says with a smile. "That hit man hasn't solved the problem."

"Not yet . . ."

Saga gives a few random blows to the boxing bag hanging from the ceiling and then looks Joona over. "During my training, I saw a film of a bank robbery and how you rendered the suspect harmless with a broken pistol."

"I was lucky," Joona says.

"Right."

He laughs and she comes up to him, circles him with fancy footwork and then stops. She reaches out with open hands and meets his eyes. She waves at him to come on, waggling her fingers. She's wanting him to take her on for a round. He smiles as he understands her reference to Bruce Lee: the waving hand. He shakes his head but doesn't break eye contact.

"I've seen how you move," he says.

"Then you know," she says shortly.

"You're quick and you'll get in the first blow, but after that—"

"I'm cooked," she answers.

"It's a good thought, but—"

She makes the same gesture again, a bit more impatiently.

"But you will come in much too hard," he says, amused.

"No, I won't," she says.

"Try it and you'll find out," Joona says calmly.

She waves once more, but he doesn't seem to care. He gets up and turns his back to her as he heads for the door. She goes straight for him to land a right hook. He bends his neck slightly and the blow sails over his head. As a smooth continuation, Joona spins around and draws his pistol while taking her down to the ground with a kick to the kneecap.

"I have to tell you something," Saga says.

"That I was right, right?"

"Don't flatter yourself." She glares at him as she gets up.

"If you head in too hard—"

"I wasn't heading in hard," she says. "I held back because I'd just thought of something important."

"I get it!" He laughs.

"I don't give a shit what you think you get or don't get," she says. "My idea is to use Penelope as bait."

"What are you getting at?"

"I started to think about how she wants to go somewhere else and then at the moment I was about to hit you, I got an idea. I couldn't knock you out if I had to talk to you."

"So talk," he says.

"I realized that Penelope would be bait anyway, whether we'd be involved or not. She'd lure the hit man to her."

Joona stops smiling and nods slowly.

"Keep talking," he says.

"We don't know for sure if the hit man can listen in to our communication, if he can hear everything we say via RAKEL . . . but it's probable since he found Penelope on Kymmendö," Saga says.

"Right."

"He'll find her one way or another, that's what I think. He doesn't care if she's under police protection or not. We'll do everything we can to keep her placement a secret, but it's hellish to protect her without radio communication."

"He will find her," Joona says.

"That's what I was thinking. Penelope will be bait, no matter what. The question is: Are we going to be ready when he comes? She gets just as much protection as planned, but if we put the stakeout guys from Span to watch the place as well, maybe we can catch this guy."

"That's entirely possible. You're thinking in the right direction," Joona says.

the safe apartment

Carlos, Saga, and Joona are heading down the long hallway to Säpo headquarters. Verner Zandén is already waiting for them, and without unnecessary greetings, he speaks the minute they've shut the door behind them.

"Klara Olofsdotter at the International Prosecutor's Office is in on this. I don't have to tell you, this is a big stakeout for CID and Säpo. But who the hell are we trying to catch?"

"We know next to nothing about him," Saga says. "We don't even know if he's working alone or if he's part of a team of professional killers from Belgium, or Brazil, or even leftover operatives from the KGB or from the former Eastern bloc."

"It's not very difficult to listen in on our radio communications," Carlos admits.

"This man knows Penelope's being protected and it will be difficult to get at her," Joona says. "But there are always small chances: at times a door must be opened, guards change, people bring her food, she'll have to meet her mother, confer with a psychologist, and she's planning to meet Niklas Dent from the NHS—"

Joona stops talking when his cell phone rings. He checks the display and clicks it to voice mail.

"Of course, our first priority is Penelope," Saga says. "But even while protecting her, we feel we might have a chance to catch this man who's murdered so many of our colleagues."

"I don't have to remind you that he's extremely dangerous," Joona says. "None of us will meet a more dangerous human."

The secure apartment, at Storgatan 1, has a window that faces Sibylle-gatan with a view over Östermalm Square. There are no apartment buildings across the street and the closest building is at least one hundred meters away.

Saga Bauer holds the steel door open at street level for Dr. Daniella Richards to lead Penelope Fernandez from an iron-gray police bus. Armored Säpo guards surround them.

"This is the most secure aboveground apartment in all of Stockholm," Saga explains.

Penelope doesn't seem to notice her words. She just follows Dr. Richards to the elevator. Security cameras proliferate around the entry hall and the stairwell.

"We've put in motion detectors, an advanced alarm system, and two encrypted direct lines to Central Control," Saga tells Penelope as the elevator heads up.

On the fourth floor, Penelope is brought through a heavy door to yet another locked door, which yet another uniformed officer opens, letting them into the apartment.

"This apartment has tremendous protection against fire," Saga says. "It has its own electrical generator and its own ventilation system."

"You're safe here," Dr. Richards says gently.

Penelope raises her face and looks at the doctor with an empty expression.

"Thanks," she finally says, almost soundlessly.

"I can stay with you if that's what you want."

Penelope shakes her head. Dr. Richards and Saga wait for a long moment before they turn to leave.

Penelope locks the door behind them and then walks over to one of the bulletproof windows with a view of Östermalm Square. The window is opaque from outside. She looks down and understands that some of the people moving about on the square must be police in disguise.

She slowly touches the window. She can hear nothing from the outside world.

The doorbell rings.

Penelope jumps and her heart starts to pound.

She walks over to the monitor, finds the intercom button, and presses it. The female officer's face appears and she says that Penelope's mother has arrived.

"Penny? Penny?" her mother's anxious voice asks from behind the officer.

Penelope presses the combination to the door lock and hears the mechanism tick an answer before she can open the heavy steel door.

"Mamma," she says quietly. The sound of her own voice drops into the apartment's oppressive silence.

Penelope lets her mother into the room, then closes and locks the door. After that, she can't seem to move. She presses her lips together and feels her body start to tremble. She forces all feeling from her face.

She glances up at her mother but doesn't dare meet her eyes. She waits for her mother's tirade and accusations because she wasn't able to protect Viola.

Claudia has stopped and takes a slow look around.

"Are they taking good care of you, Penny?" she asks.

"I'm fine now."

"But they have to guard you."

"They are, so I'm safe here."

"That's all that matters," Claudia says in words almost beyond hearing.

Penelope tries to swallow her tears.

"There's so much I have to take care of now," her mother says, and turns her face away. "I . . . I just can't realize that I have to arrange Viola's funeral."

Penelope nods slowly. Her mother reaches out her hand to touch Penelope's cheek, but Penelope startles back and her mother jerks her hand away.

"They tell me that it will be over soon," Penelope says. "The police think they'll get that man . . . the man . . . who killed Viola and Björn."

Claudia nods and looks at her daughter with a face so naked and unprotected that Penelope is surprised to see her smile. "Just think, you are alive!" Claudia says thickly. "Just think, I have you again! It's all that matters now . . . It's the only thing that matters."

"*Mamma.*"

"My little girl."

Claudia reaches out her hand again, and this time Penelope does not shy away.

77

Jenny Göransson is in charge of the stakeout. She's positioned in the bay window of an apartment three floors up on Nybrogatan 4A. She's waiting. The hours pass. No one has reported anything. All seems quiet. Routinely, her eyes sweep in surveillance of the square and up to the roof of Sibyllegatan 27. Some pigeons startle and fly up and away.

Sonny Jansson is positioned on that roof. He must have shifted and scared the birds.

Jenny contacts him and finds out that he had moved to look into another apartment.

"I thought they were in the middle of a fight, but then I realized they're actually playing Wii and jumping around in front of the television."

"Return to your position," Jenny says drily.

She lifts her binoculars to peer at the dark area between the kiosk and the elm trees again. She's decided it could be a potential hot spot.

Blomberg calls in. He's undercover as a jogger running down Sibyllegatan.

"I see something in the cemetery," he says in a low voice.

"What?"

"Someone is under the trees, about ten meters from the gate."

"Check it out, Blomberg, but be careful," she says.

He jogs past the horse stairs by the Military Museum's gable and on into the cemetery. The night is warm and green. He moves silently onto the grass next to the gravel path and thinks that he'll soon stop and pretend to stretch. Right now, he just keeps going. There's a rustling among the leaves. The light left in the sky is blocked by branches and it's dark between the gravestones. He is startled by seeing a face near the ground. A woman of about twenty. Her hair is stubby and dyed red and her green military backpack is lying next to her head. Blomberg begins to see more clearly as another person, a black-clad, laughing woman, pulls up the other woman's sweater and begins kissing her breasts.

Blomberg carefully moves away and reports back to Jenny Göransson: "False alarm. Lovers."

Three hours have passed. Blomberg shivers. It's getting chilly. The dew is forming on the grass as the temperature drops. He rounds a corner and pulls up abruptly in front of a middle-aged woman with a well-worn face. She seems extremely drunk as she wobbles on her feet. She's walking two poodles on a leash, jerking back angrily as the dogs eagerly sniff the ground and want to pull away.

Near the edge of the cemetery, an airline attendant passes by. The wheels on her blue carry-on clatter against the asphalt. She gives Blomberg a disinterested glance and he hardly glances back although they've been colleagues for more than seven years.

Maria Ristonen hears the sound of her own heels echo along the wall. She's pulling her carry-on toward the entrance of the subway to check on someone almost hidden near the entrance. The carry-on gets stuck in a cobblestone and skitters sideways. She has to stop and as she bends down, she checks out the person in the shadows. He's very well-dressed but he has an odd look on his face. He seems to be waiting for someone and he eyes her intently. Maria Ristonen's heart begins to beat harder and she hears Jenny Göransson's voice in her earpiece.

"Blomberg has seen him, too, and he's on the way," Jenny says. "Wait for Blomberg, Maria. Wait for Blomberg."

Maria feels she can't hesitate too long. The normal thing would be to walk along again. She tries to move more slowly and now she's nearing the man with the odd look. She'll have to walk past him and then her back would be to him. The man draws back farther in the shadows as she approaches. He has a hand inside his jacket. Maria Ristonen feels the adrenaline pump through her veins when the man suddenly steps toward her and pulls something out that he's had hidden. Beyond the man's shoulder, Maria sees Blomberg take a stance, weapon suddenly in his hand. Jenny shouts that it's a false alarm. The man holds only a beer can.

"Bitch!" The man spits beer toward her.

"Oh God," sighs Jenny in Maria's earpiece. "Just keep on going to the subway, Maria."

The rest of the night passes without incident. The last nightclubs close and then only a few dog owners and aluminum-can collectors go by. Then the newspaper delivery people. Then more dog owners and a few joggers. Jenny Göransson can hardly wait for her relief at eight a.m. She gazes at Hedvig Eleonora Church and then at Penelope Fernandez's blank window. She looks down at Storgatan and then back toward the priory, where the film director Ingmar Bergman grew up. She pulls out a stick of nicotine gum and studies the square, the park benches, the trees, and the sculptures of the hunched woman and the man with the slab of meat on his shoulder.

There is a small movement near the high steel gate guarding Östermalms Saluhall. Gourmet food stalls have reinvigorated the interior of the huge redbrick building. Now the weak shine of glass in the entrance is briefly hidden by dark movement. Jenny Göransson calls Carl Schwirt. He's on a park bench between the trees where the Folk Theater had once been. Two garbage bags of scavenged cans sit between his feet.

"I don't see a damn thing," he replies.

"Stay there."

Maybe, she thinks, *maybe I should let Blomberg leave his spot next to the church and jog down Humlegårdsgatan to check this out.*

Jenny peers through her binoculars at the entrance again. She can now see the vague image of someone on his knees inside the black grille. An illegal taxi has driven the wrong way on Nybrogatan and swings around. Jenny watches the light from the car's headlights slide along the redbrick wall of the Saluhall. The light flicks across the entrance, but now she sees nothing. The car stops and reverses.

Idiot, she thinks as the taxi drives backward until one wheel goes up on the sidewalk.

Then the headlights shine onto a display window farther along the street, and that window glass throws a reflection right into the entrance.

There *is* someone behind the high fence.

Jenny needs only a second to understand. The man is adjusting the scope on a rifle.

She drops the binoculars and radios Central Control.

"Alert! I see an armed man!" she almost shouts. "Military-grade rifle with scope, at the entrance to the Saluhall . . . I repeat! A sniper at ground level at the corner of Nybrogatan and Humlegårdsgatan!"

The man at the entrance waits patiently behind the bars of the gate. He has been surveying the empty square for some time and waiting for a homeless collector of cans on the park bench to leave, but decided to ignore the homeless man when it appeared he was going to spend the night on the bench. Under the cover of darkness, he unfolds a tubular barrel with the absorbing shoulder support for a Modular Sniper Rifle. With precision ammunition, the sand-colored semiautomatic rifle is accurate for distances of up to two kilometers. Calmly he mounts a titanium flash suppressor on the barrels, pushes in the magazine, and lowers the tripod in front.

He had slipped inside the Saluhall just before it closed for the night. He'd hidden in a storage area until the cleaners had finished and the guards had left, and as soon as the place was locked and all the lights were off, he'd moved into the Saluhall itself.

It took only a short time to disconnect the building's alarm system from the inside. Then he was able to slip into the outer entrance, which was protected from the street by a large wrought-iron fence.

He'd been protected from all sides in this deep entrance, like a little hunter's hut, behind the fence. He has a clear view out but can't be seen at all if he remains still. If anyone happens to come near the entrance, he can simply back away to disappear into the darkness.

He aims his rifle at the building where Penelope Fernandez is located. He seeks her room using his electro-optic scope. He's patient, slow, and systematic. He's been waiting a long time. Soon it will be morning and before light comes, he'll have to retreat, reactivate the building's alarm system, and wait for tomorrow night. His instinct tells him that she will be drawn to the window to look out sometime, assuming the bulletproof glass will protect her.

He adjusts the scope and then the headlights of a car pass over him. He turns away for a moment and then returns to his observation of the apartment at Storgatan 1. There is a heat signature behind the dark window. The image is blurry and vague, weakened by the distance and the bulletproof glass. A worse target than he had expected. He tries to get a fix on the center of this blurry outline. A pale rose shadow moves in the speckled violet, thins out, and then appears again.

He is interrupted. Two figures have materialized from somewhere on the square, and they run directly at him, pistols out and close to their bodies.

östermalms saluhall

Penelope wakes up early and sleep is gone. She lies in bed for a while, but then gets up and starts some water for tea. She thinks about the watch the police have on her and wonders how long they can afford to keep it up. Perhaps for only a few days. If police officers hadn't been killed, they might not even have given her that. It would be too expensive.

She takes the kettle of boiling water from the stove and pours water into the teapot. She drops in two bags of lemon tea, takes the pot with her to the dark living room, and puts the teapot and cup down by the window nook. She turns on the green glass lamp hanging there and looks down into the empty square.

Two people pop up from nowhere and go running over the stone pavement. Then they fall flat and lie still. It looks odd, like a puppet show from up high. She quickly switches off the lamp. It sways from her jerky movement and bangs against the windowpane. She moves to one side and looks out again. A SWAT team is running along Nybrogatan and she sees a sudden pop of light in the entrance to the Saluhall. At the same moment, it sounds as if someone has thrown a wet rag at the window, which thumps as a bullet goes through the glass and into the wall behind her. She throws her body on the floor and crawls away. Glass splinters from the green lamp are all over the floor. She doesn't notice that she's cut her palms.

Stewe Billgren had always had a very quiet job at CID. However, right now he's in the passenger seat next to his boss, Mira Carlsson. They're in Alpha Car, an unmarked car slowly proceeding up Humlegårdsgatan. Stewe Billgren has never found himself in an active position, though he's wondered many times how he might handle it. This situation was beginning to wear on his mind, especially since the woman he was living with had come out of the bathroom with her pregnancy test and triumphantly shown him the results.

Stewe Billgren's entire body aches from playing in a soccer game yesterday, and experience has taught him the pain will only get worse over the course of the day.

Shots snap out somewhere. Mira has just enough time to glance out the window and ask, "What the hell was that?"

A voice over the radio yells that two officers are down, shot, and lying in the middle of Östermalm Square. Group 5 is ordered in from Humlegårdsgatan.

"We've got him!" Säpo's chief of operations shouts. "There are only four doors to the Saluhall and—"

"You're sure?" Jenny Göransson's voice demands.

"Nybrogatan entrance, one in the corner, and two on Humlegårdsgatan."

"Get more people there!" the chief of Central Control is yelling to someone.

"We're trying to get a layout of the Saluhall."

"Move Groups 1 and 2 to the front door," someone else yells. "Group 2, go in, Group 1, secure the entrance!"

"Go! Go! Go!"

"Group 3 to the side entrance and support Group 4," Jenny says. Her voice sounds focused. "Group 5 already has orders to go inside. Alpha Car! Come in now!"

Ragnar Brolin, chief of Central Control, calls Alpha Car. Stewe Billgren glances nervously at Mira Carlsson as he picks up the call. Brolin's voice is tense as he orders them to drive to Majorsgatan and await further orders. He swiftly explains that the area of operation has expanded and that they will probably have to provide fire support to Group 5.

The radio repeats again that the situation is critical and that the suspect is now inside the Saluhall.

"Damn," Stewe whispers. "I shouldn't be here . . . I'm an idiot!"

"Calm down," Mira says.

"I just found out my girlfriend is pregnant. I just found out last week. I'm going to be a father!"

"Congratulations."

He can feel himself breathing more quickly. He bites the side of his thumbnail and stares straight ahead. Through the windshield, Mira watches three heavily armed police officers rush from Östermalm Square down Humlegårdsgatan. Two of them click off the safeties from their laser-scoped automatic guns and head inside the building. The third runs to the other side door to force open the wrought iron fence.

Stewe Billgren stops chewing his thumbnail and feels the blood drain from his face as Chief Brolin calls their car again: "Alpha, come in!"

"Answer," Mira commands Stewe.

"Alpha, Alpha Car!" yells the chief impatiently. "Come in!"

"Alpha Car here," Stewe answers unwillingly.

"We can't wait any longer for more people." Brolin is almost screaming. "We're going in now. You have to back up Group 5. Clear?"

"Clear," Stewe replies, and feels his heart pound.

"Check your weapon," Mira says tersely.

As if in a slow-moving dream, Stewe takes out his service pistol, opens the magazine, and checks his ammunition.

"Why do we—"

"We're going in there!" Mira says.

Stewe shakes his head and mumbles, "He's killing police like flies—"

"Now!"

"I'm going to be a father and I . . . perhaps I should—"

"I'll go in," Mira says. "Use the car as a shield. Watch the door. Keep in radio contact at all times and be ready if he comes!"

Mira clicks off the safety on her Glock and climbs out of the car without looking back at Stewe. She runs to the closest door through the broken fence, pokes her head in and back for the briefest of looks. The officer from Group 5 waits in the stairwell for her. Mira takes a deep breath, feeling fear pour through her body, and then steps through the narrow door. It's dark. There's a slight smell of garbage from the storage area on the first floor. Her colleague meets her look and motions for her to follow and secure the line to the right. He waits a few seconds and gives her the sign for the countdown: three, two, one. He turns into the Saluhall and runs through the door to crouch behind the counter in front of him. Mira follows and concentrates to catch any movement from the right. Her partner presses against the counter, which holds wheels of cheese the size of car tires. He's murmuring into his radio. The little pinpoint light from his scope dances on the floor in front of his feet. Mira moves up to his right and peers around. The gray light of morning filters down from the glass ceiling twenty meters above her head. She raises her Glock. The room is full of shining stainless steel surfaces. She sees a large air-dried ox fillet. Something wavers among the reflections. She intuits a narrow figure with shining wings. An angel of death, she thinks in the split second before the dark Saluhall is lit by the muzzle fire of a silenced automatic rifle.

Stewe Billgren huddles behind his armored, unmarked car. He's pulled out his SIG Sauer and it's resting on the hood as he lets his gaze sweep rapidly back and forth between the two entrances to the Saluhall. Sirens are screaming nearer from all directions. There is the small nattering sound of a pistol from behind the wall. Stewe jumps. He prays to God that he'll be safe and wishes with all his heart that he could just run away and quit being a policeman.

when it all goes down

In his apartment on Wallingatan, Joona Linna wakes up. He opens his eyes and looks outside at the light early summer sky through his open curtains. He never closes them, preferring natural light.

It's early in the morning.

Just as he turns over to fall back to sleep, his phone rings.

He knows what's happening before he sits up to answer. He listens to the excited voice telling him the latest developments in the operation while he opens his safe and takes out his Smith & Wesson. The suspect is in Östermalms Saluhall and the police have just stormed the building with no strategy at all.

It's been six minutes since the alarm was sounded and the suspect retreated toward the center area of the building. The leader of the operation is now trying to close off the surrounding area while still continuing to guard Penelope Fernandez.

A new SWAT team heads into the entrance from Nybrogatan. They swing left past the chocolate counter and among the tables in the fish restaurant. Chairs are still upside down on the wooden surfaces. A chilled display counter shows lobster and turbot on crushed ice. The officers' footsteps echo up from the floor as they rush forward. They spread out and take cover behind pillars. As they wait for further orders, someone can be heard moaning deeply in the darkness. A colleague sounds badly wounded and must be lying in his own blood.

The rising sun's light is spreading through the sooty glass windows in the ceiling. Mira's heart is thudding. Two heavy shots had just been released, followed by four quick pistol shots and then two more heavy shots. One police officer is quiet and the other one must be terribly wounded. He's screaming he's been hit in the stomach and needs help.

"Can't anyone hear me?" he pleads.

Mira sees a reflection in the window. A figure moving behind a display of hanging pheasants and reindeer shanks. She signals to her colleague that someone is right in front of them. He calls the chief of operations to see if any police officers are in the middle hallway. Mira wipes sweat from her fingers and regrips her gun. The obscure figure is moving very oddly. She goes closer, bent over, pressing her side against a vegetable counter. She smells the green of parsley and the earthy scent of potatoes. Her Glock shakes slightly in her hand. She lowers it, takes a deep breath, and nears the corner of the counter. Her colleague gestures toward her. He's preparing an operation with three other officers who've already gotten in from Nybrogatan. He's moving toward the suspect along the counter with the wild game. All of a sudden, a high-speed automatic rifle fires from the direction of the fish restaurant. Mira hears the wet, sucking sound of a bullet going through the protective vest and the body armor of boron carbide of an older officer and into his body. The empty cartridge of the high-speed automatic rifle clangs on the stone floor close-by.

The hit man sees his first shot enter the policeman's chest and blood spurt from between his shoulder blades. The man is dead before his knees buckle. As he slides sideways to the ground, he pulls one of the tables with him. A salt-and-pepper stand clatters to the floor, and the shakers roll beneath a chair.

The hit man doesn't pause. He's running as fast as he can toward the center of the building and automatically calculates lines of fire. A police officer must be hiding behind a tiled wall next to the fish counter. Another is approaching through the hallway of wild game. The hit man whirls around and fires two quick shots while he heads for the kitchen of the fish restaurant.

Mira hears two more shots. Her young partner crumples, and blood spurts from the exit wound between his shoulder blades. His automatic rifle smacks the ground, and he falls back so hard that his helmet shakes loose and rolls across the floor. The barrel of his fallen gun points toward Mira. She moves away fast and crawls along the floor next to the fruit counter. Then chaos as twenty-four police officers storm the Saluhall—six pouring through each door. She tries to radio in, but can't contact anyone. With an astonished blink, she sees the hit man less than ten meters away. He's going toward the fish restaurant. Mira steadies her Glock in two hands, aims, and fires three shots at him.

A bullet plows through the hit man's left forearm as he's storming through the swinging doors to the kitchen. He keeps going along the grill, blundering through some hanging steel pans and toward a narrow metal door. Warm blood runs over the back of his hand. He knows there's some serious damage, especially to the back of his arm. This was hollow-point ammunition, after all. But he can also tell the artery is untouched. Without looking down at his wound, he opens the door to the warehouse elevator, scrambles through and out the facing door. He finds himself in a narrow hallway and kicks open another gray metal door, heading toward morning light beyond. Eight cars are parked on an asphalt inner courtyard. Rising around him are the high, smooth walls of the Saluhall like the backside of a yellow theater curtain. He folds up the accessories to his weapon and runs to an older-model red Volvo that has no automatic ignition. He kicks out the back passenger window on the driver's side and reaches in to open the door. The sound of automatic rifle fire still resounds inside the Saluhall. He sits down behind the steering wheel, breaks open the column and then the lock, pulls open the ignition, and, with his knife blade, starts the car.

the shock wave

Stewe Billgren has just watched twelve heavily armed police officers split up to run through two doors into the Saluhall. He's been frozen with his pistol aimed at the closest door since Mira ran inside with Group 5 less than ten minutes ago. Now she finally has some backup. He stands stiffly up, relieved, and goes to sit in the driver's seat of Alpha Car. Blue lights flash on walls all the way down to Sturegatan. A new movement in his rearview mirror makes him glance up. The hood of a red Volvo pokes out from an entrance to the building beside the Saluhall. It comes slowly forward across the sidewalk and turns right onto Humlegårdsgatan, nearing his own car. It passes and turns onto Majorsgatan right in front of him. The early-morning light reflects back from the windows and he can make out only a vague impression of the man behind the wheel. He looks away toward the square and watches an officer shout urgently into his radio. Stewe feels the urge to go over and ask about Mira when several things click into place in his mind. The man in the red Volvo had to let go of the wheel in order to shift. His black jacket looked shiny, as if it were wet. Stewe's heart stutters. The left arm was wet. He couldn't see the driver's face through the reflections, but there were no reflections in the back side window because the window was gone. And the glitter around its edge was broken glass.

The hit man had broken into the Volvo to escape and his left arm was bloody.

Stewe reacts immediately. He radios the leader of the operation even while the red Volvo is driving up Majorsgatan. He gets no answer. He starts his engine and shifts his car into gear without a thought for his own safety. The moment he turns onto Majorsgatan, the Volvo speeds up. The hit man realizes immediately that Stewe is on his trail. Both cars now speed up. They are on a narrow street past the neo-Gothic Holy Trinity Church and approaching a T intersection. Stewe is shifting into fourth gear and closing on the Volvo. He plans to force the driver to stop by swerving into its side. The light façade of the church seems to approach too fast. The Volvo swings right on Linnégatan so rapidly his wheels swerve up onto the sidewalk beneath a red awning to crash through some café tables. Splintered wood and metal scraps fly up. His left fender is torn loose and sparks on the concrete. Stewe slides around the curve and so gains a few seconds. He shifts up and closes in on the Volvo even as they are speeding down Linnégatan. The fender tears loose from the Volvo and smacks into Stewe's windshield. He involuntarily ducks, slows a second, but speeds up again. A taxi honks at them from a side street. They both swerve into the opposite lane to pass two slower cars. There's hardly time to see the roadblocks around Östermalm Square. Gawkers have begun to gather.

The wider road next to the National Historical Museum gives Stewe a breather and he tries to reach the leader of the operation again.

"Alpha Car!" he yells.

"Roger," a voice says.

"Suspect is in a red Volvo on Linnégatan heading toward Djurgården," Stewe calls into the radio.

He drops the radio and it bounces on the floor as his car hits a wooden barrier in front of a sandpile. His right front tire lifts off the ground and he slides to the left, passing the hole where the asphalt has been broken up. He disengages the clutch and matches the drift in the other direction, slides past the opposite lane, and is in control of the car again. He hits the gas.

He's pursuing the Volvo down tree-lined Narvavägen Boulevard, which had crossed Linnégatan. A bus brakes hard to miss the Volvo. It slides into the intersection and the back end swings around to hit a light pole. Another car swerves to avoid the bus and helplessly drives right into a bus shelter. Glass splinters rain down onto the sidewalk. A woman throws herself away from the car and falls down. The brakes of the bus are still squealing, its tires thunder up onto the safety island, and the roof of the bus knocks off a large, overhanging tree branch.

Stewe keeps following the racing Volvo past Berwald Concert Hall. He's coming closer just in time to see that the driver is managing to aim a pistol at him. He stamps down on the brake at the same moment the shot goes through the window near his head. The interior of Stewe's car instantly fills with flying glass. The Volvo drives over a parked bike with a placard advertising Linda's Café. There's a big bang as the bike bounces up, then over the hood and roof and on into the air. It lands directly in front of Stewe to be crushed beneath his wheels and thwack up momentarily against his undercarriage.

They're speeding through the sharp curve to Strandvägen, right over the safety island between the trees. Stewe hits the gas as he pulls out of the turn and his tires spin. They're racing through early rush-hour traffic, leaving the sounds of squealing brakes and the thud of minor collisions behind. They come up to the left by Berwald Concert Hall, over the grass-covered safety island and onto Dag Hammarskjölds väg.

Stewe pulls out his pistol and puts it down next to him. He reasons that he'll reach the other car at Djurgårdsbrunnsvägen. At that point he'll try to head him off, and then it will be time to take the man out. They're passing the American embassy, hidden behind a high gray fence, at about 130 kilometers an hour. The Volvo, its tires smoking now, jerks from the road and turns to the left just past the Norwegian embassy. It goes up over the sidewalk and between the trees. Stewe reacts a touch too late and is forced to swing wide, right in front of a bus, over the sidewalk, up onto the lawn, and through some low bushes. His tires whack on the curbstones of the Italian Cultural Institute. He crosses the sidewalk and slides to the left on Gärdesgatan, where he immediately spots the Volvo.

It's stopped in the center of the Skarpögatan crossway.

Stewe believes he sees a glimpse of the driver through the back window. He grabs up his pistol from the seat and releases the safety. He drives slowly up to the Volvo. Blue lights flash from all the police cars streaming from Valhallavägen beyond the Sveriges Television Building.

The Volvo driver bails quickly from his vehicle and then he is only a black-clad figure running down the road between the two stately embassies of Germany and Japan. Stewe is almost out of his car when the Volvo explodes into a fireball. The shock wave hits his face and the blast deafens him. He hears the world as if cotton wool were stuffed into his ears, but he drives on into the unbelievable quiet, up onto the sidewalk, even directly across the smoking hulk, but he can no longer see the suspect. There is no other place to go. He speeds up, crashes through a high fence, stops as the street dead ends, leaves the car, and runs back with his pistol ready.

The man is gone. The world is still unbelievably silent, except for an odd high-pitched whistle as if a strong wind were blowing. Stewe scans the street quickly up and down. The embassy buildings sit behind gray steel wire. There was nowhere the man could go except into one of these buildings by using a code or even climbing over one of the high fences.

People are emerging from their buildings to see what caused the explosion. Stewe looks around, takes a few steps, then quickly turns around again. This time, he spots the suspect immediately, on the grounds of the German embassy. He walks casually, matter-of-factly, to the main entrance. The door swings open and the man steps inside. Stewe Billgren lowers his arm and tries to calm down from a feeling of total frustration. He tries to control his breathing. The German embassy sits on a piece of land that is diplomatically considered part of Germany itself. He cannot enter without an express invitation. Swedish jurisdiction stops at the gate.

the german embassy

A uniformed officer is stationed ten meters in front of the barrier on Sturegatan by Humlegårdsgatan when Joona Linna drives up. The policeman tries to direct him away, but Joona ignores him and parks at the edge of the road. He shows his ID, bends underneath the plastic tape barrier, and then starts to jog toward the Saluhall.

He'd received the call only eighteen minutes ago, but the gunfight is over and the ambulances have begun to arrive.

The leader of the operation, Jenny Göransson, is receiving a detailed report regarding the police pursuit of the suspect, which has concluded in the part of town called Diplomat City. It appears that the suspect has entered the German embassy. Saga Bauer is talking to a colleague outside the Saluhall. The officer is wrapped in a blanket. Saga catches Joona's eye and waves him over. He walks toward the women and nods a greeting.

"I was sure I'd get here before you," Joona says.

"Too slow, Joona, you're too slow."

"Yes, I am." He grins as he replies.

The policewoman in the blanket looks at Joona and says hello.

"This is Mira Carlsson from Span," Saga says. "She was one of the first into the Saluhall and she thinks she hit our man."

"But you didn't see his face," Joona states.

"No, I didn't," Mira confirms.

Joona looks at the entrance to the Saluhall and then turns to Saga.

"They assured me that all the buildings nearby were secure," he mutters bitterly.

"They assumed these were too far away—"

"They assumed wrong," Joona says.

"Yes," Saga agrees, and gestures at the building. "He was behind the fence of this entrance and he was able to fire a shot through Penelope's window."

"So I heard. She was lucky," Joona says softly.

Barriers were up in the area around Östermalms Saluhall and small numbered signs marked the first findings: a shoe print and an empty cartridge from a full metal jacket American-made precision bullet.

Farther inside the open doors, Joona can see some tomatoes scattered across the floor along with a battered-looking magazine from a Swedish AK-5.

"Stewe Billgren, our colleague from Span," Saga continues, "followed the suspect to Diplomat City and reports that he walked into the German embassy through the front door."

"Any possibility he could be mistaken?"

"Maybe . . . we're in contact with the embassy and . . . wait"—she quotes from her notebook—"they say that they have not 'registered any unusual activity within the embassy grounds.'"

"Have you talked to Billgren yourself?"

"Yes." Saga looks at Joona seriously. "His hearing was damaged when the suspect blew up the stolen car. He can hardly hear a thing. However, he's absolutely certain what he saw. He clearly saw the suspect enter the German embassy."

"And perhaps he went on through and back out on the other side."

"Well, we have our people surrounding it now and a helicopter in the air. We just need permission to enter the building."

Joona takes a quick look at the Saluhall. "That can take a while." He takes out his cell phone and says, almost to himself, "I'm going to have a chat with Klara Olofsdotter."

Klara Olofsdotter, the main prosecutor for the International Prosecutor's Office, picks up the phone on the second ring.

"I know it's you, Joona," she says without a greeting. "And I know what's going on."

"Then you also know we must get inside that embassy."

"That's not so easy. This is always a damned sensitive area, excuse my language. I've talked with the ambassador's secretary by phone," Klara Olofsdotter explains. "She insists that everything is absolutely normal at the embassy."

"We know the suspect is inside," Joona says.

"How could he have gotten in?"

"He might be a German citizen demanding his right for help from the embassy. They've just opened. He could also be a Swedish part-time employee or he has the pass code or . . . some kind of diplomatic status. Maybe he has immunity or he's being protected by someone. We just don't know. He might even be a close relative to the defense attaché or the ambassador, Joachim Rücker, himself."

"But you don't even know what he looks like," she says. "How could we identify him even if they let us inside?"

"I'll get a witness," Joona says.

There's a moment of silence. Joona can hear Klara Olofsdotter breathing on the other end of the line.

"All right. Then I'll find a way to get you in," she says at last.

the face

Joona Linna and Saga Bauer are in Penelope's protected apartment. No lamps are lit. The morning sun shines through the broken window. Penelope Fernandez sits on the floor with her back against the innermost wall and she's pointing at the window.

"Yes, that's where the bullet came through," Saga corroborates.

"The lamp saved my life," Penelope says as she lowers her hand.

They're looking at the remains of the window lamp, its hanging cord and its broken plastic socket.

"I turned it off to see out a little better. Something was going on down on the square," Penelope says. "The lamp started to sway then and he thought it was me, right? He thought it was me moving and the heat was from my body."

Joona turns to Saga. "Did he have an electro-optic scope?"

Saga nods and says, "According to Jenny Göransson, he did."

"What's that?" Penelope asks.

"It seeks heat—you're right, the lamp saved your life," Joona answers.

"Good God in heaven," Penelope whispers.

Joona looks at her calmly and his gray eyes glitter.

"Penelope," he says slowly. "Actually, you have seen his face, right? Not this time, but before. You said you didn't, but . . . now I want you to nod if you believe you can describe him."

Penelope wipes her cheeks quickly and looks up at the tall detective. She shakes her head.

"Any description at all?" Saga asks gently.

Penelope listens to the detective inspector's voice and his mild Finnish accent and wonders how he can be so sure that she's seen the man's face. She *had* seen him, but she's not sure she can describe him. Everything had happened so quickly. She had only a glimpse of him. Rain was on his face. It was just seconds after he'd killed Björn and Ossian.

She wishes she could erase every memory.

But the man's tired, almost concerned face is lit up again and again by the white flashes of lightning.

Saga Bauer walks over to Joona, who is near the window, reading a long text message he's just received.

"Klara Olofsdotter has been speaking with the chief justice who has, in turn, spoken with the German ambassador," Joona says. "Three people will be allowed into the embassy for one hour. This hour will begin in forty-five minutes."

"We'd better hurry over there right now," Saga says.

"No reason to hurry," Joona says as he leisurely looks out over the square.

Journalists swarm around the barricades protecting the Saluhall.

"Did you tell the prosecutor that we have to go in armed?" asks Saga.

"We have to coordinate everything with the German security force," Joona replies.

"Who's going in?"

Joona turns to her. "Maybe . . . who tracked him down?"

"Stewe Billgren," she says.

"Yes, Stewe Billgren," Joona says. "Can he identify him?"

"Stewe didn't see his face. No one has seen his face," Saga replies. She turns back to go and sit down again next to Penelope.

They sit together quietly for a long while, leaning back against the wall. Saga calms her breath and speaks slowly as she asks the first question.

"What does he want from you? That guy who's after you—do you know why all this is happening?"

"No," Penelope says slowly.

"He's after the photograph you taped to your door," Joona says, though his back is to Penelope.

Penelope lowers her head and nods.

"Do you know why he wants that photograph?" Saga asks.

"No," Penelope answers, and begins to cry quietly.

Saga waits another moment and then says, "Björn tried to blackmail Palmcrona—"

"I didn't know anything about that." Penelope interrupts her. "I didn't agree to any of that."

"We've realized that," Joona says.

Saga takes Penelope's hand gently in hers.

"Did you take that photo?" she asks.

"Me? No, not me . . . the picture came to the Swedish Peace . . . you know, I'm the chairwoman and . . ."

Penelope falls silent.

"Did it come in the mail?" asks Joona.

"Yes."

"From whom?"

"I don't know," she says quickly.

"Was there a letter with it?" Joona asks.

"No, not that I know of."

"Just an envelope with a photograph."

She nods.

"Do you still have the envelope?"

"No."

"How was it addressed?"

"Just my name and the Swedish Peace . . . well, not the post office box, just my name."

"So it was addressed to Penelope Fernandez care of the Swedish Peace and Reconciliation Society," Saga says.

"And then you opened the envelope and took out the photograph," Joona says. "What did you think at that moment? What did the photograph mean to you?"

"Mean to me?"

"What did you see when you looked at it? Did you recognize the people involved?"

"Yes . . . three of them, but . . ."

She falls silent.

"Tell us what went through your mind when you first looked at the photo."

"Someone had seen me on TV," she says, and she collects her thoughts for a second before she continues. "I thought that this picture is just so typical. Palmcrona is supposed to be neutral, but here he is, he goes to the opera and sits and drinks champagne with the head of Silencia Defense and a weapons dealer who sells arms throughout Africa and the Middle East. It's totally scandalous."

"What did you plan to do with this picture?"

"Nothing," she answers. "There's nothing I could do. It's just a photograph, but at the same time, I remember I thought, at least now I know where he stands."

"I see."

"It reminded me of the idiots at the Immigration Office. They'd just deported a helpless family seeking asylum. Yes, they celebrated with champagne and patted themselves on the back for booting out people who sought refuge in Sweden, a family with a sick child . . ."

Penelope falls silent again.

"Do you know who the fourth person is? The woman in the picture?"

Penelope shakes her head.

"It's Agathe al-Haji," Saga says.

"Really?" Penelope grimaces.

"Yes."

"Why is she . . ."

Penelope falls silent and her dark eyes stare at Saga.

"Do you know when the picture was taken?" Saga asks.

"No, but of course the arrest order against al-Bashir was issued in March 2009, and . . ." Penelope stops abruptly and her face flushes scarlet.

"What is it?" asks Saga.

"The picture was taken after that," Penelope states, her voice shaking. "Right? The picture was taken after the arrest warrant."

"What makes you say that?" asks Saga.

"That's what makes it so important . . ." Penelope muses and the color fades again from her face.

"It's the deal with Kenya," she says with trembling lips. "That's what the photo is all about, isn't it? It's the Kenya contract, and Palmcrona's just agreed to it. The selling of ammunition to Kenya—I always knew there was something wrong there."

"Keep going," Joona says.

"Kenya has ongoing business with Great Britain. Delivery of ammunition will go to Kenya all right, but it'll end up in Sudan and Darfur!"

"Yes," Saga says. "That's what we believe is happening, too."

"But it's forbidden! This is terrible . . . it's treason, it's against international law . . . Beyond that, it's a crime against humanity . . ."

Penelope thinks a moment, her face in her hands.

"So that's why all this has happened," she says quietly. "Not because Björn attempted blackmail."

"That was the catalyst. It alerted these people to the fact that this photograph existed."

"I had assumed the picture might have been an embarrassment," Penelope says. "Embarrassing, yes, but not much more than that."

"When Palmcrona called them about the blackmail attempt, they went on alert," Saga explains. "Until then, they knew nothing about any photograph. Now they were worried. They did not know how much or how little it revealed. All they knew was that it was not good. We're not sure exactly what they reasoned . . . perhaps that either you or Björn was the photographer."

"But—"

"They couldn't know how much you both could prove. But they wanted to take no chances."

"I understand," Penelope says. "And that's still the same situation now, isn't it?"

"Yes."

Penelope nods.

"They think I might be the only witness to the deal," she says.

"They've invested a great deal of money," Saga says.

"They can't get away with this," Penelope says softly.

"What did you say?"

Penelope looks directly into Saga's eyes and says clearly, "They can't pump ammunition into Darfur, they just can't do it! I've seen what happens. I've been there twice—"

"They don't really care. It's only about the money," Saga says.

"It's not! It's about . . . it's about . . . so much more," Penelope says and turns her face to the wall. "It's about . . ."

She falls silent remembering the crunch as a clay figure is broken underneath the hoof of a goat. A small woman made of sun-baked clay crumbled into dust. A tiny child laughing and crying out, "That was Nufi's ugly mother! All the Fur are going to die! They're all going to die!" All the other children smiling and taking up the chant.

"What are you trying to say?" Saga asks.

Penelope looks at her, looks into her eyes, but does not answer. Her mind has gone back to Darfur.

After a long, hot car ride, she'd arrived at the refugee camp in Kubbum, southwest of Nyala in Janub Darfur, West Sudan. She'd barely arrived before she and Jane and Grey had to get down to work trying to save the lives of people caught up in the Janjaweed raids.

During the night, Penelope had awakened when she heard three teenage boys shouting in Arabic that they were going to kill slaves. They belonged to the militia. They walked down the middle of the street and one of them had a gun. Penelope had peeked out the window. They were bragging about how they'd walked up to an old man selling sweet potatoes and shot him in the head point-blank.

The boys kept walking down the street shouting and then had pointed at the house where Penelope and Jane were staying. Penelope held her breath. She heard their stomping feet on the veranda and their excited voices.

Suddenly, they kicked in the door of the barracks and started down the hallway. Penelope dived under the bed to hide. Completely still, she had recited the Lord's Prayer silently. Furniture was knocked over and stomped on. Then she heard the boys walk back out into the street. One of them laughed and yelled that slaves were going to die. Penelope crept back to the window again. The boys had Jane by the hair, pulling her, until they threw her down into the middle of the street. The door to the other barracks across the street was flung open and Grey came out swinging a machete. The thin boy went to meet him, although Grey was about two feet taller than the boy and much more muscular.

"What do you want here?" Grey demanded.

His serious face was slick with sweat.

The thin boy said nothing but simply raised the pistol and shot Grey in the stomach. The bang echoed between the buildings. Grey stumbled and fell down backward. He tried to get back up, but then kept still with his hand pressed to his stomach.

"One dead Fur!" yelled one of the other boys gleefully. He still had Jane by the hair.

The second boy forced Jane's legs apart. She struggled but still talked to them in a calm, hard voice. Grey yelled something at the boys. The thin boy went back over, yelled something at Grey, pressed the gun to his temple and fired. It clicked and he tried six more times. The pistol was empty. The group of boys suddenly began to look doubtful. Other doors in other barracks opened and African women started to pour out. The teenagers let go of Jane and began to scuttle away. Penelope saw five women chasing them. Penelope grabbed her blanket from the bed, unlocked the door, and rushed out into the street. She ran over to Jane to wrap the blanket around her and help her up.

"Go back inside, all of you!" Jane yelled. "They might be back with more ammunition! You shouldn't be outside if they come back!"

All that night and the next morning, Jane stood working at the operating table. Not until ten in the morning was she able to go to her bed convinced Grey's life was saved. That evening, she worked her usual schedule and by the next day, the routine in the hospital tent had returned to normal. The small boys helped her, but they were more guarded and sometimes they pretended not to hear her when they thought she was too demanding.

"No," Penelope whispers.

"What did you say?" asks Saga.

Penelope thinks that these people must not be allowed to export ammunition to Sudan.

"They can't get away with it," she says, and then is quiet.

"You were safer in the underground room," Saga says.

"Safe? No one can keep me safe," Penelope replies.

"We know where he is. He's inside the German embassy and we've surrounded the building—"

"But you haven't gotten him yet," Penelope says louder.

"He's probably been wounded. Shot in the arm. We're going to go in and—"

"I want to go with you," says Penelope.

"What?"

"Because I *have* seen his face," she replies.

Both Saga and Joona start and Penelope looks directly at Joona.

"You were right," she says. "I have seen his face."

"We don't have much time. Perhaps you can just give us a sketch of the suspect," Saga says anxiously.

"That won't be enough," Joona says. "We can't go into an embassy with just a sketch."

"But with a live witness who can point him out?" Penelope says, and she stands up to look Joona in the eye.

83

Penelope stands between Saga Bauer and Joona Linna behind an armored police bus parked on Skarpögatan beside the Japanese embassy. They're barely fifty meters away from the German embassy. She feels the weight of the protective vest dragging on her shoulders and the tight fit around her chest.

They have to wait five minutes. Then three people will be admitted into the German embassy in an attempt to identify and arrest a suspect.

Silently, Penelope accepts the extra pistol Joona slides into the holster on her back. He adjusts the angle so that, if needed, it can be drawn out quickly.

"She doesn't want that," Saga protests quietly.

"It's okay," says Penelope.

"We don't know what will happen," Joona says. "I hope that everything will go smoothly, but if it doesn't, this little backup might make a difference."

Swedish police, Säpo's officers, SWAT teams, and ambulances are everywhere.

Joona Linna looks over what remains of the burned-out Volvo. Only the charred chassis is still in one piece. Parts of the car are strewn all over the street crossing. Erixson has already found a detonator and traces of explosives. "It's probably hexogen," Erixson says as he pushes his glasses back up his nose.

"A bomb," Joona says as he looks at his watch.

A German shepherd is nosing around the legs of a policeman and then lies down on the pavement and pants with its tongue hanging out.

A SWAT team escorts Saga, Penelope, and Joona to the gate, where four expressionless German military officers wait.

"Try not to worry," Saga says softly to Penelope. "All you have to do is identify the suspect and you'll be brought out again immediately. The embassy security guards won't arrest him until you are out of the building."

A strong-looking, well-built policeman with a freckled nose opens the gate and lets them onto the embassy property. He gives them a friendly greeting and introduces himself as Karl Mann, head of security.

They follow him up to the main entrance.

The morning air is still cool.

"I hope you've been well briefed. This man is an extremely dangerous killer," Joona says.

"We understand. We've been informed," Karl Mann replies. "However, I have seen nobody except employees of the embassy and other German citizens here all morning."

"May we have a list?" Saga asks immediately.

"All I will tell you is that we've been reviewing the tapes from our security cameras," Karl Mann tells them. "We think your officer was mistaken. Perhaps this fugitive got in over the fence, but instead of entering the building, he probably ran around it and kept on going."

"A possibility," Joona says calmly.

"How many people are here in the embassy right now?" asks Saga.

"It's open for business and there are four appointments scheduled."

"Four people?"

"Yes."

"And how many employees are here?"

"Eleven."

"And how many security guards?"

"Five, at present," he says.

"No other people?"

"No."

"No carpenters, no painters, or—"

"No."

"So twenty people in all," Saga says.

"Do you wish to look around on your own?" asks Karl Mann quietly.

"We would prefer to have someone with us," Saga replies.

"How many?" asks Karl Mann.

"As many as possible and as heavily armed as possible," Joona answers.

"So you really believe he is that dangerous." Karl Mann smiles. "I can put two men at your disposal along with myself."

"We don't know what to expect, but—"

"You said he'd been shot in the arm," Karl Mann points out. "I must say I'm not exactly afraid."

"And it's possible he never actually got inside. Or maybe he's already left," Joona says quietly. "But if he *is* here, we might lose some people."

Silently, Joona, Penelope, and Saga, accompanied by the three policemen carrying automatic rifles and shock grenades, begin to walk through the corridors on the main floor. Renovations had been carried out throughout the building during the last few years while embassy business had been moved to Artillerigatan. However, in spite of the fact that the last few touches were being completed, embassy personnel had been moved back. It still smelled like paint and newly sawed wood. Some of the floors were still covered with protective paper.

"We would like to see your visitors first," Joona says. "Not the regular employees."

"I expected that," Karl Mann says.

Penelope feels strangely calm as she walks between Saga Bauer and Joona Linna. Somehow she does not believe she will meet her pursuer here. The place seems too normal and peaceful.

Then she notices Joona's caution, how his movements beside her change.

An alarm starts beeping. Everyone stands still. Karl Mann lifts his radio and speaks shortly in German.

"A door alarm is going off," he explains to them in Swedish. "The door is actually locked but the alarm is so sensitive it acts as if the door had been opened for a few seconds."

They keep walking together along the hallway and Penelope Fernandez is aware of the extra weight of the gun against her back.

"Here is the office of Martin Schenkel, our business attaché," Karl Mann gestures. "He has a visitor, Roland Lindkvist."

"We'd like to meet them," Joona says.

"Martin has requested no one disturb him until after lunch."

Joona says nothing.

Saga clasps Penelope's upper arm and they stop while the others continue on toward the closed door.

"Wait a moment, please," Karl Mann says to Joona as he knocks.

He receives a muffled answer, waits a moment, and then is given permission to enter. He does so, and closes the door behind him.

Joona looks at a room with a door covered by gray industrial plastic. A pile of gypsum board is stacked there. The plastic billows a little like a sail, just as sounds drift out from behind the closed door to the business attaché's office. There are voices and a loud thud. Penelope's thoughts fly back in time to the news reports about when this very embassy building had been occupied by Kommando Holger Meins in the spring of 1975. She remembers the demand that Andreas Baader, Ulrike Meinhof, Gudrun Ensslin, and thirty-five other prisoners from the Red Army Faction be released from their West German prison. It was in these very corridors that they ran and screamed at one another, pulling Ambassador Dietrich Stoecker by the hair and pushing Heinz Hillegaart's bloody body down the stairs. She didn't remember what they'd said or what the negotiations had been, but afterward, the German chancellor Helmut Schmidt had told Swedish prime minister Olof Palme not to negotiate with the terrorists and then two of the hostages were shot. Karl-Heinz Dellwo had screamed that he would shoot one person every hour until his demands were met.

Now Penelope watches Joona Linna step up to the door. The other two men are standing totally still. Joona pulls out his gun, undoes the safety, and then knocks at the door.

There's an odor spreading in the hallway as if someone left food burning on the stove.

Joona knocks again, listens, and hears a monotone voice as if someone is repeating the same phrase over and over. He waits a few moments, hides his pistol behind his back, and then pushes down the door handle.

Karl Mann stands directly below the ceiling lamp with his automatic rifle down beside his leg. He looks at Joona and then back at the man sitting in an armchair pushed deep into the room.

"Herr Schenkel, this is the Swedish inspector," he says softly.

Books and folders of scattered papers are spread all over the floor as if someone had pushed them off the desk in a fit of rage. The German business attaché, Martin Schenkel, is sitting quietly in an armchair watching television. A live broadcast of a soccer match is coming from Beijing. The game is between Germany's DFB-Elf and the Chinese National Team.

"Wasn't Roland Lindkvist here a minute ago?" asks Joona deliberately.

"He left," answers Martin Schenkel without looking up from the television.

Joona and Karl Mann go back into the hallway. Karl Mann is annoyed as well as disquieted. He barks some orders to his men in a hard voice. A woman in a light gray knit dress is walking quickly away down the hall over the protective paper.

"Who is that?" asks Joona.

"The ambassador's secretary," answers Karl Mann.

"We'd like to talk with her and—"

Suddenly an alarm rips the air. Over the whooping noise, a calm, prerecorded voice admonishes them that this is no drill and that they should not use the elevators as they exit the building immediately.

the fire

Karl Mann spits rapid orders into his radio as he jogs toward the stairwell.

"The top floor is on fire," he says shortly.

"How big a fire?" asks Joona as he keeps pace with him.

"We don't know, but we're evacuating the embassy and there are usually eleven people working upstairs."

Karl Mann snatches a fire extinguisher from a red cabinet and pulls out the safety stopper.

"I'll take Penelope outside," Saga yells.

"He started the fire," Penelope says. "He's going to escape when everyone's working to put out the fire."

Joona follows the three military men up the stairs. Their steps echo between the cold cement walls although they try to run as quietly as they can. They come into the hallway on the third floor where there is a stronger smell of smoke and even gray wisps curling up to run along the ceiling.

They take turns yanking open doors but they find nothing in the rooms.

"It looks like there's smoke coming from the Schiller salon." Karl Mann points as he speaks.

At the end of the hallway, smoke is streaming smoothly from beneath the double doors. It flows like water moving in the wrong direction, up the doors and along the walls to spread out at the ceiling.

A woman screams somewhere and there's a thud in the building as if there's a clap of thunder within the walls. A sharp bang snaps from behind the doors as if a large glass pane had broken from the heat.

"We have to get people out," Joona says. "There's—"

Karl Mann motions Joona to be quiet as he listens to his radio. He puts the fire extinguisher down as he answers in German. He then turns to the whole group.

"Listen up!" he says in a steady voice. "Our security cameras have spotted a man dressed in black in the men's bathroom. He has a pistol in the sink."

"That's the guy," Joona says.

Karl Mann talks again to security in a low voice to pinpoint where he is in the bathroom.

"He's two meters to the right of the door," Karl Mann explains. "He's bleeding heavily from the shoulder and he's sitting on the floor . . . but the window is open and it's possible that he wants to get out that way."

They make their way quickly over the brown floor paper, past a propped-up painter's ladder, and crowd in behind Karl Mann. It's gotten hotter here and the smoke is curling like a dark clay ball near the ceiling. It's crackling and roaring, and it feels as if the floor is quivering beneath their feet.

"What kind of weapon does he have?" Joona asks.

"They could see only the pistol in the sink. Nothing else—"

"Ask about a backpack," Joona snaps. "He always carries one—"

"I'm doing this," hisses Karl Mann.

Karl Mann signals one of his men. They all glance quickly down, double checking their automatic rifles, and then follow him into the dressing area. Joona stifles a warning as they head inside. He fears their standard attack will not suffice against this killer. They're like flies lured to a spider. One by one, they'll get stuck in his net.

Joona feels smoke sting his eyes.

A spider makes a net from two kinds of threads, he thinks. *The sticky ones to catch her prey and the threads she makes for herself.*

She remembers the pattern and can therefore jump past her own trap without getting caught.

Joona joins the military police, who have already taken shelter outside the bathroom door. One of them, with blond hair sticking out under the edge of his helmet, pulls the safety pin from a shock grenade. He opens the door slightly to throw the grenade across the tiled floor and closes the door again quickly. A deadened bang is heard and then the other men open the door with weapons drawn. Karl Mann makes a hurry-up gesture with his hand. Without a moment of hesitation, the blond policeman rushes in with his automatic rifle lifted with the piston on his shoulder. Joona's heart pounds in worry. Then he hears the blond policeman's frightened shout, almost childlike in its panic. Only a second later, there's a massive explosion. The bodies of the men are flung back from the door with smoke and debris flying around them. The door is blown off its hinges. A policeman drops his weapon and slips aside, falling to one knee. The pressure wave forces Joona backward. The blond policeman is on his back on the floor. His mouth is open and a pool of blood can be seen welling between his teeth. He's unconscious. A large splinter sticks up from his thigh. Bright red blood is pumping out in splashing drops. Joona rushes forward and pulls the policeman over and turns the man's face to one side. He makes a hurried field tourniquet with the man's belt and a ripped-off sleeve. He ignores the warmth of blood on his hands.

One of the men is crying with a frightened, quivering sound.

Civilians are being led out. Two policemen help a gray-haired man through the hallway. The man's face is sooty and he can hardly walk. A woman has wrapped her sweater around her mouth and she's hurrying through the hallway with wide-open eyes.

Holding his pistol out, Karl Mann walks into the bathroom, crunching on splintered glass from the mirrors. He finds the hit man lying on the floor. The man is still alive. His legs jerk and his arms thrash wildly. His chin and most of his face have been blown off. Karl Mann surveys the scene and calculates what might have happened. He thinks the man had intended a trap using his own grenade but had been jarred by the shock grenade. He had dropped his own instead.

"We'll evacuate everyone else," Karl Mann says, and leaves the bathroom.

Joona wipes blood from his hands. He calls the center of operations and directs them to send medical aid to the bathroom. As he speaks, he sees Penelope hurrying toward him from the stairwell with Saga right behind. Penelope's eyes are ringed in black fatigue. Saga is murmuring soothing words and tries to lead her away, but Penelope jerks free.

"Where is he?" Penelope asks with a haunted voice. "I have to look at him!"

"It's dangerous for you here," Joona says. "The fire could get here in just seconds."

Penelope pushes past Joona and steps across the littered floor of the men's bathroom. Staring around, she sees the man on the floor still flailing about with the chewed-up remains of a face. She whimpers and rushes back out to lean for support against the wall. A framed letter from former chancellor Willy Brandt slides to the floor and the glass cracks, but the letter rests upright against the wall.

Penelope's stomach lurches. She swallows and feels Saga trying to put her arms around her to move her back toward the stairs.

"That's not him!" Penelope whimpers.

"We have to get out," Saga says urgently, and leads her away.

Medical personnel have come running in. They load the blond soldier onto a stretcher. A new heat explosion can be heard. Glass shards and wooden splinters are in the air. A man stumbles along the hallway, slips, and gets back up. Smoke pours from an open door. A huge man stands silently in the hallway with blood running from his nose and over his shirt and tie. The military police herd everyone toward the emergency exits, shouting at them to move quickly. Flames suddenly shoot out from an open office door. The protecting paper on the floor catches fire and twists around as it burns. Two people are running hand in hand. A woman's summer dress has caught fire. She's screaming. An officer covers her with foam from his extinguisher.

Joona is choking from the smoke but doggedly returns to witness the devastation from the hand grenade. The hit man lies absolutely still now. Someone has wrapped his face with temporary bandages and gauze. Through the bullet wound in his forearm, dark red blood trickles down the sleeve of his jacket. A first-aid kit once attached to the wall is now on the floor and bandages have fallen out and are scattered with the dust onto the white tiles. The walls are blackened and most of the tiles have been blown loose. A toilet stall is demolished. Water pours across the floor from a broken pipe.

In the sink, there is a Heckler & Koch pistol with seven magazines of ammunition. Behind the door of another stall lies the black shape of a rough nylon backpack. It looks flattened and empty.

Yells, frightened voices, and barked orders come from the hallway outside. Karl Mann leads medical personnel in.

"I want a guard over him," Joona says, gesturing toward the hit man as the men lift him onto a stretcher and strap him down.

"He'll probably be dead before he gets to the hospital," Karl Mann says, coughing up smoke against his hand.

"Even so, I want your word he'll be guarded as long as he's on embassy property."

Karl Mann squints at Joona and then designates one of his men to take responsibility for the prisoner until they hand him over to the Swedish police.

Heavy black smoke now belches through the hallway with the sounds of loud roars and crackling coming nearer. Everyone is racing to get outside. Karl Mann squats below the layer of smoke and says shortly, "Someone from this floor is still missing."

Joona walks across a door that's lying on the floor and then to one still closed in its frame. He presses down the handle. Light shines for a second and then disappears. Only fire illuminates the smoky hallway and sparks are flying through open doors.

There's roaring and sparking and banging and crackling as metal heats and begins to writhe.

Joona gestures Karl Mann to move back. He draws his pistol, opens the door a few more centimeters, moves aside, waits a moment, and then looks in.

There's nothing but the black silhouettes of office furniture. The curtains are closed. But the eddy of air close to the floor makes Joona move away from a possible line of fire.

"Evacuate!" someone yells behind them.

Joona turns and sees four firemen who specialize in rescue work coming up through the hallway. They spread out and systematically search through the rooms.

Before Joona can give them any warning, one of the rescuers shines his strong flashlight into the room, and two eyes reflect back. A Labrador retriever begins to bark loudly.

"We'll take it from here," one of the men laughs. "Can you get out on your own?"

"There's still one missing," Karl Mann says.

"Be really careful." Joona warns them as much as he can.

"Come on!" Karl Mann shouts urgently behind him.

"I need to get just one more thing."

Joona, coughing heavily, runs once more into the men's bathroom, noticing the pattern of blood on the floor and on the walls, and hurries to snatch up the black backpack.

hunting the hunter

Penelope's legs shake. She clings to the fence surrounding the embassy and stares down at the black asphalt. She is fighting the impulse to vomit. The sight she'd seen in the men's bathroom still vibrates before her eyes: the face blown to bits, teeth all over, blood.

The weight of the bulletproof vest seems to drag her down toward the ground. Noise around her forms a cacophony. Sirens warn of approaching ambulances. Police officers shout, even scream, at one another and into their radios. She watches medical personnel hurry over with a stretcher. It's the man from the bathroom. Blood has soaked through the bandages covering his head.

Saga comes over to Penelope with a nurse in tow; she says that she's worried Penelope is going into shock.

"It wasn't him," Penelope repeats as they wrap her in a blanket.

"A doctor will be here soon," the nurse says soothingly. "Meanwhile do you need something to calm down? I can give you something if you're in good health . . ." She hesitates. "No liver problems, for instance?"

Penelope shakes her head and the nurse gives her a blue capsule.

"Swallow it whole," she explains. "It's half a milligram of Xanax."

"Xanax," Penelope repeats dully as she looks at the capsule in her hand.

"It's not dangerous and it'll calm you down," the nurse explains even as she hurries away.

"Let me get you some water," Saga says, and goes to the police van.

Penelope's fingers feel numb. She looks at the little blue capsule in her hand.

Joona Linna is still in the building. More people are stumbling outside. They're smudged with soot and reek of smoke. The cluster of shocked diplomats is collecting by the fence that separates their grounds from those of the Japanese embassy. Everyone is waiting for transportation to Karolinska Hospital. A woman in a dark blue business suit sinks to the ground and weeps openly. A policeman comes up to her and puts his hand on her shoulders as he talks to her. One of the diplomats licks his lips and rubs his hands over and over with a handkerchief. An older man in a wrinkled suit is standing and talking on a cell phone. His face is stiff. The military attaché, a middle-aged woman with hair that's dyed red, has dried her tears and is trying to help the others, but she moves like a sleepwalker. She is asked to hold up a bag for an IV drip and she does so with no emotion at all. A man with burns on his hands has been huddled in a blanket, patiently sitting, his bandaged hands over his face. Now he gets up slowly, the blanket falling to the ground and he starts to walk quietly, almost dreamily, over the pavement toward the fence.

A military policeman holds on to a nearby flagpole. He is weeping.

The man with the burned hands walks gently in the bright morning sunshine beyond the fence. He turns the corner and heads down the right side of Gärdesgatan.

Penelope draws in a sudden breath. As if drenched in cold water, she's jabbed with sudden insight. She'd never seen his face clearly, but she has seen his back. That man with the burned hands is her pursuer. He's heading toward Gärdet, the large open field near the television tower. He's heading away from the police and the ambulances. She doesn't need to see his face; she's seen his back when he sat on the boat beneath Skuru Sound Bridge. When Viola and Björn were still alive.

Penelope's hand opens and the blue capsule falls to the ground.

Penelope begins to walk after him, her heart racing. She turns onto Gärdesgatan and lets the blanket fall away from her body just as he had done. She picks up speed. She starts to hurry faster as he makes his way between the trees, moving slowly. He looks tired and weak. Penelope remembers he might have been shot. That would explain it. She thinks triumphantly that he will not be able to run away from her. Some jackdaws lift from the trees and flap away. Penelope feels filled with power. She's striding quickly over the meadow grass and sees him less than forty meters away. He's staggering and he has to hold on to a tree trunk to stay upright. The bandages are unwinding from his fingers. She's running now and watching him leave his cover in the small grove of trees to limp into the sunshine of the large, open field. Without pausing, Penelope reaches back for the pistol Joona Linna had so providentially secured to her back. She glances down long enough to release the safety as she goes on through the trees. She slows and aims at his leg with her arm straight out.

"Stop!" she whispers as she pulls the trigger.

The shot fires and the recoil jerks her arm and shoulder. The gunpowder burns across the back of her hand.

The bullet seems to disappear but Penelope sees him try to run faster.

You never should have touched my sister, she thinks.

The man is running along a path. He stops for a second, grabbing his arm, then he veers off across the grass.

Penelope runs into the open field and the sunshine. She's getting closer. She crosses the pedestrian path and lifts the weapon again.

"Stop!" she yells.

She fires and she sees a furrow of grass ripped from the ground ten meters in front of the man. Penelope feels adrenaline shoot throughout her body but she's clearheaded and focused. She aims at his leg and shoots again. She hears the bang again, feels the recoil, and sees the back of his knee punctured with debris blown around his leg from his kneecap. He screams in pain as he falls onto the grass, but he keeps trying to crawl away. She's coming closer, striding forward while he tries to pull himself upright to lean against a birch tree.

Stop, Penelope thinks. She lifts the pistol again. *You killed Viola. You drowned her and you killed Björn.*

"You killed my baby sister!" she yells out loud. She shoots.

The bullet goes into his left foot and blood spatters over the grass.

As Penelope comes up to him, he slides down, completely still, his head hanging forward with his chin resting on his chest. He's bleeding heavily and is panting like an animal.

She stops in front of him, the shadow of the birch tree covering them both. She aims the pistol again right at him.

"Why?" she asks. "Why is my sister dead? Why is . . ."

She falls silent, swallows, and gets on her knees to look directly into his face.

"I want you to look at me when I kill you."

The man licks his lips and seems to try to raise his head. It's too heavy. He can't manage it. He's about to lose consciousness. She aims the gun again, but she hesitates and pulls his head up with her other hand. She stares right into his face. She clenches her teeth as she sees again the tired features lit up by lightning over Kymmendö. Now she remembers every detail: his calm eyes after he killed people and the deep scar on his lip. He's just as calm now. Penelope has hardly time to think how strange this is before he attacks. He is so very strong and unbelievably quick. He grabs her hair and pulls her toward him. There is so much power behind his move that she bangs her forehead against his chest. She cannot move fast enough to evade him when he shifts his grip to grab her wrist and wring the gun from her hand. With all her strength, Penelope pushes and kicks her way free, but he already has her gun. She looks up at him as he aims it at her and releases two quick shots.

the white trunk of the birch tree

Only when Joona has left the stairwell and is hurrying through the main floor of the German embassy does he realize how his lungs are heaving and how much his eyes sting. He has to get out for some clear air. He coughs heavily and remains close to the wall as he jogs on. He can hear new explosions above him, and a ceiling lamp falls to the ground. He can hear many sirens. He walks out through the main entrance of the embassy with relief. Six German military policemen are deployed on the asphalt outside the door. They make up the provisional security team. Joona draws fresh, clean air into his lungs, coughing and looking around. Two fire trucks have set up ladders against the wall of the embassy. Outside the fence, there are crowds of police officers and ambulance personnel. Karl Mann lies on the grass and a doctor is leaning over him listening to his lungs. Penelope Fernandez is walking along the fence that separates this building from the Japanese embassy. Her shoulders are covered by a blanket.

At the last minute, Joona had gone back into the men's bathroom to retrieve this battered backpack. It was an impulse. He couldn't understand why the hit man had wanted to hide an empty backpack with the pistol and magazine in full sight in the sink.

He has a fit of coughing again. He opens the black nylon and looks inside. The backpack is not empty. It contains three different passports and a short attack knife with fresh blood on the blade.

Who did you cut? Joona wonders.

He peers closely at the knife blade. The blood is just starting to coagulate. He looks out over the busy people and ambulances on the other side of the gate. The woman with the burned dress is now bundled in a blanket and is being helped into an ambulance. She holds another woman's hand. An older man with a soot streak on his forehead is talking on the phone. His expression is empty.

Joona realizes his mistake. He drops the backpack and the bloody knife to the ground and runs to the fence to yell at the guard to let him out.

He rushes past police and other personnel, jumps the plastic tape barricade, and forces his way past journalists who seem to have sprung up out of the ground like weeds. He stands on the road, blocking a yellow ambulance just ready to leave.

"What wound does he have on his arm?" Joona yells as he holds up his ID.

"What?" the ambulance driver asks in surprise.

"The man injured by the bomb—he has a wound on his forearm and I need—"

"Considering his condition, it's not that important."

"I have to see his injury!" Joona yells.

The ambulance driver wants to protest further, but something in Joona's voice makes him change his mind and he does what Joona asks.

Joona climbs into the back of the ambulance. The man lying on the stretcher has a face totally covered in bandages with only an area free to allow an oxygen mask and an oxygen lead to his nose. A suction tip is hanging from his mouth. One of the ambulance attendants cuts the jacket and shirt wider open. The wound is temporarily bandaged.

But it's not a bullet wound. It's a knife cut and it's deep.

Joona jumps out of the ambulance and looks around the area until he sees Saga. She's carrying a plastic cup with water, but as soon as she sees his expression, she throws it to the ground and comes running.

He's getting away again, Joona thinks. *We can't let him get away!*

Joona pans the scene, remembering he'd seen Penelope with a blanket over her shoulders heading along the fence between the embassies and turning onto Gärdesgatan.

"Bring a gun!" he yells at Saga as he starts running along the fence. He turns to the right but can't spot Penelope or the hit man anywhere.

As if in their own little world, a woman is watching two beautiful Dalmatians play freely on the grassy lawn of the Italian Cultural Institute.

Joona races past its shining white façade, already pulling his pistol out of its holster. He realizes that the hit man had merged with the stream of people stumbling from the burning building.

Saga is yelling something behind him, but he doesn't listen. His heart is pounding too loud and there's a rushing sound in his head.

He runs faster toward a small grove of trees the killer might see as cover. He hears a sudden pistol shot. He stumbles down the slope of a dike and then up the other side, up a hill, and between the trunks of trees in the grove.

More pistol shots. The explosions are short and sharp.

Joona bats aside tree branches and then comes out onto the sunny lawn. He sees Penelope three hundred meters away. She's underneath a birch tree. A man is sitting against the tree with his head hanging down. Penelope is on the ground in front of him when suddenly she's pulled forward and then falls back. The man is aiming a gun right at her. While running, Joona throws a shot at the man, but the distance is too great. He stops to take a steady stance and hold his gun in both hands. At that same moment the hit man fires two shots into Penelope's chest. She flies onto her back. The hit man looks exhausted, but lifts his gun again. Joona shoots and misses. He runs closer and watches Penelope kick at the man to get away. The hit man looks up to see Joona coming but then looks back down at Penelope. He is looking her in the eyes as he aims the gun at her face. A shot is fired . . . but Joona hears the sound from behind. It whines past his right ear and within the same second a cascade of blood squirts from behind the hit man's back to cover the white tree trunk. The full metal jacket bullet has torn through his breastbone, into his heart, and on out of his back to bury itself in the tree behind him. Even as Joona keeps running with his gun still aimed, another shot rings out. The already dead body whirls under the impact, the bullet's entry point just centimeters away from the first one. Joona lowers his gun and turns to see Saga standing in the grove of trees with a high-caliber rifle at her shoulder. Her long hair is dappled by the sunlight breaking through the leaves and her expression is still one of deadly concentration as she slowly lowers the rifle.

Penelope scrambles back, coughing, into the sunlight. She gets up to stare down at the dead man. Joona walks over to the body, kicks away the pistol, and kneels to put his finger against the man's throat. He wants to make absolutely sure this man is dead.

Penelope unlatches the bulletproof vest and lets it fall to the ground. Joona gets up and comes to her as she walks toward him, staggering, as if she is about to faint. He catches her exhausted body as her face falls to rest against his chest.

the red herring

The man with the mutilated face died one hour after his trip from the German embassy to the hospital. He was identified as Dieter Gramma, the cultural attaché's secretary. During the autopsy investigation, the chief medical officer, Nils Åhlén, found the remains of tape on his clothing and abrasions and wounds on his wrists and neck, which indicated that he'd been tied up at the time of the explosion. When the initial crime-scene investigation was completed and tapes from the security cameras were analyzed, a reconstruction of events could be made: After arriving at his office on the second floor of the building, Dieter Gramma logged on to his computer and read some e-mail messages. He didn't answer any but flagged three of them. Then he went to the lunchroom and turned on the espresso machine before going to the men's bathroom. He was just about to enter one of the stalls when a man turned away from the mirror over the sink. His face was covered by a ski mask. The man, dressed in black, was the wounded hit man who had gotten into the German embassy with his German passport. He'd just escaped police pursuit and had blocked surveillance of the men's bathroom by taping over the security camera.

The hit man estimated Dieter Gramma's body proportions through the mirror. Dieter Gramma probably didn't have time to say much before the hit man pressed a gun to his chest and forced him to his knees to tape his mouth shut. The hit man switched his black jacket with Dieter Gramma's suit coat, and then tied him in a squatting position to a water pipe with his back to the security camera and plunged the double-edged knife through the bullet hole of the leather jacket.

Probably Dieter Gramma was so confused by the pain, fear, and release of endorphins that he couldn't comprehend much of what was happening. The hit man fashioned a piece of wire around Dieter Gramma's throat with a loop at the back. Through this loop, he threaded a long wire, took out a hand grenade, a Spräng 2000, and attached one end of the wire to the grenade, pulled the pin, but kept the handle down. If he'd let go of the handle, the grenade would have exploded within three seconds. Instead, he taped the grenade to Dieter Gramma's chest with its handle pressed down. Next, he pulled the end of the wire through a loop around Dieter Gramma's neck, wrapped it around the sink trap, and stretched it across the floor to become a trip wire.

Of course, he meant to have someone enter the bathroom, release the grenade to mutilate Dieter Gramma, and in all the chaos Gramma's mutilated body would be identified as his. Then he could just walk away.

The hit man was probably slowed by his wound and blood loss, but the priming of the trap wouldn't have taken more than four minutes from the moment Dieter Gramma entered the bathroom to the moment when the hit man dumped his gun and magazines into the sink, left his backpack with the bloody knife in a stall, peeled the tape off the security camera, stepped over the trip wire, and left the room.

He then went along the hallway, entered the meeting room through its double doors, and ignited a quick fire. After that, he went to Davida Meyer's office and was just starting to tell her the reason for his visit when the alarm went off.

For the next twenty-five minutes, Dieter Gramma was tied on his knees with a hand grenade strapped to his chest before he was noticed by the security camera. He probably tried to cry out without dislodging the grenade. The autopsy revealed that he'd broken a blood vessel in his throat and the inside of his mouth was bitten.

The door to the men's bathroom was opened and a shock grenade was tossed inside over the tiled floor. Instead of a release of shrapnel, as happens with normal grenades, a huge pressure wave slammed through the small room. Dieter Gramma hit his head on the pipe and tiled wall and passed out. A young police officer named Uli Schnieder ran into the room with his weapon drawn. The smoke made it difficult to see so it took the young man a few seconds to realize what stumbling over the trip wire meant.

The handle on the grenade on Dieter Gramma's chest had been released. The hand grenade stopped at the loop around Dieter Gramma's neck, slipped down slightly since the man was unconscious, and then exploded with horrible effect.

the visitor

Joona Linna, Saga Bauer, and Penelope Fernandez are in an armored police van being driven away from Diplomat City and along Strandvägen and, beside it, the glittering water.

"I knew his face," Penelope says in a monotone. "I knew he would keep after me and after me until . . ."

She stops speaking and stares straight ahead.

". . . until he killed me," she finally says.

"Yes," Saga answers.

Penelope shuts her eyes and lets herself rock with the gentle motion of the police van. They're passing the remarkable monument to Raoul Wallenberg, which is formed like white-capped waves or Hebrew letters blowing in the wind.

"Who was he? The man who was after me?" Penelope asks.

"He was a professional hit man," Joona explains. "Also called a problem solver or a *grob.*"

"Neither Europol nor Interpol has anything on him," Saga says.

"A professional killer," Penelope says. "So someone had to send for him."

"Yes," Saga says. "But any leads back to who did will be well hidden."

"Raphael Guidi?" Penelope asks softly. "Is he behind this? Or is it Agathe al-Haji?"

"We believe it has to be Raphael Guidi," Saga says. "It doesn't make sense for Agathe al-Haji to be behind it. As far as she's concerned, it wouldn't matter if she was seen buying ammunition—"

"It's not a secret what she does," Joona says.

"So Raphael Guidi sent a hit man, but . . . what does he really want? Do you know? Is all of this just about the photograph? Really?"

"Perhaps he assumed you were the photographer and a witness—you may have seen or heard something that would implicate him."

"Does he still think so?"

"Probably."

"So he'll just find another hit man?"

"That's what we're afraid of," Saga answers honestly.

"How long will I have police protection? Will I be in hiding forever?"

"Well," says Saga, "we'll have to plan the next steps, but—"

"I'm going to be hunted down until I can't run any longer," Penelope says.

They're driving past NK and see three young people on a sit-in strike outside the elegant department store.

"He won't give up," Joona confirms. His voice is serious. "So we will expose this whole deal. Then there won't be any reason to silence you."

"We know we probably can't do much to Raphael Guidi himself," Saga says. "But here in Sweden—"

"What could you do here?"

"Primarily, we can stop the arms deal," Saga says. "The container ship can't leave Gothenburg Harbor without Axel Riessen's signature."

"And why wouldn't he sign?"

"He will never sign it," Joona says. "He knows what's going on."

"That's good," whispers Penelope.

"So we stop the deal and arrest Pontus Salman and all the other Swedes involved," Saga concludes.

After a moment of silence, Penelope says, "I have to call my mother."

"Here's my phone," Saga says.

Penelope takes Saga's phone, appears to hesitate, and then dials the number.

"Hi, Mamma, it's me, Penny. I'm okay."

"Penny, I'm just on my way to the door. I have to get it—"

"Wait, Mamma!" Penelope cries. "Who's there?"

"I don't know," her mother says.

"Are you expecting anyone?"

"No, but—"

"Don't open it!" Penelope shouts.

Her mother says something indistinguishable as she puts down the phone. Penelope can hear the bell ring again. The door is opened and Penelope can hear voices. She waits helpless, looking wide-eyed at Saga and Joona. There's some noise on the line and a thud and then her mother's voice again.

"Are you still there, Penny?"

"Yes, I'm here."

"There's a woman here looking for you."

"Looking for me?" Penelope wets her lips. "All right, Mamma, hand over the phone."

There's a crackle on the line and then an unfamiliar voice.

"Penelope Fernandez?"

"I'm here," Penelope says.

"I have to see you."

"Who are you?" Penelope asks.

"I sent you the photograph."

"I don't know anything about a photograph," Penelope says abruptly.

"Good answer," the woman says. "We don't know each other, but I *am* the person who sent that photograph to you."

Penelope says nothing.

"We must get together as soon as possible," the woman says. There is tremendous tension in her voice. "I sent you the photograph of four people in a private box at the theater. I took the photograph secretly on November 13, 2009. One of the four people in the box is Pontus Salman. He's my husband."

the meeting

Pontus Salman's house is on Roskullsvägen on the island of Lidingö, a Stockholm suburb. A single-family house built in the sixties, it has begun to look its age, although it still shows the craftsmanship so typical of the time period. They park the car on the stone pavement leading to the garage and get out of the car. Someone has drawn graffiti on the garage door with chalk: a childish picture of a penis.

They agree that Joona will wait with Penelope in the car while Saga goes to the front door. It's open, but Saga rings the doorbell, which is in the form of a lion's head. Three pleasant chimes sound, but then nothing more happens. Saga takes out her Glock and checks her magazine, takes off the safety, and walks into the house.

Much of the house was actually built below ground level. Beyond the entryway, the house opens into a spacious room encompassing both kitchen and dining room. Its tall windows overlook the breathtaking view of the inlet flowing past Lidingö.

Saga prowls through the kitchen to look into empty bedrooms before she makes her way back to a flight of stairs going down. Music comes from a room with a brass label marked R&R. She opens the door and can hear the music more clearly. It's Verdi's *La Traviata* with Joan Sutherland.

At the end of the tiled hallway shines the blue glimmer of a lighted pool.

Saga steps softly toward the pool, listening for anything else besides music. She thinks she can hear the padding of bare feet.

She keeps her weapon close to her body and continues on. There is comfortable-looking wicker furniture and some potted palm trees. The air is warm and humid. The odor of chlorine mixed with jasmine gets stronger. She comes up to a huge swimming pool made of light blue tiles and with a glass partition facing a garden and the waterway outside. A slim woman of about fifty is next to a bar with a glass of white wine in her hand. She's wearing a golden swimsuit. She puts her glass down when she sees Saga approach and comes to greet her.

"Hi, I'm Saga Bauer."

"Which agency?"

"Säpo."

The woman laughs and leans forward to kiss Saga on each cheek. She then introduces herself as Marie-Louise Salman.

"Have you brought your swimsuit?" Marie-Louise asks on her way back to the bar.

Her long, narrow feet leave prints on the terra-cotta tiles. Her body is trim, and it appears she works to take good care of it. The way she walks is artificial, as if she is used to having people admire her.

Marie-Louise Salman picks up her glass and turns. She gives Saga a close once-over as if to make sure that Saga is really concentrating on her.

"A glass of Sancerre?" she asks, with her cool, modulated voice.

"No, thank you," Saga says.

"I swim to keep my body in shape, although I don't accept as many modeling jobs as I once did. It's so easy to become ego-fixated in my field. Yes, I'm sure you know all about it. It feels like shit when no one remembers to hurry to light your cigarette any longer."

Marie-Louise leans forward and whispers theatrically, "I had an affair with that youngest Chippendale dancer. Do you know him? Doesn't matter, all those guys are gay anyway."

"I came here to talk about a photograph that you sent—"

"Oh! I knew he couldn't keep his mouth shut!" she exclaims with exaggerated indignation.

"Who?"

"Jean-Paul Gaultier."

"The designer?" Saga asks.

"He's the one, the designer who always wore striped shirts; he had deliciously golden beard stubble and a pouty little mouth. He still hates me. I knew it!"

Saga smiles patiently. She picks up a bathrobe and hands it to Marie-Louise as she notices Marie-Louise is covered in goose bumps.

"I love to freeze," Marie-Louise says. "It makes me more desirable. At least, that's what Depardieu said to me last spring . . . or . . . I don't really remember, it might have been that sweetie pie Renaud who said that. Doesn't matter."

They hear new footsteps coming along the hall toward the pool. Marie-Louise looks nervous and seems to glance around for a way out.

"Hello?" a woman calls out.

"Saga?" It's Joona's voice.

Saga takes a step toward the hallway where she sees Joona and Penelope entering, escorting a woman with dark brown hair expensively cut into a pageboy.

"Marie-Louise," the woman says with an exasperated smile. "What are you doing here?"

"I just thought I'd come for a swim," Marie-Louise answers lightly. "Cool off between my legs, you know."

"You know I wish you'd call ahead."

"Oh, yes, sorry, I forgot."

"Marie-Louise is Pontus's sister, my sister-in-law," the woman explains. Then she turns to Saga and introduces herself. "Veronique Salman."

"Saga Bauer from Säpo."

"Let's go into the library," Veronique says, and starts to walk back.

"Can I still swim, as long as I'm already here?" Marie-Louise calls behind them.

"Just not nude!" Veronique replies without looking back.

the photograph, again

Saga, Joona, and Penelope follow Veronique through several rooms on this lower level and into the library. It's a small room with tiny window-panes of yellow, sienna, and rose. Books are lined up behind glass in bookcases, and comfortable brown leather furniture is placed around an open fireplace. A polished brass samovar dominates a coffee table.

"Please excuse me for having no refreshments, but I'm hurrying to catch a flight in just an hour . . ."

Veronique looks very tense, and she wipes her hands over her skirt before she continues.

"I must . . . I have to tell you right away that I will never testify in court. I refuse," she says, subdued. "If you force me, I will deny every-thing I'm about to tell you no matter what the consequences."

She tries to straighten a tilted lampshade, but her fingers tremble so much it ends up just as crooked.

"I'm leaving without Pontus. He won't be able to follow me," she says. She looks at the floor. Her mouth twitches and she has to collect herself before she can continue.

"Penelope," she says, looking at Penelope, "I understand you look down on Pontus as if he were pond scum. But he's really not a bad per-son, he really isn't."

"I haven't said—"

"Listen to me, please," she says. "I just want to say that I love my husband very much, but I . . . his work . . . I don't know what I think about his work. In the beginning I told myself people have always needed weapons to defend themselves. Arms have been traded as long as people have made them. And practically speaking, all countries must be armed for their own defense. But there's defense and then there's—"

She walks to the door, jerks it open, looks out, and then closes it again.

"Exporting weapons to fan flames in countries in the middle of a war . . . you shouldn't be doing that."

"No, you shouldn't," Penelope whispers.

"I understand my husband is a businessman," Veronique continues. "Silencia really needs that contract. Sudan is a large country with an uncertain supply of ammunition for their automatic rifles. They use almost exclusively Fabrique Nationale, and Belgium is not sending them any. People keep an eye on Belgium, but since Sweden has never been a colonial power in Africa, we have an unsullied reputation in the region, and so on, and so forth. Pontus saw the possibilities and moved in quickly the minute civil war in Sudan ended. Raphael Guidi put the deal together. They were just about to sign the contract. Everything was ready to go when the arrest warrant for President al-Bashir was released."

"Then it would break international law," Saga says.

"Everyone knew that. But Raphael would not cancel the deal. He said only that he would find a new interested party. It took a few months, but then he declared that the army in Kenya would be the recipient for the Sudan arms. Same amount of ammunition, same price, and so on. I tried to talk Pontus out of it. I told him it was too apparent that this ammunition would go to Sudan, but Pontus said Kenya was just making a smart move. It was a good deal for them and they needed the ammunition. I don't think he believed what he was saying, I really don't, but he passed the whole thing over to Carl Palmcrona and the ISP. If Palmcrona signs it, it'll be all right, was Pontus's explanation and—"

"An easy way to wash your hands of it," Penelope says.

"So that's why I took that photograph. I just wanted you to know who met in that private box on that night. I walked in and told Pontus that I wasn't feeling well and needed to call a taxi. While I prepared to do that, I simply snapped the picture on my cell phone."

"Brave of you," Penelope says.

"But I didn't know how dangerous! Or I never would have done it," Veronique cries. "I was angry at Pontus and wanted him to change his mind. I left the Alte Oper in the middle of the concert and looked at the picture in the taxi. It was crazy. The buyer was represented by Agathe al-Haji, who is the military adviser to Sudan's president. I mean, that ammunition was going to be pumped into a civil war that no one wanted to acknowledge."

"Genocide," Penelope whispers.

"When we got back home in Sweden, I pleaded with Pontus to get out of that deal . . . I can't forget the strange way he looked at me. He said it was impossible. He told me he'd signed a Paganini contract, and when I saw his expression, I was frightened. He was terrified. I didn't dare keep that picture in my phone. I printed out only one copy and then erased it from my memory card and my hard drive. Then I sent the photograph to you.

"I had no idea what would happen," Veronique says quietly. "How could I? I am so terribly sorry, I can't tell you how . . ."

They are all silent now. Splashing noises come from the pool.

"What is a Paganini contract?" asks Joona.

"Raphael owns several priceless instruments," Veronique says. "He collects ones played by Paganini himself, more than a hundred years ago. He keeps some of them in his home and others he loans to gifted musicians and . . ."

She runs her hands nervously over her neatly styled hair before she continues. "This business about Paganini, I've never really understood it. Pontus told me that Raphael connects Paganini to the contract. He says that Paganini contracts last forever, or that's what Raphael says. Nothing is written on paper . . . Pontus told me that Raphael prepares everything precisely. He has all the numbers in his head; he knows all the logistics, and exactly how and when each deal will be carried out. He tells each one of them what is demanded of them and how much they will earn from the deal. Once you've kissed his hand, so to speak, there is no way out. You can't escape, you can't be protected, you can't even die."

"Why not?" asks Joona.

"Raphael is . . . I don't know how to put it, he's . . . he's a horrible man," she says, her lips trembling. "He manages to extract . . . he deceives them . . . everyone he works with . . . he gets them to tell him their worst nightmare."

"How?" asks Saga.

"I don't know. Pontus said it. He says Raphael has the ability," she replies seriously.

"What does Raphael mean by 'nightmare'?" asks Joona.

"I asked Pontus if he'd told Raphael his nightmare—of course I asked him that," she said with a pained look. "But Pontus wouldn't answer and I have no idea what to believe."

They are silent again. Large, wet patches of sweat spread under the arms of Veronique Salman's white blouse.

"You won't be able to stop Raphael," Veronique finally says. "But maybe you can prevent this ammunition from reaching Darfur."

"We shall," Saga promises.

"You must understand . . . it's the lack of ammunition that keeps the lid on there after the election . . . I mean . . . if it heats up again, all aid organizations will flee Darfur."

Veronique Salman glances at her watch and tells Joona that she has to head for the airport soon. She goes to the window. The multicolored light filtering in on her face reveals an almost dreamy expression, as if she's shifted a heavy load.

"My boyfriend is dead," Penelope says abruptly. She wipes her cheeks. "My sister is dead. I don't even know how many others have died . . ."

Veronique Salman turns to face her again.

"Penelope, who could I turn to? I only had the photograph. I thought you, of all people, would be able to identify the people in the private box," she explains. "You would have known the reason why Agathe al-Haji was there buying ammunition. You've been to Darfur, you have contacts there, and you're a peace activist and—"

"You were wrong," Penelope says. "I didn't recognize Agathe al-Haji. I knew of her, of course, but I didn't know what she looked like."

"I couldn't send it to the police or the newspapers. They wouldn't understand what it meant, not without an explanation, and I couldn't explain. How could I? One thing I did know was that I was afraid to have anything to do with it, so I sent it to you. I purged it completely. I knew I could never reveal my connection to any of this."

"But now you have," Joona points out.

"Yes, because I . . . I . . ."

"Why did you change your mind?"

"Because I'm leaving the country and must . . ."

She looks down at her hands.

"What happened?" Joona asks gently.

"Nothing," she says, but she is holding back tears.

"You can tell us," Joona says.

"No, it—"

"There's no danger here," Saga whispers.

Veronique rubs her cheeks and then looks up at Joona.

"Pontus just called from our summerhouse. He was crying and asked me to forgive him. I didn't know what he was talking about, but he told me he would do anything he could to escape reaping his night-mare."

91

one last escape

A rowboat of polished mahogany bobs on Malmsjö Lake. It's floating on calm waters behind a large spit. A soft breeze blows from the east and brings the smell of manure from the farm on the other side of the water. Pontus Salman has pulled in the oars, but the boat hasn't drifted more than ten meters during the past hour.

His rifle is lying across his lap.

The only thing he hears is the lapping of water against the hull and the slight rustle of wind through the leaves of the trees.

He closes his eyes for a moment. He breathes deeply, opens his eyes, sets the piston on the floor, and makes sure it is held by the wooden bar. His hand touches the barrel heated by the sun and then he aims the barrel at his forehead.

He feels ill at the thought of his entire head blowing off.

His hands shake so much that he has to pause. He decides to aim the barrel at his heart instead.

Swallows are flying lower over the lake as they hunt insects across the surface of the water.

It's probably going to rain tonight, he thinks.

A white streak from an airplane appears in the sky. Pontus begins to think about his nightmare.

It seems to him as if the entire lake turns dark, as if black ink were spread over it.

He turns his attention back to the rifle. He puts the barrel into his mouth and feels it scrape against his teeth. He tastes metal.

He's about to pull the trigger when he hears the sound of a car. His heart flutters in his chest. Various thoughts race through his mind in less than a second. He realizes it must be his wife, since no other person knows where he's gone.

He sets the rifle back over his knees and feels the blood pound through his veins. He notices how much he's shaking as he tries to peer between the trees toward their summerhouse.

There's a man walking across the dock.

It takes Pontus a moment to realize that it's the detective who'd come to the office and showed him the photograph that Veronique had taken.

The moment he recognizes the detective, a new fear rushes through him. *Tell me it's not too late,* he thinks over and over again as he starts to row back to land. *Tell me it's not too late and that I don't have to reap my nightmare. Just tell me it's not too late.*

Pontus Salman doesn't row all the way to the dock. He's pale and only shakes his head as Joona asks him to come closer. Salman seems to want to keep his distance, and he turns the boat so the prow is pointed back toward the lake.

Joona decides to sit on the broken, sun-bleached wooden bench at the very end of the dock. He listens to the lapping of the water and the rustling of the wind in the trees.

"What do you want from me?" asks Pontus. Terror is in his voice.

"I've just been talking to your wife," Joona says.

"Talking?"

"Well, I—"

"You have talked to Veronique?" Pontus asks worriedly.

"I just need some answers."

"There's not enough time for that."

"We're not in any hurry," Joona says, taking note of the rifle in the rowboat.

"What do you know about anything?" mumbles Pontus, more to himself than to Joona.

The oars move softly through the water.

"I know that your wife took the photograph."

Pontus's face falls. He lifts the oars and water rushes over his hands.

"I can't stop the deal," Pontus says morosely. "I needed the money. I was in too much of a rush."

"So you signed the contract."

"It was watertight, even if it came to light. Everyone could swear that they'd agreed in good faith. No one would be guilty."

"But there was a glitch in the end, right?"

"Right."

"I thought I'd wait to put you under arrest—"

"That's because you can't prove it, can you?" Pontus says.

"I haven't discussed this with the prosecutor," Joona continues. "I'm sure that we can offer you a lighter sentence, however, if you testify against Raphael Guidi."

"I won't testify. I will never testify," Pontus says, and the intensity in his voice reveals his determination. "I see that you don't comprehend what's really going on here. I've signed a rather unusual contract, and if I hadn't been so cowardly, I'd already have killed myself, just like Palmcrona did."

"We'll protect you if you testify," Joona says.

"Palmcrona escaped it," Pontus says. "He hanged himself and now the next director has to be the one responsible for signing the order. So Palmcrona means nothing to Raphael Guidi. He was able to escape reaping his nightmare . . ."

Pontus's expressionless face changes into a smile. Joona studies it while he thinks that Palmcrona did not escape his nightmare after all. His nightmare must have been the death of his son.

"A psychologist is on her way over here," Joona says. "She's going to do her best to convince you that suicide is not the answer. You're telling me that the next director of the ISP will have to sign the export order, but what will happen if he refuses?"

Pontus stops rowing in circles. The rowboat continues to drift away from the dock.

Pontus says, "He can refuse, but he won't . . ."

discovered

Axel wakes up when the telephone on his nightstand rings. He hadn't been able to sleep until close to dawn, and only beside Beverly's sweating body.

Now he observes her young face and can tell that she resembles Greta: the same mouth, the same eyelashes.

Beverly is whispering something in her sleep and rolls over onto her stomach. Axel feels the warmth of tenderness wash through him as he regards this heartbreakingly small young person.

He sits up in bed and reaches for the thin volume of Friedrich Dürrenmatt's *The Visit*. There's an unexpected knock on his bedroom door.

"Just a minute," Axel calls at the same moment Robert rushes into the room.

"I thought you were already awake," Axel's brother says. "I really need your advice about this new instrument that I've—"

Robert sees Beverly in the bed and halts abruptly.

"Axel," he stammers. "What's going on?"

Beverly wakes up when she hears Robert's voice. When she sees Robert, she hides underneath the blanket.

Axel gets out of bed and wraps himself in his robe, but Robert is already backing out the door.

"Shame on you!" Robert's saying softly. "Shame on you!"

"It's not what it looks like—"

"You've been using her?" Robert raises his voice. "You've been using a mentally ill girl?"

"I can explain," Axel tries to say.

"You son of a bitch!" Robert grabs him and tries to pull him out of the room.

Axel loses his balance and knocks the lamp to the floor. Robert is still backing up.

"Wait!" Axel says. "You're wrong! I know what it looks like, but you're wrong! Just ask her—"

"I'm going to take her to the police station right now!" Robert declares. "I would never have imagined that you would—"

Robert is overcome with emotion and his eyes well up.

"I'm not a pedophile," Axel says. "You have to understand me. I only need—"

"You need to sleep with a child!" Robert says. "You're using another human being whom you've promised to protect!"

By now Robert has reached the library, and Axel has followed him. Robert falls into one of the sofas and looks at his brother while trying to keep his voice steady.

"Axel, you realize, of course, that I have no choice but to take her to the police," he says.

"I understand," Axel says.

Robert can't look at his brother any longer. He rubs his hand over his face and sighs.

"I might as well take her there now," Robert says.

"I'll go get her." Axel returns to the bedroom.

Beverly is sitting upright in bed and smiles at him while wiping away tears.

"Go on and get dressed," Axel says. "You have to go with Robert."

As Axel returns to the library, Robert stands up. They both stand while avoiding each other's gaze.

"You should stay here," Robert says.

"Right," Axel whispers.

Beverly enters the library a few minutes later. She's wearing jeans and a T-shirt. She's not wearing makeup, so she appears even younger than she is.

greta's death

Robert drives without saying anything. He stops the car at the light and waits for it to turn green.

"I'm very sorry about what happened to you," Robert says in a sad voice. "My brother told me that he was helping you by giving you a place to live until you got your own student apartment. I don't really understand why he'd do such a thing. I never believed—"

"Axel is not a pedophile," Beverly says.

"Why would you want to defend him? He doesn't deserve it."

"He doesn't touch me like that. He never has."

"What does he do, then?"

"He hugs me," Beverly answers.

"Hugs you!" Robert exclaims. "You've just said—"

"He hugs me so he can sleep," she explains in her frank, clear voice.

"What are you talking about?"

"There's nothing ugly about what he does," Beverly says. "At least not as far as I can tell."

Robert sighs and says she'll have to explain everything to the police. He wonders if he's doing the right thing.

"It's all about his insomnia," Beverly explains slowly. "He can't sleep unless he takes his pills. But he can't take his pills anymore. But when I'm there, he calms down and he—"

"But you're underage!" Robert says.

Beverly looks through the windshield at the light green leaves on the trees, which flutter in the warm breeze. A few pregnant women are chatting on the sidewalk. An elderly woman is standing still with her face turned toward the sun.

"Why?" Robert asks. "Why can't Axel sleep at night?"

"He says he's always been like that."

"I know that he wrecked his liver by taking all those pills."

"He told me all about why he can't sleep. It was when we were still in the hospital together," Beverly says. "Something sad happened to him."

Robert stops at a pedestrian crossing. A child drops his pacifier in the street and his mother doesn't notice but keeps walking. The child rips himself away from his mother and dashes back. The mother screams horribly but then notices that Robert has observed the scene and understood that the child would run back. The mother picks up her child and carries him to the sidewalk while he shrieks.

"He knew a girl who died," Beverly says.

"Who was it?"

"He only told me about it once, while we were at the hospital. He doesn't like to talk about it."

Beverly twists her fingers together.

"Tell me what he told you," Robert says. There's tension in his voice.

"They were in love and they slept together and then the next day she killed herself." Beverly glances at Robert. "I kind of look like her, right?"

"You do," Robert answers.

"When he was in the hospital, he told me that he was the one who killed her," Beverly whispers.

Robert jerks and turns to her.

"What are you talking about?"

"He said there's something he did that made her want to kill herself."

Robert's mouth drops open. "He said that? He said it was his fault?"

Beverly nods.

"He said it was his fault because they were supposed to be practicing together, and instead they had sex and she thought he'd lured her into it so he could win the violin competition."

"None of that was his fault," Robert says.

"Of course it was. He said so."

Robert sinks behind the wheel and rubs his face with his hands.

"Oh, good Lord," he says. "There's something I have to tell him."

Robert stops the car and the car behind him honks. Beverly looks at him with worry.

"What's wrong?" she asks.

Robert starts to turn the car around.

"There's . . . there's something very important I must tell him. I was behind the stage right before Axel was going to go on and I know what really happened. Greta had already played right before he was supposed to go on because she was first on the program and—"

"You were there?"

"Just a minute," Robert says. "I heard everything that happened. I know that Greta's death had nothing to do with Axel."

Robert is so upset that he has to stop the car again. His face is pale as ash as he says to Beverly, "Please, forgive me, but I really have to—"

"Do you know that for sure?" Beverly asks.

"What?" Robert looks at her in confusion.

"Are you absolutely sure that it wasn't Axel's fault that Greta died?"

"Of course!"

"But what happened?"

Robert wipes a tear from his cheek. He opens the car door.

"Just a second," he says. "I have to . . . I must speak to him."

Robert gets out of the car and stands on the sidewalk.

The enormous linden trees on Sveavägen are shedding their seeds, which dance in the sunshine. Robert has a big smile on his face as he reaches for his cell phone and punches in Axel's number. After three rings, his smile disappears, and he starts to walk back to the car with his cell phone to his ear. Only when he breaks off the call and attempts to redial the number does he notice that his car is empty. Beverly is gone. He looks around but can't see her anywhere. City traffic is picking up. Students in their cars are rushing down to Sergel's Square.

Robert shuts the door, starts his car, and begins to drive slowly as he looks for Beverly.

white rustling plastic

Axel Riessen doesn't know how long he's been standing at the window. He'd watched Robert and Beverly drive away until they were out of sight. His thoughts had gone back into the past. He forces himself to stop re-membering and walks over to his music system and puts on the first side of David Bowie's *The Rise and Fall of Ziggy Stardust and the Spiders from Mars*. He jacks up the volume.

Pushing through the market square . . .

Axel walks over to his bar and takes out one of the most expensive whiskey bottles in his collection. It's a Macallan 1939, from the first year of the Second World War. He pours himself half a glass and then goes to the sofa and sits down. He listens to the music with his eyes closed—Bowie's young voice and the sloppy piano playing—and he sniffs the aroma of oak barrels, heavy reservoirs and dark cellars, straw and citrus. He drinks and the strong liquor burns his lips as it fills his mouth. Guarding its precious taste, this liquor has been waiting through decades: generations, changes of government, war and peace.

Now Axel is thinking that maybe what just happened is a good thing. Maybe Beverly will finally get the help she needs. He has a sudden im-pulse to call his brother and tell him that he loves him, but frowns at the pathetic thought. He won't be killing himself—he's just going to meet what's coming to him soon enough and try to die on his feet.

He takes the whiskey to his bedroom and stares at the unmade bed. He's able to hear the sound of vibrations coming from his jacket, which is hanging over the back of a chair. Just then, he also hears the sound of footsteps behind him. He whirls around.

"Oh, it's you, Beverly," he says in surprise.

Her face is dusty and she's holding a white dandelion ball in her hand.

"I didn't want to talk to the police," she says.

"Where's Robert?"

"I hitchhiked home," she says. "It wasn't hard. I got a ride right away."

"Why do you hitchhike? You might have been—"

"Don't be mad. I really didn't do anything wrong. But there's something very important that I have to tell you."

The telephone in his jacket starts to vibrate again.

"Just a moment, Beverly, I have to get this," he says.

He searches through his jacket pockets and finds his cell phone. He answers, "Axel Riessen here."

A voice that seems to come from far away says, "Hello?"

"Hello," Axel says.

"This is Raphael Guidi." The voice is deep and the English is accented. "Please excuse the noise on the line. At the moment, I'm at sea, on my way to Latvia. I'm afraid that once we get out on the Baltic, we may lose our connection altogether."

"I can hear you," Axel says politely while Beverly walks over to the bed and sits.

"Let me get down to business," Raphael Guidi says. "I'm calling you because I need to know that your signature is on the export authorization. I'd already thought that the container ship would have been able to leave the harbor by now."

Axel holds the phone close to his ear. He walks into the library but can't hear much besides his own breathing. He thinks about the photograph with Raphael Guidi, Carl Palmcrona, Agathe al-Haji, and Pontus Salman. He remembers how Palmcrona had raised his champagne glass and was laughing so that his teeth shone.

"Are you still there?" asks Raphael Guidi on the crackling line.

"I am not going to sign the authorization form," Axel replies shortly, and shivers run up and down his spine.

"Maybe there's a way I can convince you to change your mind," Raphael Guidi says. "Think whether or not there's something I can offer you that would help—"

"You have nothing I want."

"I believe you may be wrong about that. Whenever I sign a contract, I—"

Axel hangs up. He slides the phone back into his jacket pocket. He's filled with discomfort, almost a premonition, and begins to walk to the hallway door leading to the staircase. As he looks through the window, he spies movement in the park: shadows among the bushes heading toward his house. Axel whirls and looks out the other window but sees nothing.

There's a clink from the bottom floor, as if one of the small panes of glass broke in the sunshine. Axel thinks the whole thing is absurd and at the same time realizes what's going on. His body fills with adrenaline, and he has heightened awareness of his surroundings. Heart racing, he moves as swiftly as he can without running. He heads straight toward Beverly in his bedroom. Beautiful sunlight is flooding in through the gaps in the venetian blinds and landing at Beverly's feet. Beverly has gotten undressed and crawled back into the unmade bed. She has the volume of Dürrenmatt on her stomach.

"Axel," she says, "I came back because I have to tell you some really good news—"

"Don't be afraid, now." He interrupts her. "Just do as I say. Hide underneath the bed right now. Don't move or make a sound. Stay there for one hour."

Beverly does what he says without question. She crawls beneath the bed.

Axel hears the tromping of feet coming up the stairs. *There's at least two of them*, he thinks. Beverly's jeans and T-shirt are on a chair. He picks them up and throws them under the bed.

His heart is pounding and his thoughts are whirling as he looks around, not knowing what to do.

He grabs his telephone from his jacket and runs out of the bedroom and into the library. He can hear the sound of feet in the hallway, also heading to the library.

His hands are shaking as he tries to punch a number into his phone. He hears the floor creak as someone rushes into the room. There's no time to call. He tries to head over to the window so he can yell into the street for help, but someone grabs his right wrist while jamming a cool instrument against his throat. He doesn't realize it's a stun gun; 69,000 volts of electricity pulse through his body.

The sparking of electricity can be heard in the room, but Axel only feels heavy blows, as if someone were beating his throat with an iron pipe. He doesn't even hear himself screaming. His brain shuts down and the world around him disappears.

The man who attacked him has already taped his mouth shut by the time Axel starts coming to. Axel finds he's lying on the floor and his body is jerking in spasms. His arms and legs are flailing. A burning bite on his throat hits him with pain. He has no chance to defend himself.

The men brusquely move Axel's arms and legs so that they can wrap him in white plastic. The plastic crackles softly and he believes that he's going to suffocate. However, air is able to come through to him. The men tape up the plastic and then lift him like a rug. Axel tries to struggle, but he's no longer in control of his own muscles. The two men carry him down the staircase, out through the front door, and into a waiting garbage truck.

disappeared

Joona tries to call Pontus Salman back to shore. The rowboat glides farther away. Joona runs from the dock to the meet the psychologist and
the two colleagues from Södertälje. He accompanies them back to the
dock and tells them to be careful, but he doesn't believe that Pontus
Salman is a danger to himself or others.

"But keep him in custody," Joona says. "I'll be in touch as soon as I
can." He hurries back to his car.

As Joona drives over the bridge over Fittjaviken, he reflects on Pontus
Salman and how Salman sat in the rowboat and told Joona how he was
convinced that Axel Riessen would want to sign the Paganini contract.

Joona had asked Salman if Riessen could refuse, but he said that
Riessen would not want to.

As he dials the number for Axel Riessen, Joona can see Veronique
Salman in his mind's eye. The disappointed expression around her mouth
and the fear in her eyes as she described how once one had kissed Raphael Guidi on the hand, there was no way out.

Those words, "the nightmare," keep returning, Joona thinks. Palmcrona's housekeeper had used it. Veronique Salman had said that Raphael made sure that everyone would tell him their worst nightmare and
Pontus Salman had said that Palmcrona had avoided his nightmare by
committing suicide.

Pontus had said, *He was able to escape reaping his nightmare.*

Joona reflects on the fact that Stefan Bergkvist never knew that Carl Palmcrona was his father. He thinks about the unbearable heat that burned the flesh right off the bones and made the blood boil—the heat that burst the boy's skull.

You can't break a Paganini contract even if you die.

Joona tries again to reach Axel Riessen on the phone and then tries the direct number to the ISP.

"Can you connect me to Axel Riessen?" he asks quickly.

"I'm sorry. He is not reachable at the moment," the receptionist replies.

"I'm a detective with the police and I need to speak to him right away."

"I understand, but—"

"Interrupt him if he's in a meeting."

"He's not here," she replies, raising her voice. "He hasn't come in this morning, and we haven't been able to reach him by phone."

"Now I know," Joona says while hanging up.

Joona parks his Volvo on Brahegatan outside the gate to Axel Riessen's mansion. The massive front door is just swinging shut as he approaches, and he races to ring the bell. The lock rattles and the door is reopened.

"Hello there," Robert Riessen says as he sees Joona.

"Is Axel at home?"

"He should be, but I just got here," Robert replies. "Has something happened?"

"I've been trying to reach him."

"Me, too," Robert says, and he lets Joona inside.

They walk up a half staircase and enter a large foyer dominated by an elaborate rose-colored glass-armed chandelier. Robert knocks on the door and then walks right into Axel's residence. They both hurry up to the private apartment in silence.

"Axel!" Robert yells.

They look around, going from room to room. Everything appears normal—the stereo system is on but no sound comes out, and a volume of the *Encyclopaedia Britannica* is lying open on the dictionary stand.

"Do you know if he was planning to travel?" Joona asks.

"No," Robert replies, but there's an odd exhaustion in his voice. "He does so many strange things."

"What do you mean by that?"

"You think you know somebody and . . . well, who knows."

Joona walks into the bedroom and takes a quick look around. He sees a large oil painting leaning against the wall with its back facing the room and a puffy white dandelion past its bloom placed in a whiskey glass, and he notices an unmade bed and a book.

Robert has already left the room and started down the stairs. Joona follows him down and to the large kitchen.

raphael guidi

Joona parks his car next to Kronoberg Park and walks to the police station while on the phone to the Södertälje police. Something is nagging him; he wishes he had been part of the group to bring in Pontus Salman.

His worry intensifies when the Södertälje officer explains that no one knows where Pontus Salman is.

"I'll call you back," the man says in a strong Gotland accent. "Just give me a few minutes."

"But you did bring him in, didn't you?" Joona asks.

"That was the plan," the officer says doubtfully.

"I was very clear that he should be held."

"No need to blame me," the man says. "I'm sure all procedures were followed."

He is heard to tap on his computer, mumble to himself, and then tap some more before he gives Joona the information: "Yes, he's in custody here. We have also confiscated his weapon, a Winchester 490."

"Good. Keep him there. We'll send a car for him," Joona says. The nearby Kronoberg Park swimming pool smells strongly of chlorine to Joona as he walks through the large glass doors.

He takes the elevator up and strides quickly through the corridor. He's almost reached Carlos Eliasson's office when his cell phone rings. It's Disa. Time is very short, but he answers anyway.

"Hi," Disa says. "Are you coming tomorrow?"

"You told me you didn't want to celebrate your birthday."

"I know, but I thought . . . just you and me."

"Sounds good," Joona says.

"I have something important to tell you, too," she explains.

"Okay," Joona says as he arrives at Carlos's door.

"I—"

"Sorry, Disa, but I really can't talk. I'm heading into an important meeting."

"I have a surprise," she says.

"Disa, I have to hang up now," he says, and opens the door.

"But—" Disa says.

"I'm really sorry, but I just can't talk now."

Joona walks into Carlos's room, closes the door behind him, and sits down next to Saga on the sofa.

"We can't reach Axel Riessen," Carlos tells him immediately.

"We're afraid these murders are all tied to the export authorization," Joona says. "And we believe that Raphael Guidi is behind the whole thing. We need an arrest warrant for him as soon as possible—"

"Arrest warrant?" Carlos repeats, taken aback. "Just because Axel Riessen hasn't answered his phone for two hours and has been delayed coming to work, you immediately assume he's been kidnapped by Raphael Guidi—who, I might remind you, is a successful businessman with an unblemished record." Carlos starts counting on his fingers. "Swedish police have nothing on him. Europol has nothing on him. Interpol has nothing. I've even talked to the police in France, Italy, and Monaco."

"But I've talked to Anja." Joona smiles smugly.

"You talked to *Anja?*"

Carlos falls silent before the entry of Anja Larsson, who closes the door behind her.

Without any introduction she begins. "During the past decade, Raphael Guidi's name has come up six times. He was rumored to be involved in illegal arms deals, illegal money deals, and unexplained deaths."

"Only preliminary investigations," Carlos objects. "That doesn't mean—"

"Should I go on or not?" Anja says.

"Please, go ahead."

"All suspicions about Raphael Guidi were squashed at an early stage in almost every case and so he was never really investigated."

"So you have nothing," Carlos says.

"His business earned 123 million dollars on Operation Desert Storm by providing Nighthawk jets with AGM-65 Maverick missiles," Anja continues. She glances at her notes to check her accuracy. "But one of his auxiliary corporations provided Serbian forces with artillery rockets capable of bringing down these same planes during the Kosovo war."

Anja shows them a photograph of Raphael in sienna-tinted sunglasses. He's in sharply pressed blue pants, with a more comfortable-looking blue shirt hanging out. He smiles broadly. He's between two bodyguards, posing in front of a smoke-colored Lamborghini Diablo.

"Raphael's wife was the well-known violinist Fiorenza Colini," Anja tells them. "One year after their son, Peter, was born, she was diagnosed with breast cancer. She underwent all kinds of treatments, but died when their son was seven."

She shows them a newspaper clipping from the Italian newspaper *La Repubblica*. Fiorenza Colini has a beautiful red violin at her shoulder with the entire orchestra of La Scala behind her. The conductor, Riccardo Muti, is poised beside her. His wavy hair shines in the spotlight. Fiorenza Colini's slim body is a shimmering column in a gown of platinum trimmed with silver brocade and an edging of sparkling crystal. Her eyes smile beneath thick lashes. Her right elbow is lifted as if her bow is traveling down and her slender fingers are placed high on the fingerboard, searching for a difficult note.

Anja shows them another clipping, this one from *Newsweek*, in which Raphael Guidi, his newborn son in his arms, stands improbably and proudly next to the American rock star Alice Cooper. The headline reads BILLION DOLLAR BABY. And in yet another, Guidi, dressed in a soft, light-colored suit, chats with Italian prime minister Silvio Berlusconi while three blond women in micro bikinis lounge beside a rose-marble pool shaped like a heart.

"Raphael Guidi supposedly lives in Monaco, but if you want him, you have to go to sea, as far as I can determine," Anja says. "He spends almost all of his time these days on his mega yacht, *Theresa*. It's easy to understand why. Lürssen built it in Bremen fifteen years ago with every luxury that could be devised."

A shot of the yacht, white and arrow-shaped, accompanies a feature on Guidi in French *Vogue*. In the photo the ship looks like a porcelain spear, and the article, entitled "Lion en Cannes," breathlessly details a lavish film-festival bash thrown on board: "*À la ville comme à la mer: Raphael Guidi et sa femme, Fiorenza, prennent le temps de faire les présentations. Kevin Costner et Salma Hayek saluent Victoria Silvstedt, l'icône* Playboy *suédoise.*"

The men wear tuxedos, the women wear little, and the ever-present bodyguards planted behind Guidi wear their habitual stolid expressions. The article takes special pains to describe the dining hall, which features toucans in birdcages hanging from the ceiling, and a male lion, pacing back and forth in a cage of his own.

They hand the clippings back to Anja.

"Let's listen now," Anja says. "Belgian Intelligence has recorded a telephone conversation between an Italian prosecutor and Salvatore Garibaldi, who was a brigade general in the Esercito Italiano, the Italian army."

She passes out copies of a hastily made translation, puts a USB flash drive into Carlos's computer, leans over, and hits Play. The recording opens immediately with an official voice giving the circumstances, place, date, and time in French. Then a small metal click can be heard and a distant connecting tone. There's a crackle, then a firm voice speaks.

"I'm listening and I'm ready to begin the preliminary investigation," the prosecutor says.

"I can never testify against Raphael Guidi, not even under torture, not even . . ."

Salvatore Garibaldi's voice disappears in a spurt of static. Then it appears again more weakly as if through a closed door.

". . . med recoil brakes or completely recoilless rocket systems . . . and a hell of a lot of mines, antipersonnel mines, antivehicle mines, antitank mines . . . Raphael would never . . . like in Rwanda, he didn't care. They used sticks and machetes—nothing with real money. But when the fight spilled over into the Congo, he wanted part of the action. He thought it would be a gold mine. First he armed the Rwanda Patriotic Front to be able to attack Mobutu forcefully. Then he turned around to pump heavy weaponry to the Hutus so that they could retaliate against the RPF."

A strange peeping sound rises through the static. It hiccups and then his voice is clear again.

"The whole deal with the nightmare, I couldn't really believe it. I was forced . . . forced to hold his sweaty hand . . . while I watched. My daughter, she was fourteen. She was so pretty, so beautiful . . . Raphael . . . he did it himself. He used the knife himself . . . he screamed at me that I was reaping my nightmare. He owned it . . . he owned my nightmare. I still . . . don't ask me to think about it again . . . I can't . . ."

There are strange sounds. Someone shouts in the background. Breaking glass can be heard. The sound recording sputters.

Salvatore Garibaldi is weeping. "How could anyone do anything like that . . . he took a fillet knife from his bodyguard . . . my daughter's face . . . her beautiful, beautiful . . ." He continues to sob and then he screams that now he wants nothing more than to die. He wants to die.

More crackling and the recording ends. No one in Carlos Eliasson's office says a word. Through the small windows facing Kronoberg Park's green slope, a playful light falls into the office.

"This recording"—Carlos clears his throat—"proves nothing. Right from the start he said he would not testify, he was not going to be a witness. I imagine that made the case evaporate and made the prosecutor end the investigation."

"Three weeks later, Salvatore Garibaldi's head was found by a man walking his dog," Anja says. "It was in a ditch by the Via Goethe, behind a racetrack in Rome."

"What happened to his daughter?" Joona asks quietly. "Does anyone know?"

"Fourteen-year-old Maria Garibaldi is still missing," Anja says shortly.

Carlos sighs and mutters to himself. He walks to his aquarium and contemplates his paradise fish for a long while before he turns back.

"What do you want me to do? You cannot prove that the ammunition is being diverted to Sudan. If Axel Riessen *has* disappeared, you cannot link it to Raphael Guidi. Give me the tiniest shred of proof," he pleads, "and I will go to the prosecutor. But I need something concrete, not just—"

"I know it's him," Joona says.

"And I need more than Joona declaring that he knows," Carlos responds.

"We need the authorities behind us to arrest Raphael Guidi for crimes against Swedish and international law," Joona continues stubbornly.

"Not without proof," Carlos says.

"We'll find proof," Joona says.

"You need to convince Pontus Salmon to testify."

"We've already picked him up, but getting him to testify will be very tough. He's already so frightened he was about to commit suicide," Joona says.

"If we arrest Raphael, maybe he'll feel free enough to talk. That is, if things ever calm down," Saga says.

"We still can't arrest someone as important as Guidi without any proof," Carlos reiterates firmly.

"So what the hell can we do?" demands Saga.

"Lean on Pontus Salman—"

"We've got to hurry. I believe that Axel Riessen is in danger," Joona says.

They are all interrupted as Jens Svanehjälm, the chief prosecutor, strides into the room.

flight

Air-conditioning has chilled his car, but that's not what makes Pontus Salman's hands shake on the steering wheel. He's already crossing the bridge to Lidingö Island. A ferry to Finland is leaving its dock and beyond Millesgården someone is burning leaves.

A few hours ago, he'd been in his tiny flat-bottomed rowboat trying to hold a rifle barrel to his mouth. The metal taste is still on his tongue, and he can still hear the scraping sound it made against his teeth.

A woman in a straggly blue punk haircut was jogging onto the dock with the detective. She'd called him gently in her middle-aged voice to come closer. She had to tell him something important. She was wearing bright red lipstick. She'd brought him to a small gray room. He found out her name was Gunilla and she was a psychologist. She'd talked to him deeply about what he had intended to do when he rowed out onto the lake.

"Why do you want to die?" she'd asked plainly.

"I really don't want to," he'd answered truthfully, surprising her.

She was taken aback a moment and then they began to really talk. He'd answered all her questions and became more and more convinced that he did not want to die. He'd rather run and he began to plan where he could go. He'd just disappear and start a new life as someone else.

The car had crossed the bridge. Pontus Salman looks at his watch and feels tremendous relief that, by now, Veronique's plane must have left Swedish airspace.

He'd told Veronique about French Polynesia and now he can fantasize: he sees her emerge from the airport carrying her light blue carry-on. She's wearing a broad-brimmed hat, which she has to hold down in the breeze. Why couldn't he escape, too?

The only thing he needs is his passport from his desk drawer.

I don't want to die, Pontus Salman thinks as he watches traffic rush by.

He'd rowed out into the lake to flee having to reap his nightmare, but he just couldn't pull the trigger.

I'll take any plane at all, he thinks. *Iceland, Japan, or Brazil. If Raphael Guidi really wants me dead, he'd have killed me already.*

Pontus Salman drives up to his garage and gets out. He takes a deep breath to smell the warm stones under his feet, the car exhaust, the fresh smell of growing plants.

The street seems abandoned with everyone at work and even the children still in school for a few more days.

Pontus Salman unlocks the door and walks in. All the lights in the house are off and the curtains are drawn.

He has to go downstairs to get his passport from his office.

Once on the lower level, he pauses as he hears something strange, as if a wet blanket is being pulled across a tile floor.

"Veronique?" he asks in a strangled voice.

Pontus Salman can see light from the pool dapple against a white stone wall. With his heart racing, he slowly, silently, walks toward the pool.

98

Chief Prosecutor Jens Svanehjälm greets Saga Bauer, Joona Linna, and Carlos Eliasson quietly, gestures them to a seat, and then sits down. The material Anja Larsson collected is spread over the coffee table in front of him. Svanehjälm takes a sip of his soy coffee and looks at the top picture before he turns to Carlos.

"You'll have a hard time convincing me," he says.

"But we will," Joona says with a smile.

"Go ahead, make my day," the prosecutor replies in English.

Svanehjälm looks like a little boy dressed in his father's clothes. His neck is thin, without any apparent Adam's apple, and his narrow shoulders slump even though he wears a well-tailored suit.

"This is complicated," Saga says. "But we fear Axel Riessen from ISP has been kidnapped as part of this slaughter that's been going on the past few days."

Carlos's phone rings so she pauses.

"I'm sorry," he says to them, and then into the intercom he snaps, "I thought I told you that we couldn't be disturbed!" He listens a moment to the voice there and then picks up the office phone. "Carlos Eliasson here."

He listens and then his cheeks flame bright red. He mumbles that he understands, thanks the caller, and hangs up.

"I'm sorry," Carlos says.

"It's nothing," Jens Svanehjälm says politely.

"I mean, I'm sorry that I have troubled you at all with this meeting! That was Axel Riessen's secretary calling from ISP. I've been in contact with her all morning . . . and she's just gotten a call from Axel Riessen."

"So what did she say—no kidnapping?" Jens Svanehjälm smiles.

"He is on Raphael Guidi's yacht wrapping up the final details on the export approval."

Joona and Saga exchange glances.

"So you're all happy now?" asks the prosecutor genially.

"Apparently Axel Riessen requested a meeting with Raphael Guidi," Carlos tells them.

"He would have spoken to us first," Saga says stubbornly.

"The secretary says that they've been on the boat the whole day to iron out any differences. He says the agreement is long overdue and he would probably fax his signature in to the ISP this evening."

"He's going to authorize it?" asks Saga as she stands up abruptly.

"That's right." Carlos smiles.

"And his plans after that? He's made plans—" Joona inquires.

"He was—" Carlos stops and frowns at Joona.

"Why did you think he would plan something special after this meeting?" he asks. "But yes, his secretary told me he planned to borrow a Forgus sailboat from Raphael Guidi to go on a long sail down the coast to Kaliningrad."

"Sounds wonderful," says Jens as he gets up to leave.

"Idiots!" Saga says as she kicks the wastebasket. "You must know he was forced to make that call!"

"Let's behave like adults here," Carlos says.

He bends down to pick up the wastebasket and the spilled trash.

"So we're done here now, aren't we?" Svanehjälm says quietly.

"Axel Riessen is a prisoner on Raphael Guidi's boat," Joona says just as quietly, but his words are rock firm. "Give us the authority to go get him."

"Maybe I'm really dense, but I see no cause for action at all," Jens Svanehjälm tells them, and calmly leaves the room.

They watch him leisurely close the door behind him.

"Sorry I lost it," Saga apologizes to Carlos. "But this makes no sense. Axel was adamant he would never sign this agreement . . . at least, not of his own free will."

"Saga, I've put two lawyers onto this case," Carlos explains. "All they found was a perfectly legitimate export deal that Silencia Defense had put together. I assure you they went over it with a fine-tooth comb—"

"But we have a photograph where Palmcrona and Salman meet with Raphael Guidi and Agathe al-Haji in order to—"

"I know all that," Carlos says hastily. "But we can't prove what we suspect. A simple photograph is not enough."

"So we're going to just sit on our asses and watch this ship leave Sweden with ammunition we know is bound for Sudan?" Saga exclaims indignantly.

"Get Pontus Salman in here," Carlos answers. "Get him to testify against Raphael Guidi. Offer him whatever you can as long as he agrees to be a witness—"

"But if he refuses?" Saga asks.

"Then there's nothing we can do."

"Actually, we do have another witness," Joona says softly.

"I'd like to meet him!" Carlos demands skeptically.

"We just have to bring him in before they find his drowned body in the sea outside of Kaliningrad."

"You're not going to get your way this time, Joona." Carlos seems to push himself back.

"Yes, I will."

"No, you won't."

"Yes, indeed I will." Joona won't give an inch.

Carlos looks at Joona sadly.

"We'll never convince the prosecutor about this," he says after a while. "But since I can't spend the rest of my life sitting here and saying no to you while you say yes, well, then . . ."

He sighs, thinks for a moment, and then says, "I'll give you permission to look for Axel Riessen in your usual role as our consultant. We simply need to check on his safety."

"Joona will need backup," Saga says.

"This is not a real police operation," Carlos says. "It's just a way to get Joona to shut up."

"But Joona will be—"

"What I want," Carlos says, "what I really want is for you, Saga, to bring Pontus Salman here from Södertälje as I've already requested . . . if he can give us a watertight case, we can go after Raphael Guidi with everything we've got."

"There's no time for all that," Joona says as he starts walking to the door.

"I'll go get Pontus," Saga agrees.

"And Joona? What are you—"

"I'm going to drop in on Raphael and have a little chat," Joona answers as he walks out of the room.

the payment

After lying huddled in the trunk of a car, Axel is stiff when he's finally allowed out. He finds he's been taken to a small private airport. The landing strip is made of concrete and surrounded by a high fence. A helicopter waits in front of a building that looks like a barracks. A tall mast sticks up from the roof.

Axel can hear the screech of seagulls as he is made to walk between the two men who have kidnapped him. He's still wearing just trousers and a shirt. There's nothing to say, so he climbs into the helicopter with the men. He sits down and fastens the harness. One of the two men is the pilot. He manipulates the instruments on the panel before him, then turns a tiny, shining key, hits another control, and presses a pedal.

The man next to the pilot spreads a map over his lap.

There's peeling tape on the windshield.

The motor hums as the engine takes hold and the rotors start to slowly rotate. The narrow blades slice heavily through the air and the hazy sunshine blinks across the windshield. The rotor revs more and more quickly.

A paper cup on the ground is blown away.

The engine has warmed up. The blades clatter deafeningly. The pilot holds the joystick in his right hand, moving it with small, square movements. Suddenly they lift.

The helicopter heads slowly straight up at first, but then it tips forward and they move off.

Axel's stomach lurches as they fly over the fence, up over the trees, and then swing so quickly to the left that it feels as if the helicopter is tipping to the side.

Swiftly they put the rolling green ground behind them, along with a few lonely roads and a house with a shining tin-plated roof.

The helicopter engine thuds and the shadows of the rotating blades flick across the windshield.

The mainland ends and the sea opens up beneath them.

Axel tries to think through what's happened. Raphael Guidi must have had everything in place. He'd phoned Axel from his yacht in the Finnish bay. He'd said that he was on his way to Latvia and heading for the open Baltic Sea, then Axel had cut him off. There could have been no more than a minute or two between the time he told Guidi he would not sign and the moment when the two thugs broke into his house and shocked him with the stun gun.

At least they didn't rough him up. They made sure he was lying comfortably even if it was in the trunk of a car.

Half an hour later, they'd stopped that car and exchanged it for another.

An hour later, they let him walk on his own to the helicopter.

The ocean beneath them moves past as swiftly as a highway. The skies above seem static, cloudy, and moistly white. They're flying at fifty meters and at great speed. The pilot talks into the radio but Axel finds it impossible to hear what he's saying.

Axel dozes for a while and can no longer sense how long he's been in the helicopter when he looks down to see a luxury yacht plowing through the rippling sea. It is huge, a white ship large enough to contain a light blue swimming pool and several tanning decks.

They drop steeply down.

Axel reminds himself again that Raphael Guidi is a very rich man and he leans forward to take a good look at the yacht. It's really unbelievable. The ship is trim and arrow-sharp and so white it looks frosted. It's at least one hundred meters long with a soaring captain's bridge, at least two stories high, on the afterdeck.

The helicopter thrashes its way down toward the rings marked on a helicopter pad on the foredeck. The backwash from the rotor blades whips along the water curving from the sides of the boat. The helicopter hovers, sinks slowly, and then settles onto the platform, softly swaying. They land smoothly and wait until the blades stop. The helicopter pilot remains in the cockpit while the other man takes Axel's arm to guide him across the platform. They stoop in the wind draft until they pass through a glass door.

The room they enter seems to be an elegant waiting room, with sofas and a coffee table as well as a darkened large-screen television. A man in a white uniform greets them smoothly and gestures toward a sofa for Axel to take a seat.

"Would you like something to drink?" he asks softly.

"Just water, please," Axel replies.

"Plain or mineral water?" asks the man.

Before Axel can reply, another man walks through the door.

This one resembles the first man who'd escorted Axel from the helicopter. They are both tall and wide with well-coordinated bodies, but this new man is so blond that his eyebrows are almost colorless, and his nose looks like it had once been painfully broken. The resemblance ends there. Axel's first captor has gray hair and horn-rim glasses. They move together as a team, silently, effectively and with no wasted movement, as they lead Axel down some steps to the suites below.

The whole ship seems strangely deserted. A beautiful little wicker suite on a platform has been neglected. The exquisite weaving has splits and jagged points that stick out from the edges of the chairs and table. Axel is surprised to see that the pool, which looked so blue from above, almost looks dusty. It clearly has not had water in it for years. It's filled with piles of broken chairs, a sofa without cushions, and some broken desk chairs.

Inside, the farther one goes in the ship, the more empty and deserted it seems. Axel's footsteps echo across the hallway's scratched marble floor.

They walk through double doors with the words SALA DE PRANZO elegantly carved into the dark wood above. The dining room is enormous. Only open sea can be seen outside the panoramic windows and a wide, red-carpeted staircase leads to the upper level. Stunning crystal chandeliers hang from the ceiling. The room has been designed to impress, but on the dining-room table there's nothing but a copier, a fax machine, two computers, and a massive collection of folders with filed paperwork.

A short man sits at a small table in the massive room. His hair is flecked with gray and a wide bald spot shines on his crown. Axel recognizes Raphael Guidi at once. Guidi is dressed casually in light blue gym shorts with a matching jacket. The number 7 is stitched to his breast pocket with a larger image on the back. He wears white tennis shoes without socks. "Welcome," he says in English.

A cell phone rings in his pocket, and Guidi picks it up, glances at the number, but doesn't answer. Almost immediately afterward, another phone call comes in, and Guidi says a few words in Italian. Then he looks at Axel Riessen. He gestures proudly to the panoramic windows and the rolling ocean waves.

"I am here against my will," Axel begins.

"I'm sorry, but there was no other way. We've run out of time—"

"What do you want from me?"

"I want your loyalty," Raphael replies shortly.

The two bodyguards grin down at the floor and then immediately wipe the expression from their faces. Raphael takes a long gulp of what looks like yellow vitamin water and burps loudly.

"Loyalty. The only thing that matters," he says softly as he looks sternly at Axel. "I know you believe I have nothing you might want in payment, but—"

"That's true," Axel answers sharply.

"Still, I believe we can make a deal . . . I believe I have something you want desperately," Raphael continues. He smiles, but there is no pleasure in the grimace. "For your loyalty I will offer something that you really, truly want. In fact, what you want more than anything else in the world."

Axel shakes his head in disbelief. "I couldn't even say what that might be."

"Oh, no," Raphael says smoothly. "What you want more than anything else in the world seems so simple . . . a good night's sleep—"

"How did you know that?" Axel gasps, then stops short as he sees Raphael's cool, calculating look.

"So then you already know that I've tried every possible way," Axel says slowly.

Raphael gestures indifferently. "You will be provided with a new liver."

"I've been on the donor's list for years," Axel says with an involuntary smile. "I call the doctors every time they have a meeting, but my liver damage was self-inflicted and my tissue type is so unusual, no donors can be found."

"I have located a liver for you, Axel Riessen," Raphael says in his sharp voice.

There's silence in the room and Axel feels his face and ears flush.

"And in return?" Axel says, swallowing hard. "You want me to sign the export authorization for Kenya."

"More than that," Raphael says. "I want us to sign a Paganini contract."

"What is that?"

"There's no hurry, there will be time to consider. It's a major decision. But before you decide, I want you to go thoroughly through the information I've accumulated about this particular organ donor."

Axel's thoughts zip through his mind at blazing speed. Axel eagerly tells himself that he can sign the export authorization and then, once he's gotten his liver, turn on Guidi and testify against him. He'd be protected by the authorities, he knows, and perhaps he would have to change his identity and all that. But he would be able to sleep again.

"Why don't we have something to eat?" Raphael asks. "I'm hungry. Aren't you?"

"Maybe . . ."

"But before we eat, please phone your secretary at ISP and let her know that you are here."

pontus salman

Saga has her phone against her ear as she stops for a moment next to the recycle bin in the hallway. She sees without noticing it the leaflike remains of a butterfly on the floor, mimicking life in the breeze from the ventilation system.

"Don't you have anything else to do up there in Stockholm?" asks an officer with a Gotland dialect when she finally connects with Södertälje.

"About Pontus Salman," she says irritably.

"Well, he's gone now." The policeman sounds contented.

"What the hell are you saying?" she yells.

"Well, I talked to Gunilla Sommer, our psychologist, who brought him into the psychiatric ward."

"And?"

"She interviewed him and decided, without reservation, that he was no longer a candidate for suicide. She felt he should be free to go, so she released him. Hospital beds cost money, you know."

"Send out a description and bring him in at once!" Saga demands immediately.

"For what? A halfhearted suicide attempt?"

"Just make sure you find him!" Saga snarls and hangs up.

She jogs toward the elevators when Göran Stone steps in front of her and blocks her with outspread arms.

"So you want to get Pontus Salman to talk to you—right?" he teases.

"Right," she says, and tries to push past, but he doesn't let her go.

"Just shake your ass a little," he says. "Or toss your hair so that you're—"

"Move!" Saga commands. She's so angry, her forehead begins to flush.

"Okay, sorry, I just wanted to help." Göran Stone laughs nastily. "But for your information, we've just sent four cars to Salman's house on Lidingö."

"What's happened?" Saga asks quickly.

"The neighbors called the police." Göran smiles. "They'd heard a little bang-bang and some screaming."

Saga pushes Stone roughly away and begins to run.

"Thank you so much, Göran!" Göran calls after her. "You're the best, Göran!"

As Saga drives to Lidingö, she tries to keep her mind blank. But she can't forget the sounds on the recording of the broken man who, weeping, described what had been done to his daughter.

Saga tells herself that she's going to exercise hard tonight and then go to bed early.

People have come out of their houses and filled the street around Roskullsvägen, so she has to park one hundred meters away from Salman's house. Curious onlookers and reporters crowd outside the blue-and-white police tape trying to get a look inside the house. Saga excuses herself in a tight voice as she pushes her way through. The blue lights of the emergency vehicles flash across the green trees. Saga sees her colleague Magdalena Ronander leaning against the dark brown brick wall and vomiting. Pontus Salman's white BMW is parked in front of his garage. Its roof window is missing. Small, bloody glass cubes are scattered over the ground and sparkle on the chassis. Through the blood-smeared side window, a man's body can be seen slumped sideways.

She recognizes it as Pontus Salman's.

Magdalena lifts a pale face to look at Saga tiredly. She wipes her mouth with a tissue. Then she blocks Saga from going to the door.

"No, no," she says hoarsely. "You don't want to go in there. Absolutely not."

Saga stops and glances toward the large house. She turns to Magdalena to ask something but stops again. She understands, then, that the first thing she must do is call Joona right away to tell him they no longer have a witness.

the girl who picks dandelions

Joona is jogging through the arrival hall of Helsinki-Vantaa Airport, located just outside of Helsinki, when his phone rings.

"Saga, what's up?"

"Pontus Salman is dead. He was found in his car outside his house. It appears he shot himself."

Joona exits the airport building and hails a taxi. He directs the driver to the harbor as he sprawls in the backseat.

"What did you say?" Saga asks.

"Nothing," Joona says.

"We have no witness now," Saga says anxiously. "What the hell do we do next?"

"I don't know yet," Joona says. He shuts his eyes for a moment.

He feels the rocking motion of the car surround him, gentle and soothing. The taxi leaves the airport behind and speeds up to merge with traffic on the highway.

"You cannot go out to Raphael's boat without backup," Saga states firmly.

"The girl," Joona says abruptly.

"What?"

"There's a girl. Axel Riessen was teaching her the violin," Joona says, and he opens his gray eyes. "Maybe she's seen something."

"Why do you think that?"

"There was a dandelion ball in the whiskey glass."

"What the hell are you talking about?"

"Try to find her," Joona says, and snaps off the phone.

He leans back against the seat and pictures how Axel was standing and holding a violin as the girl came with a bouquet of dandelion puffs. Then he thinks of the dandelion ball with its wilted stem drooping over the edge of the whiskey glass in Axel's bedroom. She'd been in such an intimate part of the house . . . maybe she'd seen something.

Joona goes on board the gray Finnish Coast Guard vessel *Kirku*, which the Finnish navy had acquired from the Swedish Coast Guard six years before. As he shakes hands with the vessel's captain, Pasi Rannikko, he is reminded of Lennart Johansson at Dalarö, the one who loved to surf and called himself Lance.

Like Lance, Pasi Rannikko is a young, tanned man with clear blue eyes. Unlike Lance, however, Pasi takes his duties extremely seriously. It's obvious that this unexpected run beyond Finnish waters is troubling him.

"Nothing about this makes me happy," Pasi Rannikko says with a frown. "But my boss is friends with your boss . . . and it appears that's all that was needed."

"I hope to have something from the prosecutor before we get there," Joona says soothingly as he feels the vibration of the ship pulling away from the dock and smoothly heading out across the water.

"The second you get your arrest warrant, I'll contact FNS *Hanko*. It's a patrol boat with twenty officers and six soldiers." He points at a blip on the radar. "She can reach thirty-five knots and it won't take her more than twenty minutes to get to us."

"That's good."

"Raphael Guidi's yacht has passed Dagö and is now just outside Estonia's territorial waters. I hope you are aware that we can't board a vessel in Estonian waters unless it's an emergency or open criminal activity is observed."

"I realize that," Joona says.

The boat leaves the harbor with thudding engines.

"Here comes the entire crew," Pasi Rannikko says with an ironic grin.

A broadly built man with a blond beard is climbing up to the captain's bridge. He introduces himself as the first—and only—mate. "Niko Kapanen, like the hockey player." He eyes Joona speculatively while scratching at his beard. Then he asks slowly, "So what's this guy Guidi done?"

"Kidnapping, murder, murder of policemen, weapon smuggling," Joona says.

"And Sweden sends a single policeman?"

"Right." Joona smiles.

"While we contribute this old baby carriage of a boat."

"As soon as we have the arrest warrant, we'll almost be a platoon," Pasi Rannikko says in a monotone. "Urho Saarinen on the *Hanko* can get here in twenty minutes if I just say the word."

"An inspection," Niko says abruptly. "I'm sure as hell that we can demand a surprise inspection—"

"Not in Estonian waters," Pasi Rannikko protests.

"What the fuck . . ." mutters Niko.

"It will all work out," Joona says mildly.

turning over the picture

Axel Riessen lies fully dressed on a bed in the five-room suite he has been given on Raphael Guidi's mega yacht. Next to him is a folder with complete information about a liver donor, a man in a coma after an unsuccessful operation. All the data is perfect—the tissue type matches Axel's completely.

Axel concentrates so intently on the ceiling that he is startled by a knock on the door. It's the man in the white uniform.

"Dinner."

They walk together through a spa area. Axel glimpses low-lying green beds filled with empty bottles and cans. Plastic-wrapped towels are still stacked on white marble shelves, and behind glass doors frosted for privacy, he can make out a gym. A double door of matte-surfaced metal slides open as they walk past the relaxation room with its beige wall-to-wall carpeting, sofas, and chairs as well as a short but massive table of polished limestone. The lighting is odd—points of light and shadow slide across the walls and floor. Axel raises his eyes to realize they are beneath the yacht's enormous swimming pool. The bottom of the pool is made of glass, and overhead Axel can see the bulk of garbage and broken furniture outlined by a pale sky.

Raphael Guidi is sitting on one of the sofas. He's wearing the same gym shorts as before, but now with a white T-shirt stretched over his belly. He pats the seat beside him and Axel obediently goes over and sits down. Both bodyguards remain behind Guidi like two shadows. No one says anything. Raphael Guidi's telephone rings. He answers and speaks on and on in a long conversation.

In a short while, the man in white silently pushes a serving cart in. Without a sound he sets two place settings on the limestone table with plates, silverware, and glasses along with large platters of grilled hamburgers, bread, french fries, a bottle of ketchup, and a huge plastic bottle of Pepsi.

Raphael continues his conversation without even glancing at the food. His voice is a dull monotone as he discusses what sounds like details about production speed and logistics.

No one says a word. They all wait patiently.

Fifteen minutes later, Raphael Guidi finishes his call and looks at Axel Riessen calmly. He then starts to speak in a soft tone.

"Maybe you'd like a glass of wine now," he says. "Since in a few days you'll have a new liver."

"I've reread this material about the donor many times," Axel says. "It's in wonderful order. I'm impressed. Everything seems to be perfect."

"There's an interesting thing about desire," Raphael begins as if he hadn't heard Axel's words. "A desire you want more than anything else in the world; myself, I wish that my wife was alive today and we could be together again."

"I understand . . ." Axel murmurs.

"But I have a quirk. I like to see desire balanced by its opposite," Raphael says.

He takes a hamburger and a scoop of french fries. Then he passes the platter to Axel.

"Thank you," Axel says automatically.

"The desire is on one side of the scale," Raphael continues. "The nightmare is on the other."

"The nightmare?"

"I mean to say . . . we live our lives with many outer trappings while inside . . . we have deep unfulfilled longings that we desire, and also nightmares that never come true."

"Perhaps we do," Axel says.

"You wish desperately to be able to sleep again, something very good, but what . . . I'm talking about the other side of the scale here . . . what is your worst nightmare?"

"I really don't know," Axel says with a smile, raising his brows.

"What are you afraid of?" Raphael shakes salt over his french fries.

"Illness, death . . . mostly pain."

"Of course, everyone fears pain, I agree with you there," Raphael says. "But as far as I am concerned, my worst nightmare, as I've begun to realize, concerns my son. He'll soon be grown up, and I'm afraid he'll turn away from me and pursue his own life."

"So, loneliness?"

"Yes, I believe so," Raphael says. "Complete loneliness is my worst nightmare."

Axel shrugs."Well, I'm already alone; the worst thing has already happened to me."

"Don't say that!" Raphael jokes.

"No, what I'm afraid of . . . oh, well, let's not talk about it."

"What?" Raphael coaxes.

"Forget it, I really don't want to talk—"

"You fear you were the reason a young girl committed suicide so long ago," Raphael says, and lays something on the table.

"Yes—"

"And who might think of suicide today?" asks Raphael quietly.

"Beverly," whispers Axel, and sees that the item Raphael has set on the table in front of him is a photograph.

It's facedown.

Axel doesn't really want to touch it, but he does and turns it over. He pulls his hand sharply back. Beverly's wondering face is clearly visible in the light of a camera flash. He stares down at the photograph, almost too afraid to understand its meaning. It is a warning. The photograph was taken a few days ago, inside his house, in the kitchen, the day Beverly tried to play the violin and then went away to find a vase for her dandelion bouquet.

103

After two hours on the Finnish navy's gray boat, Joona finally sees Raphael Guidi's luxury yacht smoothly gliding along on the horizon. In the sunlight, she appears to glimmer like a ship made of crystal.

Captain Pasi Rannikko comes over to stand next to Joona. He nods toward the huge yacht.

"How close do we need to get?" he asks intently.

Joona gives him an ice-gray look.

"As close as we can. We need to see what's going on," he says calmly. "I need—"

A huge throb of pain knifes through his temples. He falls silent and grabs on to the railing and tries to breathe slowly.

"What's the matter?" Pasi Rannikko asks with a bit of laughter in his voice. "Are you getting seasick?"

"No."

The pain shoots through his head again and he grips the rail tightly. His medicine is out of the question even if it would help. He cannot lose his focus. He cannot accept the exhaustion it would bring.

The wind of their passage cools the drops of sweat that appear on Joona's forehead. He thinks about Disa's gaze and her serious, open face. The sun strikes across the rolling surface of the sea, and in his mind he can see the bridal crown. It shines in its display case in the Nordic Museum. The braided tips gleam. He thinks of the scent of wildflowers and a church that has been decorated in leaves for a summer wedding. His heart is pounding so strongly in his ears that he doesn't hear the captain speaking to him.

"What did you say?"

Joona looks in confusion at Pasi Rannikko beside him and then out toward the huge white yacht.

the nightmare

Axel feels nauseous. His eyes are drawn back to the photograph of Beverly.

Raphael dips his greasy fries into a pool of ketchup on his plate.

Axel looks up to see a young man standing in the doorway, watching them. He looks very tired and worried. He's holding a cell phone.

"Peter!" Raphael calls jovially. "Come on in!"

"Please, no," Peter answers in a gentle voice.

"That wasn't a request." Raphael smiles, but anger quirks his mouth.

The boy walks over and shyly says hello to Axel.

"This is my son." Raphael introduces them as if they were at a normal dinner party.

"Hello," Axel says in his usual friendly way.

One of the men from the helicopter is now standing next to the bar. He's throwing peanut shells toward a happy, ragged dog. His gray hair looks like metal and his glasses flash white.

"Nuts make him sick," Peter remonstrates weakly.

"When our dinner is through, could you bring out your violin?" asks Raphael in a suddenly tired voice. "Our guest is interested in music."

Peter nods. He is very pale. There is a sheen of sweat on his face and the rings around his eyes are almost violet.

Axel makes an attempt to smile.

"What kind of violin do you have?"

Peter shrugs. "It's much too good for me. It's an Amati that belonged to my mother. She was a musician."

"An Amati?"

"Which one do you think is best?" Raphael breaks in. "Amati or Stradivarius?"

"It depends on who's playing it," Axel replies.

"You're Swedish," Raphael says. "There are four violins made by Stradivarius that now reside in Sweden. None of them were played by Paganini, however, and I imagine—"

"I believe you," Axel says.

"I collect stringed instruments that can still remember how— No." He interrupts himself. "Let me reformulate that . . . If these instruments are handled properly, you are able to hear the longing and sadness of a lost soul."

"I see," Axel says noncommittally.

"I make sure people can hear that sorrow when we sign a contract." Raphael smiles without joy. "We gather together, we listen to music, we hear that unique, sorrowful voice, and then we sign the contract. Just in the air. Our desires and our nightmares become part of the contract . . . I call it a Paganini contract."

"I understand."

"Do you?" Raphael smiles. "It is a contract even beyond death. You can never be released from it. Even a man who turns to suicide must understand his worst nightmare will still come true. I own it, but he reaps his nightmare."

"What do you want me to say?" Axel asks.

"I'm just saying . . . consider this contract to be unbreakable. And I . . . how should I put it?" he asks, hesitating. "It would not help my business if you mistook me for a kind man."

Raphael goes over to the huge television mounted on the wall. He takes a shining DVD from a pocket in his shorts, removes the cover, slides it into the player. Peter perches on the edge of the sofa. He looks around from under his brows at the other men in the room. He has very pale coloring and is fine-limbed, with a sensitive face that seems to show every emotion. His build does not resemble the broad, compact body of his father at all.

The picture flickers on the screen and then gray streaks fill it. Axel feels a gut-wrenching fear as he watches three people walking out of the door of a brick family home. He recognizes two of them immediately: Detective Inspector Joona Linna and Saga Bauer. The third person is a woman with Latin American features.

Axel watches Joona Linna take out a cell phone and make a call. He doesn't seem to get an answer. The three people have closed, stern expressions as they get into a car and drive away.

The camera moves shakily toward the door. It's pushed open, light disappears, and then the automatic viewfinder adjusts to the darkness. Two large suitcases stand in the hallway. The camera moves along to the kitchen, then to the left and down some stairs, through a tiled hallway, and finally into a room with a swimming pool. One woman in a bathing suit is lounging in a poolside chair and another, her hair in a stylish pageboy, stands and talks into a phone.

The camera pulls stealthily back and waits for the phone call to end, hidden until she finishes. Then it moves forward again. Footsteps are heard, and the woman with the phone turns her tired, unhappy face toward the camera and stiffens. An expression of naked fear crosses her face.

"I don't really want to see any more of this, Pappa," the son says in his gentle voice.

"Now, now, it's just getting started!" Raphael replies, and the boy doesn't move.

The TV goes dark for a minute because the camera has been turned off. The picture returns a moment later, jiggles, and stabilizes as if the camera is now steady on a tripod. Both of the women are found sitting on the floor with their backs against the tiled wall. Pontus Salman faces them, sitting on a chair, but his body writhes and he breathes rapidly.

The time on the camera shows that the recording was made less than an hour ago. A man dressed in black with his face covered by a ski mask walks over to Veronique and forces her face toward the camera.

"Forgive me! Forgive me! Forgive me!" mocks Raphael in a squeaky voice from his seat on the sofa.

Axel looks at Raphael in amazement, just as Veronique Salman's voice pipes up: "Forgive me! Forgive me! Forgive me!"

Her voice is shot through with terror.

"I had no idea!" mocks Raphael, and points at the television.

"I had no idea!" pleads Veronique. "I took the picture but I didn't mean to harm anyone! I didn't know how stupid I was being, I just thought that—"

"You have to choose," the man in the ski mask says. "Who should I shoot in the knee? Your wife or your sister?"

"Please, don't do this," Pontus whispers.

"Who should I shoot?" the man repeats.

"My wife," whispers Pontus. His voice is practically inaudible.

"Pontus, please!" His wife is pleading. "Please, don't let him—"

Pontus begins to sob shrilly and piercingly.

"It's going to hurt when I shoot her," the man warns.

"Don't let him shoot me!" screams Veronique, panicked.

"Do you want to change your mind? Should I shoot your sister instead?"

"No," Pontus mumbles.

"Beg me to."

"What did you say?" Pontus's expression is that of a broken man.

"Beg me nicely to shoot her."

There's a moment of silence and then Axel Riessen hears Pontus say, "Please be so kind as to . . . shoot my wife in the knee."

"I'll do both her knees, since you've been so polite," the man says, and places the barrel of his pistol against Veronique's knee.

"Please don't let him do this!" she screams. "Please, Pontus!"

The man shoots. A short bang is heard. Veronique's leg jumps. Blood spatters over the tiles. Veronique screams so loudly her voice breaks. He shoots again. The recoil makes the gun jerk. The second knee is hit and bends at an impossible angle.

Veronique screams again, hoarse and distant. Her body spasms in pain and blood begins to pour over the tile floor beneath her.

Pontus Salman has started to vomit and the man in the ski mask watches him in a wondering, dreamy gaze.

Veronique pulls herself to one side, panting, and she's trying to reach her injured legs with her hands. The woman next to her appears to be in shock. Her face has turned green and her eyes are nothing but big black holes.

"Your sister is mentally ill, right?" the man asks curiously. "Do you think she even realizes what's going on?"

He pats Pontus on the head comfortingly. Then he says, "Do you want me to rape your sister or shoot your wife again?"

Pontus doesn't answer. His eyes are rolling backward. The man slaps him across the face.

"Answer me! You want me to shoot your wife again or rape your sister?"

Pontus Salman's sister shakes her head.

"Rape her!" whispers Veronique between heavy breaths. "Please, please, Pontus. Tell him to rape her instead."

"Rape her," Pontus whispers.

"I didn't hear you!"

"Rape my sister!"

"All right. Soon enough," the man says.

Axel looks down at the floor between his feet. He's trying to close his ears to the wailing and the prayers and the raw, horrific screams. He tries to fill his mind with the music of Bach, tries to reach for spaces within his music, spaces filled with light and heavenly rays.

Finally there is no more sound. Axel looks up at the television. The women are both lying dead against the wall. He sees the man in the ski mask stand, panting, with a bloody knife in one hand and a gun in the other.

"You've reaped your nightmare—you may kill yourself now," the man says, and throws the pistol down at Pontus's feet as he walks out of the frame and around the camera.

105

Saga Bauer leaves Magdalena Ronander and steps back over the police tape. More curious onlookers have turned up as well as a van from Swedish Television. A uniformed officer is trying to part the crowd to allow an ambulance through.

Saga leaves all this behind her and walks up a stone pathway to someone's garden and past a jasmine tree. She keeps walking faster and faster, then starts to run back to her car.

"The girl," Joona had said on the phone. "You have to find the girl. There's a girl who lives with Axel Riessen. He called her Beverly Andersson. Ask Robert, his brother. The girl's about fifteen and you should be able to trace her."

"How much longer do I have to get an arrest warrant?"

"Not long," Joona had answered. "But you should make it in time."

As Saga drives back toward Stockholm, she calls Robert Riessen, but there's no answer. She calls the exchange at CID and asks for Anja, Joona's assistant, the plump woman who had once won an Olympic medal in swimming and who delights in bright, shiny lipstick and nails painted in violent colors.

"Anja Larsson." Saga hears the response after only one ring.

"Hi, I'm Saga Bauer at Säpo. We met recently at—"

"Yes, we did," Anja says coolly.

"I need information about a young woman named Beverly Andersson who—"

"Can I bill Säpo for it?" Anja's voice is frigid.

Saga snaps. "Do whatever the hell you want, as long as you get a damned number before—"

"I don't care for your language, young lady."

"Forget I asked."

Saga swears and then honks at a car that hasn't moved even though the light has turned green. She's about to click her phone closed when Anja asks, "How old is she?"

"About fifteen."

"There is no Beverly Andersson in that age group listed with any telephone registry. But the government does have her registered at the same address as her father, Evert Andersson."

"Okay, I'll call him, then. Can you text me the number?"

"I've already done it."

"Thanks, Anja, thanks so much—please forgive me for being a bitch. I'm in such a hurry. I'm worried about Joona. I believe he might do something stupid without backup."

"Have you talked to him?"

"Yes. He asked me to find the girl. I've never even met her, I don't know . . . he trusts me to figure all this out, but I—"

"You call Beverly's father and I'll keep looking," Anja says, and hangs up.

Saga swings onto the shoulder by Hjorthagen and parks to look at the number Anja sent her. The area code is for the province of Skåne. *Maybe the town of Svalöv*, she thinks as she presses the Call button.

106

Evert Andersson sits in his pine-paneled kitchen in the middle of the province of Skåne and jumps when he hears the telephone ring. He's just come in from disentangling a heifer from his neighbor's barbed-wire fence. It took more than an hour. Blood is on his hands, and he wipes them on his blue work clothes. When the phone rings, he doesn't care to answer it. Not just because of the state of his hands but because he feels that there's no one he'd really care to speak to. He leans forward, checks the ID display, and sees it's a blocked number. Probably a salesman who'll be hiding behind that. He lets the phone ring until it stops. Then it starts again. Evert Andersson takes another look at the display and finally picks up the phone: "Andersson."

"Hello, I'm Saga Bauer." Evert hears an abrupt female voice. "I'm a police officer with Säpo. I'm looking for your daughter, Beverly Andersson."

"What's happened?"

"Nothing. She has done nothing wrong, but she has some very important information we need."

"And now she's just taken off?" he asks weakly.

"Do you have her phone number?" Saga asks. Evert's slow thoughts revert to the time he'd once hoped his daughter would take over the farm after him. She would carry on tradition, she'd live in his house, she'd work in his barn, his buildings, his fields. She'd walk through the gardens that her mother had planted, wearing rubber boots like his in the mud, growing thick around the middle as her mother had done, wearing a long coat with her hair in a braid down her back.

But even as a small child, Beverly had something odd about her, which he sensed and feared.

As she'd grown, she became more and more different, as if she'd sprung, an alien, from him and from her mother. Once she'd walked into the barn when she was eight or nine years old. She sat in an empty pen using an upturned bucket as a stool and then just sang to herself with her eyes closed. She'd lost herself in the sound of her own voice. He'd thought it his duty to yell at her to shut up and stop making a fool of herself, but there was this whole air about her that bewildered him. He marked that incident as the moment he knew he would never understand her. So he could no longer talk to her. Whenever he wanted to say something, the words died away.

When her mother died, the silence on the farm was complete.

Beverly began to ramble around the countryside and would be gone for hours or even an entire day. The police had to bring her home after she'd wandered so far she didn't know where she was. She'd go with anyone if they spoke kindly to her.

"I don't have anything to say to her, so why would I have her phone number?" he replies in his strict, stubborn Skåne dialect.

"Are you absolutely sure—"

"You city folk from Stockholm don't understand this stuff." He cuts her off vehemently and hangs up.

He looks at his fingers on the receiver: the blood smearing his knuckles, the dirt under his fingernails, embedded in his cuticles, in every crack and surface. He walks over to his green armchair and slowly sits down. He picks up the shiny TV supplement to the newspaper and begins to read. This evening there's going to be a show about the program host Ossian Wallenberg, who died recently. Evert drops the newspaper and is surprised to find tears in his eyes. He remembers that Beverly used to sit beside him and they'd both laugh at the silly nonsense on *Golden Friday*.

the empty room

Saga Bauer swears aloud, shuts her eyes, and pounds the steering wheel a few times. She tells herself that she has to pull herself together and get going before it's too late, when the phone rings.

"Hi, it's me again," Anja says. "I'm putting you through to Herbert Saxéus at Saint Maria Hjärta Hospital."

"Okay. Why?"

"Saxéus had Beverly Andersson as a patient for two years there."

"Thanks, that was—"

Anja has already put Saga through to the other line.

Saga waits as the signals go through. She remembers Saint Maria Hjärta, located east of Stockholm in Torsby.

"Herbert speaking," a warm voice says in her ear.

"Hi, my name is Saga Bauer and I'm a police officer, an investigator, from Säpo. I need to reach a girl named Beverly Andersson who was one of your patients, I understand."

There's a pause on the line.

"Is she all right?" asks the doctor.

"That's what I need to know. I have to speak to her," Saga says quickly. "And it's urgent."

"She lives in the house of Axel Riessen, who . . . well, he has informal guardianship."

"So is she still there?" Saga asks, while turning the key in the ignition. She starts to pull onto the highway.

"Axel Riessen is giving her a room until she finds something of her own," he replies. "She's only fifteen, but it would be a mistake to force her to live at home."

The traffic is steady and Saga drives as fast as she can.

"May I ask what Beverly was treated for?" she asks.

"I don't know if that's helpful, but as a doctor I would say that she has a serious personality disorder, which we call Cluster B."

"What does that mean?"

"Not much," Herbert Saxéus says. "But if you ask me as a fellow human being, I'd say that physically Beverly is completely healthy, healthier than most . . . It's a cliché, I know, but she's not the one who's sick."

"No, she lives in a sick world."

"That's right." He sighs.

Saga thanks him for his time, ends the call, and turns onto Valhallavägen. The seat against her back is sticky from sweat. Her phone rings and she hits the gas to get through the yellow light by the Olympic Stadium before she picks up the call.

"I thought I would try to talk to Beverly's father as well," Anja says. "He is a pleasant man, but he's had a rough day with an injured cow. He had to comfort it, he says. His family has always lived on the same farm. Now he's the only one left. We chatted about *The Wonderful Adventures of Nils* and then he found some letters that Beverly had written to him. He hadn't even opened them. Can you believe that man? So stubborn! Beverly's telephone number was in every single letter."

Saga Bauer thanks Anja profusely and calls Beverly's number. She's already pulling to a stop in front of the Riessen house while the signal goes to Beverly Andersson's cell phone.

One beep after another disappears into the darkness of space. The sun shines through a little dust in the air in front of the church. Saga feels her body tense with determination. There's little time left. Joona will be on his own when he goes against Raphael Guidi.

With the phone still to her ear, she walks up to Robert Riessen's door and rings the bell. Suddenly someone picks up on the other end of the phone line. Saga can hear a slight rustling.

"Beverly?" Saga asks. "Is that you?"

Saga can hear breathing.

"Answer me, Beverly," Saga says in the gentlest voice she can muster. "Where are you?"

"I—"

"What did you say, Beverly? What did you say? I can't hear you."

"I can't come out yet," the girl whispers, and hangs up.

Robert Riessen is silent and pale. He leaves Saga in Beverly Andersson's room and asks her to lock up when she's done. The room doesn't look lived-in. There are just some white clothes in the wardrobe and a pair of rubber boots, a field jacket, and a cell-phone charger.

Saga locks Beverly's room as she leaves and goes into Axel Riessen's rooms. She tries to understand what Joona meant and how this girl could be important. She walks through the drawing rooms, salons, and the peaceful library. The door to Axel Riessen's bedroom is slightly ajar. Saga steps over the thick Chinese carpet, past the bed, and into the adjoining bathroom. She returns to the bedroom. Something is making her edgy. There's a nervous energy in the room. Saga puts one hand over her Glock in her shoulder holster. There's a whiskey glass on the table with the drooping remains of a dandelion.

The dust floats slowly in the sunlight in a room almost vibrating with silence. Her heart jumps when a branch from a tree outside scrapes against the window.

She walks over to the unmade bed and considers the two pillows and the disarray of the bedding.

Saga thinks that she might be hearing steps in the library and turns to leave when a hand grabs her ankle. Someone is under the bed. She twists loose, falls backward, and draws her gun in one motion while, inadvertently, she knocks over the table with the dandelion.

Saga rolls to her knees and aims, but then lowers her gun again.

The girl peers out of the darkness under the bed. Her eyes are wide open and frightened. Saga replaces her gun in the holster and sighs deeply.

"You're shining," Beverly says.

"Are you Beverly?" Saga whispers.

"May I come out now?"

"Yes, I promise, you may come out," Saga says.

"Has it been an hour? Axel told me to wait a whole hour."

"It's been more than an hour, Beverly."

Saga helps her stand up. The girl wears only underwear and is a bit stiff after lying in the same cramped position for so long. Her hair is very short, and her arms are covered with ink drawings and letters.

"What are you doing under Axel Riessen's bed?" Saga asks, keeping her voice calm.

"He's my best friend," Beverly answers as she pulls on a pair of jeans.

"I believe that he's in danger—please tell me what you know."

Beverly pauses, holding on to her T-shirt. Her face flushes red and tears fill her eyes.

"I haven't done—"

Beverly's lower lip starts to tremble.

"Take it easy," Saga says, trying to keep the tension from her voice. "Start from the beginning."

"I was in bed when Axel came in," Beverly says in a weak voice. "I knew something bad was happening. He looked white. I thought he was mad because I'd gotten a lift. I'm not supposed to hitchhike."

She pauses and turns her head away.

"Please go on, Beverly, we're almost out of time."

Beverly whispers, "Sorry." She wipes her face with her T-shirt. Her eyes are damp and the end of her nose is red.

"Axel ran into the room," Beverly says when she's collected herself. "He told me to get under the bed and hide for an entire hour and then he ran out again to the library and I don't know . . . I just saw their legs, but two guys came after him. They did something awful to him. He yelled and they threw him on the floor and wrapped him in white plastic and then they carried him outside. Everything happened so fast. I didn't see their faces . . . I'm not sure they're even human beings."

"Just a second," Saga says. She pulls out her phone. "You have to come with me and tell your story to a man named Jens Svanehjälm."

Saga calls Carlos. Her hands shake.

"We have a witness! She saw Axel Riessen being kidnapped! We have a witness!" she repeats. "She saw Axel Riessen overpowered and taken away, and that should be enough."

Saga and Beverly look at each other while Saga listens to Carlos's reaction.

"Good," she says. "We'll be right in. You go get Svanehjälm. Make sure he prepares a statement for Europol."

108

Raphael Guidi is walking through the dining room carrying a black leather folder, which he sets down on the table and pushes toward Axel Riessen.

"Pontus Salman's nightmare, as you perhaps already understand, was to be forced to harm his wife or his sister," Guidi explains. "I don't know. I've never felt the need to be so explicit before, but . . . how can I put this? Lately there have been people who thought they could escape their nightmares through suicide. Please don't misunderstand me. Usually our plans go very well. We can all be civilized. I can be an extremely generous man to those who are loyal to me."

"You're threatening to hurt Beverly."

"You can always choose someone else . . . perhaps choose between her and your younger brother, if you'd rather?" Raphael says nonchalantly as he sips his vitamin drink. He wipes his mouth and then turns to Peter and asks him to fetch his violin.

"Have I told you that I acquire only instruments played by Paganini?" he asks. "They are the only ones I care about. People say that Paganini hated the appearance of his face . . . I personally believe he sold his soul to the Devil so that others would worship him. He called himself an ape, but when he played, the women came crawling to him. It was worth the price. He would play and play so unbelievably that people said they could smell hellfire around him."

Axel looks out the wide windows at water that now seems to barely move. He knows that if he turned and looked toward the foredeck he would see the helicopter that had brought him here. Axel's thoughts avoid the appalling film he's just seen and instead search for a way out of all of this.

He feels drained. He sits still and listens to Raphael, who goes on and on about violins, Stradivarius's fixation on the clearest sound, the hardness of the wood, the slowly growing maple and spruce trees he chooses for his workshop.

Raphael stops and smiles his lifeless smile while he says, "As long as you are loyal to me, you will enjoy everything possible on one side of the scale. You will receive a healthy organ and you'll sleep better than you ever have before. In return, I demand that you will never betray the contract we are about to sign."

"And you just want the export form signed."

"I shall have that no matter what. I don't want to use force, or even kill you. That would be such a waste." Guidi waves that away. "What I demand is—"

"My loyalty," Axel states.

"Is that too much to ask?" Raphael asks. "Think it over for just a minute. Count all the people that you can rely on absolutely. The ones who you know would be entirely loyal to you."

A long pause comes between them. Axel stares straight ahead.

With a sorrowful look, Raphael says, "Exactly."

the contract

Axel opens the leather folder on the table. All the export documents are there. All the paperwork necessary to clear M/S *Icelus* from Gothenburg Harbor with its huge cargo of ammunition.

All that is missing is his signature.

Raphael Guidi's son comes back into the room. His face is pale and withdrawn. He's carrying a beautiful violin: a reddish brown instrument with a gently curved body. Axel recognizes an Amati immediately, and one in superb shape after so many years.

"I have already told you I demand certain music to accompany the deal we are about to make," Raphael says softly. "This violin belonged to the boy's mother . . . and much earlier, Niccolò Paganini played it."

"It was fashioned in 1657," Peter says. Absentmindedly he empties his pockets of his keys and cell phone as if to prepare for a great event. He discards them on the table before he puts the instrument to his shoulder.

The boy lays the bow gently on the strings, and soon he begins to play as if he is falling into a dream. Axel immediately recognizes the introduction to Paganini's most famous piece: Caprice no. 24. It is considered the most difficult violin piece ever written. The boy plays like he's swimming underwater; it moves much too slowly.

"Our contract would be very advantageous," Raphael says.

It's still light outside. The wide windows allow great light into the salon.

Axel thinks about Beverly and how she came to him and crept into his bed when he was in the psychiatric ward. She'd whispered, *I saw there was light in this room. You're giving off light.*

"Are you finished thinking it over?" Raphael demands.

Axel can't bear to look at him. He looks down instead and picks up the pen from the table in front of him. He listens to his heart race. He tries to disguise his quickened breathing.

This time he can't draw a cartoon figure saying "Hi!" He will be forced to sign his name and then pray to God that Raphael Guidi will be content and let him return to Sweden.

Axel feels the pen shake. He steadies one hand with the other, takes a deep breath, and puts the tip of the pen to the empty line on the contract.

"Wait one moment," Raphael Guidi says abruptly. "Before you sign, I need to know that I own you . . . that I own your loyalty."

Axel looks into Guidi's eyes.

"If you are truly prepared to possibly reap your nightmare if our contract is broken, you must show your faith. You must demonstrate it by kissing my hand."

"What?"

"We enter into a contract, do we not?"

"We do," Axel replies.

"Then it will be sealed by a kiss on my hand," Raphael says in a voice so twisted he could be the idiot in an ancient play.

Raphael's son plays more and more slowly as he tries to force his fingers to obey. He awkwardly shifts position but stumbles during the rapid runs. He mangles the passage again and then he gives up.

"Continue," Raphael demands without a glance his way.

"It's too difficult. It doesn't sound good."

"Peter, it's wrong to give up before you've really tried—"

"Then play it yourself," his son says with a pout.

Raphael's face stiffens so that his features are as hard as a rock formation.

"Do as I say," he says with chilling calm.

The boy doesn't move, just looks at the ground. Raphael's right hand goes toward the chain on his gym shorts.

"Peter, I thought it sounded fine enough to continue," Raphael says menacingly.

"The bridge is crooked," Axel breaks in with a voice barely above a whisper.

Peter looks at the violin and blushes.

"Can you adjust it?" he asks.

"Of course. It's easy enough, and I can do it for you if you want me to," Axel says.

"Will it take a long time?" asks Raphael.

"No," Axel says.

Axel puts down the pen and takes the violin from the boy. He turns it over and feels how light it is. He's never held an Amati before, let alone one the master Paganini had played.

Raphael's phone rings. He looks at it and then stands straight up while he listens.

"That can't be true!" he's exclaiming with a savage expression.

A twisted smile plays across his lips. He barks something to his bodyguards, and together they turn to head up the stairs.

Peter watches Axel loosen the strings. The violin creaks. The dry sound of Axel's fingers brushing against the instrument vibrates through the sensitive sound box. Axel carefully adjusts the bridge a fraction and then tightens the strings again.

"Did that work?" asks Peter.

"Of course," Axel says as he tunes the strings. "Try it now and see."

"Thanks," Peter says.

Axel is sharply aware of Peter's cell phone on the table behind him as he says, "Start again. You've just finished the first run, and next comes the pizzicato movement."

"I feel embarrassed," Peter says, and turns away.

Axel leans back on the table, reaching behind him, finding the phone and trying to pick it up. It slides around a little on the smooth surface.

Peter has his back to Axel. He's lifting the violin to his shoulder and setting the bow to the strings.

Axel manages to get the phone in his fingers and keeps it hidden in his hand as he moves slightly to one side.

Peter draws the bow in only one note. Then he stops. He turns around and looks past Axel.

"Hey, wasn't my phone there?"

Axel lets the phone slide out of his hand before he turns and picks it up.

"Do I have any messages?" Peter asks.

Axel glances at the telephone. There is full coverage, even though they're out at sea. He realizes that the ship must have satellite transmission.

"No messages," he says, and puts the phone back down.

"Thanks."

Axel remains next to the table as Peter begins again to play Caprice no. 24. It's much too slow, and more and more out of rhythm.

Peter has some talent and it's easy to tell he's practiced a great deal, but this piece is beyond him. Still, the sound of the Amati is so wonderful that Axel would have enjoyed listening even if a small child plucked the strings.

Peter plows through the music but he's finally so lost he stops. He tries again. Axel decides he will try for the phone again and saunters to one side. He doesn't have enough time as Peter hits a false note, stops playing, and turns back to Axel.

"This is very hard," he exclaims. But he's ready to try again.

He starts, but it's still all wrong.

"It's not working," he says as he lowers the violin.

"Keep your third finger on the A string. It's easier to reach—"

"Can't you just show me?"

Axel looks at the phone on the table. A reflection from the sun sparkles outside and Axel turns toward the panoramic window. The sea has become remarkably calm and smooth. He can hear thudding sounds from the engine room, a constant noise he's surprised to notice now.

Peter hands Axel the violin. Axel puts it to his shoulder, tightens the bow slightly, and then starts the piece from the very beginning. Its flowing, sorrowful introduction pours at high speed into the room. The Amati's voice is not strong, but it is wonderfully soft and clear. Paganini's music sings out, circling in higher and higher reaches as one melody chases another.

"Oh my God," Peter whispers.

The voice changes to sound in a hissing prestissimo. It's playfully beautiful and at the same time filled with difficult fingerings and quick jumps between octaves.

The music already lives in Axel's mind. All he has to do is let it out. Not every note is perfect, but his fingers instinctively know the way and dance quickly over the fingerboard and the strings.

Vaguely he hears Raphael yelling something from the captain's bridge and there's a thud overhead that shakes the crystal chandelier. Axel continues to play—the quivering notes are like sparks of sunlight over the sea.

Steps come thudding down the staircase. When Axel sees Raphael with sweat pouring down his face and a bloody military knife in his hand, he stops playing abruptly. The gray-haired bodyguard runs behind Raphael with his rifle up and ready. It's a Belgian Fabrique Nationale SCAR.

on board

Joona Linna is next to Pasi Rannikko and peering through a pair of binoculars. The first mate stands beside them. They all watch the enormous luxury yacht now dead in the water before them. It rocks slightly although the wind has died down. The flag of Italy droops. There's no movement on the ship, as if all aboard are suspended in Sleeping Beauty's hundred-year sleep. Whitecaps have disappeared from the surface of the Baltic Sea, and it is so calm the smooth water mirrors the light blue sky.

The cell phone rings in Joona's pocket. He hands the binoculars to Niko and answers.

"We have a witness!" Saga is screaming on the other end. "The girl saw everything! Axel Riessen has definitely been kidnapped. The prosecutor has already issued a warrant—you can go on board and search for him!"

"Good work!" Joona says.

Pasi Rannikko looks at Joona expectantly as he puts his phone away.

"We have the authority to arrest Raphael Guidi," Joona says. "He's accused of kidnapping."

"I'll radio FNS *Hanko*," Pasi Rannikko says, and rushes up to the communication radio on the bridge.

"They'll be here in twenty minutes," Niko says excitedly.

"Request for backup," Pasi Rannikko says into the microphone. "We have an arrest warrant to board Raphael Guidi's boat and take him in . . . Roger, that's correct . . . Yes, but hurry! Top speed!"

Joona has the binoculars again and sweeps his gaze along the white stairs from their platform on the deck, past belowdecks, and then back up to the afterdeck with its closed umbrellas. He tries to get a glimpse through a set of overwide windows but they are too black. He follows the railing and then back up the next set of stairs onto the large terrace.

Shimmering hot air filters through vents on the roof of the captain's bridge. Joona swings his binoculars back to the black windows and stops. He thought he saw movement behind the glass. Something white is hurrying along behind the panes. For a second it looks like a huge wing, bent feathers pressed against the glass.

The next moment, it appears to be cloth or white plastic.

Joona blinks to clear his vision and looks again to find himself staring into a face lifting its own binoculars.

The steel door to the captain's bridge slams open, and a blond man runs out and jumps down the stairs to race across the foredeck.

These are the first people Joona has seen on the yacht.

The second man is dressed in black. He hurries to the helicopter pad and unfastens the lines around the helicopter's base. He opens the door to the cockpit.

"They've listened in on our radio," Joona says.

"We'll change channels," Pasi Rannikko calls back.

"It doesn't matter anymore," Joona says. "They're not going to stay. They're going to try to get away on the helicopter."

He hands the binoculars to Niko.

"Fifteen minutes to backup," Pasi Rannikko says tensely.

"Too late," Joona states swiftly.

"Someone's already in the helicopter," Niko calls out.

"Raphael knows we have his arrest warrant and can come aboard," Joona says.

"So do we board the ship right away?" asks Niko.

"That's what we'll have to do," Joona says, giving him a quick glance.

Niko snaps a magazine into an automatic rifle that is as black as dirty oil. It's a short-barreled Heckler & Koch 416.

Pasi Rannikko takes his own gun from his holster and hands it to Joona.

"Thanks," Joona says as he quickly checks the ammunition and looks the gun over. It's an M9A1 semiautomatic. He recognizes it as similar to the M9 used in the Gulf War, but the magazine is slightly different and there's a fastener for a lamp and a laser scope.

Without speaking again, Pasi Rannikko aims his ship toward the aft bridge of the yacht, which is just above the waterline. As they near it, the yacht seems to rise higher and higher, almost like an apartment building. Pasi puts his engine into reverse to slow, whipping up the wake, and Niko throws fenders over the side. The hulls bang against each other and sparks fly.

Joona climbs aboard even as the boats veer away from each other. Water churns up between them. Niko jumps and Joona catches his hand; his automatic rifle bangs against the railing. They run together toward the stairs, force their way past the debris of scattered wicker chairs and old wine boxes, and race up.

Niko turns for a second to wave at Pasi Rannikko, who is roaring away from the yacht.

111

traitors

Raphael Guidi is on the bridge with his bodyguard, the one with gray hair and glasses. The navigator looks at them both with such fright as he nervously rubs his hand across his stomach over and over.

"What's going on?" demands Raphael.

"I ordered the helicopter to get ready," the navigator quavers. "I thought—"

"Where's that damned police boat?"

"There," he says pointing aft.

Close under the yacht's afterdeck, beyond the swimming pool and the winches for the lifeboats, the gray naval boat is bumping close and churning up a wake as it reverses its engines. "The radio call . . . what did they say exactly?" Raphael demands.

"They said they didn't have much time. They called for backup. They said they had an arrest warrant."

"How can they!" Raphael howls and looks around.

Down on the helicopter pad they can see the pilot already in the cockpit. The rotors have just begun to move. And they can hear Paganini's Caprice no. 24 being played in the dining room beneath them.

"Their backup is coming," the navigator says, and points to a spot on the radar.

"I see. How much time do we have?" Raphael asks.

"They're moving at about thirty-three knots, so . . . ten minutes?"

"No danger," says the bodyguard, glancing at the helicopter. "We can get you and Peter out of here. Only three minutes until—"

The blond bodyguard runs onto the bridge. He's shouting, and his face is white.

"Someone's on board! Someone's on the ship!" he yells.

"How many?" The gray-haired man is now totally alert.

"I only saw one. He has an automatic rifle. No special equipment."

"Go stop him."

"Give me a knife!" demands Raphael.

The guard pulls out a knife with a channeled gray blade. Raphael takes it and whirls on the navigator. His eyes tighten.

"Did you or did you not tell me they would wait for backup?" he screams. "You told me they would wait!"

"That's what they said—"

"Then what are they doing here? They have nothing on me!" Raphael says. "They have absolutely nothing!"

The navigator steps back as he shakes his head. Raphael barges closer.

"Why the hell are they here if they have nothing on me?" Raphael keeps screaming. "There's nothing—"

"I don't know, I don't know," the navigator screams. "I can only tell you what I heard—"

"What did *you* tell *them*?"

"Tell them? Me? I don't understand—"

"Don't mess with me! Just tell me what the fuck you told them!"

"I didn't say anything!"

"Coming from you, that's strange . . . most unusual, very strange indeed. Don't you think so?"

"I only listened in as I was told to, I didn't—"

"Why don't you confess!" Raphael roars as he leaps toward the navigator and pushes the knife deep into his belly.

There is little resistance as the knife slides through his shirt, his fat, and into his intestines. Blood is channeled past the knife and spatters on Raphael's hand and arm and even onto his gym clothes. A confused expression comes over the navigator's face as he tries to step backward to get away from the knife, but Raphael looks deep into his eyes.

The beautiful music still filters up from the dining room. Unbelievably rapid notes dance up and down the scale.

"It could be Axel Riessen," the gray-haired bodyguard says abruptly. "Maybe he was bugged . . . maybe he's in contact with the police . . ."

Raphael jerks the knife back out of the navigator's body and throws himself down the stairs.

The navigator stands still, holding his stomach as blood drops onto his black shoes. He tries to walk, but slides to the ground instead and lies there, staring mutely at the ceiling.

Raphael's bodyguard is running behind him, holding his rifle ready to fire as they both run down the carpeted stairs.

Axel stops playing when Raphael comes roaring in, pointing to him with the bloody knife.

"You traitor!" he roars. "You betrayed me!"

The bodyguard suddenly fires his rifle at the window, the bullets slamming through while the brass casings clatter down the stairs.

the blade of the knife

The gray-haired bodyguard continues down the stairs with his weapon steadily aimed at the windows. Smoke trickles from his rifle and the casings are still bouncing down the stairs.

Peter has curled into a ball and holds his hands over his ears.

Silently the bodyguard slips out a side door.

Axel is backing away between the tables, holding the violin and its bow, and retreating as Raphael points at him with the knife.

"How could you ruin everything?" he roars as he tries to catch up to Axel. "I'm going to cut up your face, I'm going to—"

"Pappa, what's going on?" screams Peter.

"Get my gun and get on the helicopter! We're leaving this boat!"

The boy nods. His face is pale, his chin wobbles. Raphael skirts around tables toward Axel. Axel moves backward and throws down chairs between them.

"Load it with Parabellum, hollow-point!" commands Raphael.

"How many?" the boy asks. "One magazine?"

"Yes, that's enough—but hurry!" Raphael yells as he kicks aside a chair.

Axel is trying to get through the door on the other side of the room. He turns the lock one-handed, but the door won't open.

"I'm not finished with you!" howls Raphael.

Axel shakes the door again with his free hand and then sees the bolt high up. Raphael is barging closer. The knife glistens in his hand. Axel reacts impulsively and whirls around to hurl the beautiful violin at Raphael. It tumbles in the air, red and glowing. Raphael jumps aside and trips but still lunges as he tries to save the instrument. He almost catches it, but fumbles although he's broken its fall. The violin skitters across the floor with a sibilant whisper.

Axel has gotten the door open and rushes out into a cluttered hallway. There's so much trash he can hardly get through. He clambers over a heap of lounge-chair pillows and over a pile of diving masks and wet suits.

"I'll get you!" Raphael is following him with the knife in one hand and the violin in the other.

Axel's foot gets caught in the mesh of a rolled-up tennis net. He crawls away, kicking at it as Raphael draws nearer.

Short, hard bursts of automatic fire can be heard outside.

Raphael pounces, driving the knife down at Axel, but he misses as Axel kicks himself loose. He scrambles to his feet and knocks over a foosball table to block Raphael, then rushes again down the hallway to the door at the end. His hands fumble with the lock and the handle, but something blocks it shut. He shoves. The door opens a crack.

"You can't get away from me!"

Axel tries to press himself through the gap, but it's too narrow. The edge of a large shelving unit stacked with clay pots is in the way. Axel throws his whole weight against the door and the unit beyond scrapes a few inches. He can feel Raphael behind him. He shoves once more and finally can squeeze his body through. He tears his hand on the lock but he can't notice. He must get out of there.

With a scream, Raphael stretches out and swipes down with the knife. The blade rips Axel's shoulder. It burns with pain.

Axel stumbles into a room with a glass ceiling that looks like a forgotten greenhouse. He runs again, feeling for his shoulder, covering his fingers with blood. He stumbles over a withered lemon tree in a pot and rushes on, bent over, along rows of dead plants with dry, rustling leaves.

Raphael is kicking powerfully at the door. He grunts at every kick. The pots shake as the shelving unit is shoved aside, bit by bit.

Axel searches frantically for a hiding place. He crawls under a dirty plastic sheet hanging down from one of the banks of plants. He keeps crawling past buckets and tubs. He prays Raphael will give up soon and escape from the boat with his son.

There's a thundering boom from the door, and a few pots smash on the floor. Raphael wrenches his way into the room, panting hard, and nudges against a trellis with withered grape vines.

"Come out and kiss my hand," he calls.

Axel holds his breath. He tries to retreat farther but there's a massive metal potting bench in his way.

"I promise I'll give you everything!" There's a wide-stretched, oily smile on Raphael's face. He prowls forward, searching among the shelves and past the dead stumps of bushes. "Your brother's liver is waiting for you. All you have to do is kiss my hand and it'll be yours."

Axel's stomach lurches and, shaking violently, he leans against a metal cabinet. He's blocked. His heart races and he hears a roaring in his head. He tries to remain silent. He searches everywhere and then discovers a hatch just five meters away, a hatch that must open onto the foredeck.

The helicopter's engine is roaring louder.

Axel plans to crawl under the table and then run the last few steps. He peers closely. The door is held shut with just a hook. He begins to shift to one side.

He lifts his head slightly to estimate the distance. But then he freezes. In his concentration, he lost track of Raphael, who has crept up behind him. He hears Raphael's rasping breath and smells his sweat. And he feels the cold edge of a knife against his throat. It burns where the blade touches Axel's skin.

114

the final fight

The gray-haired bodyguard slides out of the dining room silently, glides through the doors, and then runs quickly along the glass-covered section of the deck, holding his camouflaged weapon ready. The lenses of his glasses sparkle. Joona sees him sneaking up behind Niko and knows he will get Niko in a few seconds.

Niko's back is unprotected.

The bodyguard raises his automatic weapon and shifts his finger to the trigger.

Joona stands up, rigid, and places two shots into the middle of the man's chest. The bodyguard staggers and catches the railing to keep himself from falling overboard. He looks around wildly to see Joona coming. He raises his weapon back up to shoot again.

Joona realizes that the man wears a bulletproof vest under his black jacket.

Joona has already sprung at the man and knocked his weapon before slamming his gun into the base of the man's nose. The bodyguard's legs collapse. He staggers back, head thudding against the railing, his sweat and snot scattering about the deck. He flops down completely.

Joona and Niko run along the yacht on each side of the dining hall. They can hear the helicopter's rotor blades revving even more.

"Hurry up! Get aboard!" someone is shouting.

Joona runs as close to the wall as he can. He pauses to take a look around the corner to the foredeck. Raphael Guidi's son is already in the helicopter. The shadows from the rotor blades flutter over the decks and railings.

Joona hears noise from overhead and realizes that Raphael's other bodyguard has spotted him. The blond man is just twenty-five meters away and he's already aimed at Joona. There is no time to react. A bang rings out and Joona feels a flick like the stroke of a whip across his face. His surroundings fade to white. He falls over some lounge chairs without being able to stop himself and sprawls on the floor unable to keep his neck from striking the railing. His hand hits a bar, knocking his weapon from his hand so hard that his wrist feels broken. The gun falls over the railing and clatters down to the deck below.

Joona blinks as his sight returns. He creeps along the wall. He still feels confused and for a moment doesn't realize what's happened. Blood trickles down his face. He has to get up, he has to have Niko's help, he must find out where that bodyguard has gone.

He rubs his bloody cheek. It burns from pain and he feels along his face to understand that the bullet scored it.

It's a surface wound, but nothing more.

He hears an odd ringing in his left ear.

His heart pounds.

As he stands up, protected by the metal wall, his head feels a familiar ache.

It is the warning that precedes a migraine.

Joona presses a thumb against his forehead between his eyebrows and closes his eyes, trying to force the pain away.

After a moment, he opens them again, tries to see Niko, the helicopter, and beyond the foredeck and the railing.

The Finnish navy's well-equipped vessel is approaching like a black shadow on the smooth sea.

Joona twists free a long rod of metal from the broken lounge chair. At least he will have something in his hand when he has to face the bodyguard.

He presses tightly against the wall. He spots Raphael and Axel out on the foredeck. Moving backward toward the helicopter, they're oddly fused together. Raphael has an arm slung across Axel, the beautiful Amati in his hand a bright red against Axel's chest. With his other hand, he holds a knife blade to Axel's throat. Their hair and clothes flutter in the draft from the rotor blades.

The man who shot Joona is creeping sideways to locate him again. He's not sure if he scored a direct hit to the head; it happened so quickly.

Joona slides backward to get away, but his headache slows him down until he comes to a stop. He can move no more.

Not now, he thinks as he feels the sweat on his back.

The bodyguard edges around the corner, weapon ready. He catches sight of Joona's shoulder and glimpses his throat and his head.

Then blond-bearded Niko Kapanen barrels around another corner with his automatic rifle raised. The bodyguard is too quick. He whirls and lets off four shots in a row. Niko doesn't even feel the first one hit his shoulder but he's thrown back when the second hits his stomach. The third misses, but the fourth strikes Niko in the chest. He falls on his side, along the edge of the raised helicopter platform. He's so shocked from his wounds, he doesn't realize his finger is still on the trigger as he falls. The bullets aren't even aimed and fly out over the water as he empties the entire magazine in two seconds until his weapon clicks.

Niko draws a ragged breath and his eyes roll back in his head. He drops his weapon and dazedly sees the massive bolts on the underside of the helicopter pad. He notices that rust has forced its way through the white paint at the cracks of the large nuts, but he doesn't notice that his right lung is filling with blood.

He coughs weakly and fights against losing consciousness. He spies Joona hiding behind the wall to the dining room with no weapon but a metal rod in his hand. Their eyes meet. Niko gathers his last strength and kicks his automatic rifle over the deck to Joona.

Axel is terrified. His heart races. Gunfire all around makes his ears ring. He can't help trembling under Raphael's knife, his body held as the man's shield. The knife has cut into Axel's skin and blood runs down his shirt. He can see the bodyguard getting closer to Joona Linna's hiding spot, but he can do nothing.

Joona reaches for Niko's carbine and pulls it toward him. The bodyguard crouching near the helicopter pad lets off a blast toward him. The bullets ricochet every which way. Joona jerks out the empty magazine and, from the corner of his eye, sees Niko rummage through his pockets. Niko looks drained of blood and he can barely move. He has to stop a moment, his hand pressing against his stomach. A bodyguard yells at Raphael to hurry and climb in the helicopter; it's about to lift off. Niko fumbles in a pocket on the leg of his pants. A candy wrapper flutters away. Still, his fingers close over one stray bullet. Niko coughs and looks at the full metal jacket bullet in his palm, then he tosses it to Joona. The bullet rolls across the metal floor, flashing in the sunlight. Its bronze hull and tip of copper shine.

Joona grabs it and shoves it into the magazine as fast as he can.

Niko's eyes are shut now. A bubble of blood appears between his lips, but his chest is still rising and falling with shallow breaths.

The bodyguard's heavy steps clunk across the deck.

Joona shoves the magazine into the carbine, slips in the one bullet, lifts the weapon, waits a second, and leaps out of his hiding place.

Raphael is still pulling Axel with him. Raphael's son yells something from within the helicopter and the pilot is waving at Raphael to get in.

"You should have kissed my hand when you had the chance," Raphael murmurs into Axel's ear.

The Amati gives off a deep sound as Raphael pulls it into Axel's chest.

The bodyguard is strolling toward Niko and bends to send a bullet into his face.

"*Jonottakaa!*" yells Joona in Finnish.

He sees the bodyguard whirl to shoot at Joona instead. Joona leaps to one side to concentrate on the line of fire since his one bullet must count.

It all happens in seconds.

Behind his shield, Raphael keeps a firm grip on his knife. The increasing draft from the helicopter rips at their clothes. Rivulets of blood are sucked from Axel's neck. They see Joona crouch, shift the muzzle of the carbine slightly, and fire.

Jonottakaa! Joona thinks. *Get in line, boys!* He feels the hard recoil bang against his shoulder. The full metal jacket bullet leaves his weapon at eight hundred meters a second. Making almost no sound, the bullet plunges into the bodyguard's throat and exits in a spray of blood before it plunges again into Raphael's shoulder and out to fly over the water.

Raphael's knife arm is shocked from the hit and the knife tumbles to the deck.

Axel Riessen falls away.

The bodyguard looks at Joona in surprise as his blood spurts from his throat to pour over his chest. He tries again, groggily, to lift his weapon, but he can't. An odd sound emanates from his throat. He coughs, and this time blood splutters from his mouth and down his chin.

He sits down abruptly. He lifts his hand to the hole in his throat. He blinks two times and then his eyes fix, wide open.

Raphael's face has drained and he wavers in the strong, pulsing draft. He still clutches his violin. He stares malevolently at Joona.

"Pappa!" Peter yells. He throws a pistol to his father.

It strikes the deck and bounces once before landing at Raphael's feet.

Axel has dragged himself up against the railing, his hand pressing against his throat.

"Raphael! Raphael Guidi!" Joona yells. "You're under arrest!"

Raphael is only five meters from his helicopter. The pistol is at his feet. His gym clothes flap on his body. With effort, he bends for the gun.

"You are under arrest for weapon smuggling, kidnapping, and murder," Joona shouts clearly.

Raphael straightens with the gun in his shaking hand. His face is covered in sweat.

"Put down your weapon!" Joona orders.

Raphael is aiming the shaking gun. The pounding of his heart interferes. He meets Joona's eyes.

Axel yells at Joona to run.

Joona remains absolutely still.

Everything then happens at once.

Raphael lifts the pistol toward Joona and pulls the trigger. The pistol clicks. He tries again and fails. He chokes on a ragged breath when he understands that Peter never put a new magazine in the pistol. He understands his son has thrown him an empty gun. The loneliness he has always feared wraps itself around him. And now it's too late. He cannot drop the weapon and give himself up. He feels three soft thuds against his body as a bang sounds over the sea. Raphael feels only as if someone has struck a fist against his chest. Then he loses all sensation in his legs.

The helicopter will wait no more. It lifts straight into the air, leaving Raphael Guidi behind.

The Finnish navy's ship has drawn alongside the yacht. The three sailors once more fire in unison; once more, all three bullets strike Raphael with one explosive bang. Raphael Guidi's body twitches as if he wants to move but he can't. He falls.

His back is warm, but his feet are already ice-cold.

Raphael stares up at the helicopter quickly rising into the hazy sky.

Peter looks down at the yacht growing ever smaller beneath him. His father is sprawled inside the concentric rings of the helicopter pad, which now look like a target.

Raphael Guidi holds Paganini's violin to his bloody chest. The red pool beneath his body widens. His eyes are now blank in death. Joona is the only person still standing upright on the deck of the yacht.

He watches the helicopter fly away.

The sky is bright and empty. On the shining surface of the ocean, three vessels bob together in a moment of quiet.

Soon the rescue helicopters will arrive from Finland. Right now, though, it feels like the moment after a performance when the last note fades away, the audience is still enthralled, and the thunderous applause is about to erupt.

the conclusion

Joona Linna, Axel Riessen, and Niko Kapanen, along with the gray-haired bodyguard, are being transported by rescue helicopter to Surgical Hospital in Helsinki.

At the hospital, Axel is curious about why Joona did not duck when Raphael picked up the pistol from the deck.

"Didn't you hear me yell at you?" Axel asks.

Joona tells him that he'd already spotted the navy snipers and trusted they would fire before Raphael.

"But they didn't," Axel says.

"You can't be right all the time," Joona says with a grin.

Niko happened to be awake when they looked in before they left. He joked that he felt like the hero Vanhala in the book *The Unknown Soldier.*

"Go, Sweden!" he says to them. "And brave little Finland didn't do so bad, either!"

Niko's injuries are no longer life-threatening, but he knows he still faces several operations over the next few days. He will grumble about having to be in a wheelchair when he is released to the care of his parents, and he will be unhappier still when he realizes that it will take at least another year before he can play hockey with his sister again.

Raphael Guidi's bodyguard was arrested and booked into Vanda jail while the judicial wheels began to grind.

Joona Linna and Axel Riessen travel home to Sweden.

The large container ship M/S *Icelus* was never allowed to sail from Gothenburg Harbor. Its cargo of ammunition was unloaded and stored in a customs facility.

Jens Svanehjälm began his proper procedures but, except for the wounded bodyguard, all the people responsible for the crimes were dead.

They never had enough proof to charge anyone else. Only Pontus Salman was found to be mixed up in the illegal export of weapons, and the only suspected criminal in the ISP was its previous general director, Carl Palmcrona.

The government official Jörgen Grünlicht was investigated, but there were never any charges leveled at him. The conclusion was unhappily reached that all the politicians in Sweden and the people working for the Export Control Committee had been in the dark themselves and had just acted in good faith.

Investigations against two Kenyan politicians were handed over to Roland Lidonde, the anticorruption general and the state secretary for Governance and Ethics. It was assumed, however, that he would find that the Kenyans had also acted in good faith.

The supposedly innocent owners of Intersafe Shipping did not know that the ammunition was supposed to go on to Sudan from Mombasa Harbor, and the Kenyan transportation company, Trans Continent, was also unaware that trucks scheduled to travel to Sudan would be loaded with ammunition. Everyone had acted in good faith.

Axel Riessen feels the stitches in his shoulder as he climbs out of the taxi to walk the last steps up Bragevägen. Under the bright sun, the asphalt appears pale, almost white. As he puts his hand to the gate, the outer door of the house opens and Robert comes out. He'd been waiting at the window.

"God, what you've been through!" Robert says, shaking his head. "I've been on the phone to Joona Linna and he was telling me this crazy story—"

"You know how tough your big brother is," Axel says, smiling.

They hug and for a moment hold each other tightly. Then they walk together to the house.

"We've set the table for lunch in the garden," Robert says.

"How's your heart? It hasn't given you further trouble, has it?" Axel asks as he follows his brother.

"Actually, I was scheduled for surgery next week," Robert answers gravely.

"I didn't know that," Axel whispers.

"I'm getting a pacemaker instead. I don't think I've ever mentioned it to you—"

"So, an operation."

"Well, anyway, it was canceled."

Axel looks at his brother and he feels a dark twist in his soul. He understands who had booked Robert's operation and that it was meant never to succeed. The details of the patient in a coma had come from Robert's medical data. He would have gone into an induced coma on the operating table. Axel would have been given the donation from his own brother.

Axel has to sit abruptly on a hall chair. He feels the flush of guilt. Tears come to his eyes.

"Aren't you coming?" Robert says easily.

"Yes, of course."

Axel takes a deep breath, stands up, and follows his younger brother through the house and into the garden. Underneath the shade of the big tree in the center of the garden, a table set with their finest tableware is waiting on the marble paving.

Axel starts toward Robert's wife, Anette, to greet her, but Robert takes his arm to steer him away.

"Remember when we were kids? We had fun together," he says quietly, looking serious. "Why did we grow apart and stop talking? What happened?"

Axel looks at his brother in surprise. He notices the wrinkles in Robert's face and the stubbly hair around a large bald spot.

"Life happens—"

"No, there's something else," Robert says. "We must talk about something I could not discuss over the phone."

"What could that be?"

"Beverly told me that you blame yourself for Greta's death," Robert says.

"I refuse to discuss that."

"But you must listen," Robert insists. "I was backstage at the competition. I heard everything. I heard Greta with her father. She was crying the whole time. She'd played a passage incorrectly and her father was furious she'd lost the competition."

Axel breaks free of Robert's hold.

"I already know—"

"Let me tell you what I have to tell you," he says.

"Go ahead, then."

"Axel . . . if only you'd just said something. If only I'd known you blamed yourself for Greta's suicide. I was the one who overheard her father. It was his fault, his fault and only his fault. They had a horrible fight, and he said horrible things to her. He told her he was completely humiliated. He said that she'd shamed him and that he didn't want her as his daughter any longer. She was to leave his house. He would no longer finance her at the music academy. She was to drop her whole world here and go back to her drug-addicted mother in Mora."

"How could he ever have said such a thing!"

"I'll never forget Greta's voice," Robert continues bitterly. "How frightened she sounded. She pleaded that she'd done her best. She said that everyone makes mistakes and there'd be other competitions . . . That this was the only life she knew, the only one she loved."

"I always told her there would be other competitions," Axel says slowly.

He looks around, dazed, and doesn't know what to do. He slowly sits down on the marble patio and holds his face in his hands.

"She was crying and said she'd kill herself if he didn't let her keep her life in music, let her stay at the academy and continue to play."

"I don't know what to say," Axel whispers.

"You should thank Beverly," Robert replies.

beverly andersson

It's drizzling as Beverly stands on the train platform inside Central Station. Her journey south will be in a summer landscape wrapped in gray fog. It's not until she reaches Hässleholm that the sky will clear again. She changes trains in Lund. Then from Landskrona, she takes the bus to Svalöv.

It's been a long time since she was last home.

She remembers that Dr. Saxéus assured her that things would go well.

I've had a long talk with your father, the doctor had said. *He really wants you to come home.*

Beverly is now walking across a dusty square. She pictures herself as she was two years ago: vomiting on the square because some boys had forced her to drink illegal booze. They'd taken shameful pictures of her and then dropped her off on the square. Her pappa did not want her at home after that incident.

She keeps walking. Her stomach ties in knots when she sees the country road open before her. The road leads to her farm three kilometers away. Cars used to pick her up on this road. Now she doesn't remember why she would agree to go with them. She'd imagined she had seen something in their eyes: a special shine.

Beverly shifts her heavy suitcase to her other hand.

Down the road, dust flies up from an approaching car.

She thinks, *I know that car.*

She smiles and waves.

Pappa is coming! Pappa is coming!

penelope fernandez

Roslags-Kulla is a small church made of reddish wood. But it has a tall, beautiful clock tower. The church is in the quiet countryside near the Vira factory, just a bit farther away than the heavily trafficked roads in the Österåker district. The sky is clear and blue and the air is clean. The wind blows the scent of wildflowers over the peaceful cemetery by the church.

Yesterday Björn Almskog was buried at Norra Cemetery, and today four men in black suits are carrying Viola Maria Liselott Fernandez's coffin to her final resting place. Following the pallbearers, two uncles and two cousins from El Salvador, Penelope Fernandez and her mother, Claudia, walk with the priest.

They gather around the open grave. One of the cousin's children, a girl of about nine, looks at her father questioningly. When he nods to her, she lifts up her recorder and begins to play Hymn 97 while the coffin is lowered into the ground.

Penelope Fernandez holds her mother's hand while the priest reads a passage from the book of Revelation.

And God shall wipe away all tears from their eyes; and there shall be no more death.

Claudia looks at Penelope and straightens her collar. She pats her cheek as if Penelope were still a small child.

As they return to their cars, Penelope's phone buzzes. It's Joona Linna. Penelope disengages her hand from her mother's and walks to the shade underneath the large trees to talk in private.

"Hello, Penelope," Joona says in his characteristic voice, singsong but serious.

"Hello, Joona," Penelope replies.

"I thought you would want to know that Raphael Guidi is dead."

"And the ammunition to Darfur?"

"We've stopped the shipment."

"That's good."

Penelope looks around at her relatives and friends; her mother, who stands where she left her. Her mother, who won't let her out of her sight.

"Thanks," she says.

She goes back to her mother who watches her anxiously. She takes her mother's hand again, smiles, and they walk together to the cars. She stops and turns around. For a second she'd thought she heard her sister's voice right beside her. She shivers and a shadow passes over the neatly mown grass. Her young cousin with the recorder is standing between the gravestones looking at her. Her headband has slipped free and her hair is loosened in the summer breeze.

saga bauer and anja larsson

These summer days never end: the nights glow like mother-of-pearl until dawn.

The National Police Board is having a party for employees near Drottningholm Palace.

Joona Linna sits with his colleagues at a long table beneath a big tree.

In front of a Falun-red dance platform, a band dressed in white suits is playing the traditional Swedish folk song "Hårgalåten."

Petter Näslund is dancing the *slängpolska* with Fatima Zanjani from Iraq. He's saying something and laughter lights up his face. Whatever he's saying, he seems to be making Fatima very happy.

The song is about a time when the Devil came to play the violin. He played so well that the young people never wanted to stop dancing. Finally they were so exhausted, they started to weep. Their shoes wore out, their feet wore out, and soon only their heads were left hopping to the Devil's music.

Anja is nearby on a camp chair. She wears a flower-patterned blue dress and stares morosely at the dancing couples. However, when she sees Joona get up from the table, her round face flushes.

"Happy summer, Anja," he says.

Saga Bauer is dancing over the grass between the trees. She's chasing soap bubbles with Magdalena Ronander's twins. Her flowing blond hair with its entwined colored ribbons shines in the sun. Two middle-aged women pause to admire her.

"Ladies and gentlemen," says the leader of the band after the applause dies down. "We have a special request."

Carlos Eliasson smiles and looks at someone behind the stage.

The singer smiles. "I have my roots in Oulu, and I am going to sing a special Finnish song for you. It's a tango called 'Satumaa.'"

Magdalena Ronander is wearing a wreath of flowers in her hair as she heads toward Joona and tries to catch his eye. Anja stares at her feet. The band starts playing the tango.

Joona has already turned to Anja and he bows slightly. He asks quietly, "May I have the honor?"

Anja's face, and even her neck, blushes bright red. She looks up at him and nods seriously.

"Yes, yes you may."

She puts her fingers on Joona's arm and throws a proud glance at Magdalena. She steps onto the dance platform with her head high.

Anja concentrates on her steps at first, a furrow on her brow, but soon she relaxes and her face is calm and happy. She had fashioned an elaborate arrangement of her hair on the back of her neck, even sprayed it heavily to keep it in place, but now it looks just right. She follows Joona's lead, and her steps become lighter and lighter.

As the sentimental song nears its end, Joona feels a nip on his shoulder, which doesn't hurt.

Anja gives him another nip, a bit harder, and he feels forced to ask, "What are you doing?"

Her eyes are shining brightly like glass.

"I just felt like it," she says honestly. "I wanted to see what would happen. You never know unless you try . . ."

At that moment, the music ends. Joona releases her and thanks her for the dance. Before he can escort her away, Carlos hurries over and asks Anja for the next dance.

Joona steps to one side and watches his colleagues dance, and others, dressed in summer white, gather on picnic blankets, eating and drinking happily. He decides to head to his car.

Reaching the parking lot, Joona Linna opens the door to his Volvo. In the backseat, there's a huge bouquet waiting, wrapped in gift paper. Joona climbs into the car and phones Disa. The call goes to voice mail.

Disa sits in front of her computer. She's in her apartment on Karlaplan. She's wearing her reading glasses and has a throw draped over her shoulders. Her cell phone is on her desk next to a cup of cold coffee and a partially eaten cinnamon bun.

The photo of a worn cairn of stones in the middle of a green meadow is on her screen. The stones mark a mass grave of cholera victims near Skanstull in Stockholm.

She's tapping notes into a document on her computer. She stretches her back and lifts her coffee mug halfway to her lips and then thinks better of it. She gets up to brew a new pot of coffee when the telephone on the desk buzzes.

Without reading the name of the caller, she shuts it off. She stands by the window, looking out. She sees dust dancing in the sunlight. Disa feels a tightness in her throat. She sits back down at her computer. She intends never to speak to Joona Linna again.

joona linna

There's a festive feeling in the air as Midsummer draws near. The traffic is light on Tegnérgatan as Joona slowly walks along. He's stopped trying to reach Disa. She's turned off her phone and it's obvious she wants to be left alone. Joona passes the Blue Tower and then turns down Drottninggatan, which is lined with antique stores and small shops. At the new occult bookstore Aquarius, an old woman pretends to admire the display. As Joona passes by, she gestures toward the glass and then begins to follow him.

It takes a few moments for him to realize that he's being followed.

He stops at the black fence by Adolf Fredrik Church and turns around. The woman is ten meters behind him. She's about eighty years old. She peers at him and holds out a card.

"This is you, isn't it?" she says as she shows it. "And here is the crown, the bridal crown." She holds out another.

Joona walks over to her and takes the cards from her hand. They're playing cards from one of the oldest card games in all of Europe, tarot.

"What do you want from me?" Joona asks calmly.

"Nothing at all," says the old woman. "But I have a message for you from Rosa Bergman."

"You must be mistaken. I don't know anyone by—"

"She's wondering why you pretend that your daughter is dead."

It's early autumn in Copenhagen. The air is clear and cool when a group of men, discreetly transported in four separate limousines, arrives at the Glyptotek Museum. The men walk up the stairs and enter. They walk past the fruitful winter garden beneath its high glass ceiling. Their footsteps echo on the stone hallway floor as they pass antique sculptures and enter the magnificent concert hall.

The audience is already seated. The Tokyo String Quartet is in its place on the low stage. The musicians hold their legendary Stradivarius instruments, the ones once played by Niccolò Paganini himself.

The four late-arriving guests find their seats around a table in the colonnades to one side of the hall. The youngest is still almost a boy, a fine-limbed blond man whose name is Peter Guidi. The other men wear expressions that are determined but also one step from fear; they are prepared to enslave themselves. They are all soon going to kiss his hand.

The musicians nod to one another and start to perform the Schubert String Quartet no. 14. It begins with great pathos, a deep emotion held in check, a power restrained. A violin calls, painfully and beautifully. The music takes a breath one last time and then it all pours out. The melody seems happy, but the instruments have, at the same time, an underlying tone of sorrow as if it were breath left behind from many lost souls.

Every single day, thirty-nine million bullets are made. Worldwide military spending, at the lowest estimate, is $1,226 trillion a year. In spite of the fact that enormous amounts of armaments are manufactured, the demand never lessens and it is impossible to estimate the volume. The nine largest exporters of weapons in the world are the United States, Russia, Germany, France, Great Britain, the Netherlands, Italy, Sweden, and China.

Lars Kepler is the pen name of a literary couple who live in Sweden.